D0562299

DINA'S LOST TRIBE

DINA'S LOST TRIBE

A NOVEL

BRIGITTE GOLDSTEIN

iUniverse, Inc.
New York Bloomington

Dina's Lost Tribe
A Novel

Copyright © 2010 by Brigitte Goldstein

All rights reserved. No part of this book may be used or reproduced by any means, graphic, electronic, or mechanical, including photocopying, recording, taping or by any information storage retrieval system without the written permission of the publisher except in the case of brief quotations embodied in critical articles and reviews.

Certain characters in this work are historical figures, and certain events portrayed did take place. However, this is a work of fiction. All of the other characters, names, and events as well as all places, incidents, organizations, and dialogue in this novel are either the products of the author's imagination or are used fictitiously.

iUniverse books may be ordered through booksellers or by contacting:

iUniverse
1663 Liberty Drive
Bloomington, IN 47403
www.iuniverse.com
1-800-Authors (1-800-288-4677)

Because of the dynamic nature of the Internet, any Web addresses or links contained in this book may have changed since publication and may no longer be valid. The views expressed in this work are solely those of the author and do not necessarily reflect the views of the publisher, and the publisher hereby disclaims any responsibility for them.

ISBN: 978-1-4502-5107-5 (sc)
ISBN: 978-1-4502-5108-2 (dj)
ISBN: 978-1-4502-5109-9 (ebk)

Library of Congress Control Number: 2010912018

Printed in the United States of America

iUniverse rev. date: 10/05/2010

To Sharon Rebecca

who dwells in fields of gold

PART I

MIRROR OF AN ERRANT SOUL

Dina's Tale Begins

I breathe! I breathe free! We all can breathe free at long, long last. The pall is lifted, the stranglehold gripping my throat loosened. I fling open the shutters in the early morning mist. My nostrils widen, my lungs fill with the clear mountain air streaming in with the rising sun. My heart beats with joy; my voice soars like a lark's. The echo of my voice resounds with "The mountains skip like rams; the hills like young sheep!" It is here, on this blessed piece of earth, in this valley ringed with granite turrets that we shall build our lives, our future. Not so much my future anymore as your future, my sons. This is your inheritance, my bequest to you. May all that is past remain behind us; let us embrace the future. The Lord G-d of Israel has seen my affliction. He has heard my entreaties and has forgiven my sins. The G-d of Moses who freed the Israelites from bondage in Egypt and guided them to the Promised Land, in that spirit, he has set me free as well. This mountain valley is our promised land, my sons! True, I was accorded this gift—some may regard it as a gift, when in reality, this precious piece of earth is my just reward —through the good offices of a Christian holy man now in Avignon, the erstwhile inquisitor of Pamiers. But I am certain it was the G-d of Israel who used him as His tool to carry out His divine will. I have no doubt it was He, the Eternal, who softened his heart toward a woman in distress. Like Job, she was beaten down, lost everything, endured humiliation and servitude; now she has been restored to life through the grace of G-d. He heard of her plight, He heard her moaning; He answered her prayers. Let us rejoice, my sons! Let us praise the G-d of Israel, our benefactor.

In my years of darkness, those friendless years devoid of hope, you, my sons, were my only light, my consolation. You made my dark world luminous. You made an unbearable fate bearable. You even brought me moments of joy—when I held you in my arms, when I saw you growing into manhood. And now you too are free from the curse of your birth. The mark of shame has been wiped from your forehead. You are no longer outcasts, bastards; no one will ever again shun you, spit at you, curse you. You are free men now! Do you understand what this means?

Then why the muttering in the shadows? Why the doleful miens? The suspicious stares? Why the doubts, the whispers, reproachful glances—yes, even secret accusations? I see the questions in your eyes. I feel them burning in my back. I sense them even when you lower your eyes at the table or when I pass you in the fields, as you build your homes here in this mountain valley. I know you would not confront your mother openly. But I am not so blind as not to sense what tears at your souls. You want to know what made me do what I did. You have a right to know. He was the man who fathered you. You are flesh of his flesh. His blood flows in your veins. But that is all; he is nothing else to you. You owe him nothing—no loyalty, no love, no respect, no honor. Remember it was he who condemned you to the status of bastardry; he left you exposed to the scorn and derision of the lowliest of peasants. He dishonored your mother, kept her in a perpetual state of degradation and bondage, lower than the swineherd in the village. Remember, it was your mother who raised you, who instructed you in the teachings of her people. It was she who told you about the glory of our forefathers, of Abraham, Isaac, and Jacob. She taught you about Moses the lawgiver, she recalled the stories of David and Solomon, the kings of the ancient Israelite realm. She also nursed you on the many stories of persecution and suffering my people, your people, had endured since the destruction of the Holy Temple in Jerusalem. She told you these stories in secret, for these heretic villagers scoffed at our scriptures, what we call Tanakh and Christians call the Old Testament. The man who was your father paraded as a good Christian, a priest ordained in the Roman Church. In reality, he was the devil in priestly garb, a wolf in sheepskin, a fornicator and a deceiver, a depraved miscreant from whom no woman in this mountain region was safe.

Why should I feel remorse for what I did, for having brought him to justice when the time was propitious? For years he hid his heretic faith. Only I knew that he was a traitor to the Church. So little did he think of me; he had no care that I might denounce him. So sure was he that I was his slave, that he controlled not only my body, but also my mind and my soul. I did not rejoice when the flames of the Inquisition devoured the body he had indulged and had mingled with mine, nor did I mourn. My body and mind remained mute, my heart numb, insentient like stone. Only much later, when the realization set in that he was gone, never to return, that never again would he enter my bed at will, never again would my body be degraded by his lewd desire, I broke down in tears of joy.

Harsh, hardhearted words? Maybe. And an even harsher punishment for behavior that might seem nothing more than all too human weakness! A priest's fiendish nature was, of course, of little concern to the Church. The Inquisition was after greater aberrations. The shibboleth was heresy. *Death by fire was the fate of those convicted of spreading heretical beliefs, teachings contrary to those of the Church that would undermine the power of the Holy See. This was not my concern, of course. I wanted to be rid of the priest. I wanted to be free. Surely not through a death as terrible as the one he ultimately endured. But in the end, it was the only way, the only way I would be delivered from an odious existence. The Inquisitor of Pamiers was kind to me and kept his word; even after he had become pope in Avignon, he remembered his promise. You may think I made a pact with the devil, that I sold my soul to the prince of darkness. Some of the villagers shouted "Judas!" at me from the carts that carried them to the stake. I owe no justification to the world, to my tormentors. Only to you, my sons, do I owe anything. To understand what moved me, you have to know the whole story, how I came to such misfortune. I seek neither your forgiveness nor your pity, only understanding, to wipe the slate clean. Let me relate what happened, not only to me, but also to you, my sons, so you can judge whether I had cause to do what I did. At the same time, I want you to know where you come from. I want you to be aware of the story of your family. I want you to tell this story to your children so they can tell it to their children and on down through the generations. So it will never be forgotten, I want you to enjoin your children and their children to tell this story like the story that is being told every year by my people about their delivery from bondage in Egypt.*

My life was changed forever on the 22nd day of July of what Christians call the Year of the Lord 1306. But my people use a different counting. They begin with the creation of the world, and that day of villainy fell on the tenth day of the month of Av in the year 5066. This date is burned into my memory forever. I was sixteen years old.

Before I go on, I must explain to you the significance of this particular day in the history of our people. The ninth day of that month, Tisha b'Av in our holy tongue, is a very somber day. Every year on that day, they sit in sackcloth and ashes on the floor of their houses, mourning the destruction of the temple, the House of G-d, which once stood in Jerusalem. Twice this holy place was laid waste on that same day in the calendar. The Babylonians, an ancient people dedicated to war and conquest, erased and plundered the temple our King Solomon had built and forced the people into exile. Then, many centuries later, after they had returned and rebuilt the holy of holies, the Romans, heathen ancestors of the Roman Church, ransacked the holy city and its temple, expelled the Jewish people from their land, and dispersed them among the heathens.

It was one day after this day of mourning that the royal order, which had gone out from the north, reached us here in the south. The decree stated the express will of the king of France, the fair Philippe, fair of face and evil of heart, who had only recently become overlord of the southern parts of French regions, that all Jews must leave his kingdom forthwith.

The writing was in clear, unaffected, medieval Occitan, a language still spoken today in the area of southwestern France called Languedoc. It had been copied in a careful hand onto a modern notebook as commonly used by French students. The history of the expulsion of the Jews from France by Philippe the Fair was not new to me. In fact, one might say, I was an expert on the subject. I held a professorship in French medieval Jewish philosophy at a well-known university in Chicago. My reputation as a scholar of this period rests firmly on a long list of publications. But in all my years of research in French, German, Spanish, and Italian archives, I had never come across any reference to a Jewish woman separated from her family and people during that great upheaval of the expulsion. Unable to consult a reference work or notes, I felt lost like a wanderer in a strange forest. Where could this have come from? Was there more? I leafed through the empty pages of the notebook, looking for more, with a palpitating heart. Nothing. So-called discoveries of old manuscripts were not uncommon and somebody—whoever had sent this to me—wanted to get my endorsement for some scheme. Then again, very few people were fluent enough in Occitan to produce such a text. The language certainly had an aura of authenticity. I kept flipping the pages as if to make the information appear by magic. I flung it down several times only to pick it up again. I jumped up from the desk chair in the small hotel room where I was staying and reached for the telephone to call room service. The voice that answered was not too delighted by that late night disturbance. An eternity seemed to pass before someone knocked on the door. Finally, a sleepy boy presented me with the cognac I had ordered. As I fumbled for some change in my pocket, I almost tipped over the glass. Alone again, I gulped down the golden liquid and immediately began to feel its calming effect. I took a deep breath, washed my face in the sink, and set my mind to the conundrum at hand, but mercifully fell asleep before the demon seized me again.

Upon enquiring the concierge the next morning, I was told that a boy from the neighborhood dropped the package off and disappeared quickly. It all smacked far too much of a B movie scenario. It simply made no sense, especially since I had come to Toulouse at the request of someone I knew very well, or had known very well when we were children. In fact, we were first cousins. As adults, we had gone different ways. Besides, I was ten years older and had flown the family coop that much earlier.

The letter with the urgent request was from my cousin Nina. It reached me just as I was preparing to depart for my summer vacation at a quiet lake in upper Minnesota. My vacations always consisted of quiet time spent writing, to which I looked forward after the bustle of teaching and other university business that made it difficult to gather the thoughts, or summon the muse, during the academic year. So a sudden trip to Toulouse, even though the town was dear to me, having taught and done research at the university there, was at that moment not exactly opportune. Besides, how could I know that the letter actually came from my cousin Nina? Since we had never been in the habit of corresponding—we kept abreast of each other's movements and vagaries only through the family grapevine—I could not tell whether it was her handwriting. Then again, if someone wanted to deceive me for some reason, that someone would, it seemed to me, have used a typewriter rather than composing a letter by hand. Then there was one other consideration that made me decide to put off my writing vacation by the lake and look closer into this matter. My cousin Nina Aschauer had disappeared without a trace in the mountains of southern France five years before. No one knew of her whereabouts, not even her mother. I had often wondered whether she was still alive. Now this sign of life.

The letter contained several indications that it actually came from her, and that in fact it could only have come from her. It addressed me in German with "Lieber Henner" before going on in English. I am professionally known as Henry Marcus, and my friends call me Hank. The name of my birth, Heinrich Markus, had never become known outside the family circle, and certainly not my family nickname of Henner. The only other person who would know this name, a not very common form, was Nina's mother, who lived in New Jersey. My parents and the other family members who had come to America as refugees from Germany in 1941 had all passed away. The idea that Aunt Hedy, this lonely, aggrieved woman, would compose such a letter was absurd. What reason would she have? Her English, too, was never all that good, and the postmark was from a French town.

Besides an urgent plea for me to come to Toulouse without delay, the letter also contained some precise instructions regarding what to do and where to go when I got here. She needed money, a sizable sum of money, and it had to be in francs. Maybe I could somehow make a withdrawal from her bank account in New York? A rather illusory suggestion. In fact, the whole tone of the letter had something unreal. I would have to dip into my own funds, which I was willing to do, if only for my Aunt Hedy's peace of mind. The rest of Nina's instructions were unequivocal. I was to check into a specific hotel near the Toulouse railroad station, a place, as it turned out, with the ambience of a flophouse. I should wait for her to contact me there. She was sorry, but she could not meet me at the airport.

Despite misgivings, I was willing to put up with this disruption to my encrusted routine. After all, she was family and my favorite cousin. Actually, she was my only cousin, and until we lost sight of each other, we always had a close relationship. She was the reason that I looked forward to family gatherings on holidays and especially on Passover when we stayed together for the entire week. She was like a little sister to me, and I felt protective of her like an older brother. If she was in trouble, and it certainly sounded like she was deep into something perilous, and needed my help, I would not and could not leave her in whatever lurch she was in. So I sallied forth like the knight in shining armor to rescue the damsel in distress. Yet, I could not suppress a creeping sense that I might indeed be embarking on a kind of quixotic adventure. I was sober enough to make one more attempt to verify the authenticity of the handwriting, just to make sure that I wasn't falling for some con scheme whose purpose I was as yet unable to fathom. I decided to use the stopover in New York to pay my aunt in New Jersey a visit.

Surprisingly, I found her in an almost elated disposition, in contrast to the doleful mood I had left her in during a visit several years before. She too had received a letter from Nina—the first sign of life in five years. Nina assured her that she was well and apologized for not having been able to write sooner due to circumstances she would not or could not describe. She asked her mother's forgiveness and patience. Hopefully they would see each other soon. Where this reunion would take place, she did not specify. A comparison of the letters showed that the handwriting was identical, and Aunt Hedy assured me that it was indeed Nina's. I examined both envelopes and noticed one discrepancy, which I kept to myself. The postmarks differed. The letter to me had been posted in the town of Augen, and the one to my aunt bore the stamp of the town of Montauban. Both towns are located in the same region in southwestern France and not all too far apart. Yet, it made me wonder what might be behind this, especially since I had been asked to come to Toulouse. Did she move from place to place? And if so, why? There was no return address on either letter. Why the mystery? Why this holding back of information? No word to either me or her mother about where she had been for almost five years. What she had been doing in all that time remained a mystery.

"You know, Henner, Nina came back a changed person from her sabbatical year in France," Aunt Hedy told me.

"That was at the University of Toulouse in 1972, wasn't it?" I said. "I remember you telling me."

"Exactly. She came home sick in body and soul, Henner, as if she had caught something. But that wasn't really it." Aunt Hedy shook her head, still not understanding.

"Could have been psychological," I ventured.

"Could well be. That low-grade fever she couldn't shake for weeks kept her here at home until the High Holy Days were over. She finally went back to teaching in New York, but reluctantly, it seemed to me. There was a listlessness about her that frightened me. Of course, I didn't say anything. I saw her quite often then, especially on Shabbat; she would come over and stay till late Sunday. I was just happy to have her with me.

"When the semester was over, she told me she had to go back to France. She packed and left, just like that." Aunt Hedy threw her hands in the air. She had received a postcard from Toulouse and a brief letter from a town called Oloron Sainte Marie. Brief notes asking her not to worry, she was all right. After that, nothing more.

"As you know, Henner," my aunt said not without pride, "she was at the start of a very promising, some said brilliant, career."

I remembered the family grapevine abuzz with bulletins of Nina's rise in the academic world. Her dissertation in feminist historical studies, a developing field at that time and all the rage, had catapulted her to the top. Her pioneering opus, if I remember correctly, bore a somewhat pompous title, something about gender, female sexuality, and modernization in pre-World War I Pomerania.

The reviews my mother sent me hailed it as a landmark, a breakthrough in feminist scholarship. "A brilliant tour de force," one reviewer rhapsodized—with revelations about how the introduction of modern farming equipment into Pomerania freed rural women from their traditional roles as beasts of burden, permitting them to pay more attention to their appearance and thereby express their sexuality more openly. She demonstrated conclusively, at least to some people's satisfaction, that the new equipment led to more tightly delineated divisions of labor on the family farm, permitting men to take greater control of farming operations, displacing women from the field and relegating them to the house and yard. The resulting tension, she concluded, widened the rift between the sexes. A major conflagration was prevented only when the domestic conflict had to be temporarily placed on the backburner, so to speak, under the impact of the wave of national enthusiasm that swept up even these peaceful, remote, Pomeranian farming communities in August 1914, in the rush toward the outbreak of the Great War.

Old-fashioned historian and philosopher that I was, I chuckled a bit at what sounded to me like pretentious garble. But I kept that to myself. My aunt, though proud of her daughter's success, seemed a bit leery of this topic herself, even if for a different reason. She still remembered vividly the not-so-distant history that had driven our family from the Baltic seaport of Stettin in Pomerania, now Szeszin in Poland, where my mother and aunt's Jewish clan had lived for generations. She also remembered the country folk's enthusiasm for the Nazi regime and its Führer, which even surpassed the fervent patriotism they flaunted at the outbreak of the war in 1914, as Nina described the events in her thesis.

My mother shared her sister's reservations. "Why Pomerania of all places?" she said to me on the telephone. "And what have those peasants ever done for the Jews, except spit at us?"

I too thought it an odd choice of topic, but we all held our peace, and I wished my cousin every success in the world. And success was hers. She was swamped with offers from academic institutions far and wide. She chose New York, perhaps in part to stay close to her by-then widowed mother. But when she was offered a postdoctoral fellowship at the University of Toulouse, she took her paradigm to southern France to apply it to the pastoral community of the French Pyrenees.

My aunt and I sat in silence for a while, lost in our thoughts of Nina. We were probably thinking the same thing without saying it out loud. The Pyrenees! Aunt Hedy's coffee tasted as good as it smelled, and the home-baked cake—did she know I was coming, or did she always have some on hand?—took me back to those Sunday afternoon family get-togethers, the coffee klatsches, that filled the heart and soul with a sense of homeliness or *Gemütlichkeit* that Germans are so fond of.

"Do you have a little time?" Aunt Hedy brought out a stack of photo albums.

"Well, I have to catch the plane. Nina is waiting," I brought forth meekly, still inebriated with the nostalgia the *Kaffee und Kuchen* had stirred in me. "I should visit more often. But, you know, academic life … it's hectic and all those schedules and deadlines. My wife left me supposedly for that reason; she couldn't put up with it."

"Of course," said Aunt Hedy, all understanding, but also insisting that I stay just a little while longer. "You and I are all what remains of this family, and I not too much longer."

After some thought, she added: "Well, now it seems that Nina … but neither one of you has offspring. This is probably the end of the Aschauer/Markus/Danziger lineage."

My mother and Tante Hedy had been known as the Danziger sisters in their youth in Stettin, inseparable wherever they went, even on outings with gentleman callers, of whom there were quite a few—I was frequently given to understand. From their early childhood, and probably before, the Danziger family had spent summer vacations at the popular Baltic seaside resorts, and sometimes on the isle of Rügen. But no matter where they decided to go in any particular year, going back to a time long before the

First World War and continuing through the Weimar period, many of the resort hotels displayed signs at their front entrance inscribed in large letters with *Juden unerwünscht!* This forced these undesirable Jews, whether recognizable through dress and practice as religiously observant or outwardly conformant to the wider society, to lodge together in their own boardinghouses. This is where the Danziger sisters met their spouses. My father, Kurt Markus, came from what was then called an assimilated, educated, upper-bourgeois Jewish family in Berlin. Hedy's husband, Aaron Aschauer, came from a family of Posznanian *beheijmes handler*, horse and cattle traders. The Aschauers were religious Jews; the Markus's were more in the category of Yom Kippur Jews, as more regular synagogue goers called those who showed up only on High Holy Days. But the closeness of the sisters brought and held the two branches together, and even in America, they stayed close and continued the tradition of celebrating the Jewish holidays together.

We leafed through one album. It was tempting to linger over the images of our arrival in America and subsequent progress from the city to the suburbs. I was especially drawn into Nina's childhood and school pictures. We flipped through the pages in haste. As much as I yearned to indulge my nostalgia awhile longer, I could not stay for more. My Air France flight to Paris was to leave from Kennedy Airport in three hours, and there wouldn't be another until the next day. What if the limo got stuck in traffic, which was always a possibility on the Beltway in Brooklyn. The urgency of Nina's letter suddenly gripped me as well. Nina was alive, but apparently in some kind of trouble. She was reaching out to me for help. I couldn't let her down.

The transatlantic flight afforded me some time to kick back and relax. These last few days had taken me on an emotional rollercoaster that took me light years away from my usual activities.

I closed my eyes, hoping that sleep would alleviate the pounding in my temples. But sleep did not come. The thought of Nina kept me awake. One picture in my aunt's album remained vivid in my mind. It had been taken at a family gathering on Passover about fifteen years ago. The occasion remained distinct in my memory. It was about a month or so before Nina's graduation from college.

The photo was in black and white, but I remembered how fixated I was on her bright blue eyes sparkling with enthusiasm as she told the family about her plans for future study. Her rosy cheeks and blondish wavy hair, tamed into a ponytail, gave her that refreshing wholesome look that was still in style in the early sixties. A quibbler may have pointed out some imperfections and found her mouth a bit too broad, her chin too strong, and the bend in her nose not quite up to the classical ideal, but to me these spoke of elegance and character. She had about two inches in height on me and was slightly on the pudgy side. Although pudginess ran in the family—I too leaned in that direction—in Nina's case it was likely the result of college life. In later years, her figure was always rather slender, at times too much so.

Her chosen field was European history, she proclaimed, adding "in the broadest sense."

"Don't worry, Henner," she said, turning to me with a coquettish laugh. "I won't be competing with you for laurels."

Later that day, on an afternoon walk together, she reiterated that her interests ran in a different direction.

"A very different direction," she repeated in a somewhat patronizing tone, as if reassuring a hurt child. Without specifying further, she unleashed a series of adjectives like broader, innovative, creative, progressive, interdisciplinary, and even drastic.

"I am looking for an entirely new, you might say groundbreaking approach," she concluded with the serious mien of a visionary. I took it all in good humor. If anything, I found her youthful zeal endearing. She was twenty; I was thirty and a good deal ahead of her in the race for academic laurels.

After that, I saw her only twice more, each time at a funeral. First her father succumbed to a long illness, and then, not too much later, my parents died in a tragic accident.

Over the years, I was kept abreast of Nina's exploits. I heard about her year in Paris where she studied medieval French history. *Odd,* I thought. *That's rather close to my area for someone who proclaimed to be branching out into unexplored realms.* Somewhere along the way, she also managed to put in a year of work/study in Israel. More and more, her itinerary was confined to crisscrossing the continent from Rome to Vienna to London to Munich. Eventually her travels landed her behind the Iron Curtain, in East Berlin and other places in the German Democratic Republic. Everywhere she ransacked the archives, collecting mountains of data, which she recorded painstakingly on little note cards for her dissertation. Determined not to perish, she published with a vengeance, and as an expert on the history of women and modernization, her name became the most cited in what then came to be called "gender studies."

Sometime during those years, I got married, relatively late in life and for a short time only. I met my wife at a small Midwestern college where we were both junior faculty. She taught sociology, and I mainly a required course in Western civilization to which was added Introductory French History when the need arose. Judaic studies was not much in demand in that geographic area. For me, this was a temporary stint, a way station on the path toward a call from more prestigious institutions, a steppingstone at most. She was perfectly happy in the role of respected member of the educated social circle of this Protestant town whose residents were primarily of German and Scandinavian descent. She did get me to hang up my tweed jacket from time to time and don more formal attire. My bowtie too had to give way to a striped cravat so I wouldn't look too "goofy" at dinner parties and cultural soirées. What she couldn't change about me were my eating habits. How often did I have to hear that my refusal to eat most of the fare, especially the meat, being served at such gatherings made her look bad? After a while, I found ways to wriggle out of these engagements with excuses about publishing deadlines for papers and books, which she called my "eternal scribbling."

Her idea of a summer vacation at the lake clashed with my need to spend this time in European archives. We were incompatibility personified. But the row that broke the camel's back came when we gave thought to starting a family. I wanted to raise my children Jewish, which would have required a commitment from her to convert to Judaism. On this point, I was as adamant as she was opposed. Neither side would give in. A compromise was obviously impossible. So that was the end. We should have clarified this matter ahead of time, but I wasn't thinking with my head. All I saw at first was a pretty, smart, vivacious woman. She had style and wit and was so different from me in most ways. Why she married me, I still haven't figured out. But it was soon behind me when I was offered a position at a major university on the West Coast.

Convinced that I wasn't marriage material, I devoted myself assiduously to teaching and scholarship. I had several lady friends, though no lasting relationships. I resisted my family's urgings to look for a "nice Jewish girl."

It was just as well that Nina couldn't attend the ceremony. Aunt Hedy conveyed regrets for both of them via telephone. Nina was detained behind the Iron Curtain, but I knew they wouldn't have come at any rate.

Finally, the humming of the airplane motors made me doze off for I don't know how long. Actually, it must have been a deep, exhaustive sleep. I was awoken by the sound of my own panting and heaving. Anxiety netted my brow, and I was disoriented at first. It took several seconds before I knew where I was and that it was a dream that had so shaken me. I usually forget my dreams immediately—if I dream at all. This time, the details of the images lingered crystal clear in my mind.

From an elevation, I looked down on a boulder-strewn hollow, shadowed by ragged, mountains like growling giants. In the remote distance was a herd of cows grazing in sun-bathed green pastures, dotted with yellow dandelions and light blue cornflowers. Adjoining the pasture, a field of poppies added a touch of scarlet to the panorama. The contrasting scenes were rolled out before my eyes like the broad canvas of a panoramic nineteenth-century alpine painting. But my attention was drawn to the barren, desolate landscape in the foreground. There was a human figure zigzagging between the boulders, stumbling, ducking, tripping over rocks, grappling, hurtling forward, yet always running in place. As I zeroed in on the figure, it turned out to be a boy, a young boy of maybe nine or ten. He was panting, out of breath, but seemed determined to push on as if he wanted to escape some invisible pursuer. Instinctively, I knew his goal was the green meadows far beyond. But the boulders had suddenly turned into a horde of warriors who began to beset the boy with slings and arrows. He ducked, bobbed this way and that. He opened his mouth to call out without emitting a sound. He sank to the ground and began to weep, breathing heavily. The horde closed in on him, and I awoke.

What an odd dream, I thought, annoyed. I tried to distract myself with the movie showing onboard the plane. Then I got up, stretched my legs in the aisle, moved up and down on the balls of my feet. Finally, I gave in. There was no denying, no evading the meaning of this dream. I knew all along that the boy was me, at the age of ten, running from the Nazis. In reality, I was, of course, not alone when my family made the arduous trek across the Pyrenean Mountains from Vichy France into neutral Spain. The meaning of the dream was rather obvious. Only, in all the years since, I had never been plagued by dreams or nightmares about this chapter in my life. Maybe there is something to the old saw that we relive our youth when we get older. I had been too busy adjusting to and embracing American life, studying, building a career, and since I was ambitious, a scholarly reputation. Like everyone else around me, I was, of course, always conscious of what had been done to the Jewish people, especially once the enormity of the Nazi crime was revealed to the world. Maybe that's why I fled into the period of the Middle Ages—the Golden Age of Jewish Culture according to one Jewish historian—only to find that there may have been a flowering of Jewish learning in many fields in medieval Spain and France. The relations between Jews and the gentile world were not much better than in more recent times.

But I digress. Here I was on my way from New York to Paris, from where I would go on to Toulouse, following an urgent appeal from a cousin who had suddenly rematerialized after a five-year absence from the world. And on this flight over the Atlantic to the Continent, a passage I had made many times before, a dream evoked a childhood trauma I thought I had long ago overcome. Now the past flared up in my memory as vividly as if it had been yesterday! Somehow I was sure it all had to do with Nina. And then I remembered something my aunt had said as we were parting, something I had forgotten in the rush to catch the plane. She said: "Before she left, Nina said she had to find Valladine."

Dina's Tale 2

They came in the deep of night. "They always come at night," my father said. "No need to worry though; they will also go away again by daybreak," he added. He pointed out that the Jews have lived through episodes like this many times before and the seneschal was a trusted friend. Whether he really did not worry or just wanted to put my brothers and me at ease, I don't know, but if he thought this was just another raid or that his friend, the seneschal, would stand by him, this time he was mistaken.

It was the night of Friday to Saturday, Shabbat, our day of rest. The hour of midnight had passed when a great commotion in the street awoke us.

"In the name of the king! In the name of the king!" Coarse shouts roared through the narrow, winding alleys of the Jewish quarter of Toulouse. The stomping of boots as from a hundred foot soldiers resonated on the pavement. Hoofs clanked on the cobblestones, swords rattled, the din reverberated in our hearts. An army of horsemen and foot soldiers moved from house to house, rousing the residents with merciless ferocity. Windows shattered, doors splintered under the force of ramming blocks. Our house was at the far end of the crammed

quarter to which the Jews were relegated, and we waited with bated breath for the horde to reach us.

"Open up, in the name of the king! Open up!" To the confusion of noises were now added men's voices, some we recognized as our neighbors'. All arguing was crushed with brutal force, with the hilt of the sword, the kick of the boot. Women's shrieks and children's cries raised the general din. To this day, I cannot forget how my heart raced and my body trembled as the king's guardsmen drew closer to our abode. My father still put his faith in his friendship with the seneschal. Maybe he was aware of how serious the situation was and he merely tried to rein in our fears and keep his household from breaking out in a panic. When it was our turn, he walked with firm stride to the gate and opened it before any damage could be done. There he stood in the gate of his house, robed in Shabbat white, a knit skullcap covering his head, his grizzled beard swaying as he repelled those intent on violating the sanctity of his property. His dignified bearing, the image of a prophet to my eyes, made my heart overflow with pride and love for the man who had raised me and surrounded me for the sixteen years of my life with his protective love.

"I demand to speak to his lordship, the seneschal," he said with a resolute, calm tone as he barred the clamoring horde of guardsmen from entering our courtyard with his body.

"Hear that? This one wants the seneschal," mocked one of the soldiers. But my father's firm stance apparently gave him pause, and he did not try to push his way in. Nor did any of the others, especially since my brothers and several of our gentile servants joined now in blocking the entrance.

"In the name of the king! In the name of the king!" was all they could shout, and by then more meekly.

"The seneschal is a servant of his majesty, the king of France. I want to hear from him exactly what the king's will is."

The captain of the guard stepped up and made a respectful gesture toward my father.

"Don Elazar," he said, "we are simply here to carry out the king's orders. All members of the Israelite community are to be taken from their homes to the town's dungeon. That's all I know."

"But why? There must be an explanation, a reason for this sudden nocturnal assault," my father insisted.

"Sorry," said the captain. "We were not given any reason."

The captain spoke with a certain tone of regret and even respect. He had known Don Elazar ben Simeon de Sola e Lunel for a goodly number of years. He had witnessed many times the yearly event when my father, as one of the elders of the kahal of Toulouse, presented himself on the Thursday of Holy Week at the cathedral door with a tax of thirty pounds of wax. On this occasion, it was also the custom for the townsfolk to box that Jew's ears to remind him of the Jews' guilt for the crucifixion. This was a popular local custom, going back to the time of the early Crusades, a sporting event for which half the town turned out. The fortitude and dignity with which my father bore the insults and abuse meted out by the good people of Toulouse had gained him a certain respect among the magistrates and guardsmen who surveyed the proceedings and made sure the mob did not get out of hand.

"Go get the seneschal!" the captain ordered one of his men.

The seneschal came, but he too had no explanation. Orders of the king! There was nothing to be done.

Meanwhile, our brethren with their wives and children were being shackled and led away, one by one, into another Babylonian captivity. So it seemed to me.

Only one day before, we had been sitting on the floor of our house, wrapped in sackcloth, our heads strewn with ashes. I could still hear my father intoning the lilting plaintive of Ekha, *the prophet's lament over the destruction of Jerusalem and its temple. How apt were these familiar sentiments. Did the G-d of Israel once again abandon His people?*

For these things I weep: Mine eye runs down with water;
Because the comforter is far from me; even he that should refresh my soul,
My children are desolate, because the enemy hath prevailed.

I watched my father and the seneschal gesticulating in an animated exchange. There was nothing he could do. It was the king's will, the king of France, Philippe le Bel, sois-dit. *He conspired with the pope. The mob was on their side, ready to seize the opportunity to loot the Jews' property.*

The adversary has spread out his hand, upon all her treasures.
Mine eyes do fail with tears, Mine innards burn,
My liver is poured upon the earth,
For the breach of the daughter of my people.

We were taken to the fortress at the point of the sword. We had no weapons to defend ourselves. What good would it have done anyway? We were surrounded, helpless. The townspeople lined the streets even at such an early hour, taunting us with their venomous insults.

All our enemies have opened their mouth wide against us;
Terror and the pit are come upon us,
Desolation and destruction.
Mine eye runs down with rivers of water,
For the breach of the daughter of my people.

We sat leaning against each other, for comfort and for warmth in the chill, damp cell. My brothers, the twins Natan and Samuel, held me tight between them, spreading their strong bodies over mine as a shield against hate and the darkness that drew us in. What would become of them? *I wondered. I was the gosling whose birth had deprived them of their mother. Though they were young falcons then, not yet ready to take wing, they were old enough to prepare studiously for the day. In due course, they had, like our father, become astute merchants and scholars learned in our laws. Will the exile provide fertile ground for them to prosper again?*

They have chased me sore like a bird,
That are mine enemies without a cause.
They have cut off my life in the dungeon,
And have cast stones upon me.

The little sleep we found was disturbed as the early morning light pierced the narrow slit in the fortress wall. A mob had gathered outside. Shouts of "Death to the Jews! Death to the murderers of Our Lord!" chilled me to the bone.

Thou hast heard their taunts, O Lord,
And all their devices against me;
The lips of those that rose up against me,
And their mutterings against me all day.

In amazement, I watched my father and brothers together with the adult men of the kahal rise and gather in the corner. With their faces turned toward the slots through which the sun began to push its rays, they said their morning prayers. Their prayer shawls were among the few things they had carried with them. Their faith in the G-d of Israel was unshaken.

They hunt our steps that we cannot go in our broad places;
Our end is near, our days are fulfilled;
For our end is come.
Our pursuers were swifter than the eagles of the heaven.

Later, the seneschal had food brought in, which had been taken from our houses and pantries. My father said, "See what a good man he is. He won't cause us any harm." When he came back, the seneschal gathered us around to proclaim the king's will. All persons of the Jewish faith were henceforth banned from the kingdom of France and ordered to depart immediately. All property was to be left behind and was to revert to the crown. The king would personally assume all debts owed to the Jews. The king's guards were to make sure that the Jews take no more than they can carry on their backs and no more provisions than what would last for a three-day journey.

"Depart ye! Unclean!" men cried unto them.
"Depart, depart, touch not."
Yea, they fled away and wandered; men said among the nations:
"They shall no more sojourn here."
They chased us upon the mountains;
They lay in wait for us in the wilderness.
The breath of our nostrils, the anointed of the Lord,
Was taken in their pits, of whom we said:
"Under his shadow we shall live among the nations."

A great moaning rose from among the people of Israel. Cries of "What are we to do?" were heard. Some suggested that death at our own hands was better than exile. Others suggested that the baptismal was better than the loss of all they had labored for. Some were even seen leaving with the captain of the guard, proclaiming their willingness to embrace the Christian faith and to atone for the sins of their people. My father's angry rebuke of the greedy cowards, as he called them, seemed to make the walls tremble. "We must place ourselves into the hand of the Lord G-d of Israel!" he thundered. "He is testing us for a reason known to Him alone. But we shall not fail Him. He will also lead us and shield us in this adversity."

Remember, O Lord, what is come upon us; behold and see our reproach.
Our inheritance is turned unto strangers, our houses unto aliens.
For this our heart is faint; for these things our eyes are dim.

The people rallied around my father. Even the faint-hearted were swept up by his steadfastness. They hailed the faith of their fathers and swore never to lose their trust in the G-d of Abraham, of Isaac, and of Jacob.

Thou, O Lord, are enthroned forever.
Thy throne is from generation to generation.
Turn us unto thee, O Lord, and we shall be turned;
Renew our days as of old.

And so, banished from the place of our birth, with little to sustain us except our memories of happier days, our fate in the hands of the Lord G-d of Israel, we went into exile.

My hands holding the pages began to shake. My glasses fogged up. They had come at night then too, on that November night from the ninth to the tenth. Then too, the blackguards had chosen Shabbat, the Jewish day of rest, for their assault. Booted hordes rampaged through the streets, smashed windows of Jewish-owned stores with rocks and clubs, looted and dumped the merchandise in the street. Synagogues were set on fire and went up in flames.

My father tried to calm my fears, to reassure me that this was just an incident staged by local thugs who were jealous of the Jews. We didn't know then that what my father called an incident was part of a countrywide pogrom, staged in every city and town, from the largest to the smallest, wherever Jews lived in the Third German Reich, but even as a six-year-old, I had the gut feeling that Germany was no longer our home. My premonition was quickly confirmed. At the crack of dawn, the grinding sound of hard-stepping boots ascending the stairway forebode more ill. Harsh knocks on the apartment doors of Jewish residents. We lived on the top floor adjacent to our relatives, the Aschauers. I edged up between my father and uncle who were looking down over the railing. Gestapo agents assisted by local police, two of them holding a snarling attack dog on a leash, were moving from door to door, handcuffing the men of the families. As they opened the entrance door to shove the men outside, the rattling noise of an idling truck sent a deafening echo through the hallway. Their search for a way of escape was in vain, and when the booted trench coats appeared at our door, they had to submit to the same fate as all the other Jewish males. The thugs ransacked our living quarters, smashing furniture and china, ripping pictures and paintings from the walls, tearing books and papers, presumably to uncover any subversive material or, as it seemed to me, for the sheer fun of causing harm.

We still did not know what they had done to my father and uncle, when a troop of brownshirts invaded our apartment, bellowing orders to follow them. They pushed us down the stairs, called us *"Judenschweine,"* but otherwise did not lay hands on either my mother or my aunt. Out in the street, we were herded together with other Jews, mostly women and children, and marched toward the center of the town. It was as if they wanted to give us a guided tour of the devastation they had wrought during the night. They led us past the synagogue, pride of the community, where we had prayed and studied and celebrated our holidays, now a charred skeleton, its burnt-out tower pointing an accusing finger at the leaden November sky.

Although the streets were lined with people, an eerie silence accompanied us on our march. Intermittent shouts and curses from the brownshirts were the only sounds to be heard. I did not dare look up, but felt the piercing stares of the crowd. Were they filled with hostility or pity? I could not tell. My mother squeezed my hand tight, afraid that I might be taken away. When we reached the center of town, where most Jewish businesses were located, her grip tightened even more, bringing tears to my eyes. "Don't cry," she whispered. "Don't let them see a single tear."

The devastation was heartbreaking. Glass splinters were strewn all over the sidewalks. We later learned that, with typical sick Nazi humor, they called this rampage *"Reichskristallnacht"* for all the broken glass they left in their path in cities and towns all over the country. For us, a Cossack-style pogrom had come to civilized Germany. My uncle's store, Aschauer's Men's Apparel and Custom Clothiers, had been torched. This was a loss for all of us since my father had become a business associate a few years before when he was no longer able to practice law.

"This is the end," Aunt Hedy mumbled under her breath. "We must find them and leave this place, this country, immediately."

At that moment, a trooper handed my mother, aunt, and me each a hand broom and small shovel and ordered us to clean up the *"Sauerei."* To make it "easier" for us, the booted, laughing thugs stomped on the broken glass to make sure it was all finely ground into tiny splinters. We labored for hours under the backbreaking chore without food or water. A wintry wind blew through the alleyway from the Baltic Sea. Now intermittent taunts from the onlookers were heard, especially from teenagers in Hitler Youth uniforms. As the day advanced, the crowd in general became more emboldened and their catcalls took on a more hostile tone. Toward evening, someone, apparently the mayor, called off the operation and we were told to go home.

It took my mother and aunt another week to find out that their men were incarcerated at the concentration camp of Sachsenhausen. A few more weeks went by during which there was a lot of negotiating with the authorities, most of which I didn't understand. But eventually, my father and uncle did come home—broken in spirit, my mother said—and within a few months, we packed some of our belongings and left Germany for good.

All this came back to me with a vengeance while I was reading the story of a Jewess who was witness and victim to the expulsion of the Jews from the kingdom of France in the fourteenth century. This presumed eyewitness account of a historical episode so familiar to me unexpectedly touched me on a level much deeper than anything I had ever gleaned from archives and libraries. This second installment of this woman's story—I still didn't know the name of the author, so I just dubbed her the Jewess of Toulouse—had been delivered to the front desk of the hotel while I was out for a walk.

Unable to bear being confined to the stuffy hotel room any longer, I had walked out into the seedy streets of the neighborhood surrounding the hotel, but soon found myself directing my steps toward the center of town, which was more familiar to me from previous visits. Here in the historic core of the city is the cathedral, a magnificent gothic structure. Sure, it's the place where Jews would get their ears boxed on Maundy Thursday or Good Friday, but that doesn't take anything away from its architectural glory. My admiration for things medieval was always mixed with a dash of misgiving because of the treatment the Jews received from the superstitious populace. But then has it ever been any better in modern times?

I strolled across the Place du Capitole, the central square, where *tout* Toulouse always seemed to be hanging out. As I approached the arcade, I caught sight of a man whose eyes seemed focused on me. Nor did he flinch when I, for my part, gazed into his steel-blue eyes. His entire appearance was rather odd, like a transplant from another world, Micromégas descended from outer space. His tall, rough-hewn square frame was clad in a sleeveless sheepskin vest and wide trousers of coarse homespun. His sandals too were of no recognizable modern style and had the irregularities of a handmade item. His black, shoulder-length hair and his beard were interwoven with silvery filigree. The broad-rimmed leather hat cast a shadow over his brooding face. He looked like, what we would call in America, a mountain man, and I wondered what might have taken him to the city where he was like a fish out of water. Yet, most astounding to my eyes were the two magnificent specimen of snow-white Pyrenean sheepdogs flanking his sides. I had come into contact with this breed of dog before, and it had left some fond memories with me from that time when we crossed the mountains from France into Spain. The shepherds who guided us were accompanied by several of these dogs, and I remembered their good naturedness. They let me play, and even roughhouse, with them, allowing me for a few moments to forget the evils in the world from which we were fleeing.

"Vous êtes Américain, n'est pas?" the man addressed me with a stern look in the rolling French of the region. Did I look like an American? Maybe the type of suit I was wearing gave me away. At any rate, the way he mustered me with piercing, suspicious eyes told me I'd better deny the fact.

"Mais non, pas du tout," I replied in my best French accent. To prove the authenticity of my French further, I took a seat near him at a table of a café and engaged the waiter in a lively exchange about the menu of sandwiches and pastries. Since the mountain man, who at first listened intently, soon turned and shuffled back with heavy gait toward the other end of the square, I felt convinced that my attempt to deceive him had been successful.

Nevertheless, my instinct told me it was no coincidence that of all the people milling around in the square, he accosted me with this peculiar question. I decided not to take any chances of being followed and, as a precaution, took a circuitous way back to my hotel. Better safe than sorry. When I entered the lobby, the receptionist handed me the package with the second installment of the strange tale of a Jewess who lived seven hundred years ago in the mountains that separated the kingdom of France from what was then the kingdom of Aragon. Every step of the way, it always seemed to come back to these mountains—the tale of this fourteenth-century Jewess, my childhood memories of crossing the mountain, Nina disappearing in these mountains, and now this mountain man, whose appearance on the scene, I sensed, was part of this whole drama.

I had dozed off after reading the second installment of the Jewess's saga a second time when I was roused by a soft knock on the door. I checked my watch. It was half past midnight. The recurrence of door knocking in the middle of the night, whether soft or loud, began to unnerve me. I began to curse Nina for involving me in whatever scheme she was involved in or whatever game she was playing, and I was in a mood to just quit. But as soon as the thought occurred to me, I also knew that I would and could not leave. For one, Nina was apparently in big trouble, and second, I had already become too engrossed in the story of this Jewess of Toulouse. My scholarly sleuth's instinct had been activated. I couldn't let go of the trail once my nose had picked up a scent.

The rapping on the door now became more impatient, and a hushed woman's voice entreated me to open. As I cautiously opened the door just a crack, she deftly pushed her way inside and closed the door behind her.

The room was dimly lit, and all I was able to make out from a quick glance was a dark-haired woman, maybe about thirty, in blue jeans and a plain T-shirt. It wasn't Nina.

"My name is Etoile. I am Nina's friend. She could not come, but she is waiting for us. We must go without delay," she said in commanding tone of a police inspector. Her French was obviously native and southern-accented. "Don't leave anything behind!"

"Wait a moment. How do I know this isn't some trick?" I objected. "Before I go anywhere, I'd like to check out your credentials."

"Nina thought you might make trouble!" she said in a tone that seemed to me feigning exasperation. "Aren't the two manuscript segments enough proof?"

"That's exactly what I would like to talk about before I head out into the night on command."

She sat down on the bed, this time looking really exasperated. She pushed her thick, dark hair into a wool cap, which made her slightly smudged face appear more clearly. *Nice face,* I thought to myself. I couldn't help but be touched by those brown eyes that seemed to plead with me to understand her predicament.

"I promised Nina we would return before daybreak," she said softly.

"So where is Nina? May I know at least that much?"

"I'll take you to her" was all of a reply I got.

"I have to check out of the hotel," I said so as not to seem too hasty to comply. My childhood experiences of precipitous departures for unknown destinations had left a bitter taste for such ventures, and not being able to oversee the playing field caused me a good deal of discomfort. But I was beginning to develop a soft spot for this attractive woman who was apparently doing Nina a favor, and I was willing to be satisfied with the information she gave me to follow her. After all, I was eager to link up finally with my wayward cousin.

"It's already paid for. You can reimburse me later." She got up from the bed and tightened the beige trench coat draping her slender figure. *Very cloak and dagger,* I thought.

I gathered my belongings while she looked around and nervously twirled a set of keys.

"Don't forget the notebooks." She pointed at them on the night table.

"Of course not. Not for the life of me."

We descended a back staircase I didn't know existed, which took us into an inner yard that was used as parking garage. She steered toward a black Renault Quatrelle and motioned for me to put my bag on the backseat and myself into the front. Judging from the way she opened the massive wooden entrance door and closed it again, refusing my assistance once we were out in the street, she had been here before. Her familiarity with this place was clear, and it must have been the reason why Nina, or maybe she, wanted me to stay in this particular hotel.

Self-assured, yet without saying a word, she maneuvered the car through the narrow, almost deserted labyrinth of one-way streets toward the outskirts of the city. I looked at her from the side, but she kept her eyes pinned on the roadway that was still slick and slippery from an earlier downpour. Had I gone mad to follow a strange woman in the middle of the night without asking any questions and demanding to know where we were headed? She was an attractive woman with North African features, but that was beside the point. She knew about the notebooks, which she had most likely delivered to me herself. Why the mystery?

Once we were outside the city, she turned on the full headlights and sighed with relief. She turned toward me with a smile and extended her hand.

"I am Etoile Assous, Nina's friend," she said.

"Enchanté," I replied. "I guess you know who I am."

"Oh yes, I know all about you," she said with a gurgling laughter. It escaped me what she found so funny about this.

"All joking aside"—who was joking?—"Nina is waiting for you."

"Well, I have been waiting for Nina. And I'm eager to hear her explanation for this cat and mouse game."

Etoile made no reply. It was a dark, starless night, and I could see that navigating the bumpy country roads required her full concentration.

"We are getting away from Toulouse," I said, stating the obvious. She nodded.

Stating another by-now obvious fact, I said, "Nina is not in Toulouse." She nodded again.

"She is in Montauban?" I ventured a guess since that seemed to be the direction we were taking. She shook her head, indicating that my questions had to wait. I took the hint.

After a while, we reached a more passable highway and she turned toward me again with a smile. A rather pleasant, warming smile, I thought.

"Do you like playing cloak and daggers?" I asked.

"I'm sorry. I don't mean to be rude," she said. "Nina couldn't stay in Toulouse. It was too dangerous for her there."

"What, did she rob a bank?"

"Don't be silly!" she chortled.

I just nodded, too tired at this point to ask any more questions. Etoile, in contrast, seemed now quite talkative.

"We have known each other since Nina's postdoctoral studies at the university. I was a student then and we became good friends. You know the kind of friendship that is rare and that lasts a lifetime. We come from different worlds and yet we found we had much in common besides also being Jewish."

I said something to the effect that I understood well what she meant without really understanding anything.

"I was born in Tunisia." She became talkative all of a sudden. "We came to France only five years before, right after the Six-Day War between Israel and the Arabs in 1967. There was rioting in the streets of Djerba and other cities after Israel's victory. The government tried to protect us against the mob. Bourghiba even apologized to the chief rabbi. They knew it would not be wise economically to get rid of the Jews. But then they somehow figured that robbing us of all we owned would make up for the loss of revenue. They drove us out with barely more than the clothes on our backs and a hundred francs in our pockets. After twenty-eight hundred years!"

Suddenly I was wide awake. Her remark jolted me momentarily out of my stupor.

"How do you mean?"

"Don't you know? The Jewish community of Tunisia goes back to the time of the destruction of the first temple. Almost three thousand years. We were there long before the Arabs."

This was news to me, and I asked her to explain.

"Whether this is so or not, who knows? The story may be apocryphal, but there definitely was a Jewish community in the area of Carthage in Roman times."

From the way she spoke, I surmised that she was a historian. Though I would have liked to continue the conversation, my head was too swollen from lack of sleep.

While she was preoccupied with navigating the winding curves, I dozed off, being jolted awake every time she went over a bump or pothole without slowing down. She had apparently been continuing her monologue without noticing or caring for my somnolent condition.

"I was supposed to continue the family tradition and go into law," I heard her say in a brief moment of lucidness. "My grandfather was also a lawyer and a judge in Tunisia. But can you see me as a lawyer, me arguing a case in court?" Actually, I thought, I could very well see her in that role, given her eloquence of which she had furnished amble proof in the very short time we had been acquainted.

"I was more interested in history, especially medieval history. How can you not, living in this country where it's impossible to take a step without being touched by the past. It's everywhere. So that's the area of my doctorate. I'm still in the writing stage."

I simply nodded.

"I've read a few of your books."

"Oh, really?" I said. My expectation that she might be trying to suck up to me, as the students say, to get an endorsement was not met, however. No gushing praise or the like followed. It was a simple statement of fact. And why shouldn't she have read them, since we were apparently in the same field?

"Nina recommended your writings to me," she added. "She was my mentor during her year at Toulouse. We became good friends. She also got me interested in the history of women."

Oh dear, not now, I thought. *Please, it's too late at night, or rather, early in the morning. My brain is too washed out for this.*

"But, you know, the feminist paradigm," she continued, "simply doesn't work for my study of Rashi's daughters."

There she got me again. This was, of course, a different matter.

"If you will permit me, I'd like to read your work sometime."

"Certainly," she said. "But first we have a more important project to tend to."

It was almost four in the morning; the birds were chirping their morning symphony when we reached the town of Albi, a place not unfamiliar to me.

Dina's Tale 3

So we departed. We joined a caravan of exiled Jews heading south toward the mountains, toward Iberia. All were filled with hope of finding a new life and wealth in the kingdom of Aragon, in Catalonia, or even further south in Castile.

My father forged ahead with resolute stride, a shepherd's staff in hand, his grizzled beard flowing. I looked at him with pride and admiration from the two-wheeled cart that carried our meager belongings and me when I got too tired to walk. Like Moses leading the Israelites into the desert, *I thought. I loved him more than ever. He had always sheltered me so that no harm should come to me. Since my mother had died a few weeks after I was born, most likely from childbed fever, I had been the apple of his eye, his most precious jewel. The loss of his faithful companion touched him deeply, but rather than being embittered, he bowed to G-d's will. My brothers too treated me like a princess from whom they sought to avert all evil.*

I was confident that our new life on the other side of the mountains would be as prosperous and happy as it had been in the home from which we had been expelled. My father, like his father before him, had carried on a thriving transmontane trade for many decades. He had business and family connections in the great centers of commerce and learning, places with exotic names like Zaragossa, Gerona, and Tarragona, which I often dreamed about and hoped to see some day. In one of those cities, Gerona, lived my betrothed, to whom I had been promised when I was four years old. He was the son of a wealthy merchant, a partner in my father's many commercial enterprises. Every time my father came back from one of his journeys, he would tell me about Shlomo ben Gabirol, my intended, how he was growing into a fine scholar, a true prince of learning. Now, so I hoped, I would finally get to see and meet him, and we would surely soon be wed.

"A wedding?" My father shook his head. "I am afraid nothing will come of that."

"But why not? We have spoken about it for so long. You made a pact with Don Gabirol, and now the time has come. Hasn't it?" A shadow clouded my father's brow. Disappointment and a dark foreboding gripped my heart.

"This pact becomes invalid if one party is unable to meet the conditions set forth in it," he hesitantly began to explain, taking my hand in his and stroking it gently. "We had to leave everything we owned behind, and it will take years, even under the best circumstances, to accumulate enough for the dowry agreed upon."

It was only at this moment that the full extent of our situation was revealed to me. We were poor. The king of France had robbed us of all we had. All the wealth my grandfather and father had accumulated through hard, diligent work and a keen sense of commerce was gone. The king had seized the stock of merchandise, of great value, in my father's warehouses. The royal brigand had robbed us of our very existence, the fine fabrics and embroidered linens that were the mainstay of my father's trading network, which reached from Flanders to Iberia, from Occitania to the Empire. He exchanged huge bales of silk, velvet, damask, and brocade for a variety of goods and merchandise—spices and jewelry from the Orient, leather and metal goods from the north. I don't remember it all, but the value of my father's fortune was somewhere in the thousands of livres tournois *and* écus d'or. *Despite the heavy taxes levied on the Jews, we lived comfortably. Now it was all gone. Nothing was left besides a rickety wain pulled by a donkey. It was this wain, my sons, that was to add to our misfortune; or I should say, it was this wain that caused the calamity of your mother's life.*

I shouldn't blame an inanimate object for what was done to me by human hand. It is not easy for me to speak about what happened. You already know part of it. You know that I was separated from my family and my people, but you shall know how it all came about, however difficult it is for me to speak about it and to relive that night and the days and years that followed. It is not your pity I am seeking, but your understanding of the circumstances that so embittered my heart that I had to do what I did in order to lift the heavy cloud that has overshadowed my existence for so many years until now.

I was Miryam, namesake of the prophetess and sweet singer in Israel, the daughter of a merchant prince, a proud standard-bearer of his faith and his people. I was clothed in silk and velvet and nourished on milk and honey. I imbibed the lore of our sacred scriptures and the wisdom of our sages. I was tended to hand and foot. I was like a rose of Sharon, a lily of the valley. My skin was like polished ivory, caressed with sweet fragrant oils. My hair was a cascade of raven black curls. I was the betrothed of a true prince in Israel.

Now I am Dina, the name I have chosen for myself. I have become Dina, namesake of Jacob's daughter, the defiled, the dishonored, the daughter violated by the uncircumcised. Dina, the outcast, the leper, banished from the gates of the city, condemned to dwell in the wilderness like Azazel. My garments are drab homespun; my repast is gruel and curds. My body reeks of sweat, and the stench of the barnyard clings to my skin. My hands are roughened and gnarled by labor in the field and ostal. My hair is coarse and unkempt with sticky graying strands tucked under a peasant bonnet.

Now, in my thirty-fifth year, my brow is furrowed and my skin wrinkled. The light of my eyes has dimmed before its time. I am like one approaching her dotage. How did all this come about? You want to know, and you will know, my sons. I shall try to relate the circumstances of that which brought about my misfortune truthfully and precisely. I shall hold nothing back, however much it may pain me to recall. All I beg of you is to have patience with me, and if you must judge me, to do it fairly.

We were allowed only enough provisions to last three days and were therefore forced to seek the border of the kingdom of France in great haste. As our luck would have it, the rocky terrain of the foothills of the mountains was too much for the creaking wain on which I was riding. It began to skid and bump until several spokes on one of its wheels cracked a short distance from one of the villages we were trying to circumvent on our journey. Now we had no choice but to enter the village and look for a wainwright.

My brothers pulled the damaged cart into the village. The setting sun already glowed over the western mountains, but, in my father's estimate, there was still enough daylight for us to leave the village before nightfall if the repair was done immediately. At first, the wainwright claimed he had too much work to do and we should come back the next day. Come back from where? My father tried to explain the urgency of our situation without revealing that we were Jews, maybe hoping that these villagers were not familiar with our distinctive clothing. But it fell on deaf ears. The man, viewing us strangers with a suspicious eye, insisted there was nothing he could do.

Meanwhile, a crowd of curiosity seekers began to form in front of the wainwright's shop. It was immediately clear to us that this was a community of rather impoverished peasants and shepherds, who eked out their living fairly isolated from the rest of the world. But a few of them, shepherds who drove their flocks of sheep south over the mountains for wintering in Aragon, had gained a broader view of the world.

"They are Jews! Christ murderers!" a voice rose from the crowd, whose owner apparently recognized the distinctive marks on the clothing Jews were forced to display by papal decree. Before long, the rest of the villagers chimed in to form a swelling chorus. "Death to the Jews! Death to the Christ-killers!"

This did it for the wainwright.

"I don't work for Jews," he proclaimed emboldened. "You'd better get your cart out of here the way you came."

Shouts of "Death to the Jews!" rose to a deafening din, and we began to fear for our lives. We gathered our belongings and slowly made our way through the increasingly agitated throng that formed a gauntlet of piercing, hate-filled eyes. We had not yet reached the edge of the village when all of a sudden there was dead silence behind us.

We turned around. Oh, had we just moved on! Had we only gone on our way! Had we never looked back! Had we only ditched the wain, which was not much good up on the higher mountain passes anyway. I could have walked. Had I foreseen what was to happen, I would have hastened to leave this village. But curiosity got the better of us. Like Lot's wife, we turned around. We were not turned into pillars of salt, but our lives were transformed forever.

There he was. A tall, slender figure in priest's garb, his hands raised over his humble flock.

"Good people, remember what our Lord and Savior has commanded us. Be kind to the stranger in your midst! Help those in need!" This was the first time I heard his voice—strong and calm, the unctuous voice of a preacher.

Someone in the crowd made a meek attempt of objecting. We were Jews, killers of the Lord and Savior and desecrators of the Holy Host, and worse.

The priest only had to raise his arms to muffle the voices bold enough to utter agreement with the dissenter.

"Remember the parable of the Good Samaritan and what Our Lord meant to teach us. There is goodness in the most reviled of G-d's children. These people, too, though they may be of the despised race guilty of causing the death of Our Savior, were created in the image of the Creator. Even if they are too blind and too stubborn to acknowledge the true Messiah, they once were G-d's chosen people and they deserve our pity now that they are in need."

A spell seemed to spread over the villagers. Not a sound was heard as the preacher took firm, deliberate steps to where we were standing, equally spellbound and unable to move.

"I beg you to forgive these ignorant peasants, sire," he addressed my father.

"We are grateful to you for your intercession," my father replied with a respectful bow. "We meant no harm or trouble. But time is pressing and we must move on."

"Oh, not at all! It is getting late, and the sun will set soon behind the mountains which are treacherous to cross at night. You had better stay the night here. The wainwright will have your wagon repaired by morning."

My father explained that he was quite familiar with the mountain passes and that we would make camp further down the path where we would not be in anybody's way.

"I must insist that you accept my hospitality. The mountains are no place for a lady." I lowered my head to avoid the brazenness I sensed behind the outwardly compassionate gaze he fixed on me.

My father assured him of our gratitude, but we wanted to be of no trouble. By order of his majesty, the king of France, we had been ordered to leave the kingdom without delay under penalty of death.

"The king of France! Ha-ha!" The priest made a defiant gesture. "His word is nothing around here," he added with a disdainful snort. "I insist you accept my hospitality. Not even the king of France will touch a single hair on your head as long as you are under my roof. Be assured."

At last my father was persuaded that we had best pass the night in the barn of the parish house since dusk had turned to darkness by then. He declined to partake of the food that was offered, reminding the priest that we live by the dietary laws of Moses. Water from the well would be gratefully received.

We settled down for the night in the barn, still anxious, but in some way grateful for the rest before the more arduous stretch of our journey. The wainwright, who had been ordered by the priest to take the cart back to his shop, promised to have it ready before we departed in the morning.

My father and brothers were saying their evening prayers when the priest appeared before us as out of nowhere. We had heard neither approaching steps nor the door opening. He wanted to be sure that we wanted for nothing, that we weren't lacking in comfort. But he didn't mean to disturb our devotion. He was pleased to see that Jews, too, prayed to the Creator. I wondered why he was so ingratiating toward us, the people whom he had earlier called blind and stubborn when speaking to the peasants.

When my father and brothers had finished praying, the priest expressed his fascination with the prayer shawls and the phylacteries, which my father and brothers folded up and put away with meticulous care. He had never seen any of this and asked to be enlightened about their meaning and practice. I saw my father's discomfort, but he couldn't refuse our host, whose interest seemed to flag, however, very quickly, even before my father had finished his excursus.

"I don't think this hayloft is a proper accommodation for a lady," he said suddenly, cutting off my father in mid-sentence. "You must allow her to lodge inside my house. My housekeeper will prepare a chamber more befitting a lady."

I felt a growing uneasiness about being repeatedly referred to as "lady." My father again argued that we did not want to incommode our gracious host. I protested that I was quite comfortable in the barn. But then my father began to succumb to the priest's insistence. His gem, the apple of his eye, should not have to sleep on a bed of straw. He relented. He let me go. Little did he know that he sealed my fate—that the wolf in sheep's clothes, the devil in priest's garb, was laying out the snare in which to catch his prey.

My hand trembles and the pulse of my heart flutters. I must pause here, my sons, to gather enough strength to conjure up the memory of that distant night. It will be painful for me to write this down, and it may be painful for you to read this, but it must be done; it must be said for the sake of the truth and for the sake of my love for you. You were the only light in the darkness into which I was plunged then.

My heart was pounding and my head was numb. I too had to pause. Although I knew by then what was to come—Dina had prepared her readers well for the dramatic climax—I felt I had to catch my breath. So overwhelmed was I by the fate of this Jewish woman who lived seven hundred years ago.

Etoile had left this third installment next to the couch in the basement room where she temporarily quartered me at her parents' house. When we arrived in the early morning hours, she led me downstairs and politely suggested I make myself at home. Nina was still nowhere to be seen. For this I was actually grateful at that moment, for all I could think of was sleep. It must have been the notebook next to me that didn't let me rest for very long. Within an hour, I was sitting up reading, eagerly absorbing Dina's story. I finally knew her name—should I say Miryam Dina or Dina Miryam?

I needed some time to think, to let my mind wander back to the annals of history, back to a time synonymous with fanaticism and superstition, intolerance and unrestrained cruelty. (Was our world and time any different?) A period of history, called the Middle Ages by historians, I had studied for many years in archives and libraries. Now, I deemed myself lucky to be in the town of Albi. What better place was there in which to connect the centuries, a place where every stone, every building forms a bridge to the past? This city is forever linked to one of the bloodiest chapters in French history, an episode marked in history books as the Albigensian Crusade. In the century before Dina Miryam and the Jews were driven from their homes, the Inquisition, with the support of the king of France, had launched a merciless campaign against the Cathar heresy, which had large numbers of adherents in this region.

Careful not to rouse anybody, I found my way out into the streets. I remembered the narrow alleys lined with huddled houses of red brick and cross beams and bright-red tiled roofs, some standing out with shutters painted with regional pastel colors from previous visits. The early summer sun began its rise just then, daubing the ancient medieval structures in an iridescent kaleidoscope of colors from crimson to vermilion, from scarlet to pomegranate, and gradually fading out into lighter shades of coral and amber. This was Albi in all its glory, rightfully called the "Red City."

From the alleys, I walked out onto the plaça in front of the cathedral of La Sainte-Cécilie, whose massive red brick edifice holds sway over the entire town. Begun after the triumphal suppression of the Cathar heresy, the unique fortress-like exterior, its single rather graceless tower piercing the sky, always seemed to me more a bastion of Church power, a warning against errancy than a house of worship.

From a brief contemplation of the fate of the Cathars, my thoughts wandered back to Dina Miryam and her story. She also mentions heretics. Was the priest a heretic? Again and again, I went over what I had learned of her so far. It all fit so well into the history I knew. Almost too well. Was it possible that Nina had uncovered a hitherto unknown primary source, a personal account mirroring the soul and time of a medieval Jewish woman? Things like that did happen on occasion, but as a scholar, I had to be skeptical. The sudden, almost miraculous, discovery of medieval manuscripts, especially of hitherto unknown authorship, had become all too frequent of late. Many were proven to be forgeries, some cleverly manufactured and not so easily exposed, while others, the majority, were easily detectable as modern productions.

Whatever warning signal the scholar in me was sending up, the human side of me was, as the saying goes, "hooked." I wanted to be part of the life of this Dina Miryam. Her story gripped me like a well-written suspense novel. Maybe I felt a bond with her because she was a Jewish woman, or in the more poetic, now archaic, term, a Jewess. I certainly wouldn't deny that possibility. In fact, I would assert it. Had I lived in her time in the kingdom of France, I would have shared the fate of her people. I too would have been expelled.

I fancied myself that I would have protected her against the evil in the world. *Fantasy and quite unscholarly!* the scholar in me raised his voice again. But I rebuked him. *I am not here on a scholarly mission. So leave me alone and let me indulge my dreams.*

On entering the house of my hostess, I was enveloped in an enticing aroma of fresh brewed coffee and baked bread. Etoile motioned me from the kitchen to take a seat in the dining room where the table was set for three.

"Have you been to Albi before?" she asked.

"Yes, several times," I replied.

We engaged in small talk about the attractions and merits of this quaint little town. I looked around for the third person.

"Nina will be up in a moment," Etoile chattered on. "My parents have left for work already. They look forward to meeting you later."

When she saw my puzzled expression, she explained, "This is my parents' house. Didn't I say that?"

"Possibly. I was too tired to register."

"Toulouse was getting too dangerous, especially for Nina."

"I'm still waiting to find out what this is all about," I said in a tone more caustic than I intended.

"I understand your impatience."

Etoile poured me a big, round cup of café au lait and placed a warm roll with butter and strawberry preserves on the plate before me.

"You must be starved. Believe me, your wait will soon be over. I just want to leave it to Nina."

"What do you want to leave to Nina?"

I turned in the direction of the unfamiliar, slightly hoarse female voice. The woman I saw standing in the doorway wasn't the Nina I knew. True, last time I saw her, she was just graduating from college, and people change with age. It wasn't so much that she had matured, which she had as one would expect. She was haggard, and her skin was almost sallow. The sparkle had gone out of those bright blue eyes I had remembered so fondly. She looked at me with a near-sighted squint. Against my will, I averted my eyes.

"To explain to your cousin why you had him come here all the way from Chicago and then left him twisting for a week." To my surprise, I clearly detected a caustic strain in Etoile's voice as well. "But have your breakfast first," she added in a softer tone, apparently regretting the slip up.

Nina came over and took me by the hand. She did not embrace me as I would have expected.

"Henner, I'm so grateful that you are here," she said in English. Tears appeared in her eyes. She sank onto one of the chairs at the table and began to sob uncontrollably. I looked at Etoile. She put a finger to her lips. It would be best to wait. After a while, the sobs subsided. Still choked, Nina asked me to forgive her.

"I've made such a mess of my life, and other people's lives, my children's lives. And now I'm dragging you into this. But you are my only hope, the only person who will be able to keep me from drowning in this morass."

A bit melodramatic, I thought, but that was Nina all right. But what is this? She has children? I said nothing at first. I waited patiently for her to fill me in on what this "morass" was.

"For all I care, it doesn't even matter whether I go under or not," she continued. "Other lives are involved that are more important than mine."

"You have children? Now, that's a surprise!" I didn't know why it should surprise me, but it just hadn't entered my mind.

"Oh, yes. Didn't you know? I guess Etoile didn't tell you—two adorable boys." Her face lit up for a moment.

"Well, mazel tov! Your mother will be thrilled."

And like a good yenta, my next question was: "What are their names and how old are they?"

"Arnaud is four, almost five, and Bernard is two." Tears welled in her eyes once more. "I miss them so much. I have to get back to them without further delay. It's already been too long."

She chattered on with a litany of self-recrimination about what a terrible mother she was and how much she missed them.

"This makes the matter all the more urgent," I concluded. Fearful that she might go off the cliff, I directed the conversation onto a more practical subject. I could find out more about personal things later.

"In your letter, you asked me to bring a quite tidy sum of money," I said.

She raised her head and looked at me seemingly confused. It took her awhile before she grasped what I was saying, and then she gave off a nervous laugh when it finally clicked.

"Yes, of course. We do need money. I don't have a penny. Please give whatever you have to Etoile. I've been living on her good graces these last two months."

Etoile shook her head and made a dismissive gesture. But realizing the situation, I insisted that she take the money. She gave in when I said that this included remuneration for the hotel bill I owed her.

"I don't know how I will ever thank you enough," Nina said to Etoile. "I don't deserve such a friend."

Etoile told her to stop talking nonsense and get to the point.

"Let's talk about the manuscript, if that's what it is," I said. "A fascinating story. Is there more?"

"You bet. There is a lot more to transcribe, and we have little time." Nina was becoming quite animated. "That's why I need your help."

"Wait a minute. It's a fascinating story, but have you considered its authenticity? There's a flourishing market of forgeries."

"Are you suggesting that I made this up?" Nina exploded. "I'm risking my life, and you think this is some con game!"

"No need to fly off the handle!"

Her anger seemed totally out of proportion to what I thought was a reasonable consideration. It took Etoile's persuasion to calm her and keep her from assaulting me.

"He's the only one who can help you out of this mess you've gotten yourself into," the friend reminded her bluntly.

Was this the Nina for whom I had come five thousand miles because she seemed to be in trouble? This wasn't the Nina I remembered, the Nina of my youth. The woman I saw before me had the demeanor of—I hesitate to say it but cannot come up with any other description—a fearful, hunted animal. But she also seemed like a woman obsessed. She had aged prematurely. Like Dina Miryam, it occurred to me. Nina was then about the same age, thirty-five, as this forebear stated when she started writing the account of her life.

"As a scholar, I have to be skeptical," I said softly when the seas had calmed.

"Of course you must. Please forgive my rattled nerves."

She then led me by the hand down to the basement and into a tiny room, next to the one I had been assigned a few hours before. This room was furnished with just a table and two chairs and a small bookshelf. On the table was an object wrapped in a white towel, and next to it was one of the notebooks by now so familiar to me. Nina handed me a pair of white cotton gloves and put on a pair herself. Then she pointed to a chair for me to sit on. She sat down on the other one opposite me.

"This is my workroom. Etoile and her parents have kindly put it at my disposal."

As she spoke, she slowly lifted the towel from the object in the middle of the table. I felt my heart beat faster. I took several long, deep breaths. Before my eyes lay a scholar's dream: a codex of sheets of parchment held together in a frayed yellowing white leather binding. My trained eye immediately started to assess its authenticity.

"May I?"

She nodded.

It was a good thing I was wearing gloves to cover the sweat of my palms.

I brought the codex toward me and turned a few pages. When I stopped and looked closer, I gave off a sound of surprise. My amazement knew no bounds.

"It's Hebrew," I stated breathlessly. She nodded with a smile: "The letters are, but look closer."

"Is this a test?"

"It certainly is. But I'm sure you are up to the challenge."

I took out my reading glasses and focused in on several sentences. Expecting to find a Hebrew text, I was confused when I couldn't make sense of it at first. A few more attempts and the scales fell from my eyes.

"She wrote in Occitan but used the Hebrew alphabet!" I declared triumphantly.

"Bravo! Bravo!" Nina clapped her hands together like a cheerleader.

"So you have been transcribing, not copying," I concluded.

"With the help of Etoile! I learned to speak Occitan these last years, and Etoile has studied it as well. We are both proficient in

Hebrew, but it is still slow going, too slow, and time is pressing. So we hope you can help us move things along."

"*Avec plaisir!*" I couldn't stop looking at the letters, so beautifully and meticulously drawn. They were a bit faded but still clearly legible. "Dina Miryam," I said under my breath admiringly.

"You did a fabulous job," I told the two ladies. "Do you have any more than what I've already seen?"

"Aha, he can't get enough. He's already in love with our heroine," Nina giggled. "We are working on the episode in the priest's house. We found it very difficult. The emotional subject matter is overwhelming," she added with a serious mien.

"I understand. She's prepared us well for what is to come."

Eager to get started, I looked around the little room and determined that this space was not adequate for all of us to work in. I told them this much, and they agreed but saw no alternative.

"The best solution is a hotel nearby," I suggested. I assuaged their concerns about the cost. By now, this undertaking had become so dear to me I wouldn't shy away from any expense within my means. By afternoon, we moved into a suite of two bedrooms separated by a spacious living room in one of the modernized hotels located within a historic building.

"They will never look for us here," Nina said with satisfaction.

She was obviously running from someone. I remembered the tall man in shepherd's clothes with two Pyrenean hounds who had asked me if I was American in the Place du Capitole in Toulouse. At first I hesitated to mention the incident. But then I realized that it certainly was no coincidence and that the man must have had something to do with Nina and her fears of being followed.

"That was Alphonse," she acknowledged. "So he's still in Toulouse."

"Who is Alphonse?"

"My husband," she said.

What? I thought. This is getting more and more curious. *She's married—and to this creepy sasquatch? Was he the guy she had been sick over and run away from home for? And now she was in fear of her life because of him? Nina, Nina! What have you gotten yourself into? I was overcome with the same sense of protectiveness for her as when she was a child.*

Yet, the more I thought about it, I also felt that there must be something else going on. A chilling suspicion entered my mind.

"Tell me, where did you get this codex?" I asked her as we were settling down to work. "Things like this don't just lie around somewhere in the streets of France for the taking."

"I stole it," she replied. "We'll have to return it when we are done."

DINA'S TALE 4

What I now have to relate to you, my precious sons, is a matter prickly as thorns. It concerns the carnal intercourse between your mother and the man who begot you. To make good on my promise that I will be as truthful as I can, that I will hold nothing back, I have searched the recesses of memory and looked deep into my soul. In recent days, I have relived in my mind that which in all these years has festered in my heart as the horror of that night when he first took possession of my body. These are secrets that are best kept buried deep in a mother's heart. Such secrets are not lightly revealed to a mother's sons. Even my quill falters, averse to causing you so much shame. But I beg of you, be indulgent, open your hearts, have mercy. For the sake of your peace of mind and mine, the truth must be told. I shall hold nothing back.

A grain of doubt has been planted in my mind. My ruminations have taken me back to the beginning, to the night I was defiled, the night I was made an outcast. Now my certainty about what happened has been shattered. Was it truly rape that enslaved me to the priest? True, he knew me later many times against my will. But on the first night, of what happened on the night when he, the sly fox, pried me away from my father's vigilant eyes and then stole into my bed, I am no longer certain.

What I am certain of is that the priest duped my father into believing that he had my comfort at heart. My father, ever anxious his little gem should have the best, could not conceive of a man of G-d, even a priest ordained in the Christian Church, as a wolf in sheep's clothing. The housekeeper would take care of me, the priest assured him. And so she did. Used to following her master's every command, she bedded me down in a small, cozy chamber. The bedstead and sparse furnishings of a wooden chair and table took up most of the room. Worn from the day's rough journey, I sank into the softness of the eiderdown and must have dozed off even before I had finished saying the Shema *prayer. How much time had passed between dreaming of that night when the soldiers came and being roused by the sense of a strange presence near me, I could not tell. Startled by what I perceived through eyes half-asleep, I let out a muffled scream. But the priest already stood over me and placed his hand over my mouth.*

"Don't be afraid. I mean you no harm," he whispered gently. A faint voice told me by proper decorum I should fight him off; I should bar him from entering the bed with all the strength I had. But my entire body was as lead, the hand I tried to lift against the intruder too feeble to do my will. He said much more, most of which was incomprehensible and confusing to my blurred senses. His sweet talk stilled the small voice of defiance in me and wore away any will to resistance I had left. All I know is that I liked the rushing of his breath against my ear. I remember how pleasing was the tingling that ran through me when he pressed his lips against mine. I remember the sense of pleasure and longing his smooth, naked skin rubbing against mine aroused in me. I remember all of these heretofore-unknown sensations that suffused my entire body and compelled me to relinquish myself to his desire.

He cradled me and spoke soothingly to me when I gasped in pain. He promised a garden of endless delights from then on. And so it was. I finally went to sleep in his arms. I think I was even happy. But when I woke with the cock's crow and realized what had happened, when the full extent of that night became clear to me and I realized that I would not be able to look my father in the eye again, I broke down and wept bitter tears of remorse. "What have I done? What have I done?" was all I could utter. I tore my hair and buried my face in the bed of sin.

Suddenly I became aware of my father's and the priest's voices. I ran outside, unkempt and untidy. Never will I forget my father's horrified demeanor. He started to rush toward me, but the priest's cunning knew no mercy. He pulled out the white sheet stained with blood. His stance erect, his mien proud, he waved the trophy of a conquering hero. My father cringed and shielded his eyes; he winced as if lightning had struck his stooped body.

"What happened to you, my child?" my father cried out. "What have they done to my child?"

My brothers had just then finished their morning prayers on the other side of the barn. Hearing my father's moaning, they hurried to his side. Their initial expression of disbelief quickly gave way to one of shock and revulsion at the sight of me next to the priest who was still holding his banner of triumph.

"It's time for you to move on now," the priest commanded. "It's still a long, arduous way to the border of the kingdom. A patrol of the royal militia might pass any moment."

"But my daughter, my child ..." my father pleaded.

"The girl stays here!"

"No harm will come to her, you have my solemn promise," the priest assumed a most soothing tone again.

"My child, is this your wish?" My father extended his arms toward me. My heart bled, but I realized our bond was broken. I had caused our bond to break; I had cut myself off from my family, from my people.

"He made me his whore." I was barely able to pronounce the words, but they were audible enough. "You had better go now. Save yourself."

What followed made me cringe as if a quiver of arrows had slashed my chest. A part of me died then in the priest's barnyard. The sun should have refused to rise on that day, and the world should have been cast into darkness. But she rose undeterred from behind the mountains and radiated her glory over an uncaring world. Through a veil of tears and eyes blinded by the sun's rays, I saw my father fall on his knees emitting a bone-chilling cry. He tore his mantle and covered his head with dust. Close to him, my brothers followed his example.

I closed my eyes to shut out the sting of the rays of the rising sun. For a moment, there was still a flicker of hope burning in me that my brothers would rise like Shimon and Levi and avenge the outrage committed against their sister. I saw them unsheathe their knives, fall upon the evildoer, bludgeon him, and sever the offending uncircumcised member. Then the thought made me shudder. It brought back with a jolt the memory of the night, the rapture I had experienced as the priest fused his body to mine. Once again my body felt the warmth and tenderness of his touch; the pungent peasant smell still clung to my skin and aroused my innards. My heart was sagging, too limp and feeble to gather the will for vengeance. All I felt was a craving to imbibe more of the sweet, forbidden nectar that had suffused my senses with unknown delight. I had no desire but to be immersed once more in the tumultuous river of ecstasy without regard for what was to come of it.

The sound of the wailing lament, the hymn to the glory of G-d, my death knell, jolted me back into the real world. I scolded myself for the evil thoughts and desires. I looked at my brothers prostrate on the ground and in my mind exhorted them to rise, not to let the affront against the honor of the family go unpunished. But I saw their weakness. Centuries of oppression, of persecution, of massacres, of injustice against our people had turned them from lions of the desert into cowed weaklings. Life in the galut, the long sojourn in foreign lands had cut them off from the lifeblood of their nascent soil. The sword of Joshua and David had been broken over them. The constant threat to their life and limb, the cudgel of interminable restrictions and regulations on their coming and going and where they could reside, the chokehold of usurious taxes while being accused of usury, the savagery of mobs unleashed against them at the spur of a moment, all this and more had sucked the marrow out of their spines. Harsh words, but too true. Through no fault of their own, they had to bear the humiliation to survive. Standing up to authority and defying power would expose them to more violence and even death.

Never will I forget the story my father had told so often of the libel against the Jews of Blois in the reign of Louis VII. How a stable boy accused them of murder and bloodshed, supposedly to use the blood in the baking of their unleavened bread, and how the entire kahal was burned alive. No, my brothers would not take up the sword of Shimon and Levi. Nor would I have wanted them to risk their lives for a transgression in which I had to admit myself complicit. When I opened my eyes, I saw their crouched bodies wrapped in prayer shawls, still wailing "Yitgadal ve yitgadash, shemei rabba …" *For my father and my brothers, I was already dead.*

At this moment, I wanted nothing more than to see them go, for them to leave me to my fate. A sigh of relief escaped my lips when they had finally finished their lament. Their eyes lowered, and without as much as a glance back at me and the priest, they loaded their few belongings onto the mule, and with heavy gait and flaccid shoulders, they set out for the mountains. My father seemed to have aged ten years or more in this one night. Like a mourner, he leaned on his sons to steady his stride. I was dead and buried.

My eyes remained fixed on the little band until they had disappeared in the dust of the mountain path. The wainwright later brought over the two-wheel cart repaired. It remained stored away in the corner of the yard, unused until now.

"Enough!" Nina threw her pen across the table and slumped down in her chair. This passage was really getting under her skin.

Etoile started pouring tea from a fresh pot she had ordered from room service with a plate of biscuits.

"You take it too personally," she said to Nina.

"Dina Miryam has us all enthralled," I added. "It would be heartless not to feel for her."

"What do *you* know, Henner?" Nina said.

"Not a damn thing," I replied, taken aback by her aggressive tone.

"Don't you think it inappropriate to attack our benefactor?" Etoile admonished her, calm and collected as ever. "Look, we've made more progress in one day than we made in one week before. And that's due to his help. We've benefitted from his great knowledge and expertise. Shouldn't we show some gratitude?"

Etoile! She did her name true honor; she truly was a shining star at that moment. I felt a strong attraction developing for her, and, I had to admit, beyond the purely platonic. If I had been ten or fifteen years younger, I might have attempted a move. But as the matter stood, I suggested that we go out for dinner.

"I don't know about you," I said, "but I'm starved."

Etoile proposed a walk first to "clear our heads." She knew a nice little place at the edge of town that served excellent fish dishes and pasta.

"You'll love their *brandade de morue*," she promised.

And indeed we enjoyed an outstanding meal and homely atmosphere. We polished off two bottles of an excellent Jurançon white wine with the brandade.

"I haven't had such a sumptuous culinary experience in a long time," I remarked as we savored a delectable chèvre provençal on slices of baguettes complemented by a light Gaillac rosé.

"Neither have we," Etoile chuckled. "I don't know how to thank you for liberating us from humus and pita. Don't you agree, Nina?"

Nina had said very little while Etoile and I made small talk ranging from the finer distinctions between northern and southern French cuisine to the state of historic preservation in Albi and academic politics in France.

"So what do you think? Was it rape or seduction?" Nina suddenly blurted out.

"Dina herself seems to have thought the priest seduced her. He was apparently a real smooth talking Lothario," Etoile suggested.

My thoughts took a more scholarly analytical turn.

"At first she made her readers—that is, her sons—believe that she had been raped and that this was the source of her hatred for the priest," I mused. "She even takes on the name of the Dina, the famous biblical rape victim. Then, all of a sudden, she says, wait a moment, maybe it wasn't quite that way. On second thought, I might have gone along willingly."

From Nina's irritated mien I gathered that my attempt at *explication de texte* wasn't very profound.

"Stop the psychoanalyzing, Henner," she snarled. "You make it sound as if it was a case of consenting adults. It still was rape no matter how you twist it."

"Maybe she just didn't want her sons to think of their father as a rapist," Etoile suggested. While Nina turned away briefly,

Etoile rolled her eyes as if to beg me to have patience with my impetuous cousin.

"She also says that later on he raped her many times. I think we should hold off all analyzing or judging until we know the whole story," Etoile continued in a more emphatic tone.

"Who's judging?" Nina said. "It was clearly entrapment. He set the whole thing up with one goal in mind. I don't care what you say, it was rape." It was strange, and not a bit amusing, to see Nina sulk like a little girl. I almost expected her to stamp her foot next.

"Nobody is disputing this part," I assured her.

"Oh yes, typical male! Tell me that she asked for it and enjoyed it."

"I said no such thing," I protested.

Something else was going on, and I didn't think it had anything to do with Etoile, whose forbearance and kindness were above and beyond. What had I done that made her so angry with me? *Nina's troubles must be even greater than I imagined,* I told myself. *If I am to help her, I need to get to the bottom of this bizarre behavior.*

"By the way," I said following a sudden inspiration that might give a clue to the puzzle, "you never told me where you got a hold of this codex."

"Oh, didn't I? Sorry," she replied, somehow astonished about her omission. "I found it in Valladine."

We returned to our hotel after we had walked off some of the meal. It was impossible to think of doing more work that day. We spent some time watching television, but in the absence of anything of interest, we turned in early.

Hoping for a good night's rest, I picked up some reading material from the Albi tourism office, but ominous thoughts about Nina would not leave me. She had become obsessed with finding Valladine, my aunt had told me as I was leaving for the airport. Valladine! I had forgotten all about it. But now it came back to me. I remembered hearing a reference to it when the adults reminisced about our trek across the Pyrenean Mountains in the spring of 1941. Somewhere along the way, there was a place by that name that had some special significance. Now thinking back, I was sure it was the name of the place where Nina was born. As a ten-year-old, I was preoccupied mostly with other things. But I was aware that when we set out on this march, my Aunt Hedy was pregnant, and when we got to the Spanish side, she held a baby. I didn't know then what month she was in, but I remember she looked huge to me and she had trouble keeping pace with the rest of us.

Like the swaying figures closing in on the poet of a Goethe poem, the strands of memory began to intrude upon my mind weaving a canvas of images long forgotten. And like the poet, I relented and let them have free reign. I succumbed to their power. Not everything went smoothly from one side of the mountain range to the other. Human dramas were being played out along the way, which I, as a young boy, ignored for the most part. I was more interested in making myself understood with the boy of about my age from the group of shepherds who served as our guides.

Before we reached the relative safety of the mountains, our peregrinations were beset by all manner of perils and snares our enemies had laid out for us. We meandered through a dark forest of arrests and a bureaucratic maze, circumvented the shoals in a stormy river of controls and questioning, and dodged a gauntlet strewn with suspicion and hatred. Always alert for the next stumbling block, skirting, eluding, evading, ducking, always anxious about what the next day might bring, where we would find shelter and food, always uneasy at the sight of uniformed officials everywhere, the Danziger sisters covered a six-hundred mile, twenty-day obstacle course from Brussels to southwestern France.

I will never know how they managed to plot out our itinerary through the French countryside with train schedules that had become invalid, finding connections, chartering space on a flatbed truck packed with fugitives from the capital, and at one time, persuading a kindly farmer to give us a lift on his hay wagon. And all this, while lugging heavy suitcases and backpacks filled with only the "barest necessities" as my mother found no end in emphasizing.

It all began in May 1940, in the city of Brussels in Belgium, where we had found refuge a year and a half earlier after my father and Uncle Aaron had been released from the concentration camp at Sachsenhausen and we had fled from Germany. Like many refugees, my parents clung to the hope that Hitler's army would get bogged down in Poland and Germany would not risk another two-front war. In fact, the German war machine rolled into Belgium the same way it had during the last war, through the Low Countries. Only this time, they had tanks and stormed almost unimpeded all the way to Paris, trouncing Belgium along the way.

My mother came bursting into the room where I was reading before school and paying scant attention to the noises in the apartment. The adults were always chattering excitedly. I was used to it. This morning, the excitement may have been a bit above the usual, but I was engrossed in a different world, in the Old West. I was following with bated breath the adventures of Winnetou and Old Shatterhand, my childhood heroes. A few days before had been my birthday, and my father had surprised me with a worn but readable copy of *The Treasure in Silver Lake.* Where and how he had uncovered it in the Belgian capital was a mystery to me, but I didn't care much. This was the best birthday gift ever.

I had parted under tears from my collection of Karl May adventure novels when we left Germany. My mother's dictate allowed only for the "bare necessities," and *Schundliteratur* or *Hintertreppenromane,* both typical German expressions for pulp fiction, were not on the list of bare necessities.

We took some of my father's books of classical Roman and Greek literature, and some tomes of stories about shtetl Jews, among them *Der Pojaz* by Karl Emil Franzos, the Sephardic Jew from Galicia who prided himself on being a "German," and a few volumes of Yiddish stories by Sholom Aleichem and I. L. Peretz. My mother, of course, could not do without her favorite Thomas Mann novels. I was only allowed more "serious" reading material like *The Iliad* and *The Odyssey* next to *The Wise Men of Chelm* and, of course, my Siddur. For frivolous hefty Karl Mays, there was no room. My father, a Karl May enthusiast himself, like all German males, gave me a conspiratorial wink, which I took as a promise of restitution someday. That someday had come. He had made good on his promise, and I was in heaven.

This volume remained my faithful companion throughout the long journey on which we were about to embark. Actually, our departure was delayed by several months due to the interference of the Belgian police. It might have been the military. For a nine-year-old, the events of that morning were more than confusing. First my mother eked me on to pack the "bare necessities." No, I didn't have to go school today. We had to get out of the city, out of the country. The Germans were on their way and would be here any moment. That warning got me on my feet in no time. Making a stand against that gang of gunslingers would be madness. I knew we had to flee on the iron horse once again.

Just as we made ready to leave the apartment for the railroad station in hopes of finding space on a train for France, a commotion in the stairwell made us hold our breath. Shuffling footsteps and a barrage of hard knocks on the door followed. All too familiar! Uncertain what to do, we looked around. We lived on the top floor. We always lived on the top floor for some reason. There was no other way out. My father grasped my hand. I saw fear in his eyes. Then suddenly his grip relaxed and he let go. The voices outside spoke French.

"*Ouvrez! Ouvrez*!" accompanied by continued banging and shouting. No matter. My mother and aunt rushed to the door, sighing with relief. A half dozen uniformed Belgians pushed their way in, slamming the half-open door against the two women ready to welcome them. Two heavily armed soldiers seized my father and uncle at gunpoint. The others looked around and kept the women and me in check. I had learned enough French in school to understand the words, but the meaning of much that was said went over my head. Once again, they took my father and uncle away, handcuffed like criminals. And the Gestapo hadn't even arrived in Brussels yet. No luggage, just a small bag was allowed. Where were they taking them? When would they come back? The uniformed claimed not to know.

Later we learned that all the male Jewish refugees from Germany had been arrested and taken to an unknown location in France. The charge: potential collaborators, fifth columnists, possible fraternizers with the invading army, and suspicion of espionage. The irony, the complete absurdity of these charges, apparently failed to penetrate the skull of the Belgian authorities from whom my mother and aunt beseeched information. Day in and day out, they sat, with me in tow, in corridors and waiting rooms of police stations, ministries, and myriad government agencies.

"How can they be fifth columnists? How can they be German spies? We are Jews, refugees!" I heard them saying over and over again to anybody who would listen and those who wouldn't. "All we want is a chance to get away from here."

I missed my father and longed to recite my treasured book to him. I knew it almost by heart. When news reached the Belgian capital at the end of May that Paris had fallen, the thin thread of hope that had kept my mother and aunt going snapped. It pained me to see them sink into such a state of despair. Yet after a brief interlude, they managed to shore each other up and they resumed their rounds. It didn't occur to me then, but thinking back, I realize that desperation often breeds recklessness. Throwing all caution to the wind, the indomitable sisters took their case all the way to the German commandant. The reception was amazingly polite, though without resulting in the desired information. In the end, it was a low-level Belgian bureaucrat in the interior ministry who had a heart. The German refugees were interned in a place called Saint-Cyprien. He had no idea where this place was, but that was soon found out.

I remember the wind fanning my face on the moving trains. Inside, the compartments were so stuffy from overcrowding and the summer heat, I made sure to capture a spot by an open window. My flights of fancy transported me to the American West and I fancied myself on a ride of the iron horse across the vast plains described so vividly by a man who had never seen them. I was on the lookout for attacks by Indians or train robbers, but with the noble Apache Winnetou by my side, I felt no harm could come to me.

Reality was, of course, quite different and forced me to come down to earth periodically. When we passed into what was called the "Free Zone," or unoccupied France, my mother gathered me to her bosom with joy and assured me that we were safe now. When we finally arrived at the camp of Saint-Cyprien, in the foothills of the Pyrenees near the Mediterranean, we were told my father and uncle had been transferred to a camp in the foothills of the Pyrenees on the Atlantic side. The place was called Gurs. At least they had gotten away from what we had heard described as the "hell hole of Saint-Cyprien." The prisoner with whom we spoke through the barbed wire fence told us this was worse than Dachau. He had experienced both.

Just to show how misplaced my mother's optimism was, the French police caught up with us. The wagon of the train we were put on had no windows for me to fan my face. We sat on the floor crammed together, hungry and thirsty, for I don't know how long. In the end, we were unloaded and herded into a camp filled with miserable looking women and children—a godforsaken place called Rieucros in the Massif Central region. Many of the inmates were German Jews like us. How long we stayed there, I don't remember. I was told later it was two weeks. Why they let us go is still unclear to me. I became violently sick, but there were many other sickly children. Whatever bargain my mother and aunt were able to strike and with whom, I didn't know then and don't know to this day; they never spoke about it, not even later in America when their adventures had become part of endless reminiscing. I remember this was also where the farmer with the hay wagon came in, an episode about which they spoke frequently and gloatingly later on. I never quite understood the humor of this. Anyway, he took us on a bumpy five-hour ride to the nearest town that had a stop along the north-south rail line. I remember lying curled up in the back of the wagon, the rattling and shaking wreaking further havoc with my already sensitized bowels. After hours of waiting and uncertainty, we were finally on a train steaming south again. How they paid for all this was of no concern to me. I was too miserable to even stand by the open window and have the wind fan my face. Strangely enough, my condition improved in direct proportion to the distance we put between us and this backwater region of central France.

This episode convinced the sisters that even "free" France was not a hospitable place for Jews and that we had to get away—far, far away—not only from Germany and France, but from the continent. We had to go to America, they concluded, an idea I championed with all my heart. But under no circumstances would they leave without their husbands. Besides, we had no visas. And for the time being, we were pretty tired of wandering. That bit about Ahasver, the wandering Jew, was vastly exaggerated, or more likely some antisemitic legend, I thought. We had no greater desire than to settle down somewhere in a safe, warm place. My greatest longing was for a bed of my own where I could read under the covers.

With the help of the Jewish community of Toulouse, we found more or less permanent lodging in that city. What the landlady called an apartment was one sparsely furnished room, spacious though with a few dividers. The toilet, if one could call it that, was down the hall, a little stall with an opening in the floor. It took me awhile to get the hang of doing my business spread-eagle and half suspended in the air at the same time, sort of Vitruvian-man style. I had my own mattress though and was content. If the frontiersmen of the Wild West could rough it, so could I.

Toulouse was meant to be a brief way station. It turned into almost a year. The sisters were lucky, or it may have been due to their charming persistence—anyway, they found employment in the needle trade. I wasn't sure what that meant, but the fact was that they worked long hours and were gone all day and I had a lot of free time on my hand for daydreaming, at least until the end of the summer. At the beginning of the school year, I was enrolled in a school of the *Consistoire Israëlite* where I had the best time in a long time. This was primarily due to a boy named Sami Cohen. He was a few years older than I and was preparing for his bar mitzvah. He was a voracious reader like me, especially fond of adventure novels. It was he who first opened to me the world of medieval France as lavishly restored to life through the imaginations of the French romantics. We devoured Châteaubriand, Victor Hugo, and Alexandre Dumas père, as well as Eugène Suë; the swashbucklers of the Paul Févals, both père and fils, kept us breathlessly engaged. Sami also introduced me to the Arthurian legends by the medieval poet Chrétien de Troyes, the *La Chanson de Roland*, and other *chansons de geste*, next to the travelogue of Rabbi Benjamin of Tudela, who visited China before Marco Polo and all the lands in between.

By the time Sami was to become bar mitzvah, we had left Toulouse and France behind us. I don't know if he ever reached that day. He had often told me he dreamt of joining the Hagganah in Palestine. My inquiries during later visits to the city remained fruitless. He was the best comrade I ever had. I still think of him as my *chaver* and hope he realized his dream.

I too had a dream, not quite as heroic as that of my friend Sami though. One day in late October, it came true. *G-d has heard my prayers!* I called out in the middle of the street while walking home from school. I literally flew over the cobblestones the rest of the way. Even from afar, I was able to spot the familiar figures of my father and uncle at our doorsteps, chatting with the landlady. They had gotten a lot thinner, yet their gestures and their bearing were unmistakable. I wouldn't have put it that way then, of course, but I knew as even a child knows the familiar outline of a loved one.

Before their release, we would spend every Sunday on excursions to the camp at Gurs—or better to say to the gate of the camp, for we never actually got to see the inmates. But if nothing else, the Danziger sisters were tenacious. Somehow their messages got through and a regular correspondence with their husbands ensued. So they knew where to find us when they were finally released on condition that they would leave the country *toute suite*. This was, of course, easier said than done. The hell ride they had gone through in the French camps inspired in all of us a burning desire to get away from this glorious, sweet land of Vichy France, never to look back. But where to go? Who would take us in? We had no visas for any country.

Meanwhile, Uncle Aaron found occasional work as a cutter in a garment factory. My father, who didn't have such skills, took on the mission of besieging and beseeching the American consul in Marseilles. I accompanied him on several of these trips. We joined the desperate masses encamped for days outside the consulate. Again and again, they sent us away empty-handed.

I had heard the name mentioned in the adults' discussions of Vichy anti-Jewish laws. But in the spring of 1941, our household buzzed almost constantly with the name "Vallat." Vallat became a designation more abhorrent even than the devil in Berlin. He was a minister in the Vichy government who had his own plans for ridding France of the presence of Jews who had sought refuge there. Every mention of the name was followed by laments from either my mother or aunt, or both in unison: "We have to get away from here! How long can we go on like this? How long before they will get us? The French are no better than the Nazis. Where will all this end?" I hated to see them so despondent. The two sisters always seemed so competent, so up to any situation. If they felt hopeless, maybe there really was no hope.

It was about this time that I noticed Aunt Hedy's expanding girth. I didn't know too much about these things. Under normal circumstances, this would probably have been the time in a boy's development when the father would sit down with him and introduce him to the facts of life. Our circumstances just weren't normal. My friend Sami had let me in on some of the mechanics involved: "When a man and a woman get together, really close together, they make babies."

"You mean when they kiss? I've seen them stick their tongue into each other's mouths, but I didn't know …"

"No, not from kissing," Sami laughed. "That's just how they start out, and then they go further down and get naked and the male gets inside the female."

When he saw my puzzled face, he shook his head in desperation. "You know the difference between boys and girls, don't you?"

I nodded. "But I'd never thought that's what it was for. Why would they do this?"

"It's nature, man! And it makes them feel good." Sami took on the air of superior wisdom.

"Have you ever …?" I asked, eager to hear more about this from an expert.

"Well," he said more evasively now. "Sort of, not really. But I've kissed several girls," he then added quickly.

"So you mean Aunty Hedy and Uncle Aaron did this sort of thing?"

"Of course. They're married."

"And my parents?"

"How do you think you came into this world?"

I was intrigued that the adults around me should be engaging in this kind of activity. At any rate, my fear that something might be wrong with Aunt Hedy and that she might be taken away from us was allayed. I wanted to know more but did not know whom to ask.

I finally did broach the subject with my father at the end of our last trip to Marseilles. Despite our lack of success in obtaining a visa, the time I spent with my father then is still one of my most memorable experiences of that time. For the first time in a long time, we had much time together, first on the train and then in line at the consulate. Our previous trips had passed mostly in silence. I would look out the window at the French countryside of which I believed to gradually know every fleeting tree. Or I would read. My Karl May was always with me. My father was either lost in thought or in a newspaper. On this last train ride, he was at first so absorbed in a book I didn't dare interrupt him. Later he told me that it was a novel called *The Forty Days of Musa Dagh* by Franz Werfel, a famous Austrian Jewish writer. The story was based on what the Turks did to the Armenians during the Great War, he explained. To my question whether what they did was similar to what the Nazis are doing to the Jews, he answered, "Yes, in a way—but even worse, for they actually murdered the people." That was in early 1941.

We got to talking about many things—about politics, about the war, about what was being done to the Jews by the Nazis and by the French. He had no answer for my question why the world was against us. For the first time, he spoke to me not as to a child but as to an equal. In his search for answers, he began to talk about the camps. He spoke about Sachsenhausen where the Nazis took him and Uncle Aaron on the so-called *Kristallnacht*, then about Saint-Cyprien and Gurs. He spoke in detail about the horrendous conditions, especially in the French camps, about the sparseness of food, the hunger, the lack of adequate shelter, the diseases. But about how he felt or how he was treated in there, he said nothing. He shrugged his shoulders and shook his head. I could sense his frustration at not knowing how to explain the inexplicable.

"I don't even have anything to give you for your birthday this year," he said suddenly. For the first time since we had left Germany, he pulled me into his arms and held me for a good while. "I wish I could promise you that no harm will come to you or to your mother, to any of us. But I don't know, I simply don't know what is going to happen." We fell into an awkward silence and I could see the relief coming over his face when I asked him what was going to happen to Aunt Hedy.

"No, she won't leave us. She's as healthy as ever," he laughed. "It's just that she is going to have a baby. You will be a cousin."

I must have looked really puzzled, for he declared, "This I can explain!" It was with outright good cheer that he seized upon this neutral subject and began to lay out to me the facts of life in almost clinical detail. What under normal circumstances has always been a duty discharged with a certain degree of discomfiture was for my father a welcome and delightful diversion. Of all the train rides I took then, this one I remember most fondly.

My euphoria though was dampened by our failure to obtain the coveted visas. There was a definite sense, more or less justified, that time was running out, that the powers that be were closing in on us. Uncle Aaron lost his employ. The boss was afraid of getting in trouble for hiring "foreigners," a code name in France for Jews. This left the sisters as the sole wage earners. Since they were paid by the piece, the wages were meager, barely enough for the rent. Aunt Hedy was getting bigger, and her gait got heavier. Something drastic had to be done. One day Uncle Aaron came home with the news that he heard about a band of shepherds who were guiding refugees over the mountains into neutral Spain. From what he was told, they were quite reasonable, not the usual price gougers. It was decided right then to make a run for it that very night, even without visas.

Within a few days, we had made our way to a designated place in the Pyrenean foothills. The scene of that village made our hopes flag once again. Every one of the few inns was packed to the limit. Even the center square and the narrow streets leading to it overflowed with "huddled masses yearning to be free," as my father remarked, still bitter about the experience with the American consulate. It shouldn't have come as a surprise to us that we weren't the only refugees grasping at a lifeline. But the initial shock wore off quickly, and we queued up with no choice but to wait our turn. It could take several weeks, we were told. The guides took only small groups at a time for safety reasons. Also, the Spanish border guards were not too pleased about getting inundated with bedraggled refugees. Only those in transit to Portugal would be let in.

Our turn finally came. Aunt Hedy's condition was reaching a state of imminence. The leader of the guides, a wild-eyed man in what was to me very peculiar garb, looked at her and shook his head, making a clicking sound with his tongue. We were holding our breath. The situation became even more complicated when my father told him that we had no exit visas and no visas to anywhere. The man nodded his head with serious mien and turned to his cohorts, three men and a boy of about my age. They all nodded in apparent agreement with whatever it was he told them.

"We'll have to take the longer, higher pass," he explained, turning back to us. His French had a rolling quality. He wore it on his tongue like an ill-fitting, borrowed garment. "But don't worry. You'll be all right."

If his words did not reassure the adults completely, they kept it to themselves. What choice did we have anyway? We set out in the early morning as the mountain mist rose from the meadows. The sun was just beginning to lift its shiny face above the snow-capped peaks, daubing them in orange and pink. We had no mountains at all where we came from, not even slight elevations. I stared at these towering granite giants in breathless awe and wondered if the Rocky Mountains were that awesome. I kept the sense of excitement that seized me hidden from the adults though. For that much I knew—they were not likely to see our trek over these mountains as the great adventure it was to me.

There was plenty of excitement all along the way though. As we made our ascent over the rocky pathway, Aunt Hedy frequently lagged behind. She had to stop more and more often to catch her breath. Strong-willed as she was, the weight of her body still slowed her down. Uncle Aaron tried to lift her on his back. But that was a rather undignified mode of travel to her mind. Besides, he was not strong enough in his still quite emaciated condition from the starvation diet in the camp. Our guides finally unloaded one of the mules and lifted Aunt Hedy on it. This created the kind of undignified moment she feared most. It elicited a brief nervous laughter from her, but this time she acquiesced in her fate. The bags and supplies were distributed among the rest of us for carrying.

I didn't mind the extra burden, for I had already been transported on the wings of my imagination to the Sierra Nevada where frontiersmen and fortune hunters roughed it out. To show how tough I was, I stomped bravely ahead of the others. Even so, tough or not so tough, I was pleased to notice the shepherd boy sidling up to me with a smile. Close in tow with him was a huge, snow-white Pyrenean mountain dog, one of several that hedged in our party as if we were a flock of sheep. Through gestures, the boy made clear to me that he wanted to help me with the load I was carrying. His French wasn't very clear—later I learned the language he spoke was Occitan—but we got on fine anyway. From time to time, we stopped so the distance between us and the others wouldn't get too great. To pass the time, we played with the dog, rolling around in the grass. I remember the dog's soft, smooth fur felt like a huge snowball, and how tickled I was when he pushed his big, black snout playfully into my stomach. These were cherished moments of oblivion, of exuberant abandon to frolicking on a cloudless spring day.

The caravan had come to a halt in the middle of a sun-bathed emerald green pasture populated by grazing cattle and sheep. Uncle Aaron lifted his wife from the mule and placed her on the ground, all the while fanning her face with his hand. My mother walked over and pushed him aside: "This is woman's business," she said.

As my newfound friend and I walked back a few steps toward where Aunt Hedy had been bedded on the ground and my mother was ministering to her, a strange sensation of dread and curiosity took hold of me. I was equally attracted and repulsed by the moaning and deep breathing noises my aunt was making. They were of the sort that she would definitely have described at any other time as "undignified."

"She's going to have the baby! She's going to have to the baby!" My mother seemed beside herself and at her wit's end. "What are we going to do?"

While she was pacing like a headless chicken, my father and uncle conferred with the leader of the guides. There was a lot of hand waving, eye rolling, and nodding going on between them as if they were bargaining over the price of some livestock. Finally, my father took note of me and came over to where my friend and I were lying in the grass with the dog between us.

"They will take her to a nearby village, but only Uncle Aaron is allowed to come along. The rest of us will have to move on to the Spanish side of the border. We'll wait there for them to catch up with us."

My mother was very unhappy with these arrangements, but these were the conditions and she had to accept them. The baby would be born either under the care of a midwife or out here in the open countryside among the rocks and thistles. The choice was clear; there was no choice.

And so it was that Nina Aschauer came into this world.

Dina's Tale 5

They called me the priest's concubine, or La Josiva, *and worse. Never to my face though. They never called me anything to my face. In fact, the villagers rarely spoke directly to me at all, only behind my back. They tolerated my presence without demur because that's what I was, the priest's concubine. This is all I was. I had no other quality, not even in my own eyes. Miryam, the daughter of Elazar ben Simeon de Sola, erstwhile cloth merchant of Lunel and Toulouse, ceased to exist on the day her father and brothers fell on their knees, raised their arms toward heaven, and bemoaned her death. On that day, I became Dina. I chose that name for myself. I became the namesake of Jacob's daughter, the defiled one. Only she was not thrust out, cut from the bosom of her people. She was rescued by her brothers, who wreaked terrible vengeance on the defiler and his clan. How did their sister Dina feel about being rescued? Was she horrified or was she gratified by the bloodbath to redeem her honor? We are not told. Was she too beguiled by the warmth of a body, of a man's touch, his sweet whispers in her ear? Did she mourn his death or did she exult in her brothers' deed? We are not told. Would I have exulted had my brothers snuck back in the night and rescued me? Had they slain the priest and all the males in the village, would I have rejoiced? We live in different times. In our times, Jews are hounded from their homes and countries of residence; they are dispossessed at a moment's notice, at the whim of a wily king or magistrate. Jews are powerless to defend even their honor in our days.*

Would I even have desired to be rescued? Was it not I who told my father to go away, to go on his journey without me? Had I not already sunk so deep into a mire of guilt and wickedness, I could no longer look him in the eye? Did I not wish them to leave me be? The answer to all of this—I can no longer deny it—is yes. I stood there rooted to the ground, immobile, a pillar of stone. Neither the pain I was causing my father nor the curse he cast over me in parting—true the memory of both never ceased to eat at my heart and fester in my soul—had the power to sway me to at least ask him for forgiveness. I could not, and he could not. Not with my seducer standing between us. I knew he would never be reconciled to a daughter who had violated the most sacred code of conduct, the most basic laws by which he lived and which defined his world.

I was left alone in the world. Orphaned, that's what I was. I had never known my mother. I had no memory of her, so I could not turn to her for advice or consolation. Neither did I have any reason to believe that she would regard my sin as anything other than the depravity of a daughter gone bad. She was from all accounts a devout Jewess. I had no reason to doubt that she too would have recoiled at the thought of her daughter being defiled by one of the uncircumcised. She too would have pronounced me dead.

And yet, it was this man, my seducer, who was my comfort and salvation in those early bleak days. I was sixteen years old, and like most young girls, I dreamed of love. Somehow I persuaded myself to believe I had found the man of my dreams, as absurd as it seems now. With nothing else to live for, I lived for him. I lived for the nights when he came to me. I lived for the sweet words he dripped into my ear like honey that made me forget the shame and remorse that tormented my days. I lived for that very moment when he held me, caressed me with gentle hands and tender lips, making me eager for the moment when he mingled his body with mine. Later, these moments often haunted my dreams. For many years, I clung to the memory of these early moments when we soared together into a sphere above all earthly woes and set down on a river of oblivion, floating along in close embrace. It was all I had to hold on to, to somehow justify what I had done. I could not yet admit that it had been evil.

I am relating this to you, my sons, so you will understand the complete hold the priest had over your mother. How he beguiled her and made her believe that this was—I hesitate to use the word—but in my girlish youthfulness I believed it, that it was love. I made him my prince, my beloved. I fancied that I was his and he was mine in the manner of King Solomon and his beloved queen of Sheba. But as it turned out, my seducer was no prince and I would rather have been one of King Solomon's four hundred concubines than the single one of this priest.

The first weeks and months passed rather peaceably. There was not much for me to do to fill my days but to daydream and long for the nights. Sybille, the housekeeper, you know her well, took care of the chores around the house. She also took pity on me. She was kind to me, the only kind soul in the entire village. I lent a hand in the kitchen and yard whenever and however needed. In the early morning, I would make for the well to fetch water. The women I met there immediately ceased their chattering and let me pass with their backs turned toward me. I was never sure what they hated more about me—that I was a Jewess or that I was the priest's woman.

Later they accused me of being haughty and of looking down on them. This may well have been true. I had been raised in a town with some claim to a certain urbaneness, paved streets, and I lived in a stately stone house. My father's household, a veritable mansion, contained furniture carved of the finest wood by master craftsmen, wall hangings and floor coverings imported from Spain and the Orient. We slept in down bedding and satin sheets. We ate from glazed earthenware with silver spoons and drank choice wines from pewter cups. How could the miserable huts, even the better ones of the rich peasants, and their primitive wooden implements compare? Yes, I did feel superior to these crude peasants, most of them illiterate. As time passed, as the toil of village life left its mark on me, I probably became more like them without ever becoming part of them.

But in those early days, I passed much time sitting in the summer sun on the stoop or in the shade under the elm tree in front of the portal to the parish church. This perch was my lookout on the village and its daily life as it passed before my eyes. I peered into the windows of their houses and observed their lives as if enacted on a stage. The brutish, violent nature of these peasants came as a shock to me, as I had been raised in a domain of refinement. Women were respected and honored where I came from. They were not brutally beaten by their husbands for minor infractions as I had occasion to observe almost daily in this village.

Much of the women's daily activities played out in the open and in the company of other women. They sat in the round at their spinning wheels or while sorting peas and beans. Together they went on their way to gather the sheaves of wheat from the fields and took them to the mill. Even churning butter and making cheese was a communal affair in a way. No matter what they did, their mouths never closed. Their ceaseless chatter went on all day like the squawking of a flock of geese. They gossiped mostly about other women, especially married women. Which were cuckolding their husbands, with whom they were carrying on, or whose husband was on the prowl. Sometimes they also spoke, with hushed voices but still for me to hear when I pricked my ears, about the men, strangers passing through the village, who stayed a night or two in the cellar of one or the other domus as if it was a hiding place. The peasants referred to them as "goodmen" and sometimes "perfecti." These men passed themselves off as itinerant garment and glove menders, but the reverence with which they were received was hardly befitting such a lowly station. Even from a distance, it did not escape me that these men were possessed of unusual poise in demeanor; they projected an outward dignity and inner repose. Their aura of mystery gave me pause. I sensed something secretive going on, something forbidden. I decided to take note and guard a vigilant eye.

I may have been haughty in their eyes, but let those who are guiltless throw the first stone, according to their Christian teaching. I saw much haughtiness and conceit among the more prosperous, especially the women in the priest's clan, and their disdain for less well-off villagers. For me, of course, they had nothing but utter contempt. I frequently had to eat at their table, surrounded by hostile glares from sisters and brothers and a variety of the priest's kinfolk. The priest willed it so. I was his prized possession. His mother, the ruling matriarch, would not deny her firstborn anything, no matter how odious it was to her and the others. I suffered these meals in silence. I ate of the bread with beans and turnips and of the occasional trout dish, but I never let even the slightest morsel of their impure meat or fowl pass into my mouth.

Sybille, the good soul, worried about me not getting enough food when it became apparent that I was with child. I explained to her that by the laws of Moses the pig was unclean and eating it in any form was prohibited. I doubt that she saw the wisdom of this law, but she did not argue and instead sent me into the woods to gather mushrooms and nuts. These she put into a cabbage and leek soup she made only for me. I always loved her for her kindness.

The priest relished flesh of any kind. His favored dishes were roast leg of mutton and roasted game, pheasant or deer, he brought back from the hunt. Salted pork or thick bacon soup, common local fare, he dismissed as fit for the dregs only. He tried to entice me by smacking his lips, licking his fingers, and rolling his eyes seductively heavenward. He may have been irresistible as paramour; to watch him devour impure meat only aroused my disgust. After a while, he gave up. He ceased what was for him apparently a sensuous lovers' game. I insisted on a strict line of demarcation between bed and table. He respected my wish, and I had scored a victory. But the victory came at a price. He found a way to retaliate. Only later, with increased experience and greater knowledge of human nature, did I realize how deeply wounded he was. For a man who was in the habit since childhood to indulge his every whim and to have everybody around him bow to his every wish, this concession, what was to my mind a very small concession to make, hurt his vanity. It also became clear to me in time why he had become a priest. As priest in this small, remote mountain village, the place where his family held a prominent position, he was revered among the locals, men and women alike. The priesthood also relieved him of the obligation to marry. He was free to fornicate with any girl or woman he fancied.

But he was also a great dissimulator. He pretended to go along with my wish since he knew that on this point I would not yield. And although he never, not then or later, made any direct attempt to win me over to the Christian faith, he began needling me about the "superannuated Old Testament." He scorned the laws of Moses. Neither did he, I came to realize, take the laws of Christianity very seriously. Not even the prospect of an eternity in Gehenna would inspire fear in him or make him mend his ways.

The first winter in the village was a more miserable one than any I had ever experienced. The village was on a much higher ground than the town where I grew up, and that was no doubt why I felt the bitter cold, the icy winds blowing through the cracks in the windows and walls with utter severity. By this time, I was also far advanced with child. I longed for the warmth of the priest's body, but by then he came only rarely to me at night. Where he was keeping himself I did not dare ask for fear of finding out the truth that my womanly instinct could not deny. Yet, I still cleaved to the foolish notion that I was his only woman, that it was his pastoral duties that occupied his time. The closer my time approached, the less I saw of him. Later he tried to inveigle me with the explanation for his absence from my childbed, that it would not be proper for a priest to father children. This was, of course, absurd. The entire village and other villages beyond knew that the priest was keeping a Jewess in his house and bed. The sparrows whistled it from the rooftops, and the sheep and goats bleated it from mountain pasture to mountain pasture. He had never made a secret of it. In fact, he had always brazenly flaunted his conquest.

When my time came, I was alone with Sybille, good, kind Sybille. She was herself a bastard, born out of wedlock to a mother who abandoned her and ran away over the mountains after a scoundrel. The matriarch of the priest's clan took her in and put her to work as a servant from an early age. I didn't ask her about the scars she bore on her face and arms, but I surely was not wrong to presume that she had been subjected to much abuse. Only the priest showed her some kindness, this much she said, and eventually he took her in as his personal housekeeper. She probably also served his carnal needs until she became too old.

Sybille, who had remained childless, held my hand and cooled my forehead with a wet cloth during the long hours of labor. "This child seems to simply shun the light of day," she kept repeating, despairing more and more as the hours went by. Alerted by the screams, the matriarch came in and sat with me. She sent Sybille to get the midwife.

"Breathe deeply! Inhale and exhale!" she instructed. A fleeting moment of concern for her son's offspring, if not kindheartedness for the woman bearing it. "Where is this renegade son of mine keeping himself?" she wanted to know. I could only shrug and curse him for having put me in this condition.

With the help of the three women, my first son came kicking and screaming into this world at last. A high fever had me guard the bed and I was unable to tend to my child who was meanwhile nourished by a wet nurse, another woman in the village who had just given birth. For several days, I remained suspended in a realm of flickering lights and shadows. In this dazed state and with the darkness surrounding me, I did not see her, but I felt her presence. I felt the strong attraction she exercised over my mind. I prayed to G-d to let me join the woman He had taken to Him when she gave me life. But He had other designs for me in store. Most of all and immediately, I had an urgent task to fulfill.

On the fifth day, I sat up in bed with a start. Where was my son? I had to get my son, had to get him away from those heathen women. I had a task to fulfill even though I was totally unprepared and at a loss as to how to go about it. Three days! In three days, on the eighth day after his birth, my son had to be brought into the covenant with the G-d of Abraham, Isaac, and Jacob. Three days was all I could think of. It had to be done somehow; somehow I had to do it.

Within the span of a moment, the fever had left me. I fell on my knees and gave thanks to the G-d of Israel. Only He could have pulled me from death's door and given me the strength to rise from childbed to fulfill His command. He even gave me a help maid. For how else, if not for His intervention, was it possible that Sybille, the good soul, willingly became my accomplice and lent me her hand? She needed no persuading once I explained to her what had to be done. First we had to retrieve the infant. Sybille went behind the back of the matriarch to the wet nurse, who was glad to be rid of the extra mouth to feed, even if it was for meager imbursement. The next step was more complicated. What instruments were we to use? Somewhere in the back of my mind was the memory that the one performing the ritual would remove the foreskin with the fingernail. I remembered the story of Zipporah, the wife of Moses, who used a flint stone. Neither of these appealed to me. A pair of scissors from Sybille's sewing supplies that could be purified over a flame in the hearth seemed a better choice.

All these considerations paled when I thought of the pain the infant would have to endure and what to do to heal the wound. What could we use to still the pain and heal the wound? And where would we find whatever concoction would meet the purpose? My heart fluttered with such vigor, like a bird's wings refusing to take flight. I knew so little about these things and felt at my wit's end. How glad I was, therefore, when Sybille offered to visit an alchemist she had heard about. The village where he lived was about a three-hour's walk each way. There was no certainty that he was at his house or even that he was still alive, or that he would receive her, or that he would be willing to give her the required concoction. She might also be missed and would have to explain her absence to the matriarch or the priest. All these considerations paled in view of what had to be done. It was worth taking the chance. She would make up some excuse to coax him into giving her some spirits or distilled alcohol or some potion she had seen medical practitioners use in the dressing of open wounds.

Sybille returned more speedily than we had calculated. She was no youngster, but she would not let the rough mountain paths slow her pace. She was gasping for air, and her feet were bloodied with sores and blisters. A proud, weary smile appeared on her face as she tendered the flask to me. She had accomplished the task. The alchemist revealed himself to be a kindly gentleman and willing, even eager, to trade his knowledge and a flask of distilled alcohol for a log of goat cheese and a slab of salt pork. He even added several pieces of cloths specially prepared for dressing wounds, he explained. Although she did not specify to him the kind of wound for which the items were intended, his instruction to change the dressing repeatedly and dab the wound with the alcohol were faithfully heeded.

You can imagine my relief that up to this point all had gone so well. The hours of waiting for Sybille's return had been the most anguished in my life. Tormented by thoughts of all that might go wrong, I paced restlessly with the little bundle pressed against my breast. He was so small, so helpless. The thought of what I was about to do to him, had to do to him, the pain he would feel, rent my heart. But I did not waver. My greatest fear was that the priest might return before the deed was done or that the matriarch might burst onto the scene. Fortunately, none of them had much knowledge of Jewish customs and what I was about to do never entered their mind. Later on, when their suspicions were aroused, concealment became more difficult; but by then, Sybille and I had also become more practiced in the art of deception.

So the eighth day arrived. I nursed the infant a good long time to make him strong. Sybille boiled water, held the scissors over the flame in the oven. She then placed a white sheet and pillow on the table in the kitchen and laid out the instrument, the flask of alcohol, and the dressing cloths. She took the infant from my trembling hands and even offered to carry out the task. But I explained to her that I was the one who was enjoined to perform this mitzvah, G-d's command.

The palms of my hands were wet, and thick sweat oozed from my forehead. My heart raced, and my hands trembled. I invoked the memory of Zipporah, the one of the flint stone, imploring her to give me strength and steady my hand. Sybille moved her lips in fervent prayer to the Virgin Mary. We accomplished the task. The infant's screams roused the matriarch and several women, but before they entered, we had already applied the alcohol and dressing and were able to hide what we had done from their eyes. Sybille placed her finger, which she had dipped in wine, in the infant's mouth and thus muffled his scream. The women soon departed, satisfied that nothing untoward was going on.

This is how my firstborn son was brought into the covenant. Nobody in the village learned about it until much later when you, my sons, were exposed to their eyes by accident. Your father, who would surely not have approved—for him, all "Old Testament" practices were barbaric—never got close enough to you to notice. It remained our secret, Sybille's and mine. We even became very adept at it, and by the third time, I considered myself an expert mohel. *Still, after my first son's birth, I implored G-d to have mercy on me, and should he open my womb again to let it be a female child. He fulfilled my wish, but she did not live.*

"Oh, boy!" Nina wiped her forehead with the back of her hand. "She certainly doesn't mince words, does she?"

"That's for sure," I said. "Nor does she spare the reader, in this case her sons, the intended readers. She really puts them through the emotional wringer."

"We finally know how many sons she had," said Nina, "and how often she had to go through this ordeal! But we still don't know how many children she bore, how many she lost in infancy or at birth." Nina's tone was hushed as if she was speaking in the presence of the dead.

"Come, let's have something to eat. I'm famished," I tried to distract her, afraid that she might sink again into a state of melancholy. It was also true that I felt a sharp pinch of hunger after hours of almost uninterrupted, concentrated work.

"Could we just order in?" she asked meekly.

"I really don't think it's a good idea to stay cooped up all the time. We need to stretch our legs. At least I do, and you should."

"I've been cooped up for so long. I feel almost like Kaspar Hauser. *Ich bin der Welt abhanden gekommen.*"

The way she stood there in her drab homespun shift and bonnet, she reminded me of paintings of pre-industrial peasants, an appearance out of a pre-modern world. She looked so small, vulnerable as a child, with big pleading eyes. Just looking at her broke my heart. *Nina, my Nina, what has become of you?* I wondered.

"Yes," I said, reaching for her hand. "You have gotten lost to the world. But the world wants you back, and now that I have found you, I will take you back to where you belong. Come, freshen up and change. I'll meet you downstairs in twenty minutes."

While I was waiting for Nina in the hotel lobby, my thoughts wandered to Etoile. She had left us to catch up with work on her dissertation she had been neglecting for some time. *Rashi's daughters,* I thought, *that should be interesting.* In fact, more and more often my thoughts turned to this easy-going woman, so different from Nina, and I had a sense of emptiness when she wasn't with us.

Over dinner, Nina and I discussed a few loose ends about the transcription. Dina's way of making the Hebrew letters capture the sound of Occitan was not always immediately clear, and in many places her meaning required considerable guesswork. Fortunately, we both had a good command of Occitan as well as of Hebrew, so we were able to overcome most stumbling blocks. All we had to do was put our heads together. I was sorry that the discussion came to an abrupt end when the waiter, with irritatingly affectatious gestures, served our dinner, opened the bottle of wine with a grandiose display of his virtuosity, and coaxed me to taste it. *Just put the damn stuff down,* I thought to myself. But the thread had been broken.

Nina stabbed at her salad, apparently lost in thought. She then gulped down her glass of wine as if it was a shot of whiskey. Saying what she needed to say obviously did not come easy. She looked lovely though. Her hair was still slightly damp from the shower, and she was wearing the jeans and sweater we had bought for her the day before, which gave her a refreshingly modern look. I may be a medievalist, but I have never been a fan of period customary. I like modern women to look modern.

"Will Etoile rejoin us?" I asked finally. Nina gave me a puzzled look as if she didn't understand to whom I was referring.

"Your friend Etoile," I tried to jog her memory.

"Yes, of course. She'll be back as soon as she can," she replied absentmindedly. "You like her?" she said suddenly, her face changing to an impish smile.

"Yes, I do. A lovely person and a good friend."

"The best there is," she said. "Would you like to sleep with her?"

I gave off a nervous laugh, but on consideration I said: "Not that I would mind, but I'm a bit old, don't you think, and quite out of her league?"

"Out of her league? You've got to be kidding, a man with a mind as brilliant as yours!"

"I'm not talking about my mind. She has many admirers, I'm sure." Then, my curiosity having gotten the better of me, I probed, "She isn't married or otherwise spoken for?"

"You have such a wonderfully old-fashioned way of expressing yourself," she said with a laugh. "No, I think she is, as the saying goes, between relationships. Although we haven't really discussed the subject of late. Besides, most of the guys she dates are honky-tonk musicians, truck drivers, or soccer players. Something in that league. A nice Jewish intellectual would do her good."

"You haven't forgotten the customs of our twentieth-century way of life after all," I said, and then was immediately sorry when I saw her wince. "Please forgive me. I'm really sorry. I shouldn't put my foot in my mouth like that."

"No, no, don't worry about it," she reassured me, but retreated nevertheless into a pensive mood.

"You know, they still practice it," she said softly after an extended silence.

"What do you mean? Practice what?"

"Circumcision. Only, they have a skilled person now, someone like a mohel. Thank G-d I didn't have to go through an ordeal like that poor Dina."

I was totally perplexed and didn't know what to say. I stammered something incoherent like, "But, but, but …" *Better let her explain without me pulling teeth,* I thought. When nothing more was forthcoming, I burst out in German: "*Zum Teufel, Nina, laß' die Katze endlich aus dem Sack!*"

"Okay! Okay! The cat in the sack is simply that I have to go back. I can never return to my former life. Do you understand?"

I didn't understand. How could she expect me to understand?

"I have to return to Valladine because that's where my life is, that's where I belong. The codex too has to go back where it belongs."

"But what will this Alphonse of yours do to you?"

"It doesn't matter. I have to get back because that's where my children are. They can never leave the mountain."

"You are full of surprises." I shook my head in exasperation. "How many children are there again?"

"Two boys, four and two."

"He will be all right, no cause to worry," she added, referring to Alphonse. "The other villagers may be a problem. But it'll all straighten itself out in the end. We just have to finish this transcription as quickly as possible. I want you to translate it and publish it. But you can never reveal its origin."

In view of the fact that she had told me just a few days before that she feared for her life, that she and Etoile had gone through elaborate motions to hide from Alphonse de Sola, I found this statement a bit more than odd. I didn't know what to believe or think. This entire cloak-and-dagger game they had drawn me into, she now presented as a mere marital dispute in which I was serving as foil. And then the children. How convoluted could a situation be? I thought of Aunt Hedy and how surprised, and most likely happy, she would be to discover she was a grandmother. The fulfillment of her most fervent dream! Then again, would she ever see these grandchildren who apparently were condemned to live on the mountain?

"The important thing is that we finish this project," she repeated emphatically. "There's still enough of a historian in me to want Dina's story made known to the world. And no, it's not for personal gain or glory—my name won't be associated with it. I'm handing it all over to you. I hope you will run with it and translate the chronicle into English, and French if you like. With your connections, you won't have any trouble finding a publisher, especially if your name is on it. Will you promise me to do it? My heart is really in it."

Of course, I promised even though I felt by rights she should get the credit for the discovery and the scholarly work she was putting into it. I had no doubt that it would cause a sensation, and not only in the academic world.

We had left the restaurant and crossed the cathedral square and ambled toward the garden behind the Toulouse-Lautrec Museum overlooking the river. A gentle rain was falling, but it was summertime and the tourists were out in full force. Nina and I huddled under a huge umbrella I had the foresight to borrow from the hotel management. It gave us a sense of shelter, of being inside a tent cordoned off from the world.

My thoughts turned to this Alphonse with the Pyrenean mountain dogs who had accosted me in Toulouse. He looked like a statue, a permanent fixture in that square, and yet so out of place. That he should be Nina's, my cousin Nina's husband, struck me as utterly peculiar. Also that he should have recognized me as an American was remarkable. Despite my perfect French, he probably did not believe for one minute that I was a Frenchman. There was a keenness in his eyes, a perspicacity similar to that of an eagle or a fox, a trait we urban dwellers have long lost. The full beard made judging his age difficult, but it was already grizzled, so he had to be about my age. Why was I thinking of his age? What difference did it make? And then it came to me.

"Did he ever mention anything about the war?" I asked Nina.

"Who and what war?" Was she playing dumb?

"*The* war, and your Alphonse."

"Yes, he told me his brother and others from the village served as guides to help refugees cross the mountains. Alphonse was ten years old, but he already knew every trail and mountain pass. He told me that he remembers the boy with whom he played when they took my mother to Valladine to give birth."

"And you are telling me this only now, and so casually? Nina, sometimes I could just ..." I ran out of words.

"... kill me?"

"Something like this, yes." We both burst out laughing.

"It's a small world, isn't it!" I was gratified to see her for once so full of good cheer. Maybe her *mishegas,* as my mother and aunt would have called it, would work itself out for the better after all.

I too had fond memories of that shepherd boy and his snowball of a dog. Strange to think though, that he should be my cousin Nina's husband.

We returned to the hotel and said good-night. It had been a full day, and I was looking forward to curling up with a detective story I had bought in the lobby gift shop to take my mind far away from these bizarre happenings. For the time being, I had enough of all the theatrics, whether of the fourteenth or of the twentieth century. *Amazing how little the world and the human psyche have changed,* I thought.

I dozed off mulling over the strange attraction Nina's accidental place of her birth had exercised over her. Neither Valladine nor France appeared on her birth certificate. We only knew the name of the place where the guides took Aunt Hedy because the boy mentioned it when I asked where they were going. In fact, we never found such a place anywhere on a map. Nor have we ever come across any reference to such a place anywhere in a guidebook. All my aunt and uncle knew to describe was a hut somewhere in a mountain valley where they were tended to by women speaking a language they did not understand. Besides, they came by night and left by night. It may not even have been the name of a place he was referring to. Maybe it was just a word in his language I didn't understand then. I simply presumed it was the name of a place. Somehow the term Valladine entered into our family body of myths as Nina's birthplace. Unbeknownst to the adults, however, it also became, in psycho parlance, a fixation in the girl's mind. An imaginary place she longed for all her life. *Amazing, she actually found it,* I thought. *If this isn't enough to make you a believer in destiny, I don't know what is.*

A gentle rapping on the door roused me again. Nina looked like the little girl who used to be frightened during thunderstorms. She was dressed in some sort of sweat suit we had picked up. Her hair had been brushed and hung loosely over her shoulders.

"Henner, I'm so scared. Don't let me be alone."

I pulled back my covers, and she jumped in. She curled up in fetal position, and I wrapped myself protectively around her. Her body soon went limp, and she breathed deeply and evenly, content like a baby.

She was about five or six years old. I was babysitting her as I often did when our parents had gone out. She told me then about Valladine—and what a wonderful place it must be and that she dreamed about it often. I had mentioned this name to her years before when she was very small but had been unaware until then of the impression it had made on her. She had apparently created in her imagination this mythical place, which she called Valladine, inhabited by all kinds of people with distinct personalities. She even had names for them and stories about their lives, the details of which I don't remember. I was pleased that she confided in me but didn't think too much of it. A little girl's fantasy world—nothing more. Later that night after I had put her to bed, a violent thunderstorm disturbed our sleep. Nina came running into my room, crying and trembling with fear. I took her into my bed and we nestled together then too like little spoons. She soon fell into a deep sleep. I watched over her, feeling very proud and content in the role of protector of this damsel in distress.

Our parents didn't see it that way though. When they found us in oblivious sleep, hugging together, I was rudely awoken and scolded. This was not appropriate behavior for a boy of my age.

"*Es schickt sich nicht*," my aunt would say. My mother too thought that it was not proper. Their fantasies were obviously of a different sort.

Valladine was her dream world, a Shangri-La, an unknown place hidden somewhere in those mountains and untouched even by the people and livestock flowing to and fro over its passes year in and year out. Now, in retrospect, the irony was inescapable that these are the same mountains which Jews had crossed so often in both directions at various times to escape those who meant them harm. Our small family band formed a link in that long chain, stretching from antiquity to modern times, of Jews fleeing for their lives. There was, however, another side to this transhumance, the seasonal movement of livestock and people. In more peaceful times, the mountain passes served as north-south and south-north trading routes. Over the span of a thousand years, Jewish merchants in particular traveled these rough itineraries, bearing exotic goods and often ideas from far-flung corners of the known world. Along the way, they no doubt encountered and supplied with provisions the thousands of wanderers from every part of Christendom who braved the pilgrimage to Santiago de Compostella in far northwestern Spain. One of the way stations where pilgrims, sheepherders, and traders alike, and at times refugees from either direction, halted their processions, herds, and caravans, was a village on the Spanish side of the mountains called Roncesvalles.

This is also the place where we halted on our journey, which we hoped would lead us ultimately to freedom, to wait for Aunt Hedy and Uncle Aaron to catch up with us. It was also the town that is officially listed as Nina's birthplace. How this came about was but one chapter in the strange, often bizarre, series of events surrounding her birth and our desert wanderings in search of a promised land—any land that would take us in.

Nina must have heard the story a hundred times, but one morning when we met at breakfast at the hotel in Albi, she suddenly said: "Before we get to work, tell me again what happened in Roncesvalles."

Actually I would have liked to hear more of her story, but I could never turn down a request from her. On this morning, she looked lovely and rested, almost as if she was ready to come back to our world after all. But that was, of course, only a delusion, wishful thinking on my part perhaps. In my heart, I knew that she was really lost to this world, the world of the twentieth century, from the moment she was born. The episode I related to her went somewhat like this.

The Spanish authorities—actually that's much too high-flown a designation for the handful of bedraggled police and border guards whose main occupation it was to swat flies and play cards—showed little understanding of our quandary at first. To them, we were just one of the many bands of vagabonds without valid passports or visas who were illegally invading their country. The story of a sister giving birth in the mountains for whom we had to wait and, therefore, had to indulge their kind hospitality was met with incredulity if they understood any of what my parents were trying to explain with their meager Spanish. The language was a more formidable barrier than the mountains. Not knowing what to do with us, they did what one does with people who get in the way of their game of mus; they locked us up in the town jail. The cots weren't very comfortable, but it gave us a roof over our heads and saved us the cost of a hotel.

The adults were not too pleased, but I didn't mind. My flights of fancy soared once again, stimulated by the mere fact of being in

Roncevalles, the place near the pass where Charlemagne's rear guard met with such a tragic end. I was convinced if I strained my ear I could hear the echo of Roland's horn "Oliphant" crying out for help against the murderous Basque tribesmen who had ambushed them. The legend of this Frankish hero was still vivid in my mind. Only a few months earlier, in Toulouse, my friend Sami had introduced me to the medieval epic *La Chanson de Roland*, required reading for all French schoolchildren, which I had eagerly devoured.

I was sorry to part from the shepherd boy of the mountains, but after they let us out of jail so that they wouldn't have to feed us at the Spanish government's expense, I soon made friends among the police and local boys. I actually learned to play a quite formidable card game of mus. It was probably during our stay in this village that I developed a lifelong passion for card and board games. Besides mus, they taught me several other games like escoba and botifarra, which sent my mother into a tizzy with worry that I might turn into a gambler. Less disreputable and worrisome to her were the board games we played. Alquerque or Dama, like our checkers, she recognized as the game called "*Dame*" in German, which they used to play on rainy days during the summers at the Baltic seaside. To wile away the time and distract herself from the anxieties over her sister and our situation in general, she even joined us from time to time and, I must say, was quite good at it. My father played pelota, a kind of handball popular in that region, with the police chief. By the time we finally saw Uncle Aaron and Aunt Hedy coming over the mountain, we were almost sorry we would have to take leave of what had turned out to be a rather friendly and quiet place and go on once again with our journey toward an uncertain and as yet unknown destination.

Aunt Hedy was riding on a mule clutching a bundle in her arms, flanked by Uncle Aaron leaning on a staff and guided by two of the mountaineers. I didn't think of it that way then, but every time I thought of the scene later, I was reminded of depictions of the Holy Family fleeing to Egypt in paintings by Michelangelo and Leonardo da Vinci. More important, however, this was the moment, here in Roncesvalles, when I first laid eyes on the miracle that was my cousin Nina. And a miracle is what she always remained to me. She had gotten the name through a miscommunication with the Spanish clerk who registered her birth. Her mother wanted to name her Bettina, after Bettina von Arnim as well as her own mother who, for her part, had been named after the Romantic poet and friend of Goethe's. Now she settled for Niña, which became Nina. And since in my family every name had to have some association, literary or historical, my aunt and my mother were in full agreement that the name was a good omen. *La Niña*, my mother noted, was also the name of one of the ships in the fleet of the first voyage of Columbus, a good portend for our own voyage across the *"große Teich"* as they called the Atlantic Ocean. On the subject of names, believe it or not, I was named after my paternal grandfather as well as the much beloved Heinrich Heine. Since I knew little about my grandfather, I always liked to see myself as the poet's namesake. Of course, that Heinrich was born Harry and took on the more Germanic name at the time of his baptismal, his famous entrance ticket into European civilization. A lot of good it did him. To my relief, nobody ever called me by my given name. I was always Henner to my family and friends. In America, I changed it to Henry, and most people called me Hank.

Uncle Aaron, who didn't care what secular name his daughter was to bear, organized a makeshift "*Hollekrasch*" ceremony, sometimes called "*Hol Kreisch*," an archaic Jewish baby-naming ceremony no longer practiced anywhere as far as I know, definitely not in America.

Anyway, as the only Jewish child present, I received the honor of holding the baby as the ritual prescribed. My uncle wrapped her in his prayer shawl and handed the bundle over to me. Sporting a fedora, he recited the first verses from each book of the Chumash, the five books of Moses, and finished with the last verse in the book of Deuteronomy. I was to lift the bundle up like an offering, and when he asked what the baby girl's name was to be, I was to call out full throttle her Hebrew name. I felt my heart pulsating in my throat—so scared was I of dropping the tiny creature.

He shouted at the top of his lungs as if he wanted to reach the ear of the Almighty in heaven: *"Hollekrasch, wie soll es heißen das Mädele?"*

I shouted as loud as I could: *"Es soll heißen Mirel Rifke bat Aharon ve Hedwig."*

"No, no!" my uncle yelled, waving his hands. "Your aunt's Hebrew name is *Yo-he-ved*. Let's do it one more time."

"Hollekrasch, wie soll es heißen das Mädele?" he shouted, lifting his head and forming a hand funnel like the mountain men do when passing on messages from peak to peak.

This time I gave it my all, taking a deep breath between each word as if I too wanted to reach the ear of the Almighty: *"Es soll heißen Mirel Rifke bat Aharon ve Yoheved!"*

According to custom, the question and the answer were repeated three times. The old-fashioned names came from the baby's maternal great-grandmother and her paternal grandmother. It was then up to me to declaim the first paragraph of the *Shema* prayer, and my uncle followed up with the appropriate blessings. Being a Kohen, a descendant of the biblical Aaron, he also recited the priestly benediction.

The sisters, Clara and Hedy, clapped their hands and chanted, "*Siman tov und mazel tov.*" They wiped their eyes and heaped praise and kisses on me. My uncle expressed his appreciation with a smile and a comradely slap on my back.

"Gut gemacht!" he said, which in the American idiom would be something like "good job." He even rewarded me with a few pieces of candy he pulled from his pocket.

Glowing with pride, I looked around for my father. He stood in the corner among the local onlookers with folded arms and said nothing. His raised eyebrows and puckered mouth told me that all this was superstition to him. I was sure I heard him mutter sneeringly under his breath, *"mishegoyim, mishegas,"* expressions he had ironically learned from his superstitious brother-in-law. Our new friends in the village probably thought the same thing with the equivalent expressions in their own language, but unlike my father, they joined enthusiastically in the applause. Some women came up and offered us freshly baked Sunday cake. The good feeling all around made it a festive occasion. My father's approval would have meant a lot to me, but I refused to let his negative attitude spoil the day. The familiar lines from a psalm popped into my head: "The mountains skipped like rams; the hills like young sheep." For a moment, I gave myself over to the illusion that all was well with the world.

Nina, the centerpiece of this strange ritual, meanwhile took it all in stride and slept peacefully through the entire ceremony, oblivious of all the kerfuffle revolving around her.

The grown-up Nina now clapped her hands like a child at her birthday party when I had finished. "What a wonderful story!" she exclaimed.

Yes, it was a wonderful story, but I was eager to hear another story, a different chapter in the book of Nina.

"You made me a promise too," I reminded her.

"I haven't forgotten." She took a thick notebook from a bag under the table and handed it to me. "Here, take it—it's all here. Warts and all! No holds barred."

"A chronicle?" I quickly reached for it, fearful she might take it back, and started leafing through the handwritten pages.

"No, no, you must wait until tonight. We first have a day's work before us."

Again I found myself in a real quandary, caught between Dina and Nina. *Funny, the similarity of their names,* I thought. I was as filled with suspense about the story of one as I was about the other. But under the circumstances, Nina's story would have to wait at least until the end of the day. Maybe it was a desire to get away from both of those emotionally exhausting women that made me dream of the beautiful Etoile.

Dina's Tale 6

The winter of my first enceinte was harsher than any in memory. It began early; the autumn leaves were still aglow, and the sheepherders were just beginning to round up their flocks for the migration south when the first snows began to fall. My body was in a constant throe of shivers from the time I felt the first stirs of life inside of me to near the time of my accouchement in late spring. A ceaseless wind swept down from the ice-capped mountain peaks, denuding the trees in the forests before the leaves had time to shrivel on their branches. Its cold breath seeped through the crevices in walls and windows, beating back the stream of warmth of the fire in the hearth. A premature frost spread a drab white over the gravelly ground. In the sky, an ashen shroud veiled the sun, allowing no more than a paltry morning light to squeeze through.

Since I had grown up in the lowland, I did not know what to expect from the mountain elements. Our winters had always been fairly mild. Even when a snowfall turned to ice on the ground, the sun's rays would lap it up before long. The starkness of this mountain landscape, which yielded up but small amounts of dry firewood to my frozen hands, crept into my heart and lodged there with the granite weight of the jagged mountaintops towering over the village. I was too miserable to gloat over the villagers' groans, their decrying the elements which for them too were apparently extreme. I heard their utterances about divine retribution for harboring a stranger—and a Christ-killer at that—in their midst, but evil tongues no longer touched my soul.

During those frigid nights when even the eiderdown failed to expend sufficient warmth, I yearned for my lover, for his embrace in which to find comfort and solace. Foolishly I still regarded him as such then. But he rarely came to my chamber anymore. At first, he would still steal in like a thief in the night to satisfy his lust. But as my belly grew larger, his visits became fewer and fewer. In the end I saw him only in the daytime, mostly from the distance, and as my time neared, he disappeared altogether.

"As a priest," he said once when I seized him by the sleeve to demand an explanation, "I cannot be openly involved with a woman in your condition. What would my parishioners say if they heard about our secret?"

"Your parishioners? What secret?" I cried. "The sparrows are chanting this secret from the roofs! The dullest peasant isn't duped."

"That may be so," he replied, swatting my hand grasping at him like a pesky fly, "but, you must understand, they would never betray me. They will always be on the side of their lord and master."

I didn't see him again until two weeks after you, my firstborn, had been circumcised. He came, so he declared, to baptize the infant—not his son, but the infant. Where he was keeping himself all this time became clear to me when he introduced me to the local noble woman. As soon as I saw them together, the scales fell from my eyes. They were lovers, and he had been staying at her residence, the château high on the hill overlooking the village. I felt a pinch of jealousy seeing them consort so carefree and unabashed together, like young lovers, although neither of them was all that young and she seemed a good deal older than he. In a way, I also felt a sense of relief. My child had already become the center of my existence. The certainty that I would not have to share this boy with anybody filled me with immense happiness. The priest was too busy fornicating to claim parental rights. My child was mine and mine alone, and I vowed to guard and defend him like a lioness her young.

The lady was very gracious toward me. She took a fleeting interest in the child. Smiled at him and tickled his chest. At one point, she picked him up and I held my breath lest she unravel the swaddling cloth. But she abruptly handed him back to me with extended arms when an indelicate odor rose to her delicate nostrils. She said she had been looking forward to meeting me, especially since she had never had the honor—she actually said "honor"—of encountering a flesh and blood Jewess. Although she rarely visited the larger towns where Jews lived before the miscreant Philippe—she said "miscreant"—ordered them expelled from the kingdom, she had heard much about them. Much of it, she squinted her eyes and puckered her lips, not so favorable, she had to admit. It was for this reason that she was extremely gratified to find me to be a young woman of such charm, no different than the usual lot, maybe more beautiful than the peasant lot. How pleased she must be to find that her lover's concubine had no horns, no tail, *I thought to myself.*

She finished this long, tedious, and to my mind, forced speech with a self-satisfied smile toward the priest. He rewarded her performance with gallant applause. I am sure my impression that he had coached her was not far from the truth. I responded the way one responds to one's social betters. I managed a grateful smile and a curtsy and mumbled something about her ladyship's exceeding magnanimity. She may have been a somewhat silly woman, but I must confess, she showed herself well disposed toward me on many occasions in the years that followed. She often put the power of her position in the service of my defense to ward off the villagers' accusations and insinuations against me. Whether she did this out of the goodness of her heart, which I doubted, or abhorrence of superstition and injustice, which I doubted likewise, or whether she simply acted at the behest of her beloved priest, which was more likely, mattered little to me. Maybe I am doing her an injustice, for she could easily have been a formidable enemy. She could have been goaded by jealousy and destroyed me instead of being my advocate. But such was the power of this man over the souls devoted to him. Even a lady of higher standing than he was himself was ready to eat out of the palm of his hand. As you experienced yourself, my sons, she took a kind interest in you when you had become big enough to tend to her flocks of sheep.

The entire village, including the châtelaine, witnessed the baptismal of the priest's unacknowledged son. Only I stayed in the background, keeping my eyes anxiously fixed on the swaddling cloth. Sybille had assured me that only the infant's head would be sprinkled with holy water. Still, I held my breath.

He christened you, my firstborn, Raymond, after his father, the name by which you are still known. But for me, you have always been Avraham, for our forefather who fought idolatry, which is the name I gave you at your circumcision. By the same token, I secretly named you, my second and third sons, Isaac and Jacob, so you too would be enclosed in the covenant with the Lord G-d of Israel.

Your father baptized you in the church and gave you the commonplace local names Arnaud and Pierre. He administered the holy sacrament according to the rite of the Roman Church in which he was anointed. In truth, he was a secret believer in the Cathar heresy, as you have come to know, my sons. Once you reached the age of reason, he sought to instill in you the satanic teachings of the parfaits. But by then you were already versed in the fundamentals of the Jewish faith. What irony! And what burden for you to bear! Sons born of a Jewess and a heretical priest, both adherents of despised religions! Scorned by the rulers and the masses of Christendom!

His true belief remained hidden from most of his adoring parishioners for a long time. He administered to them the sacraments, which he scorned in his heart. Only the inner circle of Cathar heretics, which included his mother, knew he was one of their own. Yet, even they were deceived. Even they were duped by his double-faced nature.

One day, I was perhaps two years or so in the village, a host of agents from the Holy Office in Carcassonne, accompanied by foot soldiers and horsemen, came to this region. They swarmed over the villages and surrounding countryside. They stormed certain houses, broke open doors and windows, ransacked storage shacks and private chambers, rummaged through chests and coffers.

"In the name of the Inquisitor!" they shouted, drawn swords clanking, leather boots grinding the gravel. As I watched from behind the window of the priest's domus, the memory of the horde storming the Jewish quarter of Toulouse by night shouting, "In the name of the king!" knotted my stomach with fear. But it lasted only a moment, for I knew this time I was safe. It wasn't Jews they were after. They hadn't come for me this time. Hundreds accused of heresy were rounded up. Men and women of all ages, even the infirm and some older children, were dragged from their homes and shops, from pastures and fields. Their wrists and ankles clamped in irons, they were carted away like so much refuse. The few who later returned told of their fate, of endless interrogations, tortures, and even executions. Some languished in the dungeons of the Inquisition for years.

How did the henchmen know whom to arrest? How did they know the names of the heretics? How did they know where to find them? These were questions being asked in the village by the remnant of the people, even by those faithful to the Roman Church. From nowhere were these questions hurled with greater vehemence and outrage than from the pulpit of the village church. No one thundered with greater force the words: "A traitor lurks in our midst!" Every sermon began with this refrain: "A traitor lurks in our midst!" Cowed in their seats, the villagers looked around with lowered heads. Who would follow the priest's challenge to come forward?

"You know who you are, and we will find you!" He switched from thunderbolts to honey-coated pitch: "Come forward now and confess." No one stirred.

I knew who the traitor was. Only, I held my peace.

In those days, I still retained a modicum of loyalty toward him. Besides, why should I stand up for these peasants who had shunned me from the first, whose eyes had stung my back with their silent enmity, whose evil tongues wagged curses when I walked by? Only their reverence, their adulation, and maybe even fear of the priest had kept them from laying a hand on me. I was sure of it. Besides, they would never believe me were I so bold to accuse the priest of betrayal. Once again, he held us all in his demonic sway.

Even so, their fanatical hatred of the stranger, the intruder, La Josiva, the infidel, burst into the open on occasion, especially when it got confused with their superstitions and ignorance. Whispers of the evil eye made the rounds every time a child fell ill or an infant was stillborn, born deformed, or afflicted with illness. Fingers were pointed; heads nodded. That these were common occurrences long before I arrived in the village mattered little, for now they had their scapegoat. Now the inexplicable, the incomprehensible, was as clear as a mountain creek in the spring. The cause of all misfortune was as indisputable as the Holy Writ. That I too had my share of misfortunes mattered little. When G-d saw fit to gather my little girl to him in his eternal home a few days after she was born, the village hags snickered and gloated. G-d had no doubt good reason to put me through such a test, but a mother's heart breaks nevertheless.

One frosty spring day, it must have been early April, maybe around Passover—I had lost track of the Hebrew calendar—a peasant mob came to the priest's domus. He was away, as he was so often, and they were clamoring for me to appear. I was with child once again, my third, and was bedridden. I had spent the morning milking the goats, and Sybille, seeing how worn I was, made some chamomile tea and ordered me to bed. According to the Christian calendar, it was Maundy Thursday, the day of the year when my father would present himself at the entrance door of the cathedral of Toulouse to the church authorities who would then allow the good citizens of the town to slap his face for half an hour in retribution for the Jews' guilt for the crucifixion. I never quite understood this hatred. The Christian doctrine teaches that G-d sent His son to redeem mankind from original sin—going back to the fall of Adam and Eve—through his martyr's death. It was the son's ineluctable destiny. His father had so destined it. Should mankind, or at least Christendom, not be grateful by this reasoning? Had he not died on the cross, they would not have been redeemed; they would be condemned to remain forever in purgatory, if not in hell. "The true reason for their wrath was no doubt of a different nature and had to do with the Jews' refusal to acknowledge this redeemer as the Messiah," my father had once answered my childish questions.

But I am departing from the incident I wish to relate. This mob of women gathered in front of the door, foot stomping and shouting something about La Josiva and the Lord's vengeance—I could hardly be expected to comprehend the finer points of theology. I peeked through the window from behind the shutters. There on the ground, spread out on a white sheet, was the wet corpse of a young girl, which was obviously the cause of their agitation.

"What do they want?" I asked Sybille.

"It's one of the midwife's girls. She was found this morning floating facedown in the sheep meadow pond. The girl is only four years old, same age as our Raymond."

"What does this have to do with my son?" The association filled me with ill foreboding. "Where is he?"

"He's fine, playing over there on the floor by the hearth." The good soul was as desirous to soothe my spirit as ever. "The reasonable explanation would be that she must have wandered off on her own and somehow tumbled into the pond. But this is Holy Week. As you know, that's when people get hysterical." She was right. I would always stay indoors during the days leading up to the anniversary of the crucifixion. One could never be sure what the shouting, groaning flagellants who roamed from village to village, their self-inflicted wounds gushing with blood, might do to one of those they decried as Christ-killers. On occasion, one such group from our village would lead a procession to the parish house, but they were quickly dispersed by the priest's raised hands. In Toulouse, my father had endured their slaps to his face. It was a ritual, a tradition one might say, carried out in accordance with fixed rules. Humiliating and painful though this custom was, he was never threatened with death, not then. Here in this mountain village I never knew what to expect from the frenzied peasant mob. Still, I was under the priest's protection.

That year, however, the priest was absent. Nobody knew where he was. He should have been in his church leading vigil. His absence likely emboldened the villagers, and at bottom enraged them. Their irrational minds put the blame on me for his neglect of his flock at this time of the great wailing. Never before had they accused me of murder as they did now. They had placed all kinds of calamities, misfortunes, and events of ill luck at my feet, never overstepping a certain line. The death of a child, no doubt accidental, was a most serious matter.

"You stay here," Sybille commanded me. "I'll see if I can chase them away. Or at least talk some sense into their numbskulls."

"Don't arouse their anger," I said meekly. "If you rile them, they might burn the house down. We've seen it before."

Sybille was a brave soul, but she was no match for the excitable hags. No words of reason could douse the inflamed tempers. Soon shouts like "Where is our priest? Where is the reverent father? Did you kill him too?" were heard. The mob moved menacingly closer and started massing in the yard. Sybille would not be able to hold them off. I pressed my son close to my chest and retreated further into the interior of the house.

"An eye for an eye! A tooth for a tooth!" The refrain was repeated to a numbing throb. Panic choked my heart. They were obviously after my child. I had no doubt they meant to harm him in revenge for the death of the girl. I grabbed a carving knife from the kitchen and cowered behind the hearth. Come what may, my mind was made up. Then suddenly, there was silence.

A few single shouts were still heard, but the chanting had stopped. Had the priest returned? But I could not feel his presence as I always did. Besides, the voice which now rose above the rest, telling the women to go home or to church, was clearly that of a woman. As I moved toward the window, I recognized the gaunt figure of the châtelaine.

"Go! Go!" she waved her hands at them. "Prepare the child's casket and pray for its soul instead of wasting precious time." This was not the first time she had defended me, but never was her arrival on the scene more propitious. Never had I felt more intense fear for my child's and my life. All too often had we Jews been victims of excitable mobs, particularly during Holy Week.

My father often told me the story of an event that happened in his youth. It was in the last year of the reign of King Louis IX, the sainted Louis whose piety was so great he became a thorn in the side of the Jews of his realm. His mother, Blanche de Castile, had presided over the defaming and public burning of our holy books comprised in the Talmud. This infamy occurred long before my father was born, but it lived on in the Jewish memory and was passed on to future generations.

Looking back over the entire reign of Louis IX, there never was a time when Jews were not accused of some crime or other calculated to harm Christians. Among the allegations were absurdities like the sale of contaminated meat and milk as well as wine. Jews also were said to delight in desecrating the holy host, of stealing the wafers and stabbing them in perverted rituals. Christians were warned not to consult Jewish physicians, who were likely to poison them despite the fact—and maybe because of it, my father told me—that Jewish physicians were more successful in treating diseases than the Christian healers. The mostly anonymous accusers did not shy away from alleging even murder and theft, and abducting Christian children and selling them into slavery.

The incident my father witnessed as a young boy involved another, and in many ways, most vicious calumny the Christians have long propagated about the Jews of the realm. It is all the more monstrous—and I want you to remember this, my sons, and never forget it—since our sacred laws forbid explicitly the partaking of blood, be it animal or human. It seemed that any dead body found in any locality was placed at the doorstep of the kahal, and often literally so. No Jew could get a fair hearing from beleaguered judges or magistrates. Whole communities were massacred by raging mobs. Not infrequently, Jews were burned on quickly assembled wood piles, or they were herded at the point of pitchforks or pick axes swung over their heads into their houses of worship which the rabble then set on fire.

To get back to my father's story, he was then studying our sacred texts, biblical and commentary, with one of the great Jewish scholars—a rabbi renowned and revered in all of Occitania—in preparation for the day when he would be reaching the age of mitzvoth and would be called up to do the reading for the first time. One afternoon, teacher and pupil were engrossed in discussion of a particular passage when a sizeable rock came crashing through the window, striking the rabbi's forehead. Blood soaked the pages of the book they were studying. The rabbi staggered to the door, motioning for my father to hide. But even before he could open the door, a menacing horde broke through and trampled over the wounded man whom they had pushed to the floor. While my father crouched behind a bookcase, he saw one group storming the upper floor, dragging the rabbi's wife with her infant son and two young daughters out into the street. Others ransacked the belongings and laid claim to anything valuable. The rabble broke into the cellar from where they hauled kegs of wine, stores of cheese, and other victuals.

They also purported to have found something else in the cellar, which had apparently been the object of their rage. The body of a young boy, the son of a prominent magistrate, who had disappeared a few days before. It was Holy Week, and the incensement of the good Christians over their Savior's passion was approaching the habitual frenzy. Word went out from somewhere, by someone, implicating the Jews in the disappearance. The search party entered the Jewish quarter, whose inhabitants were sequestered in their homes by town ordinance, presumably for their protection against just such violence. The mob roamed the narrow alleys until they came to the rabbi's house. Someone—probably the real murderer, said my father—had guided them there.

The boy's body was carried to the town square in triumphal procession and laid out for all to see. The rabbi's half-dead body was tied to a cart and dragged through the streets. His wife and children were battered with stones and anything else that came to hand. They were spared no manner of humiliation. The end came for the rabbi and his family when it was found that the boy's heart had been cut out and his genitals mutilated. Neither the rabbi nor his wife was granted a hearing in a court of law.

Many of the Jews, among them my grandfather and his family, left this place of horror soon thereafter and settled elsewhere. Planting a victim's body in Jewish homes or houses of worship came to be an almost common practice on the part of the defamers and murderers. Some of these miscreants would confess on their deathbeds, but the murderer of the magistrate's son—and by consequence that of my father's teacher and his family—was never found or brought to justice.

My grandfather settled with his family in the city of Toulouse where my father found another teacher with whom he studied for many years beyond the day when he was counted in the minyan of Jewish adults. In the year 1278, when my father was eighteen years old, he witnessed another revered teacher, Rabbi Isaac Males, being charged by the Inquisition with proselytizing and condemned to burn at the stake in the town square. With his own eyes, my father saw him being consumed by the flames. The loss of these two teachers and the memory of the horrifying deaths they suffered at the hands of fanatics stayed with him every day of his life. I know this to be true for he told us these stories many, many times, especially during the Christian Holy Week when we had to remain sequestered in the Juiverie so as not to incite the zealotry of the flagellants even further. I recount to you these stories, my sons, because it is my fervent wish for you to always remember what has been done to the Jewish people in the kingdom of France and to tell it to your children so that they will remember and that it will never be forgotten.

"Well, they did forget," said Nina when we came to the end of the day's work.

She jumped up and began stretching and bending her body, then twisting it in a yoga position, without further explanation. I too was not in a talkative mood. I lunged into my travel bag and extracted an etui that contained my pipe and a pouch of tobacco along with a lighter and other necessary paraphernalia. Silently and with deliberate concentration, I tamped down the tobacco and lit it. After I had taken a few deep draws and Nina had disentangled herself from a pretzel position, I finally posed the question that was hanging between us: "So what is it that they forgot?"

She looked up surprised as if she had forgotten I was there and what we had been doing.

"I didn't know you smoked," she finally remarked looking at me askance as if this was a matter of utmost importance.

"So what is it they forgot?" I asked after I had settled down in an easy chair and drawn several puffs of the calming smoke.

"Oh, yes," she replied. "These are my own observations, of course, from living in the village. It is clear that somewhere along the away, in the course of the centuries, the founding mother's admonitions were forgotten. Somewhere along the line, her descendants lost the ability to read what she had written. We don't know for how many generations the knowledge was preserved. Maybe one or two, or more, but eventually it was lost in the course of the centuries. Not only the knowledge," she continued, "but also the Jewish consciousness. For all intents and purposes, these descendants are Catholics, or something close to that. They have their own way of doing things."

"Such are your speculations?" I noted, drawing deeply on my pipe and filling the room with the sweet aroma. Nina started to cough and wave her hands—whether at the smoke or at my remark was not clear. Probably both.

"No, such are my observations of a world in which I have been living for several years," she asserted with superior knowledge.

"Granted! But there's one thing that comes to mind, and that's the war. These shepherds who guided the Jews and others across the mountains, unlike many other people smugglers, didn't seem to have been driven by greed alone, if at all. They really wanted to help. Could it be—I know I'm going out on a limb here—but could it be that a glimmer, however faint, of Jewishness was still smoldering, an inextinguishable spark?"

"Who's waxing speculative now?" she laughed. "A rather romantic notion!"

"All joking aside," I replied, "let's get some chow, and then I shall be incommunicado for the rest of the night. There's a read I'm eager to get to." I patted my briefcase containing the story of Nina Aschauer.

She agreed that she too was up for a good meal. We parted and disappeared into our respective rooms for changing and freshening up before reconvening at the restaurant downstairs.

"I've done enough reading for the day," said Nina, picking up the thread when we were seated at what was by then our table in the corner by the window. "Maybe I can find something worth watching on television."

"I wouldn't bet on it. French *télé* is not much better than our American fare," I replied, distractedly perusing the menu.

"I could at least catch up with world events. I'm sure much has happened during my five years of Rip van Winkling."

"You are better off not knowing. To tell the truth, I envy you for that. The world is much too much with us as it is. A Shangri-La seems like a dream to me."

"After a long absence, you still wonder whether you might have missed out on anything," she added with a pensive nod of her head. "The last event I recall was the massacre of the Israeli athletes at the Munich Olympics. I was in Toulouse at the time, but had to get back home to America a few days later .... On top of everything, Alphonse had to come into my life then," she added after a pause.

I made no reply and focused on my *truite meunière* while waiting to see whether she would continue this thread of thought.

"But you'll find out about all that in your bedtime reading," she said finally with a suggestive chuckle. "While we're still working on this repast, maybe you could give me just the gist, a quick summary, of what has been going on in the world in the last five years."

"That's a pretty tall order. You know what Moses found when he came down from the mountain."

"Dancing around the golden calf was major enough for Moses to smash the tablets. But you just said that nothing unusual has occurred. Do I detect a bit of a contradiction here?"

"Nothing unusual, in the sense of nothing new under the sun. The affairs of the world are still the same cesspool they've always been. Or shall we say, the Philistines are still bowing to one golden calf or other."

"Wasn't that the Israelites?"

"Yeah, but that story is a parable for human behavior. No, my dear Nina, the course of history has not changed history much, not in the last five years, and not since time immemorial. It's always the same: war and intermittent peace, murder and mayhem, intrigues, conspiracies, catastrophes, poverty, greed, power hunger …"

"Stop it already!" she raised her voice shooting me an angry look. "I didn't ask for your cynical generalities about the human race. As a historian myself, I'm fully aware of the many low points in mankind's march through time. I know what you are up to. I shouldn't have given you the record of *my* progression. Now you are dying to get into it and you try to avoid any deeper discussions that might keep you from it much longer. Am I right?"

"Something on that order," I confessed.

"Okay, then give it back!" She seized the handle of my briefcase and we engaged in a short wrestling match, drawing disapproving attention from management and patrons at this stodgy establishment. I emerged triumphant and held the case over my head out of her reach. To mollify her, I promised to give her a rundown—as much as I could remember off-hand—of the highlights of what occurred while she was up on her mountain retreat, but away from the indignant glares. It was time for our by now customary evening constitutional anyway.

"What was the outcome of that Watergate bit?" she asked somewhat out of breath when we stopped at a café after a brisk walk.

"Oh, you missed that," I said. "Well, Nixon resigned from office—totally discredited."

"Really? That must have been quite a show. And the war? I presume it's over."

"You mean the one in Vietnam? Yes, it's over, over and done with. The communists took over the entire country. With all the hue and cry rocking American campuses, I often yearned to escape to a mountain myself."

"Politics had nothing to do with what I did—what I had to do."

"So what was it then?" I seized the opportunity to probe the question that had been hanging between us. "What was it that made you disappear from the face of the earth?"

"You'll find out soon enough." I felt her slipping away into a space and time from which I was barred. Then just as suddenly she returned, and with a gracious smile she fixed her eyes on me.

"Tell me about Israel. What has been going on there?"

"Not so pleasant either. There was another war. We call it the Yom Kippur War since the Arabs launched their attack on that holy day. Israel was unprepared, and we suffered great initial losses, but in the end we beat them back."

I was just about to tell Nina about the oil crisis that followed and the lines at American gas stations when we heard someone calling out our names. We turned and saw Etoile meandering toward us between the tables.

"I was looking for you all over," she gasped. The women embraced, and even I received the customary French peck on both cheeks plus one.

"When did you get back?" Nina asked, obviously happy to see her friend.

"Just now. I went looking for you as soon as I arrived."

"Did anything happen?" Nina asked alarmed.

"Alphonse brought the children to Toulouse!"

"What? How could he?" Nina's voice sounded shrill and tremulous.

"Let's get out of here," I urged.

When we reached the street, Nina was still mumbling, "How could he? How could he?"

Etoile tried to calm her with soothing, sensible words: "It's not all that bad. Maybe you should just go and talk to him. This hiding game has to stop. It's driving you out of your mind."

Nina nodded. "You're right! It has to be done."

Leaning on her friend's arm, she expressed the desire for some fresh air.

I ran back inside the café to pay for our drinks and then caught up with them but remained a few steps behind. This seemed to be a matter best handled by a woman.

When we were back upstairs in our hotel suite awhile later, I administered some cognac to Nina. It revived her senses but also brought about an extreme agitation that made her jump up. She began to pace the room and shower herself with recriminations.

"I was such a fool. How could I have jeopardized everything? And for what? For what? What did I expect? How could I have abandoned my children?"

"He won't hurt the children, will he?" I asked softly.

"No, of course not. He's just using them as bait. To make me come out of hiding. What on earth possessed me? Well, it's clear—I have to go back now. It's the only way. Henner, you will have to work on this project without me. You are much better suited for this kind of work than I am anyway."

"What do you think will happen if you return without the codex?" Etoile asked.

"That will be a problem, but maybe if I explain, if I tell them about Dina and that I am trying to bring the story of the founding of their village to life for them, they might be mollified. Whatever, it's a risk I have to take. The seneschal will understand."

At the time, I did not understand this last reference but was too preoccupied with grasping the overall turn of events to ask about it.

"What kind of life will it be for you when you get back there?" I still had hoped to convince her to come back to our century for good even though she had several times insisted she would have to go back to Valladine.

"It will be the life I chose five years ago. I love my husband and I love my children, and there is no way that Alphonse would ever leave Valladine. He did it once but then went back for good. It's a peaceful life, maybe the last outpost of a utopian dream on this earth."

"Then why don't we simply give up this project and you take the codex with you? It's hard for me to see you go, but if it has to be, I don't want you to be punished. In fact, I think it may have been the hand that guides history and human destiny that brought you to this village to discover Dina's writing so it will be revealed to her descendants."

"Who's waxing romantic now?" she said in a lighter tone with a sniffle.

I felt relieved that I had brought a glint of cheer back into her eyes. But the more I thought about it, the more plausible my theory became to me. As a historian, I was fully aware of the limits of what was knowable, about how much lay beyond human ken and out of reach. Here Etoile came to my rescue.

"Before you rush into anything with all that talk about giving up what you worked so hard to accomplish, maybe we can find a way to photocopy the codex and Henner can work from there," she suggested.

"You know we tried it before. It can't be done without damaging the parchment. The only way is copying the text by hand, and that's what we have been doing," Nina demurred.

"Then talk to Alphonse. Explain what's going on." For the first time, Etoile let show some impatience with all the whining and wincing. I was beginning to think that Etoile was right and that the cat and mouse game Nina had been playing may have been unnecessary—that either it was the product of her overwrought imagination or she had some other motive to which we were not privy.

"What exactly do you want me to do?" I asked Nina.

"I want you to finish the transcription and then translate it into French or English or both and get it published."

When she saw my doubting mien, she said, "Come on, we are more than halfway there."

"In other words, you expect me to drop everything I'm doing, my teaching load, my own research, and devote myself to your work."

"I thought it was *our* work, collaboration between us. You certainly gave the impression these last weeks that you too were entranced by this story and the woman who wrote and lived it. How often do we have an opportunity to enter into close contact with a flesh and blood woman who lived seven hundred years ago?"

Is this a séance? I thought. I didn't answer since it would only lead to more fruitless back and forth, and the briefcase next to me was beckoning.

"All right! All right! I see it's no use arguing. Of course, this woman, a Jewish woman at that, has grown on me too and I want to follow her tale to the end and, if possible, make it known to the world. But arrangements have to be made. I do have obligations. Tomorrow we'll return to Toulouse to face reality. But now, let's retire and get some rest."

The voices of two women arguing still penetrated my bedroom wall for a while. Etoile apparently didn't want Nina to return and just give up the work and decried what she regarded as her friend's impulsive decision. But impulsiveness was a basic trait of Nina's, as we already knew and of which I was to find more proof in the notebook tightly filled with a handwritten account of the events five years ago which had led her to abandon the modern world.

Thus, comfortably ensconced between ample pillows and eider downs, I began to read. Already the opening paragraph made me smile. How exquisitely Nina! Here, she started out by recalling a conversation the two of us had years earlier about the poetry of Rilke, with which we had a brief fling. I was, of course, flattered to find that she addressed this account to me, her cousin in the far distance.

Part II

Yesteryear's Snows Regained

Nina's Progress 1

Account of how I, Nina Aschauer, came to Valladine, an uncharted hamlet in the Pyrenees, begun in April 1974, with the intent of establishing a record of my life here. I am addressing this to my cousin Henner, my erstwhile confidant and closest friend despite many years of separation, since I believe that he is the person most likely to understand my motivation for the quest that brought me to these mountains.

My dear Henner:

The human eye perceives the world from an inverted perspective—it is incapable of perceiving the vastness of spaces, safe as mirror images whose forms are darkened by the shadows we cast over them. The poet's exact words elude me at the moment; this paraphrase is what I remember. I suspect my memory is producing a rather garbled version of a poem we once memorized together, you and I, and recited together in the original tongue, long, long ago in another time, another place, almost another life. I was very young then, groping for meaning and fulfillment in life, and you taught me to follow the lodestar of poetry.

"The poet's wisdom is far superior, far deeper and truer to life than the philosopher's ruminations," you, a philosophy student of twenty-two, intoned, and I, a confused bat-mitzvah girl, was impressed. You also told me that true poets are prophets, unlike mere doggerel scribblers. Back then, I probably didn't understand half of what you were carrying on about. But to me, you were a prophet; your words were like holy writ. You never belittled me, never treated me like a child despite the years between us. You never made light of my thoughts and feelings that I confided to you. You never ridiculed my childish fantasies, and you always went along with my dreams of Valladine.

Well, I never gave up that dream. As I got older, grew into adulthood, achieved highest academic honors, gained some fame in certain circles and even a measure of good fortune, and settled into the life of an Upper West Side intellectual elitist, I should have found contentment, rested on my laurels, and kept on publishing little articles later to be expanded into books, endlessly belaboring the obvious and digging up the not so obvious. Yet, I felt a void, a churning disquiet inside of me. My love affairs were never really that. I had sex. I moved in with some guy, more out of a desire to conform to the then prevailing cultural norm of free love rather than real desire. This was the time of the sexual revolution, the declared liberation of women from the bondage of monogamy and the drudgery of childbearing. Life was a frantic hunt for the fulfillment and happiness to which we felt we were entitled. I felt neither fulfilled nor happy. In time, I returned, regressed some might say, to my childhood fantasies for comfort. I pulled them around me like a warm shawl, a cocoon, a carapace against an intrusive world. I remembered my childhood dreams about Valladine, a place somewhere in the mountains between France and Spain, the place where I first saw the light of day. Finding Valladine became an obsession. And then I found it.

My life changed on a late-summer evening in the year 1972, just a few days before I was scheduled to return home from a sabbatical year at the University of Toulouse. My desk in the office I shared with several other visiting scholars was cluttered with piles of ruled cards densely filled with handwritten research notes. My project for the year had been focused on the Pyrenean pastoral society. I had spent a lot of time talking with shepherds. Was I really interested in their habits, relationships, marital customs, marital conflicts, and stuff like that? Looking back, I know I had ulterior motives for wanting to enter into their world.

I sat by the open window of my office, and the evening breeze, redolent with the aroma of chestnut and sycamore, fanned my face. I breathed in the air of solace and calm, closing myself off from the atmosphere of unrest and turmoil to which this campus was not immune. My eyes came to rest on an ancient sycamore tree in the middle of the yard, and that's when I first saw him. I turned my attention back to arranging the cards into neat, smaller piles, and bundling them according to a schematic order I had devised. Before me was the accumulated result of one year's research, of months spent in archives, libraries, and, foremost, in the field. These boxes would take up an entire suitcase, if not two, together with stacks of folders containing photocopies of original documents and journal articles. For the next few years, I would be sorting, examining, analyzing, scrutinizing the data, spreading them out like parts of a jigsaw puzzle, or, better, like many-colored strands from which to weave a tapestry of life of the past. I worked diligently and mechanically, with the routine of the seasoned researcher. And yet, unlike before, this time I felt my heart was somehow not completely in what I was doing. Despite a vague sense of futility, I carried on, and it was not until the gathering dusk in the unlit room began to strain my vision that I let my hands drop with a sigh of relief.

I lifted my eyes again toward the window, gazing absentmindedly at the crown of the sycamore tree outside. Gradually I became more fully conscious of the surroundings. He was still there. The broad figure of a man flanked by two huge white dogs aroused my interest. He was standing directly opposite my window—stiff, motionless, distinguished from the stone statue behind him only by the smoke rings rising from a curved pipe dangling from the corner of his mouth. He stared directly at my window.

I had seen him only once before on a starless night, a long way from Toulouse, in the mountains, in the flickering light of the fire of a Pyrenean sheepherder's camp. Yet, I recognized his self-assured repose that had struck me then, clearly perceptible even now. He was an odd-looking figure with his broad-rimmed slouch hat sitting atop a mass of long, jet-black loose hanging hair and a leather hunting scrip slung over his shoulder. His eyes were shaded by the rim of his hat, and only the lower part of his face overgrown with a bushy, drooping moustache was visible. His attire too seemed of another time. Only in an antique clothing store could he have gotten that coarsely spun tunic-type shirt, the wide-wale black bell-bottom journeymen's trousers and open sandals. His massive frame leaned on a rough-hewn, knobby shepherd's staff. Everything about him was of oversized dimensions. Even the two dogs flanking him were gigantic. I had encountered this sturdy, pure white breed before during several excursions to the Pyrenean Mountains. The sheepherders prized them especially for their durability and loyalty.

Suddenly the statuesque figure began to stir. At first I did not trust my eyes. But there was no mistaking, he tipped two fingers to the rim of his hat and bowed slightly in the direction of the window where I was sitting. After a moment's hesitation, I acknowledged the gesture with a slight nod of my head. Finally, he took several long strides across the roadway, the dogs trotting along in step with him. From what I was able to make out, he was headed for the entrance door of the building. Five minutes later, there was a knock at my office door. How he knew to make his way through the tangle of hallways directly to where I was, I will never know, but it hardly seemed important enough to inquire about. I opened the door and bade him enter the dusky room. He must have thought I was expecting him, which in a way I probably was. A sweet, rather pleasant aroma of pipe tobacco, mixed with the raunchy smell of the panting animals, filled the room. He removed his hat, and in the twilight, I met for the first time the firm, though melancholy veiled expression of his dark eyes that sent a rush through my entire body. "Bedroom eyes," the thought ran through my mind, followed by an immediate, silent reprimand of "Don't be silly. You are behaving like a young goose."

Outwardly I tried to maintain a lady-like, proper comportment. I offered him a seat in one of a set of comfortable fauteuils and seated myself with crossed legs opposite him. The dogs collapsed as by silent command behind their master. The resemblance between the three was quite uncanny, and I barely suppressed an irresistible laughter.

"You don't mind?" he said.

"Oh no, I love dogs," I said. Just to keep the conversation going, I quickly added, "What kind are they? They are so big."

"Pyrenean sheep dogs," he explained without really explaining. His French had the rolling patois I had encountered in the mountain region.

"Oh yes, of course!" I said in reference to our previous meeting. "You are a shepherd."

"Well, not really. Only in a certain sense. I'm the owner of flocks of sheep. My name is Alphonse de Sola."

"Enchantée, Nina Aschauer." I extended my hand. He received it as if it had been tendered as a gift. He held it in both hands and seemingly forgot to let go while his eyes remained fixed on my face.

His grip was firm. His hands felt leathery but caressing. I could easily imagine that these hands had spent a lifetime roping and sheering livestock.

"What is it that you do here, Nina Aschauer?" he asked in slightly formal, even archaic French. His voice chimed with a nasal singsong reminiscent of the sweet, lilting sound of the chalemel on which shepherds trill ancient mountain airs in the quiet of the evening.

"I am a historian and a university teacher in America. I am in Toulouse as a visiting professor." I was not sure that he grasped what I was saying. He furrowed his brow and pinched his eyes together as if straining to put everything together in his head. For a moment, I felt a sense of superiority over him—the sophisticated woman of the world versus a backwoods montagnard. However, I was put in my place the very next moment.

"That is all very well. You are a teacher. That's nice. But why …" He suddenly let go of my hand and began to draw random circles in the air. "Why, for what reason, are you going about talking to shepherds and peasants, asking them what one might consider rather … intimate questions that are no stranger's business to ask?"

"Is that why you have come all the way to Toulouse? To ask me that?" I gave off a perplexed laugh. Should I explain that I was gathering data for a book about family relations in a rural, pastoral society? Would he understand? Should I tell him that I was a recognized authority on the subject and had already written a much acclaimed book on gender relations in rural Pomerania in the outgoing nineteenth century? I realized that would be pretty useless, if not ridiculous. He would hardly understand, nor would it interest him. I noticed the pupils of his dark eyes, so soft a moment ago, had become constricted, beady like a snake's, hard and challenging. He was obviously a man used to being obeyed and having his questions answered. I had somehow crossed a line and treaded on forbidden

ground. I was an intruder on a turf he considered to be his, and he was here to hold me to account. Keen disappointment began to fill my romantic soul. He obviously had not made the trip for my blue eyes, blonde curls, and alluring figure. But the next moment, a rebellious spirit reared its head in me. I was not going to be bullied by some stranger who comes out of nowhere and denies me the right of free, academic inquiry. France, after all, was a democratic country like the United States.

"Interviewing people is part of my research," I said with a stiff lip. I sat erect, hiding behind my back the hand that was still suffused with the warmth of his touch.

"Nobody is forced to answer my questions. Those who did not want to speak with me, and there were some, simply told me no. Many of these people welcome the opportunity to talk about the joys and sorrows of their lives with someone who is sympathetic. I find that to be true everywhere."

"What purpose does it serve to be writing about the dull lives of dumb shepherds and peasants?" Disdain and derision were written all over his face. I remembered now the deference the shepherds had shown him and that they had addressed him with "Seigneur." At the time, I didn't think much of it—just took it to be a quaint regional convention. Now his derisive demeanor made me see the scene I had witnessed in the mountains in a new light. There was something imposing, imperious in the way he spoke to the common shepherds. I also realized that somehow, for some odd reason, he perceived my dealings with the shepherds as a threat, enough of a threat to follow me all the way to Toulouse and to try to intimidate me. I am not your vassal, *I thought defiantly, just barely controlling an impulse to mangle that smirk with my bare hand.*

"Is this why Monsieur came all the way to Toulouse? To ask me this question? Monsieur may find the lives of these people dull, but I

personally find all that is human fascinating. And as a historian, I find the lives of these particular mountain people doubly fascinating since they have not yet been touched by modern society. They still live in a manner close to the way people lived a hundred or maybe even two hundred years ago. The lives of these people, which Monsieur regards as dull, provide modern researchers with a glimpse into the past. Their world is a living laboratory for my studies, and there is nothing dull about that, I can assure you." I was animated by a mixture of pride and anger. "I don't know who you are, but I can tell you, it is like stepping out of the present into the past, to live in the past, to feel, to think, and experience the world in the way people of long ago felt and experienced the world! To recreate and inhabit a world that no longer exists. That is what I do, Monsieur de Sola!"

"Why would you want to know so much about dead people?"

"Because I am a historian. You may be one of those who regard history as bunk." I used the English word since the French equivalent eluded me, but then I dropped the whole matter, despairing of making this man understand anything.

He made no reply, and I just wished that he would pack up his dogs and go and leave me alone. But he made no move indicating he was about to follow that course. Instead he sat in contemplative silence for several minutes—endless minutes to my mind.

"And these books ...?" he said finally, pointing at the shelf on the wall. "These are history books?"

"Yes, most are history books."

"And they tell about the lives of people who lived a long time ago and are now dead?"

"Basically, yes." I was not sure what he was getting at, if anything. Perhaps he was just an uneducated yokel with pretensions and he really didn't understand, or he was a sly fox trying to catch me in a snare—though I could not imagine for what reason.

"You write such books? And you think you know ..." he said more to himself and fell again into silent pondering.

"Well," I began again and attempted to rise. But he quickly grasped my hands and forced me back into the fauteuil.

"That was not really why I came," he said. His voice had regained its smooth, lilting singsong, though a sarcastic undertone remained. "If Madame enjoys recording the lives of shepherds and writing books about it, far be it from me to stand in the way of the advancement of human knowledge. The reason why I came to Toulouse is really something very different. What I need to know is what Madame knows about Valladine?"

"Mademoiselle," I said.

"In that case, what does Mademoiselle know about Valladine?"

I laughed incredulously. "You came to Toulouse to ask me what I know about Valladine?"

"No, you came to the mountains and asked about Valladine," he said. The seriousness of his dark, hooded eyes froze my laughter and chilled my soul. "How and what do you know about it?" he demanded as if he had a right to question me.

"What should I know? Really nothing," I evaded. This stranger's game of what almost amounted to psychological warfare was beginning to wear me down. His constant mood shifts were unnerving to a point where I felt like an animal being pursued by a cunning hunter.

"Mademoiselle mentioned Valladine several times when she spoke to the shepherds, several times," he emphasized, gripping both of my hands to make it impossible for me to turn away. "You must know something. Where have you heard the name?"

"Who are you? What do you want from me? What have I done to you?" I was frightened that I had invited a raving maniac or lunatic into my office.

"I don't mean you any harm. Only I must know what you know about Valladine. You must know something, or you would not have asked. Where did you hear of the name?"

"It's a village or valley I heard about. It seemed interesting. I couldn't find it on the map, so I thought maybe the shepherds would be able to point it out since they wander from mountain pass to mountain pass. But not even they could confirm that the place exists. So maybe it doesn't exist in reality; maybe it's a place out of a fable."

"Since it is not on the map, where did you hear about it?"

"I must ask you to leave now. I have nothing further to say. Please, go."

He made no move.

"Why is this so important to you?" I pleaded.

"Nobody around here knows anything about Valladine—and you, you come from America, and you go around asking questions. Why?"

"Well, if you absolutely must know, I was born in a place in the Pyrenean Mountains called Valladine. So my mother always told me. Maybe it was all in her head, in her dreams. Nothing but wishful thinking. Maybe she was in a delirium from the labor. Maybe she just willed it to exist since the rest of the world was such a dismal place during the war. I was always curious to find out where this place was—if it actually existed."

"What year was that?" He had mellowed again, and the pressure of his hands, though still firm, no longer hurt me. A warm shiver went through my body.

What a peculiar man. Actually, you are the peculiar one, *I corrected myself.* All he has to do is speak softly and turn that melancholy, doggish gaze on you and you turn to putty. *But I shrugged off that thought with the recklessness of someone about to embark on a great adventure and who flippantly dismisses well-meaning admonishments about the dangers ahead.*

"That was in the spring of 1941. My parents were fleeing the Nazis, and I was born on the run, so to speak. My mother was in her eighth month and went into labor early along the way. So one of the men—the leader, Raymond by name—took her to his village further up in the mountains. I was told the name was Valladine."

When I finished, the room had turned almost totally dark; only a faint light from the street lanterns filtered through the window. I did not dare pull away to reach for the light switch. The dim stream of light in the dusk was just enough for me to see the tears gleaming in his eyes.

"She is still alive and well—Madame, votre mère?*" he asked.*

"Yes, thank you, she is quite well … in New Jersey, that's in America." Another silence ensued during which he leaned forward, still holding my hands. He gently touched his lips to my fingertips one by one, slowly, almost solemnly, lingering over each one as if he was saying a prayer.

My first impulse was to pull away. This was too weird. There was something creepy, altogether too melodramatic about this man. I tried to pull back. But with each touch of his lips, my resistance melted a little bit more until I felt that I was losing my footing and my will was no longer my own.

"I shall take you to Valladine," he murmured.

I knew not what to say, but in my heart I knew I would follow him wherever he would lead me. To maintain a modicum of dignity, I felt it incumbent upon myself to at least voice some objection, to point out some difficulty, some obstacle. I could not just follow him to a place whose existence was very much in question.

"Where exactly is Valladine? Not even the most detailed map of the hiking trails gives any indication. Nor is it mentioned in any of the official guidebooks. How do I know it exists?"

"You will just have to trust me. If we leave tomorrow morning we can be there in a few days. I know a few shortcuts through the mountains; we can make it in three days. All Madame needs is a pair of good shoes."

He spoke as if it all was settled. Only a few necessities had to be purchased. All I was able to do was point out again, rather pointlessly, that it was "Mademoiselle" not "Madame."

Then, with a sudden jolt of disbelief, I called out: "A few days' time? That's a week going back and forth!" It was a rude awakening that hurled me from the clouds and landed me with a crash on the ground of reality. "My plane leaves in three days. Thanks for the offer, but no. Maybe next time when I come back."

At that moment—was it the deus ex machina come to my rescue?—a knock at the door interrupted the exchange. Actually it was a barrage of pounding fists and wild shouts in the corridor.

"I must see what is going on," I said apologetically. He did not prevent me from opening the door. A blinding shaft of light fell into the room as a man appeared in the doorframe. Within a few seconds, my eyes had adjusted enough to make out the excited, flushed face of André Weiss, a young colleague I had befriended. Pressing in close behind him was my teaching assistant Etoile.

"Have you heard the news? Something terrible is going on in Munich at the Olympics!"

"No, I haven't heard. I was busy ..." I looked from the young man to my visitor.

"I'm sorry to intrude ... I didn't know you weren't alone ... but won't you both join us in the lounge? Everybody is glued to the télé. It just goes to show that these terrorists will shrink from nothing."

"Easy, just tell me what is going on."

"Arab terrorists ... they have taken the entire Israeli Olympic team hostage. They are making some ridiculous demands."

I looked at my visitor who rose, flanked by his dogs. His hat was again pulled deep over his face, and only his moustache and the glow of his pipe were visible.

"Oh, I am sorry. André, this is—" I began.

But my visitor interrupted gruffly. "No need, I was about to leave."

"Wouldn't you like to stay and find out how severe this crisis is?"

"Crisis! There is always a crisis of some sort or other in your world. If I were to concern myself with every crisis, I would hardly have time for the things that really matter."

"The lives of people are at stake here!" André protested. "Doesn't that matter?"

"Yes, I know. What can I do?" the man grumbled, and turning to me he added, "I shall take the liberty to call on Mademoiselle tomorrow morning for an answer. It would have been better tonight, but I see the world is intruding and cannot wait. You must attend to whatever it is that is required of you, so I shall have to defer. I shall be patient. Until tomorrow then!"

He bowed stiffly with a nod toward me, taking no further notice of my colleagues. His staff pounded out a rhythmic beat on the marble floor as his massive frame lumbered down the corridor, shadowed by his loyal, panting retainers.

I saw him only briefly the next day. In the midst of the horrible news of the standoff in Munich that ended in a massacre of the Israeli team and preparations for my imminent departure for the United States, Valladine just had to take a back seat. Alphonse de Sola was strangely disinterested in these tragic events that had the whole world under its spell. In parting, he threw out the advice to go to the shepherds next time I was in the area. They would know how and where to find him.

I felt befuddled, torn between two worlds, one based on the firm yet horrible ground of reality, the other a pipe dream, a castle in the air. At that moment, I chose what I still considered to be the real world and returned to America as planned. I had things to do, schedules to keep, books to write, courses to teach. People were waiting for me, people who depended on me. I had a life to live, damn it! I had friends to cultivate, even a love life to revive that had been put on hold for a year. I had no time to indulge in fantasies.

The Air France night flight from Paris to New York was at last cruising over the Atlantic at the designated altitude. The Fasten Seatbelts and No Smoking signs had gone off. The passengers made themselves comfortable in the tight space in which we were to be confined for the next seven hours. The din of conversation mingled with the clattering of dishes as the flight attendants squeezed the food carts through the narrow aisles. A light supper was being served before the evening's movie entertainment.

Fortunately, I had an aisle seat and was able to stretch my legs. I took out a Gauloise from a silver etui and lit it with a butane lighter. I leaned back in my seat and with eyes closed inhaled deeply, filling my lungs with the pungent fumes. Suddenly I was choked by a convulsive cough. Damn French cigarettes! I crushed the poisonous cylinder into the ashtray but could not stop wheezing for several minutes, and then only with the help of several sips of water the stewardess administered.

What was happening to me? I had been used to those coarse, filter-less weeds since my student days at the Sorbonne. This past year in Toulouse, I had even come dangerously close to becoming a chain smoker. Maybe it was time to switch to a milder American smoke.

But was it really the cigarettes that were to blame for the restlessness I had been feeling for the last few weeks? Was it only the last few weeks? When was it that my surroundings began to converge on me and threaten to tip my mental balance? If I was completely honest with myself, I had to admit that this disquiet sense of ill foreboding, the maundering discontent, the longing for something I could not put my finger on had possessed me since my arrival in Toulouse almost a year before. Then again, maybe it was always there and was now bursting through the shell that had contained it.

My restlessness compelled me to take stock of my life. Was it the expectations placed on me by my early, almost spectacular, and to me sometimes still incomprehensible, scholarly success? What do you do for an encore? One had to be prolific to stay in the game. But was this what I wanted out of life? I had suppressed all the early doubts and fears that had crept into my mind after my first work had been hailed as a "seminal, feminist tractate." But you know all that already, my dear Henner, you who has drunk of the same fount of fame for years. Just, the proud family grapevine never told you about your cousin's reservations. How could they know? I never let out a word. Like you, I gave them so much naches *and didn't want to disappoint them.*

Having thus become an instant expert on the new historical scholarship that combined aspects of gender and modernization, I was in a position to garner generous, coveted, postdoctoral research grants, freeing me to mine evidence of similar patterns of the interplay of gender, anomie, and power in other parts of the world. For a while, I even believed myself that I was some kind of wunderkind. How many people, at age twenty-five, have their pick of tenure-track positions at major American universities—and in history? For the time being, I had settled on New York, an easy distance from my mother in New Jersey. In a few years, I would make the leap to a prestigious, private university in New England or New Jersey, provided I would live up to my early promise, which everybody—that is, important people in decision-making positions—had said I would. In other words, there was a certain cadre considering me to be a solid racehorse to put their bets on. I taught classes in women's history, mostly European, and pounded away on my electric typewriter, while turning a deaf ear to my mother's reminders that my biological clock was ticking. When the time came to produce another "major" work, I had departed on a sabbatical year in Toulouse.

I was never much of a determinist. Or maybe I just never gave much thought to what might be called the ineluctability of fate. Divine providence arranging the destiny of humans on the chessboard of life was an abstract concept to me. If anything, I thought of life more as a poker game. You make the best of the hand you're being dealt. Actually, Henner, I'm making this up as I'm writing. You know me.

The year had started rather uneventfully. I had teaching obligations with time to do my research. Nothing out of the ordinary seemed on the horizon as autumn faded into winter in the southwestern French landscape. Heavy snowfall blocked the mountain passes, confining me for the time being to my home base in Toulouse. My colleagues welcomed me with warmth, and I became friendly with several of them. Almost from the moment she first bounced into my office, as if that was destined too, introducing herself as my designated student assistant, Etoile Assous conquered my heart. Our bond of friendship formed virtually instantaneously.

Time had passed very quickly, and in seemingly no time, I found myself back on that fateful transatlantic flight. My thoughts flowed along in a meandering stream, skipping and dancing in twists and turns. I tried to watch the movie but was not in the mood for the escapades of some muscular, womanizing secret agent. Then my mind suddenly began to bubble with ideas about how I would weave everything into a narrative, only to succumb again to a paralyzing languor and a sense of ludicrousness. It all seemed suddenly like a striving for wind. Under the pall of melancholy, a mustachioed face was suddenly mirrored in the stream, a pair of dark eyes, as translucent as a mountain spring, their gaze reaching into my soul.

Maybe it was the strain, physical and mental, of those last days. The packing, pieces and pieces of luggage that had to be sent from Toulouse to Paris. Several footlockers had already gone ahead to Le Havre for surface transport. One departs always with so much more than one arrives with. The prospect of having to say good-bye to the people who had become good friends. And then, in the midst of all the turmoil of organizing and farewells, exploded the thunderbolt from the Olympics, leaving us all in a state of complete numbness. For hours, the world sat glued to television sets, anxious, waiting for the crisis to be resolved. Did we not live in civilized times? Did we not have rules and regulations guiding the behavior of guests in a host country? Did we not have international laws that made the taking of hostages a crime punishable by severest retribution? Would the hostage takers, terrorists, and their sponsoring nations not fear the long arm of international justice? Surely, these people had to be insane to think they could get away with such acts. Were the Olympic Games not the symbol, the ideal of the peaceful aspirations of all nations? Here was a country trying to show the world a new face, a peaceful face, a departure from its gruesome past. Beautiful sentiments, hollow words of pious speechifying, as hollow as a drained Bavarian beer barrel. In the end, the world held its breath, stunned but powerless, a glimmer of hope for a brief moment, and then eleven unarmed men were murdered by craven miscreants. Their offense: being Jews, Israelis, invincible on their home turf but left out to dry by the world.

Was it not ludicrous to pick up life where it had stopped only a day before? How can the world continue? How come the sun did not stand still? And yet, the world got on with business as usual. The games continued after a brief reprieve. And the sun rose the next day, the same sun of which it is said that brings all evil deeds to light. The games continued, and I went on gathering up my earthly belongings to go on with the life in America I had left a year before. My bags were packed, the flight was booked; in New York my teaching load was waiting for the fall semester. I was already late and hardly had time to prepare; I would have to just keep a few steps ahead of the students, as the saying goes—and Hobie was waiting, presumably.

He would be at the airport, and we would pick up our life, or relationship, wherever it was we had left off the year before. Everything would just go on as usual. I was thirty-one years old and would soon have to decide whether I wanted children. I would have to marry Hobie first. A child out of wedlock would be too much for my mother to bear; she was chagrined enough with the name Hobie. "What kind of mother, what Jewish mother, would call her child Hobie or Hobart?" she would say with raised eyebrows, rolling out the word "Jewish" like the long strands of yeast dough she braided into challah each week. It's probably no worse than Ludwig or Otto, the names of her grandfathers, *I thought.*

I tried to imagine what it would be like being Mrs. Hobart B. Kingsley. No, I would always be known as Dr. Nina Aschauer. Strange, how little I had thought about Hobie this past year. We had written each other and had spoken on the telephone a few times, but I had not really missed him. My thoughts did not travel across the oceans to be with him. Not the way they were now traveling back to Toulouse, to that stranger who had come down from the mountains to find out what I knew about Valladine, a place that was not on the map, and somehow he seemed no stranger at all. In all the turmoil of the last days, his image never left me. He was always there even when he was gone, like a guardian angel. What was it that drew me to this strange, world-weary man, so different from any man I had ever known? Was it just the novelty? Was it the persistence with which he had returned the next day, while I was gripped by the hostage crisis, which he shrugged off as just another crisis typical of human affairs?

No amount of reasoning could make clear to him that I could not just jump off the moving train of my life. He shrugged off my protestations of responsibilities, expectations placed on me. It came to me then, in the course of this exchange with someone whose thinking ran along completely different tracks than the common Western man's, that I was not a free agent, I was not mistress of my destiny. I was not free to do as I pleased, act on impulse. I was shackled, manacled, caged in a dungeon into the custody of which I had willingly surrendered myself. Taking stock from a bird's eye view, I zeroed in on the Gordian knot of my life, which appeared to me as a reverse Faustian bargain. I felt engaged in a danse macabre with a Pascalian wager, a Kantian imperative, and a Kierkegaardian problematic, all daubed in Socratic irony and topped with a fillip of Kafkaesque parody.

That's how I began to see it then, and still see it now: a clear swath of naches and kudos running from high school valedictorian to academic laurels and highest honors. I should be proud. I did my mother and family proud. That was probably the motivating force, even though my mother would have been even more proud had I married and presented her with grandchildren.

The plane hurtled ineluctably across the Atlantic toward its destination and my destiny on the opposite shore. No, *an inner voice persisted,* your destiny is on this side of the ocean, in the mountains of southwestern France. *The steam engine of my heart pumped at full throttle, pulsating in my throat and brain. I had to follow this stranger, this man who called himself Alphonse de Sola and of whom I knew absolutely nothing, except that he wanted to take me to Valladine, the place of my youthful fantasies, the accidental place of my birth. Moreover, I came to realize that I had to follow him not only to Valladine but to any place on the face of this earth he would take me.*

When the plane landed in New York, I was in a state of delirium. Neither the cold compresses, applied by the attendants, nor the aspirin administered by a fellow traveling doctor were able to break the fever. By the time the ambulance received me and rushed me to the hospital, it had reached 101 degrees. The cause of the fever was never pinpointed exactly, as all external factors, food poisoning, and infections were positively ruled out. But it fluctuated around the danger mark for almost three days. In that time, I seem to have engaged in a struggle with someone or something, like Jacob wrestling with the angel or whomever it was he wrestled with. I did not recognize any of the people present, except for my mother. She extended her hands, and I buried my face in them, whimpering and sobbing helplessly like a child. Just when even the doctors were beginning to shrug their shoulders since none of their tricks seemed to take effect, I suddenly broke out in profuse sweat, my body convulsed, I kept emitting strange words nobody understood, and then tumbled into a long, death-like sleep from which I awoke twenty-four hours later, restored to life.

To all appearances, I was returned to life, the life I had left the year before. I plunged into preparations for my teaching assignments, settled back into the apartment I shared with the man who had been my companion for three years, and mingled with the old circle of friends, mostly academics with a sprinkling of the artistically inspired, the kind of crowd one typically finds at dinner parties and restaurants on the Upper West Side of Manhattan.

On the surface, my old routine ran smoothly along its familiar tracks. Only deep inside, in my innermost being, I knew nothing was the same and never would be the same again. I felt it daily, more and more, an aloofness I was unable or unwilling to bridge, a detachment from a world in pursuit of things that appeared in an ever more glaringly absurd light. And I absolutely refused to have Hobie touch me. Suffice it to say, I slept on the couch in my study and locked the door at night. At first I thoroughly disabused him of any notion he might be harboring that he had any marital rights, certainly not without the benefit of a marriage license or rabbinical blessing. And when he proposed, I flatly turned him down.

On weekends, which in the past had been heavily booked with concerts, lectures, readings, and visits to art galleries, I found myself drawn more and more frequently to my mother's house for Friday night dinner. Eventually, instead of taking the train back at night or the next morning, I stayed till Sunday or even Monday morning. My mother did not comment, but I could see she was pleased to have me around more. On the few occasions when I tried to open up to one or the other of my female friends, their responses were always couched in stock phrases that seemed lifted from a handbook of popular psychology. Then I was bombarded with advice, where none was requested. It all boiled down to me needing to seek help, to see a therapist. What I really needed, so they said, was to finally get married; every single one of them seemed to be Hobie's confidante and, therefore, privy to his plans for the future.

Yet, I found that I could breathe freer when I was crushed by the human masses on the subway than in the apartment I shared with him. I looked forward to, almost lived for, the moment I left for work in the morning. On such weekends as I did stay in the city, I found it difficult to hide my boredom during those interminable social engagements, always with the same wine-sipping crowd, at the same restaurants or cafés. To avoid these occasions, I started attending Friday night services at Beth Chesed. The word got out, Nina was getting religious. How little they knew about me. I had always been religious, just not observant of every jot and tittle of the law.

One evening while I was grading midterm exams, Hobie erected himself in front of me with the ominous mien of an overlord.

"We have to talk," he said. This talking business so dear to the modern academic mind was to me nothing but irksome palaver.

"What about? I really don't have time right now," I said evasively, stuffing a stack of papers in my briefcase. "These exams are overdue already. It wouldn't be fair to the students to hold them up any longer."

"Why don't we make time?" He posed himself between me and the door to the apartment. "Let's talk about what's fair, or better unfair, to me?"

His lord-of-the-manor tone was all I needed. The fact that we were sharing living space—for which I paid half—did not exactly entitle him to anything to my mind.

"You've changed since France. And I need to know what's going on. Don't give me this vacuous look. I have a right ..." He grabbed me by the arm and tried to push me back inside. "What right?" I screamed. "We are not married. We owe each other nothing. And don't touch me again." I shook off his hand, and he let go.

"I don't go around moping and trying to press you to reveal what's going on in your mind or your life." I brushed my arm as if it had been soiled. And that's exactly how I felt at that moment.

"If you have a question about what goes on in my mind, just ask," he said in a more conciliatory tone. "We've always been open with each other. At least so I thought. You said yourself that openness in a relationship is the most important thing for it to work."

"I may actually have said that kind of crap years ago." My tone was still belligerent, probably unnecessarily so. "Grow up, Hobie! For heaven's sake, cut the psychobabble. These clichés have nothing to do with real life."

"Then inform me! What's going on in real life? I seem to be left out of it." He was still blocking the entrance door.

"I really must go on with my work," I insisted. "I'm not in the mood for games."

"Games! Huh? You think I'm playing games. You're the one who's playing games. I'm asking for a straight answer. What's going on and will you marry me?"

"You know what's wrong with you?"

"What? Come on, tell me! What's wrong with me, besides that I'm an idiot to put up with these … these allures of yours."

"Oh, never mind!"

"I do mind, and you won't get off the hook that easily. Come on, what's the matter with me?" He was again striking a threatening pose as I tried to dodge around him without much success. Unable to match him physically, I resorted to insult.

"You're full of yourself and you bore me. You think a woman should fall on her knees with gratitude for being honored with your attention. Should I kiss your hand in gratitude for your marriage proposal? The answer to it is no. No, I don't want to get married, not now, maybe never … and not to you."

"Seems your mother is gaining the upper hand."

"This has nothing to do with my mother!"

"Could it be a coincidence that you've been spending a lot of time across the river lately? We can't go out on Friday nights, or Saturdays, because you have to visit your mother in New Jersey. And don't think I have any illusions. She'll do anything to turn you away from me. I just thought you were adult enough to make your own decisions."

"Well, go ahead. See if I care." He finally stepped aside, permitting me with a mock gracious gesture to pass. I had a bitter taste in my mouth but felt relieved that this affair would now be over.

A short while after this altercation and a few more similar exchanges, I packed up, moved out of the apartment, and rented a hole in the wall in the Village, near my work. I was done, over and done with Hobart Kingsley Jr. My mother was right; it was an odd name for a Jew. But then he wasn't much of a Jew, come to think of it. My mother was probably right all along that he wasn't right for me. Somewhere in the far corner of my mind, a bell went off, ringing faintly that I wasn't being fair. But I pushed this last bit of qualm out the window of my heart. My thoughts turned to the other one. What about him? The one who had given me the courage to make this break—yes, there was no doubt about it and I proclaimed it freely to myself. It even put me in an exhilarated mood. He was even less of a Jew than Hobie, who could at least claim halakhic certification through his mother. Alphonse de Sola was a French peasant, a sheepherder—or whatever. I didn't exactly know what he was ... and it mattered not one wit to me. There was nothing in New York to hold me back.

Together with the course grades for the fall semester, I handed in my resignation from my teaching position. I did not even wait for a reply from the administration. A few weeks later, I was on an Air France flight to Paris and from there on to Toulouse. It was January. The mountains were capped with heavy snow, and the passes were closed. I forged on further south. The sheepherders and their flock were still in Spain for the winter. Still I put the call out for Alphonse de Sola. I wished for some kind of Oliphant, Roland's horn, to send the echo across the mountains. Instead I put up at a local inn in a small town called Oloron Sainte Marie; there I settled in and waited. I would wait no matter what, no matter how long it would take, even if I had to wait for the thaw of spring. In my heart, I knew he would come.

I must have fallen asleep in the early morning hours. When the telephone woke me, I was still sitting half-erect in bed, the notebook in my lap, and my glasses on the tip of my nose. Nina greeted me cheerfully with the shop-worn German saying: *"Morgenstund hat Gold im Mund!"*

"You won't believe the kind of night I had," I growled. "Just give me a few minutes to turn myself into a presentable *Goldmund* if not *Narziß*."

"Okay, take your shower and shave. But hurry up. We'll see you downstairs for breakfast in half an hour."

"Jawohl, auf der Stelle!" I bellowed into the receiver, but she had already hung up.

"Did you sleep well?" she asked when we met downstairs.

"Who can sleep if you're engrossed in a riveting page-turner?" I replied grumpily.

My head was still in a fog and I was not in a mood to banter. Besides, I was never much good before I had my morning coffee. Only the smile that Etoile, radiant as a morning star, bestowed on me chirping a sweet "good morning" refreshed my soul.

We lined up with trays at the breakfast buffet to make our selection from what the French call "American style" and in America is known as Continental breakfast. Before our hungry eyes were laid out a delicious assortment of cheeses, also smoked salmon, French *confitures*, fresh rolls, a variety of breads, and croissants, as well as eggs, hard-boiled and scrambled. A veritable cornucopia. There were also all kinds of meats, which we skipped over.

Nina walked ahead of Etoile and me, affording us the opportunity to exchange silent, almost conspiratorial glances. I realized how much I had missed her calming presence while she was away in Toulouse. Her straightforwardness—what I would call her un-neurotic-ness—and not least her smiling dark eyes injected a note of lightness into my dealings with the ever irascible Nina. For a descendant of desert wanderers tracing their lineage back almost three millennia, Etoile carried remarkably little baggage.

When we were seated at our table, I munched down a couple of fresh croissants laden with butter and the inimitable French *confiture de fraises,* followed by hardy consumption of bread laden with cheese and the smoked fish. The Turkish coffee—I knew café au lait alone wouldn't do the trick that morning—jolted my nervous system back into gear. A glass of fresh-squeezed orange juice and two aspirin slowly restored me to human condition. The ladies were more dainty in their table manners.

"That was quite an indictment, Nina," I said, dabbing my mouth with the napkin and taking another gulp from the coffee.

"What do you mean? What indictment?" Nina seemed ready again to fly off the handle.

"The danse macabre thing—doesn't show us academics in a very flattering light. A bit hokey, don't you think?"

"Oh, that! Actually, I thought it was quite clever. You know me; I just couldn't resist. I just thought you would get a kick out of it." She flashed me an impish grin.

"Do I detect a pitsele academic, a little pedant here after all, speaking in allegories?" My tongue performed what was probably a rather poor imitation of the Levantine "tsuk, tsuk, tsuk" sound, meant in part to admonish and in part to tease.

"No offense to you, but it was how I felt, and I had to get out of there."

"So you pulled off a disappearing act and left even those nearest to you, those who care for you and love you, in the dark." This time my admonition was meant in earnest. "And all that, just to extricate yourself from a situation that had become distasteful to you."

"That wasn't all." Tears started to appear in her eyes. "I was also in love, as silly and adolescent as it might sound."

While I raised my eyebrows, I saw Etoile consolingly patting Nina's hand.

"What's done is done," I said. "You obviously have built a life for yourself. You have a family to which you owe your first allegiance."

I still couldn't understand why she didn't tell her mother where she was going, especially since by all accounts their relationship was by no means, as is so often the case between generations in our Freudian world, a strained one. Postal communications from this mountain hideout were complicated or impossible, she justified herself. I had to accept her word, though it was hard to swallow.

"But I do want the sequel to this sappy tale of yours," I said after a brief silence. "What happened in this place called Oloron Sainte Marie?"

She promised that notebook number two would be forthcoming in due time.

"I'd like you to stay around for another day or two," I said, turning the subject back to more practical considerations that needed to be ironed out before she went Rip van Winkle. "If you want me to take over the project, which I'm happy to do, we need to devise a modus operandi."

She blew her nose and nodded agreement.

"Here's how I think we should proceed," I began. "You decide whether my plan sounds feasible or not." She seemed to have no problem with the fact that I would have to return to America and my university first. I had an obligation to teach at least one semester. As for my own research and writing projects, I was willing to put them aside for the time being. Since it wasn't advisable to take the codex out of France without courting trouble and an official investigation as to its origin, I would store it somewhere in a safe place until my return.

"Could you hold on to it for the time being?" I asked Etoile. But she didn't seem comfortable with assuming the burden of safekeeping this rare treasure.

"Don't take me wrong," she explained. "It's just the timing. I don't really have a place of my own. Besides, my oral defense is coming up in a few months. Until all this is over and done with, I'll be mostly incommunicado. After that, I'll be happy to help any way I can."

In the end, the decision was made to place the treasure in a plastic wrapping and store it in a safe deposit box.

"One more thing," I added. "Let's at least get a copy made of the handwritten transcription so you have something to show to your mountain folk, Nina."

For some reason, she had qualms about that. An oral account by her of Dina's story would suffice, she said. Then apparently on second thought, she agreed. "The seneschal would be interested," she mumbled to herself, but clearly enough for me to catch on.

"Do you mind asking who this seneschal is?"

"He's the reigning … how shall I say? … not exactly a king, but the leader of the community. I guess one could call him the overlord. He's the older brother of Alphonse. The de Solas have been the ruling family for centuries. It's all very medieval."

"Now that's an interesting revelation," I said, pricking my historian's ears.

"You will find out more in due time. I promise. But let's keep our eyes on the task at hand. And I, I must go."

All that having been done, Nina went to the room she had occupied at the hotel one more time to gather her few belongings. When she came out, she had exchanged the jeans for the peasant garb in which she had first greeted me. The sight gave me a pinch in the heart. She was going back to a world remote from mine.

The thought of our imminent parting and the uncertainty about what lay ahead almost brought tears to my eyes.

"We will meet again," I said reassuringly more to myself than to her. As far as I could see, we had tied up all loose ends that needed tying as far as the project was concerned, but there were so many unanswered questions about Nina's life. We said good-bye with a fleeting embrace. As soon as they had left the room, a sense of utter void came over me. I would miss them both terribly. Then a thought came to me, and I rushed after them out into the street. Etoile was about to turn on the ignition of her car.

"Where and how will I find you?" I called out to Nina. "I'm sure you want to see the final result, don't you?"

"By word of mouth! Just put out the word among the shepherds in the mountains that you urgently need to find Valladine, or better Alphonse de Sola. Start out in Oloron Sainte Marie and the Grande Randonnée."

I waved and watched the car disappear around the corner into the crooked medieval alleyways of the city of Albi.

Back upstairs in the lounge that had been our workroom these past weeks, I gathered the papers, pads scribbled with notes, writing utensils, and dictionaries strewn all over. Before wrapping it in silk paper, I lifted Dina's codex gently to my lips the way Jews kiss their prayer books when they have finished praying.

"*Voici, les neiges d'antan*!" I muttered. I was holding the snows of yesteryear in my hands, the snows Nina had brought down from the mountain. Now I had to take care not to let them melt and run through my fingers before I was able to freeze them in time. It was a sacred trust she had placed in me.

Dina's Tale 7

The news came floating over the mountains with the melting ice and snow. At first I refused to lend a believing ear. Nine years had gone by—an entire lifetime to me. Then the sheepherders and their flock came streaming over the mountain pastures from wintering in the south. As was their habit, the villagers gathered around them, eagerly pressing them for news from the outside world. They heard of the debased wool prices, the vagaries of the king of Aragon's perpetual wars, the fortunes and misfortunes of their Iberian cousins, their love affairs, and, whispers, mouths shielded behind hands, about the preachings of the goodmen. The reports also spoke of exotic caravans rumbling over the mountain passes. Covered mule-drawn wagons laden with what must be assortments of merchandise, they said. What kind the scouts could not say. But they were sure of the preciousness of the items being transported by men in flowing beards and loose-fitting white garments, their heads wrapped in Moorish turbans. Thus began the rumors of the Jews' return to the kingdom of France.

Handsome Philippe had descended into Gehenna—I am sure hell is the only place where he would be welcome—in the month of November previous in the year of their lord 1314. Nobody in the kingdom of France, neither peasant nor noble, was much aggrieved over the tyrant's demise. A reign marked by covetousness and greed, pursued with an iron hand, with merciless, ruthless cruelty, who would mourn such a monarch's passing? Yet, no amount of taxing, looting, robbing, thieving, plundering, extorting, disowning, intriguing, warring, murdering, or torturing had been able to still Philippe's ravenous appetite for worldly possessions and money and more money. To his successor, quarrelsome Louis, his legacy was depleted coffers and the Templars' curse on the Capetian race. With the country all but bled dry, the new king conceived of the idea of inviting the Jews back. Nine years after his father had expelled them, robbed them, and driven them from the kingdom with nothing more than the shirts on their backs, the son wanted the Jews back. Later I heard it said that he intended their stay to be limited to twenty years. Just enough time, he seems to have calculated, for them to amass a taxable fortune from which to replenish the royal treasury before they would be sent packing again. Unfortunately for him, he did not live long enough to reap the benefit of his scheme for himself. But that's a different matter and of no concern to me.

Why the Jews would hearken to the call, I could not fathom. Maybe it was that their existence was just as precarious elsewhere as it was in the kingdom of France. Or maybe they hoped to retrieve the goods that had been wrested from them. I was certainly curious, although I saw no way for me to return to the kahal as much as I longed to see my father again. Would he even come back? Would he fall for the royal bait, the iron fist that tendered sugarcoated conditions? I wondered.

I began to wonder what would happen were we to meet eye to eye—my father and I. Was he even still alive? What if the shame I caused him broke his heart and took him to an early grave? I vigorously rejected the notion, pushed it from my thoughts. It just cannot be, I told myself over and over. And what about my brothers? Would they forgive me? I began to imagine the encounter. An increasingly vivid scenario took form before my mind's eye. Somewhere deep down, I hoped that the sight of his grandsons would melt his heart. Would it really? Was I not fooling myself? You, my sons, my beloved sons, were after all the fruit of my disgrace, the living proof of my sin. But you were also his flesh and blood. I grew more and more restless. What if, what if? I spent sleepless nights spinning dialogues as they might unfold. When I finally did sink into an exhausted sleep, the voices followed me into my dreams. A trial took place. I sat in the box of the accused, my clothes torn, my head strewn with ashes. Or was it a pillory? The charge was high treason; the verdict guilty. I heard the members of a bet din, *sitting in judgment, their heads crowned with sulphur-yellow, high-pointed magician's hats, intoning the sentence: stoning until dead. A silent scream issued from my mouth, begging for forgiveness, pleading for mercy.*

This recurrent dream was senseless. I knew it. In my father's mind and soul, I had died nine years before. He and my brothers had intoned the Kaddish over me on that fateful morning even as I confessed my guilt standing rooted to the threshold of the priest's ostal. After this pronouncement, nothing could bring me back to this world for them. In the nine years since, I had been walking upright in the shadow of the valley of death. I had settled into a life of empty quotidian occupations and concerns. I had come to accept my life as it was. I did not try to fight the forces beyond my control. The die had been cast long ago, and not without my own doing; my carnal weakness had made me succumb to the devil's lure. The Jews' return would not alter the circumstances of my existence. So I told myself a hundred times every day since the news had reached the village. My fate was no longer linked to that of my people. I was cut off from the body of Israel, a severed limb cast on the dung heap; only my heart was always with them. My G-d always remained the G-d of Israel. I never adopted the practices of the idolaters around me. In all those years, I was never remiss in affirming His Oneness before going to sleep. Never did I forget to recite the Shema *prayer with you, my children, when putting you to bed at night.*

Yet, the news had awoken in me an irrepressible, long dormant yearning to make good somehow. My desire to do penance, mixed no doubt with curiosity, grew stronger with every waking day. You were tending the châtelaine's flocks at the time. She had always taken a benign interest in you, the offspring of her priestly lover, and shielded us, you and me, from the worst excesses of the villagers' rancor, something the man who sired you always shrugged off with casual insouciance. You surely must remember the day you took a flock of sheep to a higher grazing ground and one of them got lost. Maybe you also remember, although you were very young then, that I was trying not to show too openly my eagerness to join you in the search. Don't take it amiss, but I did have a hidden motive besides wanting to shield you against a scolding from the châtelaine's foreman. I was also secretly hoping that our search would lead us close enough to the main passageway across the mountains. Overlooking the thoroughfare from a hill, we came upon a scene of vibrant traffic moving in both directions. Clergymen and laymen, merchants, artisans, pilgrims, shepherds, noblemen and noblewomen and their entourage, knights and their squires, foot soldiers, peasants, beggars, minstrels and jugglers, wandering scholars, highwaymen—in all a motley human host propelled forward by all manner of transport—populated the route. According to station and means, they traveled on foot or horseback, in elegantly appointed coaches, horse-drawn carriages, on donkeys, or two-wheeled mule and ox carts, hay wains, pushcarts, and wheelbarrows. None of the travelers leaped out to me as a member of the tribe of Israel. I saw people clad in fine apparel of satin and silk, tunics and wool surcotes and tabards dyed in brilliant colors, others in crudely fashioned homespun of drab, coarse woolen or linen cloth. I looked down from my observation post on a great variety of headgear—coif caps and berets of the lower classes and scholars, the caul meshes, wimples, and toques of noble ladies, peaked helmets of knights and squires, calottes of ecclesiastics, gentlemen's velvet caps and chaperons, jesters' long-eared hoods with jingling bells.

Nowhere did I see the flowing white or sky blue linen vestments and turbans in the oriental style that distinguished Jews and Moors from the Christian folk. Nowhere did I see the yellow badge mandated by papal decree for the Jews to obviate their mingling with Christian women. None of the women were fully veiled as Jewesses had to be. Had there been any Jews among the travelers on the highway, I would have easily made them out. It occurred to me that the papal decree was also meant to prevent a Christian man from engaging in relation with a Jewish woman. But, as with so many things, the priest snubbed this law too with his habitual disdain for authority. Laws, decrees, and rules were for the simpleminded and the guileless, for dimwits and half-wits. This is how he thumbed his nose at naïve villagers who not only worshipped the ground he walked on, but also shielded him from the arm of justice and the Inquisition with staunch devotion.

A few days after you had found your errant charge and we returned to the village, I told the priest that I wanted to go to Toulouse. He burst out laughing—and what, he wanted to know, did I expect to find there. I was unable to reply "my father," fearful of his scorn. He knew anyway, as he always knew everything.

"So you heard the rumor about the Jews, that they are coming back."

"Is it a mere rumor?"

"What difference does it make? You belong here … with your children and …," he hesitated a moment, then he place his arms around my waist, "and with me," he whispered close to my ear.

Again he tried to sweet-talk me. As was his way, he used soft insinuation rather than open confrontation. Never did he raise his voice. Why should he? That's how he navigated through life unscathed, through the devious course he charted for himself unfettered. That's how he inveigled all around him. For a moment, I felt my knees weaken; my throat narrowed and I gasped for air. I felt his embrace tightening and his entire body pressing against mine. The ground seemed to shift under me. If he were to turn me toward him then, to face him, I would be lost. Everything would be as before; nothing would change. Once again, I would be a malleable piece of clay in his hands. He, the potter; I, the wet clay on the potter's wheel, for him to form and shape according to his will. I felt every ounce of will to resist fading away. He's right, *an inner voice told me,* your life is here with your sons, and maybe even, in a certain way, with him. *My father would never embrace you as his grandsons. Even if his heart were inclined to forgive, I knew he could not. He could not go against Jewish law. He could not tolerate the infringement against the ancient traditions of his people.*

I went on with my daily life, keeping house and yard, caring for you, and in the evenings, by the low light of the hearth, teaching you the aleph-bet *and the rudiments of our holy tongue, as much as I had retained after all those many years. Even if it was true that the Jews had been invited back by the king of France and some had indeed returned, it mattered little to the people in this village, and nothing was heard or spoken of the subject anymore. Only in my mind, the questions would not let go. What if? What if my father and brothers had come back? Understandably, they would not be seeking me out. But did this mean that I should not at least try to reach out to them? For them, the matter may be closed. Not so for me. My longing for a chance to explain, which I had tried to hold back, now threatened to overwhelm me. Another inner voice reminded me that there really was nothing to explain. I had made my choice clear that morning on the doorstep of the priest's house. The book was sealed. But my desire for vindication would not let go of me.*

A force stronger than I persisted in lapping at the dam I had erected around me, eroding it bit by bit, and finally causing a breach.

"I am taking my sons to Toulouse," I announced to the priest one morning after what was by then a rare night together in my chamber, to which I submitted more out of habit than desire, and perhaps even fear of his anger were I to refuse.

"You stubborn little Jewess!" He laughed, shaking his head. Still in shirtsleeves, he stood by the open window facing the mountains. He breathed in deeply the morning air and stretched his arms over his head with obvious relish and self-satisfaction. A man perfectly comfortable in his own skin. "I misjudged you when I thought you had come to your senses."

I retreated into the corner behind the bed. This time I would not be swayed. He would not bend me to his will. I would not permit him to cast a spell over my mind.

"I must go!" I insisted. "I am not your prisoner anymore."

"Of course, you are not a prisoner. What gives you the idea you ever were?" His unctuous tone, as if he was correcting a child's erroneous notion, gave me a queasy feeling in the stomach. "We kept you here to shield you from the royal militia. What do you think the seneschal would have done had he discovered a Jewess on French soil? All these years, you were in constant danger of being found out. Disobedience of the king's order would have meant severe punishment, maybe death. The stake of the Inquisition would no doubt have been your fate. You should thank the good people of this village for never having betrayed your secret."

The arrogance of this speech, its mendaciousness, the utter distortion of what had happened made me shudder violently as it rendered me speechless. I wanted to throw the truth in his face, confront him with the crime he had committed against me, against my body and soul. He who had willfully cut me off from my family, from my people, for no other reason than to satisfy his lust, he whose concupiscence degraded a young girl to the status of whore and concubine, who forced her to live in sin, this man of the Church, who sowed my body with the semen of his lewdness, condemning the children he never acknowledged to the status of bastardy, he had the impudence to claim all he did was for my good, to protect me from the authorities. I wanted to shout it out for all to hear, declaim this man's depravity to the world. But all around in this village were his accomplices. I knew the motive for their silence. The last thing anyone wanted was to draw the attention of the king's men or that of the Inquisition to this village. The thought that it was they who should be protecting me from the authorities made me laugh.

It was their own hides they sought to protect, their heretic hides. Did he really think I was not aware of the epidemic of heresy infecting this village? Did he think I could be so easily fooled? Should it have escaped him in his conceit that the leper existence to which he had condemned me gave me a perfect perch from which to observe and register what was going in this village, especially in his house and the house of his mother? The furtive comings and goings, the secret meetings behind darkened windows, the obsequious reverence accorded certain visitors, men who seemed to shun the light of day and moved about like phantoms under cover of night. Mindless of my presence, the women while drafting water or spinning and weaving chattered away about the nocturnal visit of those they called "goodmen" or "perfects." The shepherds in the fields and pastures too often spoke carelessly among themselves about doctrines I knew the Church had declared anathema. I also heard them speak of their fears of the Inquisitor in Pamiers, of heretic brethren who had been arrested who might have confessed and named other names before they were burned at the stake. I heard the whispers invoking the memory of the murderous war that had almost completely wiped out heresy in this part of France during the reign of the sainted King Louis IX a century before. Sprinklings of what the Church declaimed as aberrant teachings were alive in a few mountain villages among the remnant of adherents. It wasn't a lone Jewess like me the Inquisition was after. It was not I who was a threat to the Church. The Holy Office cast its nets wide to reel in more defiant prey.

I had gathered this knowledge in years of silent observation. Now I was of a mind to spill it all to the priest, to expose his lies, his distortions of the truth. But I was not always sure how deeply involved he was. He was too sly and—outwardly at least—held to good terms with the Church hierarchy of which he was, after all, a part. It was hard to imagine that he was not privy to the goings on in his mother's ostal. It was even less imaginable that anything that was going on there or in the surroundings could take place without his approval. Yet, I had no proof, no certainty, and I might set myself up for abuse and possible total confinement.

"I must go and I shall go!" was as much defiance as I was able to muster.

"In that case, you shall go," he said. "Go in peace and go with G-d's blessing. Just remember, this is your home. The door is always open for your return."

He extended his hand and pulled me gently but insistently toward him. My body stiffened. This was too easy. But I did not dare resist his embrace. He stroked my hair back, away from my face, and lifted my chin forcing me to meet his eyes.

"You shall go, my stubborn little Jewess, you shall go," he fluted soothingly. "Charlot will go with you. I'll ask him to get an oxcart ready right away. After all, I couldn't let a princess walk all the way to Toulouse and alone."

I wriggled free and thanked him with a sense of uneasiness. All I had to do, I told him, was wash up and gather the children.

His "No!" struck my heart like the lash from a whip.

"No, no! You go! My sons stay here!" His tone was suddenly harsh, imperious, brooking no retort. The sheep's clothing fell off the wolf.

"Your sons? Now they are your sons?" I screamed. Yes, I lost my temper. This was more than I could bear. After years of spurning you, my sons, denying his paternity, he now claimed you as his own and with it the right to withhold you from me. I ranted, I raved, to no avail. You were the trump he held in his hands to assure my return. He knew all too well I would never abandon you; he knew you were my life, my shining lights. The evil of his design was clear. To use you as pawns and to hold you, my most precious jewels, hostage! No doubt his true aim was to dash any hope for redemption I might be harboring. The sight of his grandsons might melt my father's heart. However unlikely such a possibility was, it was a faint hope this depraved priest knew I still held deep in my heart. And who knows, he must have calculated, this old Jew might change his mind. It was a chance he would not take. Once again, I was defeated, left numb and unable to assert my will.

I set out on my journey, my heart heavy and filled with ill foreboding. Fighting back the tears, I bade you farewell, promising to return within a month's time. Sybille, my only friend and faithful companion, would look after you. That much I knew. I needn't worry on that account.

The oxcart rumbled over the gouged out surfaces of the dirt roads, whirling up the dry dust of the summer's heat. I lay curled up inside, my gaze turned away from the world, the sun's rays stinging my spine with a thousand needles. How long it had been since I left Toulouse and was stranded in this godforsaken village! For nine years, I had been confined to its immediate surroundings, never venturing further than the nearby pastures or the well at the outskirts. A few times I had ascended to the châtelaine's abode on the hillside overlooking the valley. Toulouse, my birthplace, seemed as far distant as the holy city of Jerusalem. Would my father even want to return there, the city where he had suffered so much humiliation? Despite it all, he had also loved this city. He had prospered there, in business as well as in love. The grave of his beloved wife, my mother, was there at the periphery in consecrated ground. If he were to follow the royal invitation at all, I was certain this was the town to which he would return—the town we now entered after a four-days' journey.

And so it was. Charlot stayed behind with the oxcart in the town square. He quickly disappeared among the crowded stalls of market criers, produce vendors, fishmongers, and purveyors of fowl and variety meats. Nothing much had changed here. It was all as I remembered or as it was then coming back to me. The same buskers and artistes still attracted the crowds eager for entertainment and distraction. Jugglers, magic tricksters, and acrobats, strolling musicians and danceurs, raconteurs of fantastic tales and minstrels, jesters and jokers mingled with mendicant friars and assorted vagrants, beggars, and thieves who tugged at sleeves and dipped their greedy fingers into purses at every step. At the square's edge, the hucksters of human flesh still plied their ancient trade.

Alas, there was one blank spot I noted in this teeming scene. Nowhere in this crowd were to be seen the familiar red garb and yellow rouelle the Jews of France had been forced to display since the reign of the sainted Louis. In vain did I look for a high cone hat among the itinerant Levantine hawkers who dazzled and enticed these simple folk with their exotic merchandise, the aromatic roots, fragrant oils and ointments, sweet perfumes and pungent spices, besides an array of rare notions, accoutrements, and paraphernalia that hailed from far-off lands. The Jewish merchants had evidently not returned, at least not yet. Despondency gripped my heart as I turned away.

Far from the tumult, at the edge of town, I stood before the unhinged irongate, a rusted shield of David in its center. For a moment, I thought my heart stopped in my breast. Then, hesitantly, as if entering a forbidden realm, I stole into the murky alley that once was the crowded, vibrant Jewish quarter. Slowly my eyes adjusted to the obscurity of the thick walls pierced only by an oblique ray of the sun. I searched for signs of life, of human activity, but detected only packs of cats lolling about in impassible doorways and perched in darkened windows. My gaze wandered along the row of houses in which people I had known since childhood had made their home, had born children with whom I had played and prayed. Where may they be now? *I wondered. Somewhere in a foreign land, maybe a more hospitable land, beyond the kingdom of France. Did they build a new life there, a new kahal of their fellows? So many times, Jews had pulled up their stakes when forced to do so and had been able to find other shores on which to pitch their tents. So why should the Jews of France and of Toulouse not have founded a community elsewhere or have been welcomed into the fold of fellow Jews in a foreign land, merged their lives and commerce with theirs, conjoined as they are by the inseparable bond of the laws of Moses.*

At this moment, a tremor shook my entire body with such violence I had to slide down to the ground to keep from falling. The seizure ebbed within a few seconds, maybe a minute, not more, but its effect was profound when I realized what had brought it on. Once again, the sense of being alone in the world crushed me with the broiling force of a Fogony wind. Once again, the scab was torn off the wound that would not heal. Once again, I felt the pain of having been cut off from the body of my people, a severed limb left to decay among the dregs.

My heart fluttered like a little bird timorously spreading its wings for the first time. I moved slowly down the narrow alleyway devoid of human life. The bleak stare of the moldering tenements dispirited my soul. Yet, I was compelled to forge ahead. I slithered along the grimy pavement toward a spectral realm as in a shadowy dream. Every stone so familiar, yet strange, remote, from a past vaguely remembered, another life in another time, a childhood become a faded memory.

Gradually, the alley widened into a cul-de-sac ringed with several solid stone edifices. These were the residences of the elders and the wealthy of the community, the dignitaries, of which we had many. Unlike the frail tenements of our less well-off brethren, these structures seemed to have withstood the gnawing tooth of time and neglect much better. Only the gardens were dense with tangled thickets of rampant growth. My family's mansion loomed over the square with the same stark mien as it had in olden days. Only back then, in days of yore, yard and house were filled with activity, with life, where now nary a bat was astir.

I don't know how long I was standing in front of my father's house. Maybe several hours. Only the chill of descending dusk and the sound of Charlot's hasty footfall on the pavement roused me from my reveries.

"Come away from this eerie place!" he called out. "There's nothing here for you or anybody else!"

He had found cheap lodging for the night and admonished me to come with him to the inn. The next morning, we should return home. I was only too willing to follow the first demand. I too felt the need for a good night's rest after the long journey and the brusque encounter with the past. Both had drained me of all vigor. But, I told him I could not leave so soon. Charlot, as you know, was a kind-hearted man, a simple shepherd and loyal servant in the priest's household, who had always treated me with a certain deference. In his eyes, I was even someone approaching the status of a lady. Now that my safety had been placed in his hands, he took his charge very seriously. I must say I was deeply sorry when he later fell victim to the Inquisition. He was a good man, and though of simple mind, he was a far better man than many of those who poisoned his mind with heretical ideas, those shadowy drifters who called themselves goodmen and perfects.

After a restless night on a straw pallet at the inn, under Charlot's watchful eye, I returned to the Jewish quarter as I did the following day and then the following, five days in succession. Each day was as quiet as the one before. It was obvious. The Jews of Toulouse had not heeded the royal invitation. Despite a profound melancholy, even disappointment, I also felt a sense of pride. My people would not permit themselves to be pushed around like pawns by the whims of kings. True, one always hears of a few who bend to the coercion and submit to the baptismal, mainly, I presume, out of attachment to their worldly goods. But they were always the few, and I doubt there were many—if any—in our community. And yet, I nurtured the hope in my heart that maybe they would come back sometime in the future. Maybe they were held back by other businesses they had established in the meantime. My thoughts ran along those lines then. Later I learned that many did come back. They reconstituted their communities in towns like Carcassonne, Narbonne, and also eventually in Toulouse. But I will tell you more about this further on in my accounting.

During all those hours, for five days in succession, that I stood, or rather sat on the gravelly ground in front of my father's house, it was once again impressed upon me with crushing force how alone I was in the world. My strangerliness, my sense of homelessness and of not belonging, struck me once again with crushing force. Rootless as the existence of the Jews may have been, and perhaps always will be, they had their community, their common fate, their common faith, a bond that held them together in their direst straits. They were never really alone.

As for me, I was dead and buried. I had ceased to exist. My father had mourned my demise. The thought frightened me so much that I did not dare pass through the gate to my childhood home; it was as if it were sacred ground I was unworthy to tread. I remained outside, my face pressed against the lattice, an outcast beggar looking in. Unmindful of the warm rain washing over me, I tried to discern some sign, some spark of life from within. My mind roamed from the kitchen with adjacent sculleries and pantries in the back of the ground floor, where lavish meals had been prepared every week for the holy Shabbat; to the festive hall where elaborate holiday celebrations—I tried to conjure up the picture of my father presiding over sumptuous Pesach Seders that were the pride and envy of the community—were held; to my father's library, a much-admired collection of the wisdom the Jewish people had produced through the ages. Mounting in my mind the staircase leading to the private chambers, I searched for the room at the end of the hallway that had been my sanctuary. But here my memory failed. Try as I may, I was unable to conjure up the images of happier days, of the time when my father read to me the stories of our Holy Scriptures, when he taught me to read and write in our holy tongue. Here my imagination forsook me; the pictures would not rise from the nebulous blur swathing them. Even my father's face eluded me. My memory seemed shrouded in the fog of time. Or perhaps it was the fog of guilt, the guilt of having failed my father and having caused him such intense pain.

"Now isn't she laying it on a bit too thick?" Etoile looked exhausted after so much moaning and groaning as she called it.

"Have some *rachmones*," I admonished her playfully. "Just try to put yourself into this poor woman's shoes."

"Yes, but she wears me out. Enough for today!"

"As well she should," I said, showing little mercy for Etoile for my part.

Etoile switched off the typewriter, arranged the reams of paper we had produced in a neat pile, and flung herself with an exaggerated sigh on the rickety sofa in the corner. We had made good progress on this first day of our renewed collaboration in transcribing "Dina's confession," as we now called the project. I put some water in a teakettle on a small wood-burning stove for our late afternoon tea and biscuits, before a more serious repast at a local inn in the evening. It warmed my heart to watch Etoile acting in a perfectly natural, almost uninhibited way around me, as if we had been good old buddies from way back. And maybe we were. Not wanting to spoil the idyll, I kept the crush I had on her in check. Amorous entanglements, especially unrequited ones, would only get in the way of our work. We had pitched our tent in a little country house, fittingly we thought, a medieval farmhouse though it had recently been equipped with electricity and indoor plumbing and other modern conveniences for which we were both grateful. It also afforded us the use of an electric typewriter. Meals had to be prepared on a wood-burning stove that required a steady supply of firewood we took turns gathering and chopping. There was no work Etoile shied away from. She was always ready to pitch in and hold up her end, which reinforced a gratifying sense of comradeship between us. This was truly a girl with whom one could chop wood—pardon the pun.

"You have to remember to whom she's speaking and the purpose of her writing this down. Not that I think she's trying to manipulate her sons or that she's being deceitful. Her suffering is no doubt genuine. But she also has to justify her actions, and a little hyperbole won't hurt."

"Of course, I know that." Etoile waved her hand in a weary gesture. "Don't take me too seriously at the end of a hard day's work. You said yourself you find this enterprise emotionally draining."

When she saw what must have been a troubled look in my face, she added, "Don't worry, I'm delighted and grateful for the opportunity. So don't mind me if I'm a bit washed out at the end of the day."

"I understand perfectly," I said in a tone I hoped didn't sound too patronizing. The thought of the possibility of having to forgo Etoile's company stung my heart. Nor, for that matter, could I do without the expertise she brought to the task. Our skills were perfectly matched.

"Let's go get something to eat at the village inn," I said. "A hearty meal and a robust vintage will do us both good."

"You're right, she obviously seeks to justify whatever it was she did to the priest in the end," Etoile observed. The conversation inadvertently turned back to Dina once we were seated in a quiet corner of the inn and were waiting for our *brandade de morue*—this traditional cod fish concoction had become our daily staple—which we were looking forward to washing down with a nice bottle of dry Puligny-Montrachet.

"Then again, she also wants to impress her sons with her Jewish heritage," I interjected. "She was born into a wealthy, pious family, far superior to those churls in the village who disdain her. That's her message. The despised wretch they see is really a princess, an Oriental princess of ancient lineage, and her sons can be proud of her."

"Yes, and she tries to transmit—as best as she can under the circumstances—her heritage, her religion to them. Of course, I love her!" Etoile burst out in protest as if I had doubted her devotion to our heroine. "I love and admire her more than Rashi's daughters who had the privilege and good fortune to pass their lives berthed securely within their community. Even if that community was under threat from Crusaders and other fanatics, they never were severed from the body of the Jewish people, as our dear Dina Miryam likes to speak of herself."

"Have you noticed that we have been using the present tense when we speak of Dina Miryam?" I mused.

"Yes, she obviously has us in her thrall, just as she had Nina enthralled, and probably still does. So we'd better push on," she declared. Her dark eyes gleamed with the fire of a true believer in a cause—maybe a little with the fanaticism of someone filled with a crusading spirit for justice, it crossed my mind. But then, very quickly, the ardor faded into that almost impish twinkle that had endeared her to me from the start, during our first meeting the year before in the Toulouse hotel room when I followed this stranger into the dark of night.

I did not have the heart to voice the doubts that had crept into the critical scholar's part of my brain. Was Dina Miryam for real? Was she the author? And if so, could she have been the sole author? Was there another, maybe later redactor, who might have collected the story from an oral tradition? Several aspects of the narrative had aroused my suspicions. Especially the historical account seemed a bit too sophisticated to have come from a woman with minimal exposure to the world outside a mountain village. In many places, the narrative fit in almost too perfectly with what we know about this period in French history. But at the moment, that hardly mattered. Any scholarly analysis had to come later. Our task at hand was to deal with transcribing the raw material such as it was presented in the codex.

"Yes, let's press on," I nodded, lifting my glass of the golden vintage. "To Dina, *l'chaim*!"

"And Nina!" she added, taking a big gulp.

"Yes, of course. Lest we forget. It's been a long time now."

Several seasons had come and gone since that summer when Nina had gone back to her husband and children in the mountains.

She had taken a great risk by leaving the folio in my hands. I was often awake at night wondering how the community she had described as a "virtual laboratory for medievalists"—which meant to me that they were of a close-minded, superstitious mentality—had received her back. Would they punish her for having removed a sacred object, and in what way? Medieval modes of punishment were all too familiar to me. How severe would the punishment be? My imagination was filled with scenes of all sorts of tortures, confinement in dark dungeons, dank walls to which prisoners were chained. I saw Nina tied to pillar and post. Pilloried in the village square—I presumed there was such—where the villagers would spit at the victim or worse, as was common seven hundred years ago and much later as well. I tried to imagine daily life in this secluded mountain outpost, a Shangri-La, as Nina said, with its own archaic customs and laws. Yet, all the knowledge I had accumulated now appeared to me as mere bookish learning. Learned paradigms, modern-day projections unto the past, conjectures, interpretations, theories, the good old Procrustean bed of scholarship were far removed from real-life, flesh-and-blood people. I almost began to see the wisdom of Nina's tongue-in-cheek parody of theoretical tangles that cut the scholarly mind off from the real world. This much was clear to me: even people cocooned in a peaceful enclave would be capable of cruelty to punish a perceived transgression of the rules governing the community. Finishing the task and then somehow finding Nina and returning the folio to its rightful owners became all the more urgent.

A considerable amount of time had already been lost due to the fact that I had to return to Chicago to get my affairs with the university in order before I was able to free myself from my duties for an indeterminate period of time. I had stored the folio in a safe deposit box at a bank in Albi. Smuggling it out of France was neither possible nor desirable. Neither the law nor my scholar's conscience would permit me to do that. To what extent this project, or should I say the life of Dina Miryam, and to no less degree that of my cousin Nina, had taken hold of my life was brought home to me by the fact that when confronted with choosing between this project and my scholarly career and reputation, I jettisoned the latter. Unable and unwilling to reveal the reasons for my request for an indeterminate leave, I did not hesitate to simply forego my obligations to the institution where I had taught and enjoyed the status of a stellar scholar for twenty years when my department turned me down. I did not even give it a second thought at the time. Looking back, I realize that such spontaneity was very much unlike me, or maybe the punctilious scholar always playing by the rules and churning out articles and books like clockwork, maybe that was a taskmaster who had for a long time suppressed the real me. Then again, my scholarship, the knowledge I had accumulated, the expertise in arcane languages and in a generally obscure history, came in as indispensible tools for tunneling through the shaft of time to reach a Jewish woman who had left an extraordinary account of her life, albeit obscured for centuries by being no longer accessible to her descendants and who nevertheless guarded it as a sacred treasure. I hope it is not waxing too metaphoric when I say that I also regard our transcription and subsequent translation into French and English as an act of restoring Dina Miryam of the mountain to her people, to reconnect this severed limb, as she liked to describe herself, to the body of her people.

Nevertheless, I had put off my return to France until the following spring. In the hope of finding favor with my superiors at the university—I could easily have applied for a sabbatical, but that would have meant revealing my whereabouts, the nature of my research, and a time limit for my absence—for an indefinite leave, I discharged my obligation and taught two courses in the fall semester. Fortunately the subject matter required little preparation on my part: an introductory philosophy course and the history of Jews in the "golden age" of Spain, which wasn't as golden as a nineteenth-century German Jewish historian glorified it to have been. Easy enough. The testing and grading were done by teaching assistants. As I said, my request was turned down. Rumors made the round that Professor Henry Marcus was going through a mid-life crisis, male menopause, or whatever the current psych-fad was in vogue then. I didn't care. I cashed in my retirement fund and stashed it in a knapsack. I took a substantial loss, but it was still enough so I wouldn't have any financial worries for quite some time. Later I deposited most of it in my already established bank account in Albi. I dissolved my apartment and tossed out much of the junk that had piled up over the years. Most of my books and a few items I was not yet ready to part with I shipped to New Jersey for storage in Tante Hedy's basement and garage.

With these formalities out of the way, I booked my flight for France without telling anybody. On my way to the airport, I paid one more visit to my Tante Hedy.

"Not to worry! Nina is doing fine," I assured her without letting show through my own fears about Nina's well-being.

"So where is she? Where has she been all this time? Why didn't she write? She should have known how heartbroken I would be to think that something might have happened to her."

I took her hands into mine and eased her down into Uncle Aaron's favorite leather chair. Sitting opposite her on the ottoman, my mind was racing through all that I had learned about Nina, trying to decide how much of it I should tell my aunt.

"I must go see her," I heard her say.

"You will, you will. Just not yet. You see, Nina is in Valladine." I waited a moment to give her a chance to absorb the bombshell.

"Where? You mean that place in the mountain? How can that be?"

"Yes, she found it. She found the place of her dreams. Remember how adamant she was about finding it? Well, she did. And that's where she has been all these years. She couldn't write because there's no post office."

"You saw her there? You have been to Valladine?"

"No, I met Nina in Albi. She had come down for some work she was doing and wanted my help. A translation of a medieval document."

She shook her head. "I still don't understand why she would cause her mother so much grief."

"Oh, I have some good news!" I wasn't sure how happy it would make her to learn that she had been left in the dark about Nina's marriage and motherhood, but I had to let her know. "You remember the guides who helped us over the mountains?"

"Of course, I do, Henner. What a silly question!"

"Well, Nina got married to one of them … the boy, the one who was my age. She met him in Toulouse and fell in love. It was apparently because of him she left everything behind and went back to France. As she told you, to find Valladine, and him." I paused and then ventured softly, "You are a grandmother. They have two boys, about four and two."

I felt her hands trembling in mine. Tears trickled down her cheeks. She stared in front of her, mute and obviously at a loss what to say or do.

"Well, that's wonderful news—a bit unexpected, but wonderful," she finally brought forth. With an abrupt jolt, she sat up erect and withdrew her hands from mine with puckered lips. She wiped her tears and then ran one hand through her hair with a sweeping motion down to her neck and let it come to rest at her throat.

"So, where is she now?" she wanted to know. Her eyes were now firmly locked into mine with a probing gaze as if she didn't entirely trust me.

"She is back in Valladine with her family. I will finish the work she asked me to do and then get in touch with her again. Communication is a bit outmoded in that area. She will get the message through a line of shepherds, maybe by ram's horn," I said jokingly, but she was not cheered.

It broke my heart that I had to tell her it was better if she didn't go to France as yet. But the fact that her long-lost daughter was alive, and in a way well, hopefully relieved her of some of the anxieties she had felt for so many years.

My own anxiety about the uncertainty how all this would play out were considerably alleviated by Etoile's welcoming smile that greeted me at the Toulouse airport. The hiatus had given her the opportunity to complete her own work, and she was now a freshly minted Ph.D. in medieval French philosophy and culture. It also afforded her a secure spot on the unemployment line and, fortunately for me, she now had all the time in the world to devote to our project. We decided to locate in the area of Pamiers, where the Inquisitor Jacques Fournier had once held sway against the remnants of the Cathar heretics. I had worked in the town's archives in the past, and it might have been propitious that I was known and respected in its medieval section.

We retrieved the folio from the bank vault in Albi. The teller looked with consternation at the pile of banknotes worth a few thousand dollars that I had dumped on his counter from a suitcase, requesting it be deposited in the account I had previously opened. The poor churl had to count it all. I had considered moving the account to Switzerland where they are used to people coming across the border with suitcases filled with cash of various currencies. But then I decided to keep my funds in France, out of loyalty to the country or maybe aversion to the other country. Whatever it was, I did have to submit to an interview with the bank director to reassure him that the money was not stolen and that I was retiring in the area. Of course, it wasn't quite legal according to American laws, but I had become uncharacteristically reckless and was apparently willing to risk everything, even break the law, for what had become my mission, an obsession even. I was ready to burn all bridges behind me for "the project." And how fortunate was I to have found such a compatible and capable companion.

"Have you any news from Nina?" was the first thing I asked as we were driving away from the airport.

"Not a word. Nothing at all." The crease that clouded her naturally sunny face told me that she too was concerned about what might have happened to her friend, my cousin, after she had left her at the Place de la Republic in Toulouse. Alphonse de Sola was there in the company of his dogs, but since she stayed at a distance, Etoile did not see whether the children were with him at that time. She saw him crush Nina to his mighty chest, enclosing her completely for a moment before the two of them disappeared together from her sight.

"She had told me not to worry. He loved her, she assured me, and he would let no harm come to her."

"Still, we don't know what his position in the village is. What power he might hold in what I presume is a medieval type hierarchy."

"She once told me that Alphonse is the younger brother of the village elder, a man named Raymond whom she referred to as the seneschal. He seems to rule pretty much with an iron hand. She didn't want to tell me too much of what goes on there. When she spoke about life in the village at all, which was not often and then only in vague terms, she liked to depict it as a kind of utopia, an idealized society. It may be how she wanted to see it."

"A veritable Shangri-La, huh?" I shook my head, skeptical about the possibility that such a world could exist.

"Alphonse is apparently the only one, or one of few, who ever had any contact with the outside world. She once mentioned something to the effect that he even fought in the French Foreign Legion, either in Indochina back in the 1950s or in North Africa. But he returned to the village, not liking what he saw and experienced in the civilized world."

"Can you blame him?" I mused. After a pause, I added: "I seem to remember a Raymond, maybe ten years older than Alphonse, who guided us across the mountain passes. He was the one who took Aunt Hedy to Valladine when she went into labor—Alphonse let out the name of the village, probably inadvertently, while we were waiting in Roncesvalles for Nina to be born. He could be regarded as having assisted in her birth, although there was a midwife, as Aunt Hedy told the story, who was apparently very adept in her trade. A pretty nice chap by all accounts. I also remember that he took very little from the Jewish refugees for his service of getting them across the mountains. Not exorbitant sums like the other so-called guides, who were mostly *ganavim* who exploited people in desperate need."

"Well, that was nice. But we have no idea what goes on in the village in general. What are the prevailing rules in this mountain retreat? For all we know, absconding with sacred objects may be an act of treason, as it is in our world, and you know what that means in medieval justice …"

We chewed on that for a while in silence.

"Let's get to it then," I finally said. "I hope it's not too late already after all these months. Let's keep the faith, as they say in America. She wanted us to do it. Let's hope and work." I tried to be upbeat, mostly to keep my own heart from sinking and, as I presumed, to keep Etoile from giving up. In reality, she held up much better than I did under the emotional strain and time pressure.

"Never lose hope! Never give up!" she punctuated my remark.

Our hope that Nina's fate had not been sealed as we had secretly feared, and that she was still alive, received a considerable boost a few weeks later.

At some point, Etoile went to Toulouse for a few days to take care of some formalities at her university department so she could receive her diploma. I welcomed the break from the strain Dina's writing put on my eyes and decided to jump from the fire into the frying pan, as it were, to peruse some records in the archives of Pamiers pertaining to the early decades of the fourteenth century. My entire life's work had been a solitary treasure hunt in such repositories of records of the past. And what hoards my rifling through medieval vaults had yielded! I was, therefore, surprised about how forlorn I felt without Etoile at my side, and I realized once again how indispensible her companionship had become to me. Yet, I wouldn't call it love, for I liked our relationship just the way it was. I had no desire to touch her, to take her in my arms, or to go to bed with her. At least that's what I told myself. I knew full well that along the way she would be visiting an old boyfriend or fiancé, occasional lover, or whatever he was to her besides her auto mechanic and jack-of-all-trades. They had known each other since their childhood in Tunisia, she told me. He lent us a hand with moving into the house. He even fixed a few plumbing problems without charge. He was young and athletic, but not particularly handsome, at least not to my mind. *She could do better*, I thought. The stuffy old professor in me envied her free spirit and casual approach to sex. The sexual revolution, as free love was called in the early 1970s, never caught on with me. I had become so used to a state of celibacy after the disaster of my marriage that the platonic relationship in which I found myself with Etoile was just fine. So I told myself. Was I protesting too much?

All this went through my head as I was preparing to settle down one evening with a Dumas novel when the object of my contemplation burst into the house several days earlier than expected, cradling a big brown envelope in her arms.

"Tu sais quoi j'ais dans mes mains?" she gasped, out of breath as if she had run all the way from Toulouse. My curiosity aroused, I didn't even notice at first that she had addressed me in the familiar *"tu,"* and I quite naturally responded in the same mode.

"I have no idea, but it looks like some kind of package you're holding in your shaking hands."

"It's from Nina! It was dropped into the mail slot at the department a few weeks ago."

"Let me see this!" I practically ripped the envelope from her hands.

"Hey!" she protested. "It's addressed to me!"

We wrestled over it like children unwilling to share a precious find or toy. When we came to realize the childishness of this game, we burst out laughing. Was it an embarrassed laughter? Something inside me didn't want the game to end.

"Let's get serious," she said as she finally pulled out what looked like a thick handwritten letter in French. It was addressed to both of us. Although somewhat irregular and not as tight as usual, the handwriting was clearly Nina's. She was obviously alive and able to write, at least as recently as a month ago. How well she was, we hoped the letter would reveal to us forthwith.

Nina's Progress 2

Nina became the good luck charm of passengers and crew on the Portuguese freighter that chugged, huffing and puffing, across the Atlantic in the summer of 1941. In the months we had been hanging about in Lisbon, first besieging and beseeching the American consulate daily for entrance visas to the United States, then searching for a carrier that would take us there, she had turned into a smiling, gurgling, teething, and all-round happy, little creature. Once on board, I claimed her as my plaything with which to relieve some of the boredom of the seemingly endless voyage. Our living quarters below deck afforded scant comfort, but our needs and expectations had been shrinking with each leg of our wanderings. We had learned to make do, roll with the punches, and be face up for whatever lay ahead. My mother and aunt were coiled up on their cots, incapacitated by the surging waves for much of the voyage.

At long last, we sailed through the Narrows into New York Harbor. The sight of the lady with the torch, not a sword as Kafka thought, as it had done for millions of huddled masses before us, and presumably since, inspired us to burst out in rather undignified wailing and howling, except for Nina who lay in her makeshift crib, oblivious to the momentous moment. Suddenly she too began to wail and carry on, probably for reasons of her own, most likely stomach pangs. Or it may have been that the sudden calming of the waters, after the constant ebb and flow of the high seas, disturbed the rhythm to which she had become accustomed. She had been such a good little girl during the voyage, I had dubbed her "little trouper," proudly applying the American vernacular I had just learned while studying the new language we would have to master in our new homeland.

Our life in the *goldene medineh* of America got off to a rocky start though, as one would expect at that time. I don't know what my parents expected, surely not that the American government would roll out the red carpet and shower us with handouts. In fact, we were lucky to have been taken in at all. Many German Jews had been turned away previously. It may have had something to do with the fact that my Uncle Aaron Aschauer's status was listed as stateless and he was therefore not subject to the German quota of admissions that was already filled (never mind that we had been declared stateless by the German rulers as well), and the rest of us got in somehow on his coattail. Whatever, it wasn't important to me. We had made it to safety, which was all that counted. And I was happy to have finally landed in the land of the Old West without a notion of how far this west was from New York.

Despite much moaning over dearth and wont in the new country, there was no longing for a return to the "flesh pots" of Europe. Unlike the Israelites fleeing from slavery in Egypt, we had no leader to take us across the "big pond"—*der grosse Teich*, in my family's usage. We were like shipwrecks or driftwood swept ashore, left to fend for ourselves, to find a place to live and work, any kind of work, to scrape together a living day by day. But we were grateful to be alive and far from the murderous arm of the Nazis. By then, it was late fall of 1941. The news from Europe, as much as leaked out, made our skin crawl. The immigrant German newspaper *Aufbau*, which we read avidly, raised the specter of escalating Nazi measures against the Jews, of the noose tightening around Jewish life not only in Germany but in the conquered territories as well, of mass arrests and transports to the East. Only later did we learn the full scope and details of the crime. But even then, we realized that the hell from which we had made a narrow escape was far more horrific than we could ever have imagined. We could not but be grateful for being able to breathe freely with our physical survival assured. The daily challenges of making ends meet—"struggle for survival" would be an overstatement—seemed a piece of cake, in American lingo, by comparison to what the Jews stranded on the Continent had to go through.

After a brief stay in a fleabag hotel, we moved into an apartment in the Washington Heights section of Manhattan. The "Fourth Reich" was what some wags had dubbed the area due to the large number of *Yeckes*, Jewish refugees from Germany, who had settled there. Not really funny to my mind and not without a grain of malice. Four adults and two children in the two-bedroom, fifth- floor walk-up was not ideal, but others in the neighborhood had more children and were packed in more tightly. All in all, we counted ourselves lucky. The apartment had running hot water and a private bathroom, luxuries we had forgotten existed. I was enrolled at a local public school where the lingua franca was a *Kauderwelsch* best described as "Germanglish." Many of the immigrants proudly abjured the once-venerated language of Goethe and Schiller in favor of the idiom of their newly adopted country. These efforts often amounted to a heroic struggle with merciless syntactical windmills. The syntax, rolled out in thickly accented guttural tropes, chimed more like the turgid prose of a Thomas Mann than the crisp copy of a Hemingway. Yet undaunted by the fact that their opaque utterances frequently baffled native speakers, the newcomers had no qualms about correcting the natives' usage of their mother tongue. So even if they butchered the English language and overlaid it with pronounced foreign inflection, English it had to be and English it was, at least out in public. At home, in the intimacy of the family, we, like many of our compatriots, still cultivated the language of poets and thinkers, which, so the sisters emphasized on many occasions, had sadly, hopefully only temporarily, been mutilated by a horde of barbarian usurpers.

In the afternoons, I attended Hebrew school in preparation for my bar mitzvah. It swelled my comb to note that my knowledge in Judaic subjects was far superior to that of my fellow pupils, many of whom came from families new to Jewish observance. Thanks to my uncle, Aaron Aschauer, who had been instructing me in writing and reading our holy tongue whenever possible in the course of our wanderings, I found myself in the position of star pupil of my Hebrew class.

"Don't let it get to your head!" warned Uncle Aaron when I dropped a disparaging remark or two about the level and quality of instruction. I was already well versed in the prayers while the others still cut their teeth on the *aleph-bet*. The sense of superiority I felt must have shown in the way I was always strutting around with a pile of books under my arm.

"Don't be *hochnässig*," said Uncle Aaron. "Being stuck up will isolate you from your peers and eventually make you feel very alone." He had often told me about his accomplishments at the yeshiva he attended in his native Poznan. But he had previously left out the part where he was shunned by his fellow students, not for being the class primus, but for the sin of overweening pride, as his rabbi explained to him.

My father had attended a classical gymnasium in Berlin where he excelled in the study of Greek and Latin, and I never heard the end of that. No wonder I felt I had to emulate both my father and uncle and be the best in everything, and for their sake straddle the divide between Hellenism and Judaism. To my chagrin, this extended to sports as well. By his own frequent accounts, my father had been the top swimmer and soccer player in his school. *Mens sana in corpore sano* was a maxim my father preached with earnest conviction. Our peregrinations in the desert had afforded little opportunity for calisthenics though, never mind swimming or soccer playing, except for the brief period when we played pelota in Roncesvalles. Exercise such as we got came primarily from long foot marches over hilly terrains. Now that we were finally settled on safe ground, the body had to do its part as well. I no longer had any excuse to evade the injunction of the time-honored Latin saw.

"If G-d had wanted me to be an aquatic animal, he would have grown me fins," I protested as I gasped to keep from drowning while my father ran alongside the pool at the YMHA, exhorting me with shouts of "Don't breathe!" and "Stretch out!" It was a desperate struggle to live up to my father's expectations.

"The Torah enjoins a father to teach his son to swim," he proclaimed, trying a different tack when the Roman wisdom failed to hit its mark and I showed little aptitude for physical prowess.

"And how would you know that?" I quibbled, going on the offensive, as I felt my lungs filling with water and chlorine burning my eyes.

"Your Uncle Aaron told me," he replied. "Therefore it must be so. You'd better not get cheeky with me."

Uncle Aaron was the undisputed *chochem*, the authority in things Jewish in our family. My father was the *chiloni*, the secularist. He was the unquestioned authority in matters of classical learning. The Danziger sisters, not to be outshined, staked their claim of know-how on the province of German and French romantic literature, though they were not shy about going beyond that particular ambit when the occasion presented itself.

The tug-of-war for control over my body and soul was finally settled with my father conceding that priority should be given for the time being to preparing me for my bar mitzvah. I had no problem with this arrangement since my natural disposition ran more toward the brainy than the physical. I did learn to swim eventually and later even taught Nina, who soon outdid me in speed and endurance in the lap lane.

Soccer was a lost cause, however. My father had to admit that I would never reap any glory on that field. In high school, I made up by reaping glory on the debating team, the Latin club, the school paper, the chess club. All areas he valued as well. My mastery of the game of kings more than compensated for my physical deficiency. I did him proud after all.

For the next two years, I was placed under Uncle Aaron's protective wing. He not only coached me in chanting my Torah and Haftarah portions, but also preserved me from the sin of overweening pride. He gently guided me toward the recognition that my classmates were taking offense at my stuck-up attitude. And as he had predicted, I soon noticed that they kept away from me and called me *Streber*, a German word for someone who strives to achieve, mostly used in a derogatory sense. Instead of the admiration I felt I deserved, I reaped their disdain.

Ironically, it was the fortunes of war that were soon to turn into our good fortune. In December 1941, three months after our arrival, Japan's attack on Pearl Harbor brought the United States into the war. Until then, the adults had been working odd jobs, many menial, whatever could be gotten, but now an opportunity arose for putting their sartorial skills to good use once again. My mother and aunt were able to quit their employ as usher and cashier respectively at a midtown movie theater. Uncle Aaron no longer had to spend irregular hours pumping gas, which was becoming scarcer anyway. My father quit his job as elevator man at either Gimbel's or Macy's, I never could tell which was which, and gleefully chucked the ill-fitting service uniform into which he poured himself every day under vigorous protest. All four found steady employ in the garment industry, producing uniforms for the United States armed forces. As millions were drafted, the demand was nearly inexhaustible. My father, the lawyer, was the odd man out. But he realized that getting back into the practice of law was an illusion. Necessity made him acquiesce. He even became quite skilled in the art of precision cutting heavy fabric for tailoring.

By the end of the war, the foursome had pooled enough savings through thrift and diligence for us to move across the river to New Jersey. A dry-cleaning and alteration business expanded gradually to several branches and eventually into a flourishing haberdashery, dry goods, and mill end enterprise. The two family units were now able to afford separate apartments, though at the insistence of the sisters, door to door. The mid-fifties saw the realization of Uncle Aaron's dream for the reestablishment on American soil of the firm Aschauer and Markus, Fine Men's Clothiers.

A few years before then, they had already achieved the "American dream," that great mansion in the sky. Not quite stately, but still spacious enough, our house, in one of those developments that were springing up then in the suburbs, was, as one would expect, only a few doors from the Aschauers' residence. Also about that time, I began to spread my wings, though my range was strictly limited at my mother's insistence to a daily commute to Columbia University.

"So this is in a nutshell the history of the Markus-Aschauer clan in America," I concluded as Etoile, seeing the state of inner turmoil the narration had stirred in me, pushed a cognac in front of me. I lifted the glass as in a toast: "A success story, by any yardstick of the needle trade! The future held boundless promise for continued prosperity and bourgeois contentment. The tragic events that were to leave me an orphan and Tante Hedy a widow lay still far off.

"This may sound like an idealized picture of a family, but in broad outline, it is quite accurate," I told Etoile, who had not expressed the slightest doubt as to the veracity of my tale.

The close sisterly ties were the cement that held us all together. True, my father had moments of griping about having to make his living in the *shmatte* business, though a good living it was. He was, after all, university educated, the Humboldt University no less, and an attorney at law. But the difference between Anglo-Saxon law, prevailing in America, and Roman law, in which he was trained, would have required him to start all over again. At other moments, he tried to impress me with stories of his youth as a dashing flâneur on Berlin's grand boulevards, Unter den Linden and Kurfürstendamm.

"Those days are gone, and you should be the happier for it," my mother would chide him.

"Yes, you're right," my father would grumble, and in a defiant undertone he would add: *"Es sei wie es wolle, es war doch so schön—damals."*

"Ja, ja," my mother would sneer back. "Not even he could foresee the future of the fatherland." The "he," I found out later, was the venerated Goethe. I never ceased to marvel over the instant recognition of literary allusions among the adults in our family—but then it was a rather common phenomenon in German Jewish families to recite the beloved poetry and to correct each other if one made a mistake. Trading literary allusions was a commonplace pastime practiced even in the course of the most trivial conversations.

"You backwater provincials just lack all appreciation of what Berlin once was," he would sulk. But his petulance never lasted long, and he faced up to the reality that the Berlin he once knew was no more. Then again, who could blame him for wanting to hold on to the memory of those halcyon days of his youth, redolent with intellectual excitement, not to speak of the excitement brought about by the game of *cherchez la femme*?

"Your father was quite the *Schürzenjäger*," which roughly translates to ladies' man but literally means apron chaser, "before she tamed him," my aunt would comment. Berlin of the ill-fated Weimar Republic was, with all the economic hardships and political violence of the time, an electrifying intellectual scene. Some detractors of the time decried it as a cesspool of profligacy, an abyss of debauchery—the Babylon on the Spree. But it was also, and maybe more so, the capital of *Kultur* in Europe, the magnet for all that was creative and innovative in the arts and in science after the Great War, my father tried to impress upon me. "It was a time when the Jews came into their own in Germany, marching in the *avant-garde* of almost every field of endeavor."

My father was not the only one who hankered after the past and took special pride in the achievements of the members of the tribe. At the Leo Baeck Institute in New York, which was founded to preserve the heritage and history of the Jews in German-speaking lands, as the saying went, my father found a circle of *Seelenverwandten*, of soul mates, and an outlet for his intellectual energies. They all loved America, my father explained to me, but its culture was not theirs. In their hearts, they were still citizens of that better Germany, that antebellum Europe of their youth on the hill. "Not better than America, you must understand," he emphasized, but better in the sense of what the old continent had turned into. Only gradually did they come to realize that the much-vaunted German-Jewish symbiosis was more wishful thinking on the part of the Jews, and that their love for the fatherland and culture had always remained unrequited. It had always been a one-sided love affair.

My aunt and mother were much more skeptical. They shared the appreciation of German culture, but only up to a point. Nobody did them one better in reciting by heart the German poetry of the Dioscuri of Weimar, as they referred to Goethe and Schiller, of an almost mythical time. Then there were Eichendorff and Mörike and the poetess they called "die Droste," not to forget our very own revered Heinrich Heine. But the country of *Dichter und Denker* (poets and thinkers) had become the country of *Richter und Henker* (judges and executioners). The sisters shared none of the nostalgia. For them, there was no looking back, not even to those memorable summers of their childhood and youth at the Baltic seaside resorts.

"Remember, even then, long before the Nazis, they didn't want us. Remember the signs outside their hotels and pensions, *Juden unerwünscht*?" the sisters would remind him. "And that was long before the Nazis came to power," they would intone with the admonition of superior knowledge.

"I know all that." My father for his part would throw up his hands in exasperation and either change the subject or leave the room.

Uncle Aaron had no such problems. In the eastern province where he grew up, the Jewish and gentile worlds were much more clearly delineated. His was a world steeped in Jewish observance and tradition, which came in handy as stakes with which to pitch his tent anywhere in the world.

But this is to be Nina's story. The family history merely is meant to provide the "context," in postmodern jargon, the nest within which her early life unfolded, the milieu in which she was bred. Her later outstanding scholarly successes and her great learning in manifold areas have already been made known. Without resorting to psychoanalysis, for which I have neither qualification nor inclination, I shall recall episodes of her childhood, as much as I have become privy to them and inasmuch as they give a glimpse of her passion, one might say obsession, in her quest for a godforsaken Pyrenean village. I use this word, *godforsaken*, as a manner of speaking, rather than literally, for G-d must have truly been the guardian of these villagers—or their lineage would have become extinct long ago. It's a story of romantic obsession. Maybe if she had been born in some other, more ordinary way station, one less mysterious, one that could be pinpointed on a map, like Toulouse or Roncesvalles, her fantasy world would not have sprouted around a fabled place with quite such fecundity.

To all appearances, Nina Aschauer's formative years were quite ordinary; that is to say, she had a typically American upbringing. She could have been the poster child of the clean, athletic, popular American teenager of the fifties. The fact that she attended a Hebrew day school was no hindrance to her playing basketball, competing in swimming and track and field, and being very good at all of it. She was also an all-round good student in academic subjects. As the star of her Hebrew class, she seemed to follow in my footsteps, I am proud to say, though to her advantage, she lacked my cockiness. Talent for languages seemed to run in the family.

This was one face of Nina I remember—a puerile child who grew into a nubile teenager, though I was already away from home by that time and saw her only during family get-togethers. But I also remember, maybe more vividly, the other Nina. The little girl who lived in a dream world, who spun fables set in exotic places, which she peopled with fantastic characters engaged in intense human dramas before falling asleep at night. In rare moments, when we were together alone at home, she would let me have a glimpse of this world.

While we were still in our refugee apartment, I was frequently called upon to babysit when our parents went out on the town, which was with few exceptions every Saturday night. They would attend the theater or a movie, but their favorite locale was the Roseland ballroom in midtown. As soon as the stars came out, signaling the end of Shabbat, they were on their way downtown. Both couples cut very elegant figures on the dance floor, especially in the Viennese waltz and the Argentinean tango. But they could sway with equally matchless grace to the rhythms of the foxtrot and swing, much in vogue back then. In the old country, they had garnered numerous prizes in amateur competitions. I never heard the end of the stories of the times when they were pitted against each other in the final round. Either couple would win out over the other, mostly gentile, competitors. I vaguely remember the trophies on a shelf in our living room in Stettin. To their chagrin, they had to be left behind.

Neither Nina nor I ever felt any inclination to follow in, pardon the pun, those footsteps. Maybe it was the absence in American life of the preponderant German institution called

Tanzstunde into which all middle class German boys and girls, mostly the offspring of "better" families, were enrolled *de rigueur* upon reaching the age of sixteen.

Even the fads in dance, like the boogie-woogie and later rock 'n' roll, anathema to our parents, had little appeal for either Nina or me. It was almost uncanny how alike we were in tastes and preferences. The difference in age proved no barrier in bringing us close together. I acted as Nina's mentor and protector as well as confidant. On second thought, I should probably restate this. It was she, headstrong as she was from an early age, who chose me as her mentor, protector, and confidant. I was also her link to Valladine.

Nina never had enough of listening to the story of our crossing the mountains from France into Spain and the circumstances of her birth along the way. She pressed her mother for details about the people and their lives in the mysterious village called Valladine. No matter how often my aunt would tell her that she had been in no condition to observe her surroundings and all she could tell her was that the people were kind, Nina would not let up, at least not as long as she was at an age when children naturally keep asking the same questions over and over. When she understood that her mother simply didn't recall much about the place, she pumped me for information about what the boy, whom we dubbed the "shepherd boy," had said while we were waiting in Roncesvalles. I told her that the language barrier made communicating difficult and that we engaged mostly in universal pastimes like board and card games to wile away the time.

Eventually, Nina withdrew into herself and created her own mountain universe. Her Shangri-La was of elaborate design, complete with castles, fortifications, multitudes of dwellings from huts to mansions, inhabited by characters of every description who acted out the fates she assigned to them. I humored her and enjoyed stoking her imagination even further.

When I came to the end of recounting this story to Etoile, I must have fallen into a deep silence while pondering the import of what I had just related. This stroll down memory lane affected me more deeply than I would have thought. It was as if I had unlocked the gate to a dormant garden and weeded out a dense mesh of overgrowth, all the while becoming entangled in the underbrush.

"Can I get you some tea or coffee?" Etoile's voice jolted me out of my reveries.

"That would be nice," I replied, still half lost in thought. "I must admit, I was flabbergasted," I continued more to myself, "when I heard from Aunt Hedy that Nina had gone off on what sounded to me like a wild goose chase in the French countryside—that she had tossed everything to the wind, all her achievements, her academic career just getting off to such a promising start. I had presumed, if I ever thought about it at all, that she had outgrown her childish obsession. How could she do all this for a quixotic quest for a fabled village that wasn't on any map and may not even exist? Almost like a search for an elusive grail. Sounds nice and exciting in romantic legends, but people don't do such things in real life."

"It was her stay here in Toulouse, I'm sure," said Etoile. "She asked me and everybody else repeatedly if we had ever heard of a place called Valladine. Of course, I hadn't. Nobody had. Then she told me she had to find this place. She made it sound so urgent, almost as if it was a matter of life and death.

"Then she went off to the mountains, presumably to study the living conditions of pastoral societies for a book she was planning.

I didn't think it odd then because that was her métier. Now I think it was a pretext to get close to the shepherds who might point her toward this village.

"Disappointment was written in her face each time she returned. Nobody seemed to know anything about such a place. But then this strange, impressive man—he looked like a giant who had escaped from the pages of a medieval saga—with his huge white dogs appeared at the university.

"I don't know what they talked about that night in her study. I just saw him stomping out of the building. A few days later, Nina left for the United States as she had planned. I thought that was the end of it. I didn't hear from her again until that night when she knocked on my door five years later."

"Well, we've read her account of that episode and what followed," I said. "I'm still puzzled that she should have fallen madly in love with this bizarre fellow. Love at first sight. Go figure."

"He's quite attractive in his mountain man way." Etoile made a gesture of the *connaisseuse*, touching her lips with her thumb and finger held together. I yielded to her on this point since she was obviously so much better versed in "matters of the heart" and what constituted manly attractiveness than I was.

"Looks like we now have the continuation of the saga in hand." I turned to the letter. "Or shall we call it a Pyrenean melodrama? Love on the mountain, perhaps? Whatever, let's delve into it."

To Henner, my dear cousin, and Etoile, my faithful friend, greetings and love!

I hope this finds you both well. For my part, I am as well as can be expected. I am addressing both of you, confident as I am that you are by now, with the onset of spring, back at work on our common project, as promised. I hope all went well for both of you—that Henner was able to get a sabbatical or time off some other way from his duties at the university without too much hassle and that congratulations are in order for Etoile on completion of her exams and that she is now a proud owner of a doctorate of philosophy.

I hold you both in my heart with great love and gratitude for the dedication you have shown in the past. Not for a moment do I doubt your determination to make the voice of our medieval heroine, the great and wonderful Dina Miryam, known to the world. Her story deserves to be heard as an inspiring example of what a woman can do in times that test the human will and fortitude.

Maybe one day the inhabitants of this village will show us the same gratitude when they hear the voice of their ancestress speaking to them in their own tongue. So far, most of them are still unable to comprehend what I, and by extension you, am trying to do. All they know is that the object of their veneration, their talisman, the book they have always held most sacred is gone from the village, and they cannot forgive me for the infraction. I am the guilty party in this, I don't deny it. Maybe it was hubris on my part wanting to cut through the thicket of superstition that has grown around Dina's codex in the course of the centuries since the forebears of the present inhabitants lost the ability to read or even recognize the Hebrew lettering. How long ago this happened is hard to tell. It could have been only two or three generations after the matriarch's passing. There is, of course, no record, just oral traditions, stories that have come down through the generations, and are still being told, no doubt in embellished and altered form as they have been filtered through the stream of time. But most of those stories I have heard have little to do with the story we have uncovered so far in Dina's narrative. They have no notion of a matriarch who had been granted this piece of land. They have no awareness of the commune's Jewish origin, nor is there any mention of a libidinous priest, the Urvater, and of the rape of the Urmutter. To their mind, the founders were refugees from the plague that occurred years later. Even about the Black Death they know very little. How they will take Dina's story once they get to hear it in what will be to them a brutal revelation, whether they will even understand it, I cannot predict.

Alphonse understands, to some extent at least. He thinks it will be good for them to hear the true story. He thinks it will be good to shake their idealized image of the founders. What an exciting prospect! So he says. Maybe he just means to humor me and bows to my scholarly curiosity out of love. Don't think that I don't have qualms. I am often plagued by doubts. Is it not arrogance? By what right are we setting ourselves up as judges over these people? Yes, their thinking is marked by what the modern world would call superstition. In many ways, they are backward. Theirs is a medieval mindset. But that's what makes them so fascinating. Their society is a historian's dream. Their laws and customs are clearly circumscribed and strictly upheld. They are by no means completely ignorant. They know there's a world outside, beyond the confines of their mountain village. But most prefer the secluded life in the mountains.

Alphonse is somewhat of an outsider almost. He frequently forays into the world beyond—I don't mean the netherworld. To keep informed, he says, and to guard against any intruders into the realm. As one who brought a foreign wife into the community, he has to tread with special care though. Even before then, he was already looked upon with suspicion. He is one of few residents of Valladine who spent an extended period, almost ten years, away from the mountain commune. As a young man, he had yearned to see the world—like the story of the one who went out into the world to learn how to be fearful. He and two friends snuck away in the dead of night. Together they joined the

French Foreign Legion and fought in the French wars in Indochina. His comrades lost their lives parachuting into Dien Bien Phu during Operation Castor. The loss of his comrades affected him deeply. For a long time, he was consumed with rage against this so-called civilized modern world. But a return home was not possible at first. Deserters faced excruciating punishments if caught, and they were almost always caught. After the humiliating French defeat in Indochina, he served in the Algerian war until the French withdrew from there as well. Looking back, he now feels that it was cowardice for him to have stayed in the legion. Rather than wasting the best years of his life for a cause he didn't believe in—the spirit of adventure had long worn off, and all that was left was a daily struggle for survival—he now feels he should have taken the risk and attempted to get away. But back then, it just didn't seem feasible. His heart was filled with pain over the personal loss of his friends and disgust at the evil he witnessed. So he hurled himself into the fight with the ferociousness of a dragon slayer. But which was the evil side and which the good? The question bedeviled him. A clear answer eluded him. He settled on blaming the parties in equal measure and condemned them all. It was the modern world that was rotten to the core. A pox on both houses kind of thing. Not that he would put it in such terms.

Overwhelmed with longing for the pristine world of the mountains, he eventually found his way back home. His "Wanderjahre" *had come to an end. Except for occasional forays to the lowland, he remained true to his oath never to leave the mountains again. But whether he likes it or not, the world did leave its mark on him. I can see it every day. Everything he does, the way he approaches problems and dilemmas—yes, these do exist even in this secluded enclave—makes him stand out in comparison to the almost fossilized mindset of the villagers. The evil and cruelty he had seen men do to each other had also opened his eyes to the barbarity of some of the customs being practiced here. No longer did he take everything for granted and accept matters as they are just because they had been sanctified by centuries of practice. He has come to regard life in the village and the villagers themselves with a rather critical eye. But he keeps his thoughts to himself, only sharing them with me when we are alone, and then in hushed tone. The concept of First Amendment rights has not yet reached what still is—frankly speaking—a primitive, backward outpost.*

In spite of its flaws, he still considers the medieval mindset to be less harmful than the modern. My attempts to set the record straight, to enlighten him on the legendary brutality of medieval warfare, only arouse his anger. Like the wanderer lost in a dense forest lacks the broader perspective of the lay of the land, he lacks the broader perspective of history. The difference in our outlook came as a revelation to me when I ran up against his stubborn refusal to believe the stories I told him of cruelty and torture, of rampant exercise of power, fratricide and patricide even, excesses of religious fanaticism and superstition and torture that were a matter of course. Feudalism, investiture, crusades, serfdom, inequality—concepts of this kind are completely meaningless to him and to the people of this village. I quickly learned that such historical constructs created by modern historical researchers as scaffolds on which to hang and sort out so-called facts like socks on a laundry line—and you know the unsolved mystery of the matching pair—have no existence in their reality. The famous, somewhat shopworn, Procrustean bed comes to mind, if you will pardon my penchant for mixing metaphors. It has long been clear to me that academic jargon fails to encapsulate human drama as it plays itself out in real life and acts in the lives of real people in history. Forgive me if I have made this point before. Although I like to think of myself as a lapsed historian, it's a habit not easily divested.

Convincing Alphonse of the universality of evil in history was not easy. I had to speak in common language. Not dumb the narrative down, but illustrate my point through concrete examples. Even so, it was hard to convince him that I wasn't making up the stories about the Church and the Crown's cruel suppression of heresy in the Albigensian Crusade that took place not far from here. I cited details of the Crusades to the Holy Land, the massacres of Jews along the way, the torture chambers of the Inquisition and the flaming stake, just as a few examples, but he just shook his head in disbelief and insisted that it couldn't be true. "Why would I make this up?" I asked him. "To exonerate the modern world? Hardly."

Our mindsets are literally centuries apart. I had to reach into the trove of human legends, draw out episodes, anecdotes, chronicles, tales, sagas, fables, yarns spun through generations, ancient lore, folklore, eyewitness accounts, contemporary annals—in sum, stories and epics sprung from the mouths of the people. You know them all. These were stories he could comprehend.

The record of mankind, I persisted, is replete with wars and cruelty in every age and every generation. The technology changes, some may say it advances, but man's ingenuity to inflict suffering and death with whatever is at hand has never changed. This is not to say, I told him, that the record is not also replete with expressions of longing for peace and harmony among peoples and nations. Our Holy Scriptures, I told him, give ample testimony of both. Maybe only in a place like Valladine, a haven far from the world, this longing can be fulfilled and turned to reality. Academics would call it a utopian experiment—another concept that meant absolutely nothing to him. I tried to reassure him that here at least, the experiment seemed successful, as it had lasted for so many centuries. Yet, as I have come to know the village and its people, I noticed that even here, rankling, rivalries, envy, and greed are far from being absent.

But I transgress. Philosophical and historical considerations aside, let me first take up where I left off in my account of how I came to

Valladine. As I told you, I burned all bridges behind me. I had to if I wanted to reach my goal. I set out on the road with one single-minded purpose to find Valladine and, admittedly, to find Alphonse. Nothing else mattered. My life up to then, so it appeared to me, had been one long wait in the antechamber of my true destiny. All that came before had been a mere prelude to this. Only I had no idea what this "this" actually was. I had no idea where I was going. Like Abraham, I felt called up to take a journey into the unknown, following some mute yet compelling voice into the mountains, toward a rendezvous with destiny. (I can see Henner rolling his eyes and pulling out his imaginary mini-violin at so much schmaltz.) But that's what goaded me on, irresistibly. Somewhere in these mountains, he was waiting for me. I knew it. At this point, my longing wasn't so much for Valladine anymore. True I still wanted to find the mythical place of my birth. But what spurred me on was something else. I felt an overwhelming desire in every fiber of my body, a desire for this strange giant of a man with the two huge furry white dogs. In the image I had of him, he was always flanked by these dogs. They came with the package, so to speak. Yes, I know it was all irrational. But isn't that what love is—irrational, devoid of reason? Now that I have used the word love, I still wouldn't say I was in love. For that I was too old. I was obsessed. Maybe it's the same. (Wouldn't you say so, Henner? Maybe Etoile is better equipped to figure out what I mean and can explain it to you.)

So I embarked on that road. I am repeating myself. Forgive. I embarked on that road in every sense of the word—physically, psychologically, metaphorically. I was single-minded in my pursuit. Like a Don Quixote, I sallied forth on my quest unperturbed, without regard for the consequences for me and others. After all, it wasn't totally new territory. I had been there before, in the mountains. The shepherds would help me. They were likely to remember me. They would put out the word. This time I had a name of a specific person

I was looking for: Alphonse de Sola, a man they all knew well. The word would go out, and he would come for me. It would be as easy as that. He would descend from his lofty heights and sweep me up. Or so I thought. As it turned out, I soon ran up against an insurmountable wall, almost literally. One lesson I learned: the best-laid plans still have their way of going astray.

I did roll my eyes and shake my head at so much purplish prose. Even Etoile, who was much more forbearing than I, agreed that Nina's style was a tad overwrought; maybe a bit reminiscent of Dina's. To my mind, it was more than a tad. We, therefore, decided to paraphrase Nina's account henceforth and clothe it in more down-to-earth terms. We would retain her more memorable phrases, of course, just tone it down a bit.

"And she had the nerve to say Dina was laying it on too thick." I slumped into the fauteuil with a heavy sigh. "I think I could use a nice warming cognac before going on."

"Maybe I should take over the reading and type it up later. You just kick back, as you say in America, and lend me your ear." Etoile handed me a double and fluffed up a pillow for me to sink my aching head in.

"You're treating me like a sick person," I protested, but meekly, not minding being fussed over by her caring hand.

"In a way, you are. If you don't mind my saying so, you seem to handle Dina's verbal excesses much better than your cousin's. Maybe she's too close to home, or too close to your heart?" She gave me a probing glance.

"Touché!" I winced. "Down the hatch!"

Nina stormed the *sentier* of the Grande Randonnée, a well-trodden walkway across the mountains. Christian pilgrims have been trudging along this route for a thousand years on their way to Santiago de Compostella in northwestern Spain. In modern times, this stretch had been incorporated into a trans-European network of hiking trails popular among nature lovers and fitness enthusiasts. It was early March and the path was still encrusted with a thick layer of snow. But Nina was undeterred. Her gaze and mind were firmly fixed on the horizon. Unlike Lot's wife, she was determined to turn her back on the Sodom that was the modern world and never give it another look. Her disdain of the lowland fortunately did not make her refrain from bringing along necessary gear and provisions. A pair of sturdy boots and warm field clothing, a pup tent, a thermal sleeping bag and blanket, she figured would be sufficient to survive in the wilderness for a week or two, by which time Alphonse would surely have found her. And indeed, she made good progress at first. She braved the elements for several days and spent the nights curled up in her tent and sleeping bag. But the further she penetrated the mountainous terrain, the more formidable became the barrier of snow and wind. The shepherds were nowhere in sight. For a moment, she considered leaving the straight path and fanning out onto the snowy pastures. An intensifying snowfall saved her from such folly and made her realize the danger of getting stranded or lost in a wind-blown desert of ice and snow.

Five days after she had set out from Pau, she checked into a *chambre d'hôte* in the town of Oloron Sainte Marie. After a warming bath and a long rest in a kingdom of fluffy down, she had time to contemplate her situation with a clearer head. She should have known better than to let herself be guided by pure impulse. It was too early in the year for the great transhumance to have taken place. The return of the shepherds and their herds from the south was still weeks, maybe even months, away. Her more impetuous side was angered by the delay, while another, shall we say more reasonable side of her, actually thanked the weather for having brought her back to earth.

Sitting by the fireside in the lounge of the bed and breakfast, wrapped in a blanket and sipping hot tea, she began to reflect on the situation she had gotten herself into. As the stiffness in her limbs softened, she felt a soothing calm enveloping her mind and body. Her thoughts wandered back over the past few weeks. It was only two weeks since she had packed up and left her life in America, her friends, her profession. She had no regrets. Only the thought of her mother made her heart ache. She had never really explained to her what was going on, where she was going and why. It suddenly occurred to her how her odd, frequently erratic behavior must have pained the woman who had always loved her unconditionally. All she told her when saying good-bye was that she had to find Valladine. This was the first mention to her mother after many years. She had probably long forgotten this place where she spent two nights without ever really seeing it. The place held no particular significance except as a way station, a forced stop on our flight toward freedom.

A sudden desire overwhelmed her for a heart-to-heart talk. She had to do what she did, but she also wanted her mother's approval for the step she had taken. More than her approval, she wanted her blessing for all that was likely to befall her in the time to come. So she wrote to her about her search for her birthplace in the mountains, about her encounter with this man, Alphonse de Sola, who said he would take her there. This was the first mention of that name to her mother. She asked her mother's forgiveness for not speaking to her of how she despaired over having turned him down out of a sense of obligation, which she now regarded as having been misguided.

"I never told you how much I dreaded resuming the routine of my life, my oh-so-successful career in America," she wrote. "Would you have understood my desire to find Valladine? Would you have approved? Maybe what held me back was the fear you might laugh it off as a childish lark. I feared you would not understand my motives and think me foolish."

In the next paragraph, she regretted her meek attempt at justifying herself and putting the blame on her mother. Instead she resorted to a different tack, one she knew her mother would understand better.

"Maybe it was *beshert*," she suggested. Fate may well have had a hand in bringing her together with this man who was so completely different from all the men she had known in her life.

However brief the conversation with him had been, she had felt a bond forming between them as they spoke. She was sure it was mutual. This may have been the reason for his angry outburst when they parted. She had to return. She had to have another encounter with him. She had to find out if her feeling was real or if she had imagined it all in a fever trance. Again she begged for her mother's forgiveness— "a thousand times"—and promised to write again soon. No return address. No follow-up.

The letter Aunt Hedy had shown me was frayed and wrinkled, the writing faded from blotches of tears. Reading the letter became her daily ritual. Someday, G-d willing, she hoped, Nina would make good on her promise.

After she had posted the letter, Nina wandered restlessly around Oloron Sainte Marie. Ever curious, she investigated the town's history and medieval architecture and was bowled over by the richness of ancient treasures she uncovered in this out-of-the-way place. She became friendly with some of the inhabitants, especially the merchants. But her daily, seemingly aimless, amblings also caught the eye of the local police chief. The sleepy little town provided little excitement, and there were few infractions of the law and few diversions. A woman, who was a stranger at that, might spell some welcome trouble.

It did not escape Nina's attention that she had come under constant surveillance from the eye of the law. Wherever she went, she felt the police chief's piercing stares in her back or directly into her face. By then she had already exhausted the sites worth seeing and she withdrew to the indoors at the bed and breakfast where she was staying. She even played with the idea of taking up such medieval women's activities as knitting or embroidering. The continued inclement wintry weather dashed all hopes for a chance in the foreseeable future of another foray into the mountains.

She never did take up needlework, which wasn't her thing anyway. On the positive side, the imposed respite had at least a calming effect on her nerves. She was able to wind down, sort things out. Her thoughts turned once again to those last days in Toulouse. For a long time, they remained fixed on the encounter with Alphonse de Sola, the mountain man, and then on the events that followed when she was back home in America. Her previous life in the bustling metropolis, with its coffeehouse scene of intellectual pretense, as she called it, had become a surreal urban landscape—something out of a movie—to which she could not find any connection.

She reached for pad and pen and began jotting down random thoughts as they occurred to her. Scenarios and characters vacillated before her mind's eye, first in the shape of elusive frazzles of yarn, but gradually, ever so gradually, the various strands began to smoothen out into distinct forms and colors. Painstakingly, as was her habit when collecting pieces of history, she laid out the narrative skeins in chronological order and finally knitted them together into a coherent chronicle, even if a bit overwrought in parts, that ended with her departure from America. She then made a fair copy in her characteristically impeccable handwriting. The result was the tightly written account in the notebook she presented to me in Albi the night before she returned to Valladine.

Nina's second letter, the one we now held in hand and which she wrote from the village after her return there, showed none of her customary neatness. Not only was it written on irregular shreds of unnumbered grayish paper, almost like pieces of cheap French toilet paper, the handwriting in pencil reminded me of what we used to call "chicken scratch." The letters were falling over each other in any direction and were often hard to decipher. Etoile even thought she could detect signs of numerous abrupt breaks and restarts in the writing, as if she had been surprised by someone and had to hide what she was doing. Oftentimes, sentences began with "as I was saying" or "as previously noted," without a clear antecedent. There were numerous cross-outs and overwrites. Anybody who was familiar with her previous work would be profoundly disturbed, despite the fact, or maybe even more so, that only Nina could have written this account.

Without a word, Etoile gathered up the pages with slow, deliberate movements, taking care to keep them in the right order, and began numbering them in the right-hand corner. She then tapped the stack to even the edges as much as this was possible and stuffed it back into the envelope it had come in. We both knew what we had to do. Time was pressing. An ominous air settled over us. Intimations of doom made us press on. Would we be able to finish the project? We had to give it our best shot. Only the timely return of the codex might prevent irreparable harm. We had no way of knowing if it wasn't already too late. All we could do was finish the work and then do our best to find Alphonse de Sola in the mountains.

DINA'S TALE 8

What happened after my return from Toulouse is, no doubt, indelibly imprinted in your minds forever. How could your souls not have been afflicted by the venomous bolts being hurled at your mother? How could the torrent of threats, accusations, and insults not have left their mark on you? Such rants did not accord with the priest's habitual comportment. Imagine my surprise to be thusly received! I had rather expected he would welcome me back with his customary lupine graciousness, a triumphant sneer perhaps on his face, but not this. Hadn't he assured my return when he kept you hostage? The violent outburst puzzled me. I could not comprehend what was going on in his mind. The mask of civility had always stood him in good stead in his games of deception. Considerable time passed before I was able to surmise what was behind his loss of control—why at that moment he dropped his guard.

You, my sons, did not speak up; you withdrew. You went back to tending your flocks with demure silence. Maybe you thought this was just a domestic squabble between the priest and his concubine. But this concubine was your mother. You were old enough and big enough to intervene, to form a protective shield around me. I don't blame you for your sheepishness. Nobody could escape the priest's demonic spell. You had no way of knowing how it was that your mother had become a slave to this man. You also had no way of knowing what ensued later, during the night. My hand still shakes as I write this so many years later. But I must reveal this to you now so you will understand why, when the opportunity arose, I acted as I did. It is not easy for me to speak of this to my sons, of the violence my body and soul suffered that night.

My troubled spirit had barely calmed, and my body, still worn from the day's long journey, had found some rest, when wild pounding on my chamber door startled me out of my first slumber. Before I had time to get up to open the door, he had already broken in. There he stood, looming in the dark, panting like a wolfhound thirsting for his prey. My battered body would have given testimony to the violence, to the chastening it endured that night, but even in his rage, he was careful not to touch my face. No visible marks, no bruises, no scratches. Had this act of brutality come to light, it would have been his word against mine. And my word counted for naught in this village.

More degrading than the bodily harm he caused me were his words. Yes, these words hurt more deeply than anything. It's the words I shall never forget nor ever forgive. The pain he inflicted on my body eased; the wounds healed. The assault on my people, however, carved an abysmal wound on my soul that would fester forever. Had the villagers overheard the epithets he hurled at me, they would have cheered him on, would have chimed in. For these were the same and similar words they had been saying behind my back all those years I lived among them. I was the Jew whore, the Christ murderess, Jewish pig or bitch, witch, Satan's bride. These are just some, no need to list them all. But his rant did not end with personal offense. The entire Jewish people were pilloried, as swine and lepers of mankind, their faith defamed. Most inexplicable to me was his accusation that I was spreading "the vomit of Judaism." Why would he say that?

Yet, as I think back, this was also a night of great wonder, the night of my liberation. What happened then was so wonderful, so miraculous I can only describe it as a gift from the Eternal, blessed be He. This night of deepest degradation was also the night when I became free, hard as it may be to comprehend in light of all that I have told you. This was the night when the G-d of Israel heard my pleas for atonement and freed me from bondage. The Eternal, blessed be He, lifted my weakness of the flesh that had shackled me to this man for so long. "Subjection" was the word the priest used repeatedly in the course of his violent assault. He wanted total subjection to his will. He seemed to have forgotten it was his silver tongue that had allured and enslaved me to him, his tender touch, the carnal pleasure he aroused in me, which made me forget all else at the moment when our bodies became one, that moment I yearned and lived for all these years. No more! The priest's evil tongue had shaken something loose inside of me, as if a sheet of ice broke off a mountain crag under the melting rays of the springtime sun, hurtled down the ravine, and shattered into a thousand pieces on the valley floor.

The tether that had tied me to him had snapped. No longer did my body yield to his embrace. It was a miracle! In the flesh, I was still in the land of Egypt and outwardly in bondage. The G-d of Moses did not part the seas for me; he did not take me out of this place where I was a stranger and always would be a stranger. Not then, not yet. The Promised Land lay still far away in the future for me. My life went on as before. Many years would pass before my final liberation. But my soul was free, my spirit was free, and most of all, my body was free.

In the years to come, the priest still had his will with me, though less and less. He seemed preoccupied mostly with other matters. He never apologized for his behavior, never said a single word about it.

I submitted to him on those now rare occasions when he entered my chamber at night, but my body did not succumb. He resumed the pose of the smooth gallant. To me he had become a low, repulsive lecher. So when his visits became less and less frequent and when they finally ceased, I was relieved.

Never would I forget this night, the night when he unveiled his true face. Never would I forgive the humiliation, the punishment he sought to inflict on me for asserting for once a tiny, ever so slight measure of my own will. Blessed be the Lord G-d of Israel who closed my womb from this time forward—the second miracle for which I gratefully bend my knees to the Eternal every day of my life. The evil priest may have been forcing his body onto mine, but my womb was no longer receptive to his seed. No longer was my body encumbered with endless cycles of miscarriages and stillbirths. It surely must have been a sign that the Eternal had forgiven my sins.

Yet, I could not help but wonder what had caused the wolf to shed the sheep's mantle in which he usually cloaked himself. He knew I would come back from Toulouse whether I found my father and brothers or not. So why would he do this? Why the rage? Such choler was not his way of approaching situations displeasing to him. I was still pondering this mystery when my attention was drawn to remarks you, my sons, made at the table. Remarks muttered under your breath, but caught by my ears which had been sharpened by years of hearkening to people's whispers. My suspicions aroused, I drew closer. I demanded to know the meaning of what you were hinting. Slowly the pieces began to fall into place.

The ripples of goings-on I had stowed in my mind in the course of a decade—nocturnal comings and goings; cloaked men hugging the shadows; hushed gatherings behind latched doors and shuttered windows; a clandestine world of secrets and stealth—rose to a torrent that pushed open the floodgate behind which they had been contained and spilled over into my consciousness. So much became clear to me now from what you told me about what had occurred during my absence. What I had suspected for some time was confirmed. The priest was one of those men whom they referred to as the "perfecti." This meant that in the eyes of the very Church he purportedly served, in which he had been anointed, he was a heretic, a traitor. He was a follower of those who called themselves Cathars, the pure ones. Not a mere humble believer among them, but a goodman, a perfect, one of their leaders. I had heard about this sect, but not being an adherent of the Christian Church, I had no interest in what I saw as squabbles and doctrinal disputes between equally reprehensible parties. The priest had never tried to convert me to his beliefs. Never had he discussed religious matters with me. He knew better than to come to me with baptismal water. Basically, I think, it was a matter of indifference to him. He preferred subjecting me to him in other ways. He showed the same indifference toward you, his sons. Though he baptized you at birth according to the Roman rite, he never called you to him to instruct you in the tenets of any faith, Roman or Cathar. He never even thought it necessary to teach you to read and write. You were to remain illiterate shepherd boys by his decree.

What I learned eventually about the beliefs of the Cathars was nothing short of astounding to me. The conduct expected of the perfect, the goodman, stood in stark contrast to what I knew of the priest's habits. After an initiation ritual they called "consolamentum," the perfect vows to abstain from eating meat, eggs, or cheese, and—I burst out laughing when I heard this—sexual intercourse. The perfect was to foreswear the pleasures of the flesh of all kind. But why should I have been surprised? I always knew him to be a hypocrite and dissembler.

Let me now return to the subject of what transpired during my absence from the village when I had gone to Toulouse to look for my father and brothers. From what you told me, the priest apparently was seized with a sudden inspiration to instruct his sons, unacknowledged though you were, in religious truths, not the truth of the Roman Church to which he was bound by a sacred vow, but in the beliefs of the heretics, who were the sworn enemies of that same Church. I did not then and I do not now take a stand as to the veracity of either. It's a matter of indifference to me. They are both fallacy and aberration to my mind. If asked which of the two I deemed the more vile, I would say the heresy. The heretics not only decried the practices of Rome and denied papal authority, for reasons that may or may not be valid, but their teachings most of all derided and reviled our Sacred Scriptures. They spit on our Torah and the revelation given to our lawgiver Moses on Mount Sinai. For the heretics, our scripture is not only an "old" testament superseded by the "new" but still a valid precursor as the Church teaches, for them it is the work of the devil, the evil force which exists in parallel with the force of good. Or some such thing. I never cared to penetrate the finer points of this errant thinking.

A few days after I had left for the city, the priest called you together to sit with him under the willow tree in the sheep meadow, a perfect sanctuary shielded from spying eyes by the tall hedge enclosing the pasture. Since he knew little about you, just seeing you around the yard and fields, he apparently took you to be a bunch of waifs left to grow like wild mountain goats. I don't really believe this to have been so. He knew very well whose offspring you were. Only he took little interest in your upbringing until that time. So he had no idea what you had learned besides shearing sheep and tending goats and donkeys. As you related to me later, he began by telling you how evil this world was. He pointed out its irredeemable corruption and sinfulness. Opposed to this, he told you, was another world, a parallel world, the kingdom to come, a different realm that was all good. The history of the world was a constant battle between good and evil, between the good angels and the bad angels, he told you. The Roman Church was evil incarnate. The Church was the emissary of the evil one who had created this temporal world. So far, you nodded politely. His persuasive eloquence might even have drawn you to the heretical faith, as were so many of the simple shepherds. But he made one miscalculation. You were not simple shepherds. True, the existence of good and evil was quite obvious. Even a mountain village far off the world's center stage had its dramas and morality plays. But when he came to telling you about who created this evil world, you would not remain quiet. The notion of two creators engaged in an eternal battle—the force of evil, creator of the world we live in, and the force of good, creator of the world beyond, something like heaven and earth—went against everything I had taught you about the one and only G-d, the G-d of Abraham, Isaac, and Jacob, the sole creator and supreme ruler of the universe, blessed be He. I believe it was Jacob who first spoke up. For the first time, the priest learned about the Shema, *the prayer that confirms the oneness of the Eternal, and which I had been reciting with you every night before you went to sleep since I had nursed you at my breast. Besides his utter contempt for our Holy Scriptures and the people of Israel for refusing to bow to Jesus Christ, who in the heretics' universe was some kind of angel, it must have come as a shock to him to realize that he had no control over the mind of his concubine or that of her sons. Not only had I instructed you in the faith of my fathers, I had also acted to bring you into the covenant of Abraham. Herein, then, lay the crux of the matter, the core of his unruly anger. It was a bitter pill for him to swallow—in matters of conscience, he would never rule over either you or me.*

Life went on as before nonetheless. The seasons came and went according to their eternally fixed flow. I began to feel the passing of time in my gait and bones. My complexion had become tawny, and my skin had lost its suppleness from the black winds sweeping mercilessly down from the mountains. You, my sons, were growing into handsome, strapping rams. You were my light and my pride. It was for you that I was alive. And I continued to pass on to you what little knowledge I had of the Jewish faith. I taught you the aleph-bet *even though we had no books at hand in the Hebrew script. I told you the stories contained in our Sacred Scriptures, the origin and history of our people as much as I was able to call to mind. I told you about Abraham and his wife Sarah, who left their homeland to be free to worship the One. I told you about their son Isaac, and especially Jacob, from whose twelve sons descended the tribes of Israel. I told you about the enslavement of the Israelites in Egypt, of Moses, the liberator and lawgiver. I told you about the glory days of our people under King David and his son Solomon who built the temple in Jerusalem. I also told you about the destruction of the temple and the exiles and their return, and then the final destruction of the holy place in Jerusalem and the dispersion of the Jews among the nations. I also told you about the centers of learning they established in those foreign lands, how they prospered through diligence in spite of many hardships, of persecutions, and the calumnies brought against them in every kingdom where they dwelled. Then I told you of King Philippe IV, the one they called the Fair, in reality a devil incarnate, a rapacious fiend. He coveted the Jews' belongings and banished them from the kingdom to slake his thirst for worldly goods.*

You, my dear sons, always listened to the stories I told you with keen attentiveness. You were eager to learn about the world that existed beyond the narrow confines of the village where you matured. You desired more and more details of our people's at times glorious, yet often arduous march through the conduit of time and yearned to drink from the fountain of Jewish wisdom. Often your questions strained my humble knowledge. I gave you as much as I was able to extract from my memory without benefit of books. In the village of your birth, they branded you bastards, shunned you as if you were lepers, but you knew you were their betters, of far nobler birth, than those dolts who were so easily ensnared in the whispers of heretics lurking in the shadows.

A few years after my return from Toulouse and the incident with the priest, strangers started to make their appearance in the village. They were not the kind of strangers who would occasionally pass through this part on their way to somewhere else. These people seemed to be on official business. Some of them carried halberds before them and were dressed in the soldierly mail coats and leather jerkins imprinted with the emblem of the royal house, others with the emblem of the papacy. These troops milled around the center square, but at first did not speak with the villagers. Of more imposing, dignified bearing was a group of men clad in black velvet robes and head covering of the same material. They strode about with important airs and probing mien. Much of this I observed without fully grasping the meaning of their presence at the time.

Through the cracks of the window shutters, I saw them eventually approaching some of the people in the village. Then the priest came out of his church. They spoke with him for a long time. There was much gesturing and pointing. Then there was a round of handshaking under jovial parting. The priest and the officials seemed to have reached a cordial understanding about whatever it was they were inquiring. Then I heard, maybe I didn't hear them since I was too far away, but I saw the officials talking to the soldiers. A few of them rose and went to the house of a certain peasant. They came out with him and his family. Their hands were shackled. They took them away, and they were never seen again.

Such a scene was repeated several times over the next few years. The officials, accompanied by a troop of soldiers, came to the village, usually in the spring. They spoke with the priest, who pointed to a house or several houses, whose inhabitants were then taken away and never returned. The sequence of these events made me wonder. The next time the visitors came to the village, my curiosity won out over my reticence to be seen by public officials, and I moved closer toward the church and hid behind a column. The priest hurried down the church steps greeting the black-robed grandees with welcoming, outstretched arms. The ensuing conversation took place in a light manner as if they were on a casual errand. While the officials nodded, the priest spoke of heresy and heretics, foes of the true faith, while pointing in the direction of several houses on the outskirts of the village. True to the pattern I had observed previously, the soldiers were dispatched to the houses the priest had waved his hand at, and the entire household was arrested and taken away. This was my moment of revelation. The scales fell from my eyes. The priest, whom I knew to be not only a heretic himself but one of their perfects, an insinuator, a preacher of the Cathar gospel in clandestine places, was betraying the simple folk among his own followers to the authorities. Of all the depravities I had seen him commit in the past, handing his flock over one by one to the Holy Inquisition surely was the most wicked of treacheries. A Christian might have called him a Judas, but I simply murmured "blackguard," gnashing my teeth in disgust, "most fiendish of blackguards!" under my breath. My body still shudders in disgust at the memory of this man's touch. My skin burned with the sting of a thousand scorpions. My belly emptied bitter bile. I had no reason to feel sympathy for these villagers who had never shown me any kindness. Yet I could not help being incensed over this betrayal by the one whom they had venerated and elevated to the status of an idol.

I hope you will understand that the events as they ensued from then on took an inevitable course. If there was a divine hand guiding human affairs—and who would doubt it?—then a deed as abject as the priest's could not go unavenged. Someone had to unmask this false messiah. Someone with a clear vision had to rise and denounce the traitor. These peasants were far too blinded by the devil's allure to see him clearly for what he was even then. They would go to their death before facing up to the truth. Retribution had to come. And retribution came in the summer's heat of the year 1320, the year 5080 by our counting and the fourteenth year of my captivity.

The ecclesiastical host heralded its approach already from far away with great fanfare. King David's entry into Jerusalem with the Holy Ark surely could not have been more tumultuary and gaudy. A noisy racket of jarring sounds—of drum rolls and tambour rattles, blaring horns and blasting trumpets, bells ringing and cymbals chiming—roused the villagers from their midday rest in the stifling summer heat. As the procession came into view and rumbled down the sloping pathway toward the village, even a blind man, at least anyone not totally blinded by adulation, could have seen the ominous sign. This visit was of no ordinary purpose. The contingent of armed guards and foot soldiers was much larger than on previous occasions. So was the number of civil and church officials.

The procession came to a halt in the open space before the village church. The magistrates, or whatever they were, and lower churchmen alighted from their horses with the aid of their squires. The apparently highest-ranking one among them heaved his bulk from inside a litter draped in flowing white linen and carried on two poles by four servants. The dignitaries were decked out lavishly in finest fabric, some in colorful silk apparel, others in black velvet robes according to rank and position. The portly one in the litter shone in purple velvet with ermine fur trim despite the heat. My father's storehouses held no finer materials than those that were on display that afternoon in this humble mountain village. The gentlemen were fanning themselves or had their servants apply moistened cloths to their burning faces.

However, there was one group of about a half dozen men that aroused my particular curiosity since they alone knelt in front of the church door and prayed. From their coarse black habits tied together with a white rope, their feet clad in sandals, and their tonsured heads, I knew they were monks. I remembered that much from seeing them on rare outings beyond the Jewish quarter in Toulouse and asking my father who these strange-looking men were. What I didn't know at the time when they came to the village—and learned only later when I too was brought to the city of Pamiers—was that these brethren were called Dominicans, the monkish order that acted as torturers and executors of the Inquisition.

Their prayers completed with a pious bow and sign of the cross, they sent out a call for the priest, who on this occasion had failed to appear at the church entrance to greet the visitors. The villagers stood around the plaça in silence, their bare heads bowed and their hats pressed against the chest. A troop of soldiers was dispatched to search the church. I knew he wasn't there. From behind my window post, I had seen him steal away. He apparently knew, either by his innate animal instinct or some other intelligence, that the wind had turned against him. This time, it was he who was the hunted. Next they came to the parish abode. I met them at the door. In answer to their question, I told them I was the priest's housekeeper and that he was away taking care of his pastoral duties. The next move I made, I came to regret. You can imagine that I was quite fearful of being discovered for who I really was. The entire power of the Church seemed to have been unleashed against a small group of helpless peasants suspected of heresy. What would they do if they discovered I was a member of the house of Israel? Without taking full account of the consequences for you, my sons, I sought only to draw their attention away from me. Somehow, though irrationally of course, I imagined my forehead to be emblazoned with the mark of King David. So when asked in which direction he had gone, I pointed toward the pastures belonging to the châtelaine.

They found him there. But they also found you, my sons. The sight of you standing chained together with him before the fat man in purple almost made me faint. The priest stood erect, his head held high, unrepentant and defiant. As you told me later, he exhorted you under his breath not to bow to the heathens. That this might implicate you as heretics surely never bothered his mind. Then I too decided that I had to stand erect, that I could not lose my mettle. I knew what I had to do. As disheartening as the outlook was, I would put every ounce of will and strength I could muster into getting you away from him and spare you the fate I knew awaited him.

The fat man unrolled a scroll from which he read with a high-pitched, thin voice—one would have expected a stentorian basso to issue from such a barrel—a litany of accusations brought against the priest and the entire village. This man's visage remained in my memory to this day. It had decadence and debauchery etched into the greasy rolls of skin, intersected with deeply carved furrows running with ruisseaux of sweat. But it was the eyes, snaky and sly. Although I was keeping in the background, I suddenly felt his gaze piercing through the crowd and zeroing in on me like an archer sighting his target. Our eyes met for only a few seconds before his continued to wander back over the crowd. I was left paralyzed for a few seconds longer. My blood ran cold like an alchemist's metallic potion and almost brought my heart to a stop. I was sure he had registered something. His bloodhound's instinct had picked up an alien presence. The brief exchange gave me a glimpse of the personification of evil and hypocrisy for which the heretics, who called themselves the "pure ones," despised the Roman Church. This part of their teachings was surely justified. But then, the accused heretic who faced him, unbending and unrepentant, though lacking the churchman's repulsive physical attributes, was as much a snake and a fox. The only difference was in the power the churchman held over this heretic priest.

For a moment, my heart wavered. His proud bearing, his handsome figure clad in the white linen robe he favored, stood in such contrast to the ugliness of his accuser. I understood all too well why these mountain dwellers were enticed to follow this false prophet. The power he had over me for many years had been, as you know, of a different kind.

But I am wandering off the subject. When the churchman had finished reading off the litany of charges against the priest and his flock, there still was much bustle, the meaning of which eluded me for the most part. The prisoners, which comprised the entire village, were made to kneel. Although I remained on the margin, I was too frightened not to comply as well. One of the Dominicans held a huge cross aloft. The rest of the friars walked through the crowd, sprinkling holy water and swinging incensories over the people's heads. The air was redolent with pungent incense and cadenced incantations. Most of the utterances were in Latin and therefore incomprehensible to me. From what I was able to gather, this was a ritual prescribed to chase away the devil, who apparently shares my aversion toward the stink of incense and the sight of crosses.

As the sun had passed its zenith, the fat one lumbered toward the litter with the flapping curtains and was hoisted into it by the pole bearers. The magistrates mounted their horses and readied to lead the party out of the mountain valley. The friars took the priest and you, my sons, into their custody. He was their treasured captive, the prized trophy of a successful hunt. How it pained me to see you linked to him! The soldiers rounded up the other villagers. They ransacked the humble huts in search of stragglers and booty. Then, with coarse shouts, occasional kicks and cracking whips, they prodded the line of prisoners into motion for the march ahead. The men went on foot, weighed down by ankle chains. The women and elders were placed on any rickety charettes, tumbrel, or hay-wains such as could be found. I rode in the cart with the priest's mother and sisters. Even then none of them spared me a good word or any word at all.

We arrived in Pamiers sometime the next day. They herded us into the town's already overcrowded prisons. Men and women were put in separate quarters. I had no way of knowing where they were keeping you. In my most terrifying visions, I saw my boys, still chained to the priest, rotting away in some foul, airless, rat-infested oubliette. It must have been the fetid stench of human excretions filling the air that knocked the breath out of me and hurled me into a black hole of oblivion for I don't know how long. In time I felt myself prodded back into semi-consciousness at the point of a lance. Shouts of "Get up!" and "On your feet!" reached my hearing as from far away. Although I have no recollection, I must have followed the command, for I found myself all of a sudden in a large high-vaulted hall.

There was much commotion. People were clustered around the space like spring shrubs. They spoke mostly in a hushed tone, but the hollowness of the room magnified their speech and turned the cavern into a veritable tower of Babel. A guard pushed me to look forward toward a huge rosette window through which the bright sunlight illuminated the room. I would have expected that these people would feel compelled to carry out their business in a more secretive, dusky manner. However, in this place at least, quite the opposite was the case. They apparently had no compunction about letting out what they were doing. In the middle of a long, carved table, flanked by more black-robed friars, sat a rather imposing figure, imposing by mere virtue of his sitting erect in an elaborately appointed high-back chair, the way I imagined a king to sit on his throne. He was clad all in purple velvet, but to my relief, he bore no resemblance at all to the fat churchman who had led our exodus from the village. That one was nowhere in evidence, likewise to my relief. This one was tall and slender and exhibited a courteous manner. His tone was gentle and unctuous as he begged me to approach the bench. After the emotional uproar of the past few days, his demeanor reassured me that I was not facing an enemy.

As the exchange between us progressed—he asking seemingly harmless questions and listening solicitously to my answers; I speaking freely, my tongue loosened without restraint—I was suddenly reminded of the priest and his similarly engaging ways. This was no casual chatter, I told myself. Where had my vow gone never to trust a Christian? Was I about to let myself be used again for some nefarious purpose? This surely must be a clever trap. As it turned out, this churchman's kindness had no other purpose than to elicit testimony from me to use against the Cathar heretics, especially against the priest. For a hundred years, the Church had attempted to uproot this challenge to its authority as the sole gateway to heaven and eternal bliss. But I had to convince him that I was not one of them first. A lone Jewess, I fathomed, was no threat to the almighty Church.

As I contemplated my situation and that of my sons, I saw an opening, an opportunity for striking a bargain. Believe me, my dear sons, I never had any forethought about acting as avenging angel toward the priest's doom. I knew the fate of those convicted of heresy—they always were convicted and put to death on the stake. I had no plans of being an instrument of the Church in sealing his fate. What was the Church to me? It was this same Church that had conspired with the king to rob the Jews and expel them from the kingdom of France. It was the Roman Church that had time and again incited violence against the Jews in every part of Christendom. No, I owed nothing to this authority. And while I despised with equal ardor the Cathar heresy, which denigrated and vilified our Holy Scriptures and traditions in even greater measure than the Church,

I could not completely separate myself from the priest. He was still the man I had loved, for whom I had sacrificed everything, and whose seed had born fruit in my womb. It was only when the time came, when I had to choose between him and my offspring, that I found I had no choice. Even then I did not do lightly what I had to do. In spite of the resentment I bore him, the fire of hatred his conduct had oftentimes enflamed in me, I had once been an indulgent slave to his will. In the end, when I stood among the spiteful rabble in the narrow streets of the town, watching him on the charette as it moved toward the center where the flames of the stake lapped heavenwards, ready to consume his earthly shell, my heart bled and my eyes overflowed with tears. Whether he took notice of me in the crowd, I could not tell. His head held high, he kept himself erect, unbending and unrepentant. Even in the coarse penitent's shirt of the condemned, he was master of his fate. I even felt a bit of pride nipping at my heart.

But I am getting ahead of myself. The interrogation dragged on for many days. The inquisitor probed every detail of my story with questions and more questions, gently goading me on. Was it pity for my fate that made him turn such a sympathetic ear? I doubted it then and doubt it now. But his motives did not matter to me. I answered willingly and eagerly. I felt the load of guilt that had oppressed me for so many years lifting from me. I began by relating how I came to this village with my father and brothers on our way across the mountains to Aragon, expelled from our homeland by order of the king of France for all Jews to leave the kingdom. The inquisitor was particularly inquisitive about the night and morning after at the priest's house. Heartened by his solicitous demeanor, I held nothing back. All that had been stowed inside of me came flooding forth like a mountain brook in the springtime. I told him of the priest's perfidy and confessed my weakness of the flesh. He tilted his head, ponderously leaning it on his left hand as he listened with great interest to my telling about the Jewish custom of mourning a defiled daughter as if she was dead. There was no way for me to ever go back to my people, I explained. Yet I clung to some of their customs. His eyes widened astonished when he heard how I had brought my sons into the covenant with the G-d of Abraham. Notwithstanding of what I knew to be his disdain for this Jewish custom, I could detect a measure of admiration for my bravery in the face of great odds.

Then we came to the true purpose of the interrogation. That a Jewess lived as a priest's concubine in a mountain village may have been of passing prurient interest, surely something out of the ordinary, but this man had a more serious purpose. The Church's unity and authority in Christendom, as he saw it, hung in the balance. So we skipped over some of the idle chatter.

"What did you observe during those years in the village?" he steered the conversation into the desired direction.

"Because I was a reviled outcast from my people and a despised outsider in the village, always the hunted so to speak, I had developed a keen sense of awareness of my surroundings."

"So what was it you observed?" He was getting impatient at this point. But I did not want to divulge anything without getting something in return. What I wanted was a promise that my sons would go free. I assured him that you had not been tainted by the Cathar heresy, that I had conveyed to you the Jewish faith as much as I was able to do so considering the circumstance. I knew very well that Jews were not held in high esteem, but this was a gamble I had to take. I assured him that the priest had taken little interest in instructing his sons in heretic teachings. He seemed satisfied with this statement and promised to leave you unscathed. I should just take you away when the trial was over and go somewhere far away, up in the mountains where we could build a new life.

Thereupon I told him about all the comings and goings in the shadows, the secret meetings, the whispers, the shady characters. I sensed something forbidden going on, but for quite some time, the meaning escaped me. The participants were all very cautious. In time, I came to realize that two parallel worlds existed side by side in this village: the everyday world moving on the surface in the daylight, as in any other village in the area; the other a nocturnal world existing underground, in dimly lit cellars and caves, behind locked doors and closed shutters. The nature of this was revealed to me much, much later. At first I thought these were smugglers since there was much cross-mountain trafficking connected with the great transhumance of people and livestock that took place in the autumn and spring. The religious nature of this business became clear to me only a few years ago when I noticed the priest's strange behavior. It was then that my curiosity was aroused and I found out that the priest was the ruler over both worlds, the day as well as the night. He was an anointed servant of the Church and a perfect of the Cathars. The inquisitor was strangely amused by the fact that this man's conduct did not fit in with either calling. I thought I even detected a flicker of admiration in the churchman's eyes for a man who could pull off such roguery.

As I mentioned, the interrogation went on and on, extending over several days. The inquisitor's appetite for the minutest detail was insatiable. However, since you are sufficiently aware of these, they need not be repeated here word for word. More important for the tale I want you to remember and never to forget is another important incident, an encounter that shook me to the depth of my soul. I have often spoken to you about a Jew from Germany named Baruch, whom they called le Teutonic, and the grave testimony he gave about the disaster that befell the Jews of Toulouse, the truth of which I was later able to ascertain. The heinous, utterly iniquitous nature of the acts he had witnessed, and barely escaped himself, compels me to write it down so that future generations will repeat this story, never to be forgotten, like the story of the Israelites' exodus from Egypt is retold every year at the Passover Seder.

To this day, my heart aches with sorrow and anguish, my thoughts are haunted by stories of the wave of violence that swept over the Jews of Toulouse and other Occitan communities only a few years after the king had invited them back to the kingdom of France. Many, it seems after all, had followed the call and rebuilt their lives and livelihoods in the cities. Did my father and brothers come back? I never was able to find out and will never know. If they had resettled in Toulouse, they would have been among the many victims of the massacre that occurred there. Every night, I pray and hope most fervently that they may have stayed in the safety of Iberia. What I do know is that a terrible massacre occurred in the city of Toulouse in the month of June of the year 1320. May this date be etched into the annals of Jewish history forever, never to be forgotten. I must now turn to what I learned while I was incarcerated in the prison of the Inquisition in the city of Pamiers in July of that year about the time of Tisha b'Av, the day when Jews mourn the destruction of the temple in Jerusalem. For the Jews of France, this date also marks their banishment from the kingdom in the year 1306.

As fate, or the inquisitor, would have it, I was separated from the other villagers and found myself placed in a cell next to that of this man Baruch whom they called le Teutonic. My life in the mountain village had shielded me, and kept me in ignorance, from most of what had gone on in the outside world. Until then, I knew very little about Crusades, the Christians' wars against Muslims to liberate the Holy Land. I remember overhearing my father speaking gravely of Christian fanatics and brutal massacres of Jews in the Empire and even in the holy city of Jerusalem, which the Christians conquered from Arab invaders. This couldn't happen in the kingdom of France, he would conclude. How he could be so sure of this, I never knew, especially since he had often spoken of events like the burning of the Jews of Blois as well as the burning of our holy books contained in the

Talmud in Paris. I heard him admonish my brothers to beware of the renegade, traitors like Nicolas Domin and Pablo Cristiani who spread lies about our people to curry favor with the Christians.

My father's admonishment came to my mind when I first laid eyes on this Baruch le Teutonic. Even though he was imprisoned, for some reason I decided to exercise caution, for he may have been placed there as a spy. What gave me pause was the fact that women and men were usually kept far apart in the dungeons of the Inquisition. Here I was put in a cell adjacent to one holding this man who turned out to be Jew. Separating us was a wall with an inset iron lattice, but standing on toes made communicating possible. I was even able to size him up as I strained to make him out in the dimly lit cavern. It had been almost a lifetime since I had laid eyes on a member of my people. Those who went in and out of my father's house, tall, upright men of proud bearing came to my mind. Their garments were of the finest quality when conducting business and finer still at synagogue on Shabbat. And who would not be impressed with the linen white attire they paraded on leisurely strolls along the river when they tossed their sins into the waters on the days of awe? To my child's fancy, they were nasim, *princes of ancient lineage, more ancient and magnificent than any progeny of the Capetians.*

This one, by contrast, was a most wretched specimen of the House of Israel. The sight of this crouching, unkempt fellow made me recoil with shame and disgust. Not only was his clothing coarse and ragged, he was covered with filth and boils and scabs of all sorts. His face was disfigured by deep cuts in his cheeks, and his forehead was encrusted with dirt and dried blood. His nose seemed to have been broken in several places. His voice was croaky like a frog's, and he spoke a heavily accented, broken Occitan mingled with expressions of what I presume came from the Germanic tongue. Some of his idioms I recognized as Hebrew, albeit with what was to my ears a garbled ring. At first, everything in me resisted to embrace him as one of us, meaning a fellow Jew. He was the figure of Job, and I denied him my pity. Then I remembered that it was I who no longer belonged to the people Israel; I was the outcast. Who was I to condemn and despise this man? Wasn't I the one who had forfeited the right to the finery of dignity and honor of my people? It was I who was reduced to wearing coarse, homespun clothing. It was I whose hands were rough and swollen, whose hair, once a lustrous crown of henna, hung about her face in dull, thin, graying strings. All this I had brought upon myself in a moment of carnal weakness. How ashamed was I when I learned the truth about my cellmate's misfortune. This man, Baruch, whom I was so quick to condemn, he too was once a prosperous merchant with far-flung commercial connections and enterprises, spanning from the Empire to Italy, Spain, and France. He had fallen on hard times, not for anything he had done, but because of the hatred that evildoers held against Jews.

The man I met in prison was an abject wretch. At first, there were faint mutterings seeping through the wall like the monotonous dripping of wine leaking from a tap. Through the lattice, I saw him curled up on a straw-strewn pallet. He seemed in the throes of a seizure-like tremor. His shivering body rocked back and forth. His lips moved feverishly. Gradually his utterances began to take on more coherence. I strained to listen for the local patois. To my surprise, the words that arose from this crouched figure were all too familiar to me. These were the words that had been singed indelibly into my brain on the day my father hurled them at me like a curse, the words that had haunted me ever since. Hearing this hymn to G-d's glory, which Jews pronounce numerous times a day, ironically also over the dead, once again tore the scab off my festering heart.

I pulled away and retreated to my own straw pallet. So he was a Jew. He was a Jew, obviously destitute and in pain. Who knows why he was incarcerated? Did he commit a crime or was he just caught like me with the heretics? I tried to push the thoughts from my mind. What did I have to do with him? I was no longer one of them. I had my own cross to bear, as the Christians say. I still had to assure the release of my sons. That was my goal, and nothing would distract me from it. The inquisitor had given his word, and I would give him no reason to go back on it.

The next day, when I returned to my cell from the inquiry, his face was pressed against the lattice. He was apparently waiting for me.

"You are a Jewess," he said in accented Occitan.

"What do you mean?" I replied. Was he a spy for the inquisitor? Was this some kind of trap? But the inquisitor already knew who I was.

"Just as I said: you are a Jewess," he stated as a matter of fact.

I already knew who he was since it would be not very likely for a Christian to say the Kaddish, certainly not with the kind of fervor I heard coming from his mouth. But how would he know anything about me? We had never spoken. I've heard it said that a Jew can always pick out one of his brethren in a crowd. But I had been living in the galut, cut off from my people for so long. Could it be that I still bore a certain mark? The fat churchman who had come to the village came to my mind. He seemed to have seen something that gave him pause in the fleeting moment when his eyes met mine. I shook off that unpleasant thought. More likely was that the inquisitor had spoken to him about me, I told myself. I had to be all the more on my guard. I searched for signs in his face. The bloodstained furrows made me cringe. But his eyes bore no malice, only a wistful gaze.

"How would you know?" My curiosity got the better of me.

"You said the Shema *last evening. It was soft. But I heard you. I saw you watching me through the lattice before. Now I am watching you."*

I was totally perplexed. How could he have heard me?

"So what is it to you?" I felt no kinship with this ragged human refuse.

"Nothing in particular. Just with so many Jews dead already, we share a certain fate in common."

He was surprised that I hadn't heard anything about what had been going on, especially in Toulouse where he had just come from. But elsewhere too, in Carcassonne, Verdun, Castelsarrasin, all along the Garonne River, in the entire Languedoc, he went on, Jews were being dragged from their homes, confronted with a choice to either accept the baptism or be killed on the spot.

"So who is doing this?" I felt a knot forming my stomach. "Was it the Church or the king's men?"

He assured me it was neither of these, at least not officially. On the contrary, the pope was trying to stop it and have the criminals brought to justice. There were some monks who were agitating the populace. And in many places, they were only too willing to lend a helping hand. The main perpetrators were bands of shepherds come from the north in Normandy.

"These are young boys turned brigands and murderers. They swarm over the countryside by the thousands, presumably on their way to the Holy Land. I was put in prison for my safety. Also, the inquisitor wanted to take down an eyewitness account of what had happened in Toulouse the previous month."

He had mentioned Toulouse twice. My sense of foreboding that something terrible happened there was soon confirmed.

As Baruch related it, in Toulouse the outrages reached their pinnacle. But many other Jewish communities had been decimated by the savage hordes along their path of destruction as well. In Castelsarrasin, two hundred Jews had fallen victim to a murderous rampage. The Jews who had found refuge behind the walls of the castle at Verdun-sur-Garonne took their own lives and those of their children when the mob breached the fortress. The carnage continued in Toulouse. Baruch estimated that there were more than one hundred killed within one hour. Their houses were ransacked and their possessions pillaged. In every community and town they entered, these shepherds found support and sustenance for their murderous intent from local citizens and friars of various orders. The Mendicants especially were active in inciting the town's people. Everywhere, Jews were seized and told to either submit to baptism or face death. Most cleaved to Kiddush Hashem and chose the path of martyrdom. Some became fainthearted in the face of all the slaughter around them and submitted to the baptismal. Everywhere, in every town where the shepherds sowed their destruction, the local populace hailed the malefactors as the pavements ran with Jewish blood.

My friend Baruch—he did become my friend—did not have the mettle of a martyr. So he said with great regret. Three times he faced the choice, and each time his courage left him and he chose life, albeit life with dishonor. These were his words, for his soul was racked with remorse. "It is better," he admitted, "to die than to abandon the faith of our fathers, many of whom sacrificed their lives for Kiddush Hashem." He continued for a while heaping reproach on himself for his faintheartedness instead of going the path so many of our people had gone before. My heart ached with pity seeing him thus rueful and filled with shame. I could not help but feel a certain kinship with him. In his ears still rang the screams and agony of the dying, he said. During the night, his moans and screams that haunted his dreams pierced the wall.

What would I have done had I been confronted with such a choice? I asked myself. Would I have had the strength to resist the temptation to save myself? What would I have done had I been witness to scenes of murder and mayhem as Baruch described. What would I have done? I am certain what my father would have done. My brothers, they too would never have submitted to the waters. They were unwavering in their faith and righteousness. As I was lying awake in my cell, I prayed that they may be safe. I prayed and hoped with all my being that they had not returned to the perfidious town of Toulouse. Baruch had assured me he knew of no Don Elazar de Sola or any other Jews by that surname. As a cloth merchant himself, he was acquainted with everybody in that trade. Yes, he told me, the mansion in the cul-de-sac of the Jewish quarter was still standing, but it was still unoccupied.

My thoughts mingled with what Baruch had told me of the crusading mob's invasion of the Jewish quarter and the events so many years ago when we were roused from our sleep in the middle of the night by hammering on our doors accompanied by shouts of "In the name of the King!" But back then the king's soldiers proceeded in an orderly manner. By order of the king, there was no pillaging. The savagery of these shepherds come from the north and armed with all manner of illegal weapons like swords, long knives, lances, and javelins was beyond compare. Again the question "What would I have done?" would not let go of me. What would I have done had I, like Baruch, been torn from my bed without time for getting into proper dress and dragged by two clerics to the town's cathedral where they doused me with their holy water. True it is that most Jews did not yield to force. But I cannot find it in my heart to condemn him. He had seen the cathedral square strewn with the murdered, mutilated bodies of his kin. He had seen men's throats being cut in front of his eyes just to demonstrate what awaited him if he did not yield. He himself had suffered kicks and blows that knocked him almost unconscious and left deep gashes on his forehead. One particular blow, he said, felt as if his eyes were going to pop out of their sockets. How would I have responded? Women and children, Baruch told me, were not even given a choice. Most were put to the sword immediately in cold blood.

"G-d kept you alive for a purpose," I tried to console him. "He wanted you to be a witness, to give testimony to human perfidy."

The thought had come to me during the night. There was a reason why he had survived all those ordeals. I truly believed it then, and I believe it now.

"I believe that G-d did not want you to die," I told him. "Listen to me! You are a witness. G-d wants you to bear witness to the horrors you saw. He wants you to tell the world what happened to the Jews at the hands of a roving band of Christian religious fanatics. Don't you see? It is G-d's will. Think of it this way," I insisted when I saw him shake his head. "Why is the inquisitor so interested in recording your story? Unless he is carrying out G-d's will? Your testimony will be inscribed in the registers of the Church where it will be eternalized for generations. The inquisitor is the tool, and you are the messenger. G-d chose you both so these evil deeds will never be forgotten. So the outcry of Hevel's blood to the heavens shall be heard all over the face of the earth."

He still shook his head, and I don't know if he found any solace in my words. I will never know if this thought brought some measure of comfort to his tormented soul. What happened to him later is likewise unknown to me. I hope he found peace within himself and the world. I was released from this inquisitor's dungeon not long thereafter. The inquiry of the heretics was soon concluded. I doubt it was my word alone that sealed their fate. The priest and his faithful band of followers were handed over to the civilian authorities for trial before the magistracy without my testimony. The verdict of guilty and sentence of death at the stake was no doubt a foregone conclusion.

Yet, the inquisitor was a man of his word. He kept his promise to me. You, my sons, were released from prison on the day your father was executed. As G-d had commanded Abraham, he told me to leave this country and start life anew somewhere in a lofty place. Together we set out in search of our promised land, a place far off the stage of human folly, a place that was untouched by human hatred and intrigue, a place far removed from the battlefields of cruelty and treachery. We found such a place here in the mountains, in this virgin mountain valley high up near the clouds where we can be free all the days of our lives. Remember the covenant, remember the Sabbath, and remember the liberation of the Jewish people from slavery in Egypt.

"The Lord is my shepherd, I shall not want; He maketh me lie down in green pastures; He leadeth me beside the still waters; He restoreth my soul."

Here ended Dina Miryam's chronicle. The Psalmist's poem was cited in Hebrew. We sat silently, almost dumbfound, unsure what to do or say. Words failed to express the emotions that engulfed us as Dina's words sank into our souls. Slowly I closed the codex. I lifted it to my lips and handed it to Etoile. She enclosed it in her arms and kissed it with the fervor I had seen Sephardic women embrace the Torah scroll.

"What about the shepherds?" Etoile asked. "I've heard of the rampages and massacres, but not in such a direct way."

"It's historic. The Pastoureaux or Pastorelli movements are historically well documented. So is their anti-Jewish rioting. There were several such movements of very young people driven by religious fanaticism who decided to go on crusade to the Holy Land in the course of the centuries. They originated in Normandy, near Mont Saint Michel, from where they went to Paris and then south. They caused the greatest damage in Aquitaine. One occurred during the reign of Louis IX in the mid-thirteenth century. That one had the full support of Blanche de Castile, the king's mother. She was a very pious woman, like her son Saint Louis—whom Dina calls the sainted Louis. The most murderous outrages against the Jews were committed during the second shepherd crusade in 1320, much as Dina describes. Not only did they murder and pillage, they also burned and destroyed debt records, bills of exchange various town folk had signed with Jewish moneylenders."

"Why would the shepherds, presumably illiterate, be interested in that?"

"The records were most likely destroyed by the debtors themselves. Self-interest was probably their motive in welcoming and supporting the marauders."

"Nothing new under the sun, then as now! What about this renegade Baruch?"

"There actually was such a figure called Baruch le Teutonic. His testimony before the inquisitor of Pamiers about the great calamity that befell the Jews of the Languedoc is preserved in the Church archives. He converted, or was forced to convert, to Christianity three times. We know he relapsed twice, if that's the right word, and returned to the Jewish fold each time. Eventually all traces of him dissolve in the sand. Maybe he went back to the Empire. Not that Jews were any safer there."

"How did it all end?"

"The papacy was actually very much in uproar over the rampage and killings ostensibly committed in revenge of the blood of Jesus Christ. The pope in Avignon sent several sharply worded missives that establish his knowledge of the complicity of local clerics and notables. Even the monarchy got uneasy about thousands of out-of-control juveniles—most between fourteen and sixteen, what we call teenagers—running amok from one end of the kingdom to the other. The Jews seem to have been their primary targets, but they also burned châteaux in true French peasant tradition. Eventually, most of the guilty were brought to justice and punished by the Church and royal authorities working together. Even though, as you know, sporadic violence against Jews continued in France throughout the century, until they were expelled for good from the kingdom by Charles VI in the 1390s."

I pondered for a while the implications of this sad chapter, one of many in the history of our people. But my historian's heart could not help but feel elated at having found what we call in academic jargon a primary source dating to the actual time of the events. It was almost like a miracle.

"They called this place Valladine, the valley of Dina," Etoile broke into my thoughts. "Funny that the meaning of the name did not occur to us before. It's so obvious."

"Valladine!" I jumped up with a start. "Nina! What if it's already too late?"

"Too late for what?" Etoile refused to lose her cool.

"Too late to save her from whatever! You never know what these medieval feudalists are capable of."

"That's a strange thing to say for a medievalist." In my anxiety over Nina's fate, I failed to see the irony of what Etoile was alluding to.

"How can you be so calm and collected, so damn level-headed?"

"I'm as concerned as you are, but tonight, after a long day of keeping our noses to the grindstone, there's nothing we can do. Tomorrow, yes. How about a quiet celebration of our achievement first? We are entitled, you know. We've made it. Do you appreciate what you have accomplished? Maybe we should say a *Shehecheyanu*?"

I smiled. She always knew the right thing to say. Yes, this was surely an occasion to thank G-d for having brought us to this point.

Without Etoile, without her intelligence and knowledge, her talent for organization, her presence of mind, the calming effect of her ministrations, this project might have been arrested in its infancy.

"But let's not forget Nina's midwifery," I said out loud to distract my mind from what I feared was becoming a fixation on the female qualities of my collaborator. "It was she who liberated this baby from centuries of darkness and brought it into the light of the modern era. Our job was nurturing it and seeing it through to maturity."

"My, my, aren't we waxing metaphoric?"

"We still have to translate it into English and French," I said sheepishly.

"Everything in its own good time," Etoile admonished. "Tomorrow we'll make copies of the manuscript—I'd say at least half a dozen—and put one in a safe deposit box at the bank. The rest we'll take with us for distribution among the Valladinians, whoever might be interested up there in that presumed kingdom in the sky. Then we'll clean up this place and head for the mountains. First we have to find this place called Oloron Sainte Marie, Nina's starting point. We'll take it from there. Play it by ear, as you Americans say."

I nodded, willingly leaving all planning to her. As she had done so often during these months together, she filled two glasses halfway with some Napoléon and handed one to me. The amber gleam from the snifters put us both in a pensive mood. My thoughts wandered to the future. One day this would all be over. Our being together would end. Etoile would return to her own life, most likely to that auto mechanic or some other sporty young man. She would embark on an academic career for which she was eminently qualified. Maybe I would write her a letter of recommendation. Where would I be? The thought of returning to Chicago gave me the willies. I had burnt my bridges. There was nothing and no one to get back to. Of course, I would be busy for quite a while with translating and publishing Dina's chronicle, as we now called it. Maybe we would collaborate on the French edition. It came to me then as a revelation that I just could not imagine life without Etoile.

Suddenly I felt a singe on my arm. I twitched and involuntarily pulled away. It was Etoile's hand. Why should this casual gesture that was a natural part of her all of a sudden make me break out in a panic?

"Tomorrow is tomorrow," she picked up the thread where she had left off what seemed an hour ago. "Tonight," she said in her matter-of-fact way, "tonight we make love." I must have really looked stupefied or just plain stupid. "Haven't you ever thought about it?" she asked.

I nodded and finally got myself to say: "Frequently, and you?"

"All the time," she replied.

My momentary fear that I might have forgotten what to do was quickly dispersed. With Etoile, it was all so incredibly easy. I guess it's true what they say about riding a bicycle, I thought as we curled up like two spoons; once you know it, you'll never unlearn. You may learn a few more tricks, but you'll always remember the basics.

On the way to the bank the next morning, Etoile's Quat-Chevaux gave up the ghost. I didn't tell her of my sense of relief since I had feared all along that this jalopy would not be up to handling the mountainous terrain of our destination. She shed a few tears over the demise of her beloved "puppy." Then she called her Tunisian master mechanic. He arrived *sur-le-champ*, as they say in France, with his tow truck and hauled the carcass to wherever old cars go to die. He also arranged for us to get a new car, not really new, but a more recent model Renault that would hopefully be up to the task of scaling the heights and rounding the serpentines that lay ahead.

With this crisis overcome, we were finally ready to embark on our journey for the great unkown. Etoile seemed to hesitate though.

"What is it now?" I asked impatiently.

"If you don't mind," she replied, "I think it would be better if Armand drove us as far as Oloron Sainte Marie"

"And why is that?" I could barely conceal my irritation or whatever it was that aroused my displeasure.

"*Parce que*!" she drew out the words as if she was explaining something to a clueless child. "Because it wouldn't be advisable, I think, to leave a car parked in a small town for an indeterminate period of time." That, of course, made sense. So we set out: Armand at the wheel and Etoile in the front seat cheerfully chatting away, and I stewing with pulled up knees in the back seat. When we reached our destination, the first leg of our journey, he departed dutifully again *sur-le-champ*. We tried to find the small pension Nina had mention but to no avail. It might have gone out of business, which did not seem likely since the town was a flourishing starting point for hikers and pilgrims. Maybe the landlady had just had enough of mysterious foreigners and closed shop, Etoile suggested, tongue in cheek. So we settled into a small hotel. Etoile made a list of all the things—gear, equipment, clothing, and provisions—we would need for survival in the wilderness.

"Before we dash headlong into the backwoods," she proposed, "we may do well to pick up Nina's letter where we left off reading. It might give us some clues as to how to proceed and what turns to take," Etoile suggested. Once again, I was in awe of that woman's sagacity.

Nina's Progress 3

In mid-April, the long awaited spring began to display its first flush of bloom at last. It glorified the parks and walkways I had strolled along so many times when trees and bushes still stood in their denuded wintry state. The sun's glowing warmth signaled me to end my long hibernation in this little town. Charming as it was, I was ready to move on. The mountains beckoned. It was time for me to heed the call.

Yet another snag came up. The Easter holiday delayed my departure for another few days. The stores in town were closed, and I could not risk a long, uncertain hike without an adequate stock of provisions and other necessities. I decided to sleep in late on that Easter Sunday morning, but I was thrown out of bed by an ear-shattering glockenspiel ringing out from every bell tower far and wide. To the townspeople's ears it was probably music supreme, a jubilant symphony of bells announcing the resurrection of their messiah. My landlady greeted me at the bottom of the stairs with eyebrows raised and a stern disapproving look at my outfit of blue jeans and a sweater. She herself was a picture perfect example of haberdasherly primness. Her holiday attire surpassed even her usual Sunday finest. She was decked out in a gentian blue dress with starched white lace trim, shiny white gloves and patent-leather shoes, and a coquettish little cornflower blue hat with dark blue netting. Her left arm held a white little boxy leather handbag, and under her right arm, her prayer book was tightly pressed against her, in black leather binding and gold trim.

"Breakfast is served," she said with pursed lips. My cheerfully polite "Good morning" she left unacknowledged. She rushed out, leaving behind a delicate scent of lavender. All I could do was shrug. The enticing aroma of fresh brewed coffee and baked apple scones and pound cake drew me to the breakfast room. I served myself and settled down by the window. I took slow, pensive sips of my coffee wondering what was behind the lady's sudden about-face. During the six weeks of my stay with her, our rapport had been cordial though not particularly intimate. I am sure she had her suspicions about what I was doing in this town for so long without any discernible purpose, but as a businesswoman she wisely refrained from prying. I was a paying guest, and there weren't many others. My eyes caught sight of her as she crossed the street and melted with a flock of churchgoing women, old and young, girls of all ages, decked out in similarly festive garb. Of course, the gentlemen, who sauntered behind, wore their finest too, only theirs was in more subdued colors.

A little later, I went out for a walk in the park. It felt good to fill my lungs with spring air even though there still was a nip, and I was glad to be wearing a sweater. The bells kept on ringing, though more intermittently by then. I suddenly became aware that I was alone in the park. I was the only outsider. The entire town was apparently at Mass. Joyous singing resounded from the churches. I sat down on a bench and fed a few crumbs from the cake I had brought along to the birds pecking around in the grass. Song and bells clashed in my head. It was the feast of the resurrection. Just a few days before, the same town's people had mourned the death of a Jew who was crucified by the Romans in the province of Judaea two thousand years ago. This Jew they call the messiah. His mother was a virgin. According to their teaching, the purpose of his coming was to die for the sins of mankind which would thereby be redeemed. Yet until not so long ago, the living Jews in most European communities were confined to their ghettos during Holy Week, presumably to protect them from the wrath of the Christian faithful who considered them as Christ-killers. In even earlier times, various towns had time-honored rituals of letting out their frustrations on the Jews in their midst. All involved violent assaults and often bloodshed. There was no logic to any of this. Just as there was no logic to the blood libels hurled at the Jews in various places around the time of Passover. From medieval Würzburg in the Empire and East Anglian Norwich to modern-day Hungary, Jews had been accused of murdering Christian children for the purpose of using their blood in the baking of matzoth. One of the most vicious blood libels occurred in nineteenth-century Damascus over the disappearance of a monk. How many Jews all over the world had to pay with their lives for this lie! I don't have to tell you two about all this, but this was the path my thoughts were taking on that morning.

My mind began to wander to Passovers past, which often coincided with Holy Week and the Easter festival. This was the first year I would not sit at a Seder table with my family and friends. For the first time in my life, I would not participate in the telling of the story of the liberation of the Israelite slaves from Egyptian bondage. Even when I was already grown up, I was the one who had to recite the four questions, since I was always the youngest. I felt a pang in my heart. Who would be with my mother? Yes, she did have friends and a community, but no family members would be with her since the passing of my father and aunt and uncle. Questions and doubts concerning what I was about to do started to rise in my mind. What was I doing? Where was I going? Was I really following my heart as I had told myself? Was I prepared in all earnestness to cut myself off, not only from my life in America, but from my life as a Jew? For whatever or wherever this Valladine was, I could hardly expect to find fellow Jews in that place. Alphonse de Sola, the man whom I was ready to follow into uncharted territory, had shown very little empathy for the murder of the Israeli hostages at the Munich Olympics. I remembered very well how he shrugged this atrocity off as just another violent episode in a world of ceaseless strife, a world he despised. Maybe I should reconsider. There was still time to turn back. Suddenly the whole undertaking appeared to me as a lark, a mishegas, *as my mother would say. I don't know how long I wandered about. I was unaware when it was that song and bells had ceased and the sun had begun its descent behind the mountains. In the end, my mind was made up. I would return to America. No, I wouldn't return to academic life. I had definitely soured on that. There were other things I could do. I could buy a farm in South Jersey, breed dogs or raise chickens, plant a garden. Or I could write a novel. And why not do both? Yes, I told myself, I would pack and leave early in the morning. I felt sobered, my mind cleared as if I had awoken from a delusion. My soul was cleansed as after immersion in a purifying bath. A cloud had been lifted, and in the distance a light appeared like a guiding star.*

Night was falling when I returned to the pension. I had not felt so elated in a long time. My heart beat with fresh determination and courage. I would let go of this childish obsession with a place that, for all I knew, didn't even exist. I would go home. It was then, as I got closer to the house, that I saw two huge white puffs curled up on the front porch. When they noticed me, they rose in unison and lined up at the entrance steps like the lions in front of the New York Public Library. Their growling did not deter me from passing by them and entering. I found Alphonse de Sola in the kitchen chatting, laughing with the landlady over coffee and cake. I had gone through much inner turmoil, had turned my whole life upside down with longing for this man and his mountain utopia. Now he had arrived at a most inopportune moment. His presence irritated the heck out of me, most of all because I felt my knees sagging. I had finally convinced myself that I was chasing a chimera, and now this chimera was standing before me in the flesh. He was not quite as big and bulky as I remembered him, though still tall and muscular. Instead of the white lambswool fleece, he wore a waist-length gray jacket and knee breeches of what they call durable fabric (maybe worsted twill, or whatever), and knee-high boots. He looked like an alpine character out of William Tell, with a beret of course. His grizzled beard had disappeared, and he was merely sporting a thin moustache. All in all, he was much more physically appealing and much less the Sasquatch I remembered. Maybe that's what made me cave in, succumb so to speak, to his charm. (I know how much Henner hates purple prose; so please forgive me for resorting to such.)

Charming he was, though without being tacky or calculating. He got straight to the point, skipping long, drawn-out mating rituals. It seemed the most natural thing in the world, to him at least, that he should follow me upstairs (with just a brief "excuse us" to the hostess) and without much ado make love to me. Hadn't I come from far away for just that? Of course, I didn't know anything about Dina Miryam and her story at the time, but thinking back now, I am struck by the similarities—maybe I was destined to reenact the drama of her seduction, or was it rape? Only I cannot deny that I was a more willing participant and Alphonse had nothing of a demonic lover about him like the priest as described by Dina. Yet, like her, I was lost from that day forward, though without being plagued by her medieval guilt over the weakness of the flesh. I knew then that there was no turning back for me. My resolve vanished. I would follow Alphonse to the top of the highest mountain wherever he would lead me. None of the urbane Upper West Side Casanovas, with their adroit moves and techniques, their artifices, their gauged foreplay routines, came even close. The sexual revolution that had broken out then in the precincts of academe was a total sham by comparison. It was probably also on that first night that I conceived my firstborn son. Fumbling around with a modern invention like a diaphragm would have been simply, shall I say, anachronistic. Then there was the most amazing, I must say also most pleasing, discovery I made during this night. Alphonse, the primitive mountain man and lover sans pareil, had one thing in common with his predecessors; my lover was circumcised. Bingo! I told myself, followed by a Hallelujah!

The day after I settled the tab with the landlady, avoiding her piercing eyes, I went into town to stock up on provisions and other necessities. For some reason, Alphonse preferred not to be seen either with me or just in general around town. We agreed to rendezvous near the spot where the Grande Randonnée started its ascent into the mountains. As I left the general store, I noticed the pesky police chief stationed across the street. Although I tried to avoid making eye contact, I felt his eyes clearly fixed on me. Maybe the landlady had alerted him, had told him about my visitor and that I was leaving town. There certainly was no crime in that, I told myself. France was a free country. But I underestimated the small-town mentality, which is probably the same everywhere. Strangers, and especially those who hang about too long, always become subject to suspicion.

I stuffed my belongings into my backpack, and as I struggled to slip it on my back, I felt a hand on the straps. "I think you could use some help," he said. I thanked him, straightened up, and prepared to walk away.

"Where to?" he called after me. I had no choice but to turn around and say as politely as possible: "Hiking in the mountains. Spring has finally come."

"You waited a long time," he stated.

"Yes, it was too dangerous before." The chitchat made me nervous, but he was not letting me go yet, and I didn't dare be rude. He could easily make up some charge and put me in jail.

"Let me introduce myself," he said, extending his hand. "I am Inspector Fauré. You are American?"

I shook his hand briefly and nodded but didn't give my name in return.

"You are hiking alone?" he continued what now seemed to me an interrogation.

"I am meeting with a guide," I said, not wanting to be caught in a lie in case the landlady had been tattling.

"You have to be careful. The mountains are treacherous and infested with bandits. It's not unusual to have accidents; even murders can occur from time to time. Not all guides are trustworthy. I can recommend a reliable local guide who knows the mountains and their dangers very well."

"This one came highly recommended."

"What is his name? Maybe I know him." My discomfort level had reached a breaking point. I was ready to ask whether I was under criminal investigation when the silhouette of Alphonse appeared at the edge of the square. He looked around and then approached us with large, hasty strides.

"I thought you had forgotten our appointment," he said.

"Is this your guide?" said the inspector laughing, nervously it seemed to me. "Why didn't you say so? Alphonse de Sola is, of course, the very best. Nobody knows the mountains better."

"Inspector, you have made us lose precious time already," Alphonse said, playfully wagging his finger at the policeman. "We'd better be on our way now." He took my backpack and steered me away from the inquisitive inspector toward the road leading out of town. Somehow

I couldn't help but feel the inspector's eyes piercing my back for a long time.

If you are gleaning this letter for hints how to get to Valladine, you will be disappointed. Despite a few trips back and forth, I could never tell you anything about which path to follow. Alphonse always took me on what seemed a roundabout way, different every time. No matter how hard I have tried to commit certain landmarks to memory, I never found them again afterwards. This much I can tell you: from Oloron Sainte Marie we walked a short distance, maybe a mile, along the Grand Randonnée. Then we turned left onto a narrow overgrown path. From there our itinerary kept changing direction from east to south, and south to east. The way I could tell was by the position of the sun.

Alphonse blazed the trail. Without saying a word, he stomped ahead. He tramped down wild underbrush, making it easier for me to pass through the thicket. Frequently our path was intersected by rushing brooks swollen by the melting snow and ice. They tore down the mountainsides, and in several places the torrents made the crossing so impassible for me he had to carry me across. At nightfall we set up camp in a willow copse next to a waterfall. Very romantic! I don't know what we would have done had I not brought a pup tent and warm blankets. There was still a thin sheet of snow on the ground, and temperatures dipped during the night to below freezing. For all I knew, my mountain man had made no provisions for overnight shelter or food for that matter. We covered vast expanses of greening meadows. Shepherds and livestock hadn't come back from the southern flanks yet. For a brief moment, I wondered how on earth he had found out that I had returned and was waiting in that particular place. But the steady ascent of the terrain took its toll on my breathing. It was hardly the time for asking questions or even just conversing. Then I simply forgot to ask and it didn't matter much anymore. If I ever thought about it later, I just attributed it to some extrasensory perception he and his dogs seemed to have for tracking the presence of friends and foes.

At a certain altitude, the air became so thin I had a brief fainting spell, forcing us to pause on the shore of a beautiful glacier lake longer than he wanted to. All along, I had noticed an unexpected restiveness about him. There was obviously another side to his outwardly self-possessed calm disposition. He frequently cast a squinting look backward. He scanned the terrain as if he feared we were being followed. In fact, that was exactly what he was afraid of, as I found out later, even though the dogs would have alerted him at the first sign of the presence of strangers. There was a reason he did not want to be seen with me in town. He took the chance, as he explained later, only when he saw me with the police chief, which he rightly presumed to be an interrogation from which I was unable to disentangle myself. He knew Fauré's persistent ways. This was also the reason we had to take a roundabout way to Valladine. Of course, for all I knew, he could have been leading me on a tour of the moon. All I could think was, what have I gotten myself into? *And yet, I felt secure in the company of this man. It was as if he was my besherter. Then again, how could he be?*

Let me jump ahead from here, for this is all I can tell you about the itinerary to Valladine. To find it, you will have to rely on the shepherds and on Alphonse's sense of sniffing out the blood of an Englishman, or Ame-ri-can in this case. We just tramped on and on, higher and higher until we reached a narrow gorge from which issued a torrential stream. We entered and made our way along a narrow path under overhanging rocks. My old fear of closed spaces made itself felt. Slowly we edged along. Alphonse clutched my hand tightly with his big paw.

"It's just like this in the spring," he explained. "The bed is dry in summer."

If he meant to reassure me, it didn't work. Finally we came to the end of the gorge and walked out into a funnel-shaped, narrow clearing cut into towering boulders. A waterfall cascading from high above was feeding the stream we had just left behind us in the gorge. I looked around to see where we could possibly go from there. My claustrophobia acted up some more. Not behind the waterfall, *I thought. It's too much like the movies! But sure enough, Alphonse led the way directly into the cascading waters and into another gorge behind. This time we took only a few steps before the landscape opened up wide before us. We halted at the top of a ledge and looked down at a valley of breathtaking beauty sunken into a trough of gray cliffs that seemed to have been scooped out of the mountaintop by a divine hand.*

Here it was, spread out before my eyes: Valladine, my Shangri-La! A panorama of peace and contentment bathed in sunlight under a bright blue sky! I followed Alphonse as in a dream. We walked through the dark brown earth of freshly ploughed fields and over emerald meadows sprinkled with yellow and blue spring flowers on which grazed flocks of sheep. In the distance, red-brick rooftops hinted at the presence of clusters of human habitations. I breathed in deeply and out again, in and out. The thin mountain air entranced my senses such that I momentarily forgot the companion who had brought me to this place of fantasy.

"We must first call on the seneschal." His sonorous voice startled me out of my reverie without understanding what he was saying.

"The seneschal?" I knew, of course, what a seneschal was but didn't realize that there were still people around holding this Ancien Régime *title. There was much else I didn't know. I had no idea how much there was for me to learn, things and customs we would call anachronistic, passé, archaic, outdated, maybe antediluvian, but that's what Valladine was and is all about. I felt my historian's blood*

getting fired up. What greater joy can there be for those of us digging around in the past than to uncover a living laboratory such as this? I was not there, of course, for sociological or historical research. The question of what my purpose actually was, why I was really there, came to haunt me much later. At this moment, I was still enchanted by all the new impressions and quaint customs. And, of course, I was madly in love with Alphonse.

"Yes, he's my older brother and ruler of our sénéchaussée.*" I couldn't believe my ears. Seneschal?* Sénéchaussée? *I knew these terms from history books. Pretty quaint to my mind.*

The first lesson I learned was that this mountain utopia was ruled by an oligarch addressed by the title "Seneschal." The incumbent was Raymond de Sola, older brother of my beloved. The de Solas had been the ruling family for centuries, I was told. Guilhem de Sola, the second brother, is a "viguier," *another outmoded medievalism, while Alphonse, the youngest, is called* "sous-viguier." *None of these titles have anything to do with their original historical designation for royal emissaries in a particular region. Here they constitute an honest-to-goodness old-fashioned oligarchy. The seneschal is the supreme ruler, the top honcho, so to speak. In this case, I should add, a benevolent despot, but despot nonetheless.*

My first encounter with him turned out to be quite pleasant. He welcomed me literally with open arms. The Valladinians are a very demonstrative people who do not beat around the bush, as I had experienced already in body and soul. He had been informed that I was indeed the little girl he helped bring into this world some thirty years prior. It gave me a comforting feeling to be recognized as a native-born Valladinian. He was robed in a long, velvet, black gown with wide-slashed sleeves. His cap was likewise of black velvet with a golden tassel, academic mortarboard style. His brother Guilhem, the viguier, *wore similarly shaped garments in scarlet red. These sartorial touches reminded me of the pictures of fifteenth-century French nobility.* Les très riches heures du Duc de Berry *comes to mind; maybe not quite as sumptuous but close. At any rate, these duds stood in sharp contrast to the plain shepherd's wear Alphonse seemed to favor. I saw him later a few times in shiny green velvet in the course of official duties of which he acquitted himself, however, quite hastily.*

The second lesson I learned was that even the clear sky paradise is not without clouds brewing overhead. As history teaches us, despotic regimes, especially in the form of nepotism, will breed discontent among the churls. For every Moses and Aaron there is a Korach who will attract followers to his rebellion. My first encounter, better even face-off, with the Kohatites of Valladine occurred during the first communal meal I attended. Alphonse had warned me of the intrigues of this clan named Lunel. They live across the river that dissects the valley, but once a week, every Friday evening, the entire community assembles in the grand dining hall. To be absent without good reason was an almost unforgivable offense, though I had the distinct feeling that most everybody of the roughly four hundred souls in this village wanted to be there. My first impression of the seating arrangement—long tables and benches in a quadrangle—was that it is deliberately confrontational. The table along which the de Solas are ensconced is elevated on a platform facing down on the Lunels' table directly opposite. The flanking tables are populated by what one might call the common folk.

Of greater interest to me during my first attendance were the rituals framing this communal dinner, because some of them immediately set off a bell of familiarity, yet were eerily strange at the same time. Overall I noted a distinct kibbutz atmosphere of conviviality. This impression was further reinforced as I got to know the village and its customs better. A medieval kibbutz, to be sure, based on a fixed hierarchical structure of heredity rather than on socialist seniority.

The first order of business involved the seneschal chanting a blessing over the wine in some garbled language, presumably Occitan. (The local cru is truly an acquired taste; my palate was never able to adapt to its vinegariness.) The entire assembly, arranged according to social class, rose, seconded the blessing, and shouted something that sounded to me like "nastroviye" *but most assuredly wasn't, and then poured the ruby red down the hatch like a good single malt Scotch. By the way, the women, except for the members of the ruling house, which strangely included me, were not seated at the tables. It was their job next to wheel in huge, delicious smelling braided breads. (I think you get the picture why I was sitting there* bouche bée.*) Well, the seneschal lifted one of the huge loaves and shouted what apparently was a blessing or maybe an offering to the gods. He broke off a chunk so huge it made his cheeks bulge as he stuffed it into his mouth, whereupon everybody followed suit. While the chewing was going on, I wondered whether this was a religious ritual or just a gluttonous local custom. (Remember this was before I knew anything about the founding mother.) It was hard to discern what kind of religion, if any, they were following. Later I was told that they believed in Christianity and followed the pope (hard to believe) but had their own rituals and customs (that was clear to see). The seneschal functions as high priest and judge and is assisted by his brothers, the* viguier *and* sous-viguier *respectively. You can see I am having fun with these highfalutin titles.*

The highlight of the evening's festivities is the lighting of candles. You must remember that there is neither electricity nor natural gas on this mountain. All lighting comes from candles and torches; stoves and ovens are fed with wood and dung. Nevertheless, on Friday evenings, thirty-six tall candles are set up in the round inside the quadrangle of the tables. After lighting them, the women wail what sounds like a plaint song from a medieval passion play or a chorus of a Greek tragedy. Why so somber on what should be a joyous occasion, I still don't know. Later I had occasion to attend several funerary rites where the dirges the women chanted were of a similarly plaintive tonality. There's a little bit of everything, or one might say different strands are woven together into an idiosyncratic pattern.

Let me just briefly tell you about what happened after this very sumptuous first repast at which I was present. It will give you an idea of the feuds that, as Alphonse tells me, have been simmering for generations between the de Solas and the Lunels and on occasion will burst into an open fracas. On that evening, the strife was occasioned by my presence. We had just finished some sweet entremêts, *following a dinner of mutton and fowl roasted on flaming spits. "No roast pig?" I asked Alphonse, who assured me that pork was strictly forbidden. "We are shepherds," he said, "not pig farmers." I nevertheless pushed my portions of the meat furtively onto Alphonse's plate and nibbled on some roast potatoes and onions. Suddenly the angry voice of the head of the Lunel clan called out to the seneschal. This much I understood. The latter's face turned furiously red as he shouted something back. The seneschal and I had just been engaged in pleasant small talk, in the course of which he apparently sought to satisfy his curiosity about America. I tried to answer his questions as politely as I could. It was hard for me to see a despotic ruler behind his gracious, affable manner, and I was just beginning to feel, if not at home yet, at least at ease in this very strange world.*

Beatrice, the seneschal's consort—that's the title of the wives—explained to me in perfect French, I even thought to detect a Parisian intonation, what the shouting was about.

"Seneschal! What about the strange woman in our midst?" Lunel's voice reverberated in the vaulting hall.

"She's our guest and the future consort of the sous-viguier*!" Raymond shouted back. "And now hold your peace!"*

But Pierre Lunel, the head of the clan, did not hold his peace, nor did his myrmidons. I heard some clanking that sounded like sabre-rattling, and in fact that's what it was. Did I mention that these villagers are all armed to the teeth? Mostly, they carry shotguns and pistols in case an outsider should get too close to their valley. The lookouts who are always surveying the terrain also have huge binoculars. Very modern and unmedieval! Where they get this equipment, I couldn't tell at first. Obviously they do have contact with the outside world.

But I digress. On festive occasions, such as the weekly communal dinner, the menfolk mostly, but some of the women as well, strut about girded with swords. This is an interesting example of how two equally armed feuding parties keep each other in a deadlock. Here the feud between the farming Lunels and the herding de Solas has apparently been going on for many generations, maybe centuries, over some perceived wrong one party did to the other and vice versa without anybody remembering the exact wrongdoing. Strange how history keeps repeating itself! Different mountains, yet same mentality! As I put the pieces together eventually, the conflict seemed not unlike a Corsican blood feud or the Hatfield-McCoy wars. But any loss of life went against the common interest in a community as small as this. Eventually cool heads prevailed, and the feud moved into a phase of shouting matches such as the one I witnessed during that first dinner. The Lunels are mostly farmers, and the de Solas are shepherds. Both parties recognize that they are dependent on each other for survival.

I mention all this here to give you advance notice. The longstanding feud has some bearing on the matter of the codex. I am, of course, the guilty one; I cannot deny it. The fact that I absconded with their most sacred object gave new impetus to the old feud. As one might expect—and I was aware, having lived among these people for five years—the risk I took could not but arouse resentment, a sense of betrayal, and plain fear for the survival of the commune. It caused a panic and incitement to vendetta against the de Sola clan who had admitted the witch, for what else could I be, into their midst. As time stretched out, Alphonse's promises that the artifact would be returned found ever fewer believers. Even the seneschal, who as a more civilized man first supported my project, urged his brother to take drastic steps to stave off a full-fledged revolt.

Not for my sake but for the sake and safety of my children, I hope and pray you will soon find your way to this place. At this point, it matters no longer whether you have completed the task or not.

The last sentence made my heart sink. Here we were cuddled up in a swank hotel, swank by contrast to what we imagined the place where Nina was confined to be like, breathing in the vibes of warmth streaming between our bodies.

"A cry of despair," said Etoile, "and we were too deeply immersed in Dina's world, we didn't heed it."

"Maybe we were too steeped in our own bubble." Instinctively we moved away from each other and pulled the sheets like fig leaves over our bodies—Adam and Eve filled with shame and guilt. The anticipation of a night of lovemaking before we were to set out on the trail had been dispelled with a single stroke. The night was long and restless. We got ready before sunrise. We showered separately. I tried to catch her eyes a few times, but she busied herself with packing and kept her head down. At the door, I pulled her into my arms, and she did not resist.

"I feel as bad as you do," I said softly.

"I know," she replied, pulling back. "Later. Right now we must get to Nina."

We stopped by the supply store way ahead of opening hour and settled down on a bench in the small, green space in the middle of the square. As dawn's rosy fingers turned into gold and the sun emerged from behind the mountain peaks, the little town too awoke gradually to its daily bustle. On this morning, neither one of us had a mind for admiring this daily miracle of nature. We discussed some logistic matters and watched impatiently the hand on the clock of the church tower. Finally, the bells in the tower rang out the hour of eight, and that's when I saw him. He was walking straight toward us. Who knows how long he had been keeping watch. He looked exactly the way Nina had described him—stocky, squinty eyed, complete with bushy mustache. I always wanted to grow one of those in order to fit in better with the native French, but then my lanky frame didn't fit in well with the prevailing local physiognomy. I rose to meet him and almost said "Inspector Fauré, I presume." Instead I simply said in my best unaccented French: "*Bon jour, monsieur. Je suis à votre service.*" My intent was to stave off a drawn out ritual of cat and mouse play.

To my surprise, the inspector too cut to the chase and noted: "You are an American tourist, aren't you? May I see your passport?"

Not wanting to cause any trouble, I handed him my passport. He flipped through it, held up the page with the picture to my face, nodded a few times, and without a word put it in his pocket. We had not committed any offence or crime, and I found his behavior rather unusual and disturbing. "Are we under suspicion?" I asked, barely hiding my impatience against my best efforts. There's nothing these types like better than to encounter a seemingly nervous subject, and they never answer a question directly.

"That depends," he said. *Depends on what?* I thought.

"We just arrived here yesterday," I volunteered. "We are waiting for the shop to open to get some supplies and provisions."

"You are planning a hike? A wilderness hike, maybe?" This really couldn't be anything out of the ordinary in this area known for its scenic trails and the proximity of the Grande Randonnée. "How much time are you planning to spend in the mountains? And may I see your itinerary?"

The *épicier* across the square had already opened the iron shutters to his store and was starting to lay out baskets filled with his wares in front of the store window.

"Why should this be of concern to the police?" I asked. By then my edginess was clearly audible in my voice.

"What seems to be the trouble?" Etoile's voice chimed behind me at this moment.

"No trouble, no trouble, at all, Madame," piped the inspector gallantly. "Only a matter of precaution."

"We were counting on an early start," said Etoile. "Before the crowds, you know. But we still need to purchase provisions, now that the shop has opened."

"Yes, certainly, Madame. I understand very well, Madame." He started to walk away, but then, as if something had just occurred to him, he turned back again. *Why do these types always have to play these stupid games?* I thought. *They probably spend too much time at the movies.*

"When you have finished your purchases, I would like you to stop by the station. Very briefly. Just a formality." He had addressed himself only to Madame. "I shall return Monsieur's passport then." That fox! In my anger, I had forgotten that he had slipped my passport into his pocket.

At the station, we were informed that Inspector Fauré was having breakfast at a nearby café and would be happy if we would join him there. The whole thing was turning into a colossal nuisance. Our backpacks were heavy, so we didn't appreciate having to take more detours. But the fox held a trump card. We could leave our belongings at the station. "Under the eye of the police," chuckled a young flick, "you have nothing to worry about." *Very funny,* I thought.

"Won't you join me for breakfast?" Fauré invited us with a gallant gesture. We thanked him and sat down. Actually, it wasn't a bad idea not to start out on our trek with an empty stomach. We had been so eager to get on our way, the reasonable thing to do was far from our minds that morning.

More small talk from the inspector about the weather, the mountains, whether this was our first time, that we would enjoy the beautiful nature. The Pyrenees were more spectacular than the Rocky Mountains, he had been told. He chatted on while we consumed the breakfast of coffee, crusty baguette topped with fresh butter and *confiture de fraise*, and an ample helping of fresh country eggs and fried potatoes. No, no sausages; no ham either. Thank you. We are vegetarians, we explained.

Then, with an abrupt change in demeanor, the good inspector finally got to the point. In short, clip sentences, he laid out before us a gruesome scenario that could make any aspiring mountaineer's skin crawl. As the inspector described the situation, bandits and murderers were lying in wait along the trails, ready to pounce on their unsuspecting victims at every turn. "Unfortunately, the police are helpless," he sighed. I wondered why that should be so. Was all this merely theatrics? Only recently, he continued, a group of German hikers had been found dead, gunned down like others before them. But the police suspected that they were not killed in the place where they were found. The evidence suggested that the bodies were taken there—that is, they were dumped close to the main trail.

"You see, *Monsieur-Dame*, we are greatly concerned for our visitors' safety."

"We appreciate the warning and your kindness, but we really have been looking forward to this adventure, so to speak," said Etoile. "It would be a great disappointment for us to give up our plans at this point."

"I understand, Madame. I understand very well. Nobody wants you to give up your planned adventure as you call it. It is just a warning, but maybe you can help us."

What came next almost boggled my mind. When he had finished, I looked at Etoile whose expression was similarly baffled.

"Let me tell you a story," he began. "About five years ago, maybe five and a half years ago, a young woman came to this town, an American woman. She seemed very eager to go on a hike in the mountains. But it was early in the year and the trails were still impassible. So she waited. I had plenty of opportunity to observe her. She seemed restless, always wandering about town, round and around. I asked myself, what makes a young woman, a foreign woman, come here and stay? Could she not have left and come back later in the spring, when the snow had melted? Don't you think so?"

I glanced at Etoile. She listened without batting an eye. But I knew her outward composure was hiding the same emotions that ran through my body. What was he getting at? "Well, spring finally came. It was Easter, the feast of the resurrection of our Lord Jesus Christ. She did not attend the Holy Mass as everyone else in this town did. The people of this town are very devout. That evening, she received a visitor, a man, not entirely unknown to me, whom she described as her guide. They departed and she was never seen again." He paused and looked at us probingly.

"Could she not have left the mountains by some other way? She might have crossed into Spain," I suggested after some consideration.

"Quite possible," he nodded. "But for some reason, I have often wondered what might have become of her. And with the recent murders, the memory of this woman has come back to me even more. Her name was Nina Asch-au-er." The last name rolled slowly from his lips in disconnected guttural syllables with emphasis on the last. His eyes were firmly fixed on us. I shrugged my shoulders and shook my head.

"Your appearance here today, Monsieur, gave me hope that maybe, since you are an American as well, have come to look for her."

"Sorry, but I can't help you."

"The name means nothing to you?"

"It's a very sad story, but sorry." Only the mental image of Nina in distress up in the mountain village enabled me to present a nonchalant exterior. Maybe a bit too nonchalant! I had the distinct feeling he didn't believe me. But I also knew there was nothing he could do to break me. Arriving in Valladine with the police in tow would surely seal her fate. These murders he spoke of were no concern of mine.

"So are we free to go now?" said Etoile.

"You have always been free to go," said the gallant inspector while handing me my passport. I was sure he had already made a copy of it.

"By the way, she didn't eat meat either," he threw out as if in an afterthought.

I shrugged again, and we walked back to the station together with the inspector. We picked up our gear and made ready to get on our way finally. We had just reached the bottom of the stairs when we heard him call out behind us: "Just one more thing, if you please."

He guided us back inside where he presented both of us with something that looked like ankle bracelets.

"It's for your safety," he smiled.

"Or to spy on us," was my unconcealed surly reply. "Maybe you can listen in to our conversations."

"What do you take us for, Monsieur!" he protested in the best Gallic manner of indignation. He then turned to Etoile, who was obviously the more agreeable party and in better self-control. "It's only a beeping device. It will start sending a signal if it is removed or tampered with. In such a case, we shall presume that you are in danger and send out a search party. *Adieu.* See you in two weeks' time. You said that's when you plan to return, *n'est-ce pas*?"

I didn't remember that we had said anything of the sort. Somehow this whole spiel didn't make sense if it was our safety he was concerned about. I was sure that this bloodhound was using us to set a trap for whoever the criminals were he was after. Based on the letter, I had my own suspicion—so did Etoile, as she told me later—but neither of us would even remotely consider doing something that might endanger Nina's life.

We slipped on the devices—what choice did we have?—and started out toward the outskirts of the town. Like Nina, we felt the inspector's piercing eyes in our backs until we had entered the Grande Randonnée.

The sun was almost at its zenith when we finally began our ascent of the mountains. Etoile tried her best to dampen my rage against the sneaky inspector. No use expending precious energy on something beyond one's control. Of course, she was right as always. Still, for a long time down the trail, I was in a mood to turn around and strangle the little creep. But what would that accomplish except create more trouble and delay? The main path was densely populated with hikers marching in both directions. After a few miles, we turned onto a wilderness path going east as Nina had described.

We meandered aimlessly about for two days, keeping a lookout for flocks of sheep and shepherds. Not a single one grazed the luscious meadows we traversed. The weather was mild, and we didn't mind camping out under the stars.

"Maybe the great transhumance has become a thing of the past," I mused as we nibbled on our ration of trail mix. "Wouldn't it be a shame if such a thousand-year-old custom were to disappear."

"Many such traditions have outlived their usefulness in modern times," Etoile agreed. "But it must still exist in some form. Nina spoke about it, didn't she? And what about those interviews she did with shepherds about their way of life? Remember her little paradigm of the clash of tradition and modernity?"

"How could I forget?" I said with a sigh.

"No need to roll your eyes." Etoile playfully poked me in the side. "Besides, she told us specifically to make contact with the shepherds in the mountains, that they would pass on the message."

"Then again, the fabulous Alphonse seems to have a special nose for Ame-ri-cans, which might render the pastoral line of communication obsolescent."

We thus kept on bantering back and forth, mostly to pass the time and maybe also to hide our anxiety over Nina's fate. On the third day in the morning came our lucky break. We had just folded up our little tent and boiled water on a Coleman stove for coffee and shaving when a young boy appeared out of the thicket.

"Have you come for Alphonse de Sola?" he asked in Occitan. We looked him over briefly. He certainly seemed to be the genuine article from Nina's description—that is, his worn sandals, knee-high tunic of coarse homespun, black curls, and smudgy face fit the image I had of a young David in his slingshot days. Not that anybody knows what the future king of Judaea looked like then, and if I remember correctly, he was described as having red hair, but he too was a shepherd. This being beside the point, we nodded. Yes, we had indeed come on an important mission to seek out the aforementioned Alphonse de Sola. He signaled us to wait and disappeared in the brush with the swiftness of a marmot.

Before an hour was up, we were pounced on by two huge, fuzzy white clouds. They licked our faces and wagged their tails with such force it almost knocked the wind out of me. At least they were friendly. We had heard so much about them, maybe they had heard of us too. Who knows?

"Feda! Nivol! *A bas!*" The voice was as commanding as the figure that emerged from the thicket. He held a shotgun in a tight embrace, a veritable Davey Crockett. So there he was, the mountain man and Nina's lover, husband as she said. We finally met—again. Thoughts and impression whirled around in my head. For this unkempt and, what seemed to me, wild-eyed savage, my dear cousin Nina had tossed her previous life to the wind. She had left her mother, had abandoned a promising academic career, had foregone a life of refinement filled with theater and concerts in the culture capital of the world; she had chucked the faux Upper West Side world populated with pompous urbane Lotharios and rancorous, acrid feminists. Who wouldn't want to run away? But did it have to be to the other extreme?

His comportment was charmingly formal in the way he greeted us. We introduced ourselves, even though neither one of us needed introduction. He proved to be gracious, charming, and engaging in his dealings with us. But I simply did not want to think of him and Nina in the way she had written about their first encounter at the bed and breakfast in Oloron Saint Marie. I tried to chase the image that was rising before my mind's eye to the devil. When I expressed my ill feelings later on to Etoile, she said it was a typical male confronted with a rival.

"What do you mean rival?" I protested. "She's my cousin."

"Well now, aren't we protesting a bit too much!" Her sardonic smirk got my ire up, but I suppressed a desire of the moment to strangle her. It would only make it look as if she was right.

"I can well understand the attraction of this force of nature," she went on chirping.

"Like your Tunisian mechanic," I grunted under my breath.

But that little drama occurred later. All formalities out of the way, we got straight to the business at hand. I presented him with the codex, which he took out of the bubble wrap and pressed to his chest with a deep sigh and eyes turned skyward, as if he was thanking some deity.

"We also made several copies of the transcription."

"My brother will be very grateful to you. He is a true scholar. Of course, Nina and I thank you as well. Thank you so very much." He placed the documents and the codex carefully into the hunter's scrip he carried over his shoulder. It looked like this was it for him and that we would be duly dismissed on the spot.

"Your brother is the seneschal?" I asked.

"Yes, he is our ruler. Nina must have told you about him. He has also been her protector in this difficult situation."

"I would like to see my cousin. Her mother would want to be reassured of her well-being." From the way he puckered his lips and furrowed his brows, I could see that he was not going to grant my request—or maybe was not in a position to grant it.

"We have come this far," Etoile took up the argument. "To be quite frank, both of us have expended much effort; we applied our expertise in long hours of work. You may not be aware of this, but we put our lives on hold—if you know what this means—to devote ourselves exclusively to this cause. I think we deserve some consideration, more than just a thank-you and good-bye."

He did not answer but seemed to be mulling her words over in his head. Did he understand what she was saying? For all we knew, he didn't give a rat's ass about our lives and what it was we put on hold. We were, after all, representatives of this civilized world he detested, as we had heard.

"Nina is my wife, the mother of my children. I can assure you she is in perfect health."

"Nina is our dearest friend," Etoile persisted. "We cannot leave without knowing—without *tangible proof* that no harm has come to her." For the first time, I saw her express real anger.

He sat down on the ground and pointed at our legs. "Not with these chains you have on. Looks like Inspector Fauré got to you."

So that was it. He was already wise to the inspector's tricks.

"We had no choice but to comply," I said. "Several hikers have been murdered, he told us, and it was a precaution."

That revelation had no apparent effect on him.

"If we remove these anklets, it will set off a signal."

"He already knows where you are."

"What do we do?"

"You must return to Oloron Sainte Marie. Why you had to go there in the first place, I don't know."

I tried to explain, but he waved me off.

"No matter now. Give back these stupid things and then go to Spain. I shall meet you in Roncesvalles in two or three weeks. Wait for me there."

"How do we get there?"

"That's for you to figure out. I'll take you to Valladine from there. The whole matter should be straightened out by then."

Without further elaborating what the "whole matter" was, he packed up his bag and started to leave. Before he disappeared in the underbrush, he turned around once more and addressed me directly: "By the way, we won't have time to play a game of pelota or mus then. Maybe some other time, if you please." He winked at me and was gone. He remembered. I felt reassured. He was a friend after all.

We did as he told us to do—I could almost say as he commanded us to do. The inspector grumbled his displeasure at seeing us back so soon. Too hot and too crowded, Etoile explained. Now he had no choice but to relieve us of the chains from which he had obviously hoped to obtain very different results.

Now the question remained how to get to Spain. By train or by bus? Or by foot with the stream of pilgrims and hikers along the Grande Randonnée on their way to Santiago de Compostella? Etoile had the perfect solution, at least perfect to her mind. She called Armand to the rescue, and within a few hours, the Tunisian jack-of-all-trades rattled into town in a flatbed truck. Etoile berated him, but he just laughed it off. This was the only vehicle he had available at the moment. I was not in the mood to risk my life or that of my beloved by riding in an unsafe wreck driven by a maniac liable to fly over the serpentines in carracho speed and land us somewhere down a ravine with heads split open. No, I'd rather walk. The only concession I made, for practical reasons, was that he could drive us out of town to mislead the inspector.

So in a roundabout way, we picked up again the Grande Randonnée, which coincided with the trail to Santiago de Compostella that pilgrims had taken for a thousand years or more. In Roncesvalles, we settled in for what we expected to be a long wait. For the second time in my life, I found myself stranded in the town whose only claim to fame was the legend of a dying knight and his horn Oliphant also more than a millennium ago. During my first stay there, I learned to play pelota and various local card games like escoba and botifarra from a shepherd boy. This time we still played these games, only Etoile beat me fair and square in most every round. Even in mus, in which I once excelled, she held the upper hand. I was clearly out of practice. But there was time to get back in shape, plenty of time. As much as I yearned to see Nina and know that she was all right and not kept against her will or some other misfortune that entered my fantasy, the time I spent with Etoile in Roncesvalles was one of the happiest times of my life.

Part III

Valladine Unraveled

Stupor Mundi

To say he was the most remarkable human being I ever laid eyes on fails to capture his essence. Words crumble to mere platitudes in face of the élan that suffused his regal persona. He was the image of philosopher king, high priest, magician, alchemist, seer, sorcerer, and scholar all rolled into one. He had the bearing of a feudal lord, the probing aspect of an oriental despot, the grace of a benign potentate, even the physical strength of a medieval knight warrior. Within the mountain enclave of Valladine, Raymond de Sola, the seneschal, was supreme ruler and judge.

Nina had prepared us to expect an extraordinary man, but as is often the case, the real thing exceeded even heightened expectations. *Stupor mundi!* The epithet immediately struck my awed mind. Call it *illusion de sosies*, doppelganger figment, historian's syndrome, or plain fevered fancy: here before me stood the avatar of Frederick of Hohenstaufen, the medieval German emperor whose contemporaries endowed him with the cognomen *stupor mundi*, wonder of the world.

At the time of our first encounter, I had not yet even an inkling of this man's many other talents. Unlike potentates elsewhere in the world, he was also a master sheepshearer, a hunter, a goldsmith, a mason, and a falconer. Every inhabitant of Valladine, from the highest to the lowest, was bound to contribute to the sustenance of communal life. Every hand had to be productive, and so was the hand of the ruler.

"I believe I owe you a profound expression of gratitude, my lord," I muttered, bewildered.

"But, professor," he scolded, "no need for such formality."

"Forgive me. For a moment I felt like a time traveler. It seemed as if I had been transported several centuries back in time," I laughed nervously.

"I can assure you, you are still in the twentieth century—not a good one, I might add. Then again, previous centuries were not much better as far as the record of human actions is concerned. Human misery, caused by man or caused by nature, seems abundant in all periods of time."

We had a hearty laugh together, not that we were rejoicing in the abjectness of the human condition, rather we delighted in the art of meaningless blather, what we call banter in America. I, for my part, was truly impressed by the clarity and precision of his French.

"Yet, I love the period costumery." He made a half turn in both directions like a model to show off his attire of an ankle-length, long-sleeved double tunic touched off with a loose hanging, sleeveless surcote of black velvet. Black was apparently the color reserved exclusively for the seneschal. To my knowledge, the whole outfit went out of fashion at least five hundred years ago.

We settled down on comfortable pillows strewn over the floor in a sunbathed chamber on the top floor of his great house. Imagine my surprise to find the walls lined with shelves of books.

"What I meant to say," I resumed, alternately sipping tea and nibbling petit fours, which didn't taste like any petit fours I had tasted before, as they were uncharacteristically drenched with a strong anise flavor. "During the war, when we—my family and I—were fleeing from the Nazis, you saved our lives, and I am very pleased to have the opportunity to express our gratitude. You even assisted in the birth of our precious Nina."

"Yes, little did we know she would return one day to haunt us." He gave off another short-winded laugh. "*Vraiment*, she has been a great source of pleasure to me. I learned so much from her about the outside world, especially America as well as the history of mankind in general, the history of many time periods in various parts of the world. She is a very bright woman. The depth of her learning is astounding. Why she would fall for an unsophisticate like my brother Alphonse is beyond me. Women! Who can divine a woman's heart?

"We even studied your scriptures together. I sent Alphonse down to buy a French version since she only had an English one with her. Actually her version was bilingual: English and Hebrew. When I puzzled over the strange letters of the original she showed me, they appeared somehow familiar—familiar in the sense of not actually knowing this form of writing but in the sense that I had seen it somewhere in a text before. Then it came to. Of course! It was our sacred codex, which was being kept in a locked glass case in the great meeting hall. It was, and is, the most revered object of the people of Valladine. As seneschal, I had the authority to remove the book to my study. Nina immediately confirmed my intuition. The lettering was indeed in the Hebrew alphabet. However, she could not make out the words at first, even though she was, as she told me, fluent in that language.

"After mulling over it for several days, she declared that the text was in our language, Occitan, but written in the Hebrew letters. You can imagine how intrigued we both were! Unable to hold back my curiosity, I encouraged her to transcribe the text. She labored over it for about a year, but the progress was arduous. One day she told me she needed help. The task was too daunting for her alone. I was willing to help in any way I could, but she wanted to take the codex down to Toulouse. She needed dictionaries, she said, and needed to consult with some experts at the university. This I simply could not permit to happen. It would expose the existence of Valladine to the world. Our New Jerusalem has for centuries been a refuge, a haven; it has been a fortification against the evils of the world. When I denied her request, she betrayed me. She tricked her husband and then betrayed him too."

After a tense pause, I suggested, "But as a result of what you call betrayal, you now have the complete text in readable form and the codex is back where it belongs under lock and key."

"Yes, and for that we are very grateful to you. Now that I have read it, I have much to discuss with you about this narrative. First we must ready ourselves for the weekly communal assembly and dinner in the great hall."

"Much credit goes to Nina!" I protested. But he had already risen, and I was not sure that he even heard me. He was about to exit when he turned back once more.

"You see," he said pensively, "we have another chronicle, written in our language, which goes back to the founding of our community. However, I find many incongruities with the story told in the codex. There is no mention of a woman, let alone a Jewess, named Dina or Miryam in those pages, although she clearly states the de Sola and Lunel names as being those of her father. Also, the name Valladine derives no doubt from valley of Dina. The date for the founding as set in those pages is about the time of the terrible deadly pestilence in the middle of the fourteenth century. In our chronicle, the founders are said to have been three brothers who were fleeing to the mountains to escape the scourge. Eventually they were joined by more and more desperate souls and a community was formed, so states the chronicler."

He reached for the top of the shelf behind him and took down a large roll of curled up parchments. He struggled for a while with untying the coarse twine that held it together. He blew off the dust and smoothed out the yellowed sheets on the table before me. I bent over eagerly to examine the top folio. The writing was in an even hand obviously skilled in calligraphy. As the timeline progressed, the hand changed as one would expect, but remained neat and easily legible throughout. I was intrigued and ready to settle down for a closer reading. But the seneschal reminded me that we must put off all further examination and discussion. He still had other duties to attend to before the start of the assembly that evening.

On second thought, I too was eager to seek out Nina. Etoile had already gone ahead to her friend's living quarters. The patriarchal rules governing access to the seneschal precluded her from attending our meeting.

"There you are, finally, finally!" Nina jumped up from the floor where she had been engaged in a game with two young boys. She fell around my neck almost choking me. "The seneschal has kept you away from me long enough?"

"Yes, I had the pleasure of an audience with His Highness the seneschal—a very impressive man, by the way."

"Yes, he is. But you have to fill me in about all that's been happening."

"I will, but first won't you introduce me to these fine gentlemen, who I presume are my nephews."

"Yes, of course. We were just practicing our English skills."

"Boys," she said in Occitan. "This is cousin Henner from America. Henner, these are your nephews, or whatever, Arnaud and Bernard."

They got up and bowed their heads and mumbled something I didn't fully understand but presumed to be some polite phrase. Nina told them to run along and promised that next time their uncle would join in the English game with them.

I looked around for Etoile.

"She's in the room assigned to you unpacking your gear." Nina was reading my mind. "First tell me, how is my mother?"

"She's better now that she heard from you," I said in a somewhat reprimanding tone I couldn't suppress. "She knows she's a grandmother. It wasn't easy to keep her from getting on the next plane and storming this mountain."

"Maybe you shouldn't have told her," she replied sheepishly.

"I thought of not saying anything, but after all those years of uncertainty, not knowing, I figured she could use some good news."

"So how did she take it?"

"She was delighted," I said, padding Aunt Hedy's response a bit. "But, as I said, she wants to see you—she wants to see the kids."

"Well, maybe someday … I just don't know when and how. Somehow … it will work out. We'll see." Changing the subject, she said, "I am so grateful to you and Etoile for the fabulous job you did with the transcription. In addition to revealing the story of the founders of this community, it helped considerably with getting me back into good graces, at least those of the seneschal."

"Only too delighted to have been of help," I said with a gallant bow. "It was quite an adventure."

"In more ways than one, I understand," Nina said suggestively.

"So Etoile spilled the beans?" I was more embarrassed in front of my cousin than annoyed with Etoile.

"Look, she's my best friend and you're my favorite cousin."

"She is quite a woman, very charming," I said.

"Charming? Is that all you can come up with?"

At this moment, the object of our common admiration burst into the room, her mien unexpectedly grim.

"Another glitch has arisen," she proclaimed.

"What now? I thought all was forgiven and forgotten and Nina would be able to go on with her life—such as it is, I might add." I didn't think I could put up with anymore nerve-racking melodramas. I was overdue for a serious vacation by a quiet lake in Wisconsin.

"Here, see what I found in our backpacks!" Etoile opened the flap of her pack and revealed a tiny metal piece stuck to the canvas. "There's one in yours too."

Tracking devices! We had left our gear at the police station to meet with Fauré at the café and have breakfast with him. Time enough for his associates to plant something in our gear. The anklets, which we returned, were probably a distraction from the real thing. Or he just wanted to make doubly sure. Either way, we had been duped. This place could blow sky high any moment and we would be the ones who brought it on. Maybe there was still time to get rid of the gear if we got away from here. But how? We had a hiking trail map, but we didn't even know where on the map we were located. Valladine wasn't on the map! We were practically prisoners in this place and by no means free to come and go as we pleased.

"We have to tell Alphonse. There's no way around it," said Etoile. "He is free to leave any time and can dump the packs somewhere on the other side of the Spanish border or wherever."

"I will tell him," said Nina. "I have a lot to make up for."

Alphonse examined the devices and agreed they had to be disposed off somewhere far from the village and quickly. However, it would have to wait at least a day. It was the day of the weekly assembly. For the *sous-viguier* to be absent without explanation would arouse suspicion. The Lunel clan, who had just barely been appeased in the codex affair, would launch a challenge. Should we take the seneschal into our confidence? Alphonse advised against it. His brother was a temperamental man and didn't like such surprises. Better if he disposed of the gear by sinking it into a lake not too far away, he said.

"On second thought, never mind about the Lunels," said Alphonse after some consideration. "We had better not wait. This needs to be taken care of right away."

It was still early afternoon, and if he hurried, he could be back in time for the evening meal. What "not too far away" meant was hard for me to gauge. Two or three hours each way, Nina wagered a guess. That would make it between four and six hours roundtrip. He left about two in the afternoon. The hour for the start of the assembly was always fixed for sundown. Since it was summer, the assembly on that day would be at nine o'clock.

We spent the afternoon sitting with Nina catching up on events that had occurred since our parting in Albi, all the while nervously eyeing the trajectory of the sun. Nina gave us a brief account of what happened when she returned to Valladine without the codex. The uproar was led by the Lunel clan who almost succeeded in turning the general discontent into a rebellion against the de Sola regime. Other unrelated grievances were raised. Longstanding disputes, going back multiple generations, were suddenly revived: quarrels over land use and grazing grounds, proportionate staple contributions to the common fund and their distribution, presumed unequal water and fuel allocations, and the like. The seneschal kept them in check with soothing words and promises for reform. His back was covered, however, by what Nina called his "praetorian guard," under command of his brother Guilhem, the *viguier*, a somewhat shady character who seemed motivated by absolute fealty to his brother.

Nina herself was at first kept out of sight, condemned to house arrest and banned from the weekly assembly. She was, however, able to mollify the seneschal's anger against her with assurances that the codex was in the expert hands of her cousin, a renowned scholar in the field (what field she left unspecified) who, with the help of her good friend Etoile, another expert, would produce an excellent transcription, much better than what she would have been able to do under the limited circumstances, and that they would deliver it to them in due time. Alas, the due time of waiting was long and hard in view of the restive barbarians rattling the gate. Her children too were in danger and had to be kept under guard. Alphonse was her only solace. He stood by her, defended her when the seneschal, and especially the *viguier*, showed signs of losing their patience. When finally, at long last, word reached them that two hikers, a man and a woman, had asked about Alphonse de Sola, she knew her faith in her cousin and friend had not been misplaced.

"We worked as quickly as we could," Etoile said, patting Nina's hand. "There were many other things to take care of before we could devote ourselves exclusively to the task with due diligence."

"You did a wonderful job." Nina wiped away the tears. "And what an extraordinary woman Dina has turned out to have been. I mean, she was extraordinary from the beginning, but to be able to follow her progress both in psychological and historical terms is absolutely astounding. Isn't this every historian's dream come true? Henner, why are you so quiet?"

"Just thinking of Alphonse. I hope he'll make it back in time." This was only part of the truth however. More than this, it was Nina's account of her year of painful waiting that had left me deeply shaken. I searched my mind to where I could have shaved off some days or weeks, maybe even months. Maybe I dallied too long over this and that in wrapping up my affairs in Chicago. Instead of teaching another semester, I could just as well have disappeared. What could they have done to me? *But you did have a contract and you have always been a man of honor; you have always lived up to your obligations,* the rational self in me countered my self-flagellation. What about the fun I had wining and dining with Etoile while Nina was languishing in a dungeon? My overwrought mind made the situation out to be even direr than it really was. *You worked hard for hours every day and deserved at least a good meal at the end. You put your heart, soul, and mind into it.* Maybe my rational self was right, but I was still left with a lingering sense of guilt that somehow I could have done more to shorten Nina's ordeal.

"Stop tormenting yourself. You have nothing to reproach yourself about." Etoile enclosed me in her comforting arms when we were alone in our "nuptial" chamber. We were now consorts, or something of the sort. The thought gave us some passing comic relief, and we thoroughly enjoyed the idea as well as the privileges that went with our newly attained status. About an hour before sundown, Nina came in to take us to a shared bathroom, which to our surprise had running water for freshening up.

The evening feast began punctually at the set time. The entire village turned out in festive garb. *A medieval village, a living laboratory for a historian!* This thought was quickly follow by another, more ominous one. Out there was a gathering squall that was about to despoil Dina's mountain refuge and a way of life that had persisted in almost unaltered form for seven centuries.

I was seated at the center dais next to the seneschal and his consort, Béatrice. Etoile was at the right side table with Nina and the children. The seneschal's wife reminded me of the portraits of Florentine women in Renaissance paintings, her henna braids wrapped around her head like a crown. My curiosity was aroused. It took me awhile to come up with something to open a conversation, and when I leaned over to say something innocuous about the table arrangements, a hush went through the hall and the festivities began, to my great surprise, with a musical presentation. My chance was gone and wouldn't come again for a long time.

A quartet of musicians elicited the sweetest, lilting cadences from instruments of obviously ancient mold. For a moment, they made me forget the danger I knew was closing in on these revelers. My foot inadvertently began to tap out the drone of a wooden tambour that underscored the sweet tones of a gems horn blending with the nasal bowing of a rebec, a small primitive viol, and the grinding of a *viella à roue,* which was a medieval type of hurdy-gurdy. After a few short pieces in early music style, the players were joined by a group of young men and women dancers who gamboled about, some rattling tambourines, in front of the dais where the seneschal and his family were enthroned. My eyes wandered over to Etoile, who was joining in the general hand clapping with such enthusiasm, I feared she was about to leap in with the spirited bounce of the galliard that had followed a gliding, more decorous allemande. Only Nina was unaffected by the joyous display. Like her, I could not help but cast nervous looks toward the door behind us. Alphonse's seat was still empty. She answered my silent questioning with a helpless shrug of the shoulders.

Next on the program were the various blessings and chants over the wine and the bread as Nina had described. A somber plaintive melody, sounded on a hirtenschalmei by an old man in shepherd's garb with a white unkempt beard and weather-beaten face, added a note of drama to the seneschal's nasal ritual ministrations. He spelled out some kind of formula I didn't understand over a huge chalice of wine, which was seconded boisterously by the assembled crowd. Then he moved on to the bread, holding a huge boat-like braided loaf over his head while shouting something likewise incomprehensible. The crowd went wild over this one and burst into a series of raucous incantations that ceased only when the seneschal raised his arms and dropped them again.

Now dinner was being served. Young men and women pushed in cartloads of steaming fare. By this time, Nina's distress was so extreme, she broke etiquette and left her place and walked over to where I was sitting on the other side of the table. The absence of the *sous-viguier* would surely be noticed not only by the seneschal and his entourage but by the Lunel clan as well. But that, though potentially unpleasant, was the least of her worries. What if he ran into the arms of Fauré? I tried to calm her. Even if that fox was out there with his troops, he would hardly be a match in this terrain for a seasoned *coureur de bois* like Alphonse. Her fears were not assuaged.

Just as the seneschal turned toward Nina and asked in a soft but ominous tone, "Woman, where is your consort?" the coureur in question entered. Alphonse was unwashed and still in shepherd's garb. He waved off his brother's rebuke with almost disrespectful impatience. With a double nod of his head, he denoted that he wished to speak with him urgently. The seneschal's expression was grave but otherwise gave no hint of alarm about what Alphonse was whispering into his ear.

Meanwhile, the crowd was getting restless. Catcalls were heard from the opposite end of the hall, critical of the *sous-viguier's* late appearance and his appearance in general. Fingers were pointed at his common dress unfit for the weekly communal meal whose entrenched ritual and dress code were staunchly upheld by the entire village. Pierre Lunel, who as usual made himself the spokesman of the disgruntled, protested loudly, roughly translated to something like the de Solas's supercilious attitude. Then the assembly fell abruptly silent. The seneschal's figure loomed large. He once again spread out his arms, evoking to me the image of a Merlin or a Moses. His gaze passed slowly over the assembly that waited with bated breath for what he was about to say. Even the most quarrelsome among them seemed to realize that something extraordinary was happening. Their leader then emitted a sound the likes of which I have never heard. A guttural lowing, almost moose like, rose from deep inside his diaphragm and reverberated in the hall with shattering magnitude. The entire congregation, including Nina, her brood, and Alphonse, bowed and responded with a similar, though softer, bovine rumble. This continued for a while in a rhythmic back and forth. I guess it was the equivalent of our responsive prayer, albeit in utterances hardly human.

Somewhere in the midst of all this agitation, the seneschal had apparently communicated that a special session of the village council was to convene within the hour. I could feel the pulse of the agitated throng as it began to disperse. Raymond de Sola's voice was still hoarse when he told me: "I would like you to be present at the council meeting. Afterwards I have something important to ask of you."

Alphonse must have seen how taken aback I was. He took me and Etoile aside and filled us in on what was transpiring. Our hearts sank. Somehow we felt responsible for the storm brewing outside. Indeed, what he foretold meant nothing short of the end of a way of life, the life of this Shangri-La that had lasted for seven hundred years. It spelled the end of Dina's realm, I thought when I had heard him out. Maybe its time had long passed. It had become an anachronism, a vestige of something that had outlived its purpose centuries ago.

"Alas, I'm the bearer of grave news," he said. "A police force of several hundred is massing at the foot of the mountain. They will invade our terrain tomorrow morning. I never even made it to the lake where I had wanted to dispose of your backpacks. They didn't see me since I am able to melt into the surroundings. I got close enough to where they were camped out. From the way they were talking, I realized they had not the slightest clue of what kind of place Valladine was. They seemed to think their mission was to uproot a bandits' nest, a hideout for a gang of armed and dangerous criminals. None of them, not even Monsieur Fauré, had any knowledge of the historic importance of the place they were preparing to attack and destroy. After listening for a while to their boasting of how they would, if they could, string up the felons right then and there, I decided to step forward. The inspector recognized me right away and greeted me with a handshake like an old friend.

"'It's been a long time, but somehow I had a hunch I would find you here,' he said.

"'Why is that so?' I said.

"'The lady you accompanied on a hiking tour—when was it, five or six years ago?—she never came back. Nothing was ever heard or seen of her again. I've often thought of her and wonder what might have become of her. She seemed so impatient to get on that hike,' he explained.

"I told him to stop playing mind games. If he had anything to accuse me of, he should come right out and do so.

"'Far be it from me to accuse an innocent man,' he protested. 'But we will get to the bottom of the murders that have been committed around here in recent years.'

"At that moment, an underling came up to report that they had found two backpacks with the tracking devices in a bush nearby. Matters had clearly taken a bad turn.

"'Am I right to presume you were trying to hide these? Or even destroy what is government property?' he said, still very polite. 'We know whose they are. Neither of them has been seen since they returned the anklets. But we're not so easily fooled. Now maybe we can sit down quietly,' he made an elegant gesture toward a rickety camping chair, 'and you will tell me how you came into possession of this gear.'

"'How do you know they were in my possession? Did you find them on me?' I knew my attempt at evasion rested on a weak leg. I took him up on his offer of the seat and a cigarette to gain time to decide how to respond.

"'Let's keep this informal. So far you have not been charged with any crime. Maybe you can help us bring the real criminals to justice. We know there's a bandits' lair up there. If you are innocent, as you say, you have nothing to fear.'

"I had said no such thing. The fox never gives up his foxing ways. What alarmed me most, however, was that he thought it was all just a matter of eliminating a bunch of *desesperados*, as he called them, whom he would take down in a blaze of gunfire if necessary. He even laid his whole strategy out before me. When I realized that he was not averse to storming his target with weapons drawn and ready to open fire, I knew what I had to do.

"'You won't find a bandits' nest, as you call it, up there,' I said. He assured me that they had reliable information, and I protested that his information was mistaken or at least incomplete.

"'What you will find is an entire village. You could even call it a small town, a human habitation that has existed up there since times medieval.'

"He gave me this skeptical inspector's look of his. 'You mean to say …'

"'Yes, I do mean … Where do you think I and the lady—by the way, my wife—have been living all this time?' I went on to give him in as few words as possible a rundown of seven hundred years of Valladinc history going back to the founding during the reign of the Valois kings. You can imagine it took some effort to disperse his disbelief that it was possible in the twentieth century for a people to live an antiquated style of life without electricity and all the modern stuff.

"I told him briefly about my service for France in Indochina and North Africa, which seemed to impress him. His face lit up, and he made a hand gesture that vaguely resembled a military salute. What I witnessed there about the conduct among modern civilized human beings, I told him, only made me want to go back home to the peaceable mountain enclave of my birth. He kept shaking his head. 'Sounds like a fairy tale to me.'

"I should have foreseen that talking about our village life so vividly—my intent was to reassure him that there was no hideout for criminals and most of all to keep him away—would backfire. It only wetted his appetite. He even licked his chops like a fox in anticipation of a tasty prey.

"'This I've got to see! And don't forget, this is still a murder investigation,' he said.

"I begged him to hold back until the end of our holy day of rest. He would make no such concession and only remarked: 'What's that? On Saturday? Are you Jews? This story is getting more and more bizarre.'

"He let me go and even handed your backpacks to me.

"'We won't need these anymore,' he said, laughing when he saw me smashing the trackers.

"The police force is still at a considerable distance; they haven't found the entry yet," Alphonse said more to himself than to us.

One of the seneschal's sons approached us with the message that the council was gathering and waiting for the two of us to join them. Yes, the seneschal requested the professor's presence as well. Not a word about Etoile. It was apparently understood that she was expected to stay with the women.

"Go ahead," she urged me on when I hesitated. "I'm sure it would be exciting for a historian to sit in on a medieval town council."

"I'm afraid we are still very medieval when it comes to women's roles," said Alphonse. *As in many other ways,* I thought. With that, he pulled me into the council room, which was packed to the rafters. It seemed to me that every male villager was a council member. "Every male above twenty-five," Alphonse corrected my impression.

The seneschal called the meeting to order according to established procedure. And into the silence that ensued, he shouted, not quite as roaring as at the ceremony, but thundering enough to cast fear into the hearts of the assembled: "A disaster of unprecedented proportion is about to befall us! A disaster greater, more devastating than any that has befallen this commune at any time of its long existence—greater than the black death, greater than the religious wars, greater than the revolution, greater than any of the modern war. We have always stayed aloof from what was going on among the flatlanders. Our commune has always remained untouched by their quarrels. Most of the events taking place down there passed us by. We were able to preserve our isolation and keep our existence hidden from the world. But now we are threatened directly. I have been told that down at the tree line, hundreds of armed French police troops are massed ready to invade our territory. There is no way we can resist this force. By tomorrow morn, this commune will be no more. We must surrender if we want to avoid any bloodshed."

In the ensuing mayhem, it was Guilhem de Sola who made himself heard and silenced the pandemonium. It was the first time I heard him speak and likely the first time ever that he rose up against his brother, the seneschal.

"Silence! Silence!" he roared. "I think our seneschal is giving up too easily. My troops are well prepared to defend our domicile. I say, to the ramparts! I say, death to all intruders on this hallowed mountain!"

Wild applause and shaking of rifles and swords from the Lunel side encouraged the *viguier's* dare. His guards with grim menacing mien and spiked bayonets—I would almost call them storm troopers, but maybe Nina's Praetorian Guard is more apt—formed a human shield around him. It reminded me of a scene out of the movie *The Mouse that Roared.* Alphonse made my point, unknowingly of course, in the next go around.

"How will you fight a modern police force? Do you think shotguns and swords can stand against modern machine guns?"

Guilhem was the only one of the brothers who had never left the mountain for any length of time. He had never shown any curiosity about the world at large. His only forays into lower lying areas were for the purpose of meeting with weapons smugglers, who sold him outdated shotguns but nothing very sophisticated. He was a total ignoramus when it came to modern technology and the civilized world; he was a true naïve in worldly matters. Back in the day when his brother, not yet seneschal then, was helping refugees like us or the thousands fleeing Spain in the wake of the bloody civil war there, he engaged in dealings with smugglers who exploited people in despair and fear for their lives. When his father, who was then seneschal, found out, he meted out fifty lashes to him and each of his goons as punishment.

Even before I heard this story much later from Alphonse, the mere look of the man gave me the creeps. I thought of the murders Inspector Fauré was investigating, the reason he had been tracking our moves. What did anybody really know about this so-called *viguier* and his activities in the shadow of his brothers? They were refined and learned by comparison. They had seen the world and made the mountain their home by choice. Guilhem and his gun-toting roughnecks had the look and behavior of uncouth backwoods types. They were neither herdsmen, like the other de Solas, nor farmers like the Lunels. They certainly weren't artisans of any kind. Their contribution to the common good was soldiering in defense of the bastion. Raymond had gone along since his brother showed him absolute loyalty, until that night when the fraternal bond snapped and a flood of resentment stowed in decades of doggish submissiveness washed away a seven-hundred-year peaceable realm like torrents erode the rock formations and wash the boulders down the mountainside in the spring.

And yet, the seneschal was reticent about reprimanding his rebellious brother that night. He left it to Alphonse to keep the would-be warriors in check and to calm the rest of the mountain dwellers.

"There will be no fighting! The first one who fires a shot will be shot down by me personally!" Alphonse declared.

"For now, go home all! I know the police don't seek to destroy our village. They are investigating a series of unsolved murders that have taken place in the mountains in recent years, and we will cooperate as best as we can."

He continued to issue commands and answer questions as he herded them out into the star-clear night.

I stayed behind with the seneschal. He sat there silently, his thoughts seemingly far away. I wondered what might be going through the mind of this philosopher-king. Was he coming to grips with the possibility that this was indeed the end of life on the mountain as it had existed for seven centuries? Was he, like me, pondering the implications of the failure of this commune existing apart from the madding world for all such experiments? Seven hundred years can hardly be called a failed experiment, I reminded myself. My mind was still running along the entrenched tracks of academic thinking. His mind was far from entertaining such generalizations, as I found out pronto.

"Ah, professor, how good to see you! You are precisely the man I need at this moment."

I was pleased and not a little flattered that he should be looking to me for help or advice. "Glad to be of service," I stammered.

He took me by the arm and steered down the hall toward his library while casting about conspiratorial glances in all direction. Once we were inside, he quickly locked the door behind us. He pressed me into a chair while he remained standing, his steel-blue eyes peering down on me for a good while. Without breaking his silence, he began to take several steps back and forth. It was getting quite late by then, and I had to force myself to stay alert. The next day promised to bring much tumult and uproar, and certainly little sleep.

"So the dreaded day finally seems to have come," the seneschal began solemnly. "My only surprise is how long it took them to find us. For centuries we were safe here. From time to time, other refugees—some fleeing from natural disasters but most from human oppression and tyranny—would find their way to our mountain enclave and settle with us. This was good for our community, for they replenished our stock with fresh blood. Our isolation was never compromised. The means of communication, such as they existed, were in our favor. It was not until about one hundred years ago that the mountain terrain was turned into a playground for people eager to exert their bodies. Increasing swarms of hikers and climbers eager to put their physical prowess to the test began to penetrate ever more deeply into the wilderness areas. Sooner or later, I was sure, one or the other would happen upon our village. As our present century progressed, the likelihood of our being discovered by air increased as well. So it is no wonder that technology like these items Alphonse called tracking devices should finally have made us vulnerable to being caught in the claws of a hungry bear."

"But ..." I tried to put this as delicately as possible. "Advances in technology certainly opened up heretofore inaccessible, remote areas. This is true for all areas of the world, from the North to the South Pole. But wasn't it the series of murders in recent years that set the police on track. Is it possible ...?"

"Yes, professor," he nodded, his steely blue eyes firmly locked with mine. "Yes, professor, it is possible. It is absolutely within the realm of possibility. Some among our more zealous citizens may well have fended off some intruders who got too close to our domain. I shall be the one to bear the consequences."

He abruptly turned away. This was all he was going to say on the subject.

I started writhing in my seat. The events of the evening had changed the entire game plan, and there was much I wanted to discuss with Etoile and Nina. As matters stood, they had no way of knowing where I was. Yet I did not dare excuse myself and leave. A dense cloud of silence held us suspended. Had I gone too far? Had I overstepped a line? Very likely, but he showed no intention of letting me go yet. I felt the burden of being witness to this night of impending doom. The fate of his realm as it had existed for so long suddenly hung in the balance. I sensed a despondency, a melancholy in the man whose aura of strength and fortitude had impressed me so deeply I had called him *stupor mundi*. True, as overlord of this mini-kingdom, he had ruled with the hand of an autocrat. In this he upheld the practice his father and forefathers had passed on down the generations. Though he had even now lost none of his dignity, I felt he might be in need of a friend in this hour, someone to whom he could talk, share his thoughts.

His next move corrected once again my modern-day view of the human psyche. This was a medieval man through and through. He was untouched by twentieth-century sentimentality—melancholy yes, but soppiness, far be it from him.

He walked over to a crudely fashioned narrow table that functioned as a standing desk. With both hands, he picked up the wad of parchments he had shown me before. He lifted it in solemn gesture the way he raised the loaf of bread during the general gathering on Friday evenings and slowly turned toward me.

"There is a reason why I brought you here tonight, professor." He extended his hands holding the pack toward me. "Contained herein are the codex and the chronicle, as you know, records of the story of Valladine. I am entrusting them to your hands for safekeeping. Take them with you when you leave this mountain and put them in a place where no harm will come to them. If it is the fate of this realm that its existence will have to be made known to the world, then its history shall also be made known. Valladine shall stand as an exemplar for a better world than the one mankind has generally fashioned down in the lowlands. I herewith appoint you caretaker and prophet of this legacy."

I was totally flustered and dumbstruck as much by the honor he bestowed on me as by his grandiosity. He immediately brushed off my feeble attempt at expressing gratitude for his trust as well as doubt concerning my ability and the like.

"I am now convinced that the world should know. We must proclaim the success of a place without war, without persecutions, without oppression and suppression, a place where men have labored peacefully together with their fellows for the common good, a place where the loftiest dreams of mankind, as expressed by philosophers and poets, have lived in reality for seven hundred years."

For someone who had lived his life on an isolated mountaintop, he seemed well acquainted with the cruelty and strife that have characterized human actions since the beginning of history. It couldn't have been just the history he studied with Nina. No, this knowledge went deeper. It derived from a more personal experience; I could feel it.

"There was a time," he began settling down in a chair as if he anticipated my question, "in my early youth when the lowland exerted an irresistible allure over my imagination. Even as a very young boy, my curiosity led me to undertake frequent and at times extended forays into the lower regions. From the shepherds, I learned French and a Spanish dialect, the languages in which they told folktales and legends. They stirred in me a great longing to see the world that lies beyond the mountains. Most of all, I wanted to see the region to the south to which they moved with their herds of sheep every winter."

"What is called the great transhumance," I interjected, ever the pedantic professor.

"Yes, something like that," he said flippantly. "Spain was the land of my adolescent dreams. I dreamed of knights like Roland and warfare against forces of evil. My hero was the medieval warrior El Cid Campeador, the liberator of Castile from Moorish rule. Many a night as I was going to sleep I pictured him riding on his famed horse Babieca into battle against the Moors, his sword Tizona wreaking havoc among the ranks."

I nodded and started to say, "Yes, it's a fascinating story ..." but broke off when my eyes met his disapproving glare.

"I had no idea who the Moors were," he continued, "but it sounded all so exciting, and I yearned to walk the battlefields where my hero had fought against Moorish rulers a thousand years earlier.

"In my sixteenth year, I requested permission of my father to travel across the mountains. He sent me on my way with his blessing, but also with a warning. A war was raging in that country, not against invaders, although some of those were present also, but of countryman against countryman. He admonished me to stay out of trouble and return safely. Now I think he must have considered this an opportunity to cure me of my curiosity about the outside world. Why else would he send off his son and heir into a cauldron of seething hatred and abject brutality that was the Spanish Civil War?"

"Did he know about the war that was going on there?" I inquired. "Without means of communication ..."

"He had his spies who would report to him about the events," he retorted. "In any event, he did not succeed, at least not immediately."

He paused shaking his shoulders and swallowing as if to suppress some bitter bile the memory had caused to rise in him.

"Surely, the sight of countless burned corpses strewn among the charred ruins of Guernica would have been enough for anybody to give up the contents of his stomach and with it all notions of heroic warfare. But I still thought maybe this was just my bad luck. This couldn't be all. People surely were not always engaged in war. One night at a wayside inn, I got into conversing with two fellows who spoke bad French and even worse Spanish, but we managed to understand one another. They told me about the mountains of their homeland. They were of such gigantic height, they boasted, the Pyrenees were laughable dwarfs by comparison. This aroused my competitive spirit and, at the same time, my desire to see with my own eyes these natural wonders they called the Alps.

"Have you seen the Alps, professor?" I just nodded, not wanting to interrupt him again. He spread out his arms even wider than he did when he was blessing the weekly assembly to indicate the sheer size. "Professor, I dropped to my knees in awe when I finally caught sight of those giants. These fellows had been right. How pitiful were my Pyrenees compared to the majesty of the Alps? I even began to mock and belittle the place of my birth. I felt like a husband who had been seized with an irresistible passion for another woman. This was betrayal, adultery even, but I could not help myself, I had to have more and more of this seductress. I longed to feel the sweeping ups and downs of her gorges and ravines, winding pathways, her plunging valleys and heavenly heights. So I set out and traversed the entire mountain range from west to east. All along, I could not help but feel overwhelmed by those towering peaks. My livelihood I earned with my sheepshearer's skill, which fortunately was much in demand in that region."

He fell into a wistful silence. For a moment, he seemed transported to a different time and place. Did he remember a place of youthful pleasure, of idyllic pastures, of people going about peaceful lives, maybe of a woman he loved?

"This was in the summer of 1937!" His voice assumed a coarse, even harsh tone. "I observed much about the customs of these mountain dwellers. Along the way, I picked up some of their speech—a kind of German. It had a different resonance from one place to the next, but having a sensitive ear for human speech, I was able to learn the essentials. I learned much about their views of the world and of other human beings.

"Maybe this will answer your question about why I wanted to help the refugees who came to us during the war, at least in part. I hadn't thought of it that way before, but it is quite possible. His name was Ahieser Fortgang. A strange sound to my ears, but I never forgot it. I never forgot the slightest detail of our encounter and subsequent time together. What became of him? I cannot tell. I can only surmise. You may be better informed about this matter, professor."

I was startled. I reached for the glass of arak he had poured but had neglected while he spoke. Now I took a gulp so big I got it in the wrong pipe and almost choked with coughing. My interest was aroused. Up to then, I had still been restless, torn between remaining politely attentive and longing to return to Etoile. Now, all of a sudden, I was mesmerized.

"We chanced upon each other somewhere in the Austrian Alps. I was shearing a herd grazing high up in the summer pastures and had just finished the task. The sheep owner's wife was counting out my reward when my eye caught a large man in a black suit and broad-rimmed black hat lumbering up the footpath. *This is not good in this warm weather,* I thought.

"'*Ach, guten Tag, Herr Fortgang, wie schön!*' exclaimed the shepherdess, seemingly delighted to see him. The man so addressed was wrestling with his breath while he labored to divest himself of a huge valise he carried on his back and which made him walk in an almost horizontal position. I wanted to rush inside to fetch a glass of water, but the woman held me back, saying something to the effect that he has his own. Of course, I had no idea what she meant. Then the man, who had still not uttered a word, took out a cup from a smaller rucksack and walked over to the well and began to pump water into it. After a few big gulps, he washed his hands and sprinkled water on his face, then wiped both with a shiny white handkerchief. The woman waited out patiently what was apparently to her a familiar routine.

"'*Na also, gnädige Frau,*' he said with a bow when he finally joined us on the terrace to the cottage. She immediately plunged into a cascading chatter, and as far as I was able to understand, she wanted to know what he had brought—something nice, something special for her perhaps? He opened up the valise on the table. The revelation of its contents elicited a jubilant scream: '*Ach, Herr Fortgang*! *Wie wunderschön!*' She seemed so enthralled with the visitor and his merchandise, I almost expected her to fall around his neck.

"The two were haggling over all kinds of knickknacks, ribbons in every color and lace, blouses and lady's lingerie, buttons and buckles, pins and brooches, even elegant shoes and stockings, what have you—I don't remember all. They seemed to have forgotten my presence, and so I had an opportunity to get a closer look at this curious itinerant merchant. My experience with the outside world was limited, but this man appeared strange indeed. He was like nobody I had so far seen. Besides the dark clothing in the summer's heat, most noticeable was the bushy, unkempt beard that was framed by two even longer, carefully turned locks. They flipped back and forth during their energetic discussion of which I didn't catch a single word. He waved his hands about animatedly, and she raised her eyebrows and shook her head back and forth while picking over the offerings. It seemed she was playing hard to get. Both apparently followed a prescribed ritual. In the end, they came to an agreement. He handed over the wares of her choosing, and she handed over the money. He packed up. She waved a friendly good-bye with a '*Kommen Sie doch bald wieder*.'

"Her gaze remained fixed on him as he staggered down the rough footpath. His valise on his back may have been a bit lighter, but surely not by much. She had bought very little for all the effort he expended. Then I saw something in her squinting eyes that startled me. It was hatred, pure hatred. She had greeted him with such a friendly how-nice-to-see-you, and now I heard her mumbling to herself: 'Oh no, you won't come back. You and your kind will soon get what's coming to you.' These may not have been her exact words, but it was something to this effect. I didn't immediately understand it all, but with time I was to learn.

"I made my presence known by rattling the coins in my pocket.

"'Oh, you are still here,' she said surprised, quickly putting a smile on her face. 'Did you see what that Jew was just trying to do?'

"No, I didn't see. All I saw was a business transaction; nor did I know what a Jew was. I had never heard of a *Jud* as she spit out the word like venom. Her attitude alone aroused my interest and sympathy for the itinerant peddler. Without another word, I grabbed my rucksack and hurtled down the path after him. I quickly caught up with the subject of that woman's disdain and of my curiosity. He sat on a stone by the wayside, breathing heavily. When he saw me coming, he tried to get up, but the valise held him down.

"'You are too old to be carrying such a heavy load,' I said, regretting my tactlessness the very moment.

"He waved off the hand I extended to him to help him to his feet.

"'I'm used to it,' he said. 'Don't worry. I'm grateful to you for your kindness. There's very little of that nowadays.'

"I offered to accompany him. He tried to dissuade me for a while, but since I insisted, he relented. We traveled together on foot until our occupations took us in different directions and we parted. To my surprise, he was very loquacious along the way. The fervor with which he spoke about his people and their religion contrasted sharply with the subdued demeanor I had seen him display in the presence of the shepherd woman. Of course, I knew about the biblical stories and was amazed that descendants of Abraham and Moses should be alive in our day. All this being well and good, I still didn't know what a *Jud* was."

He paused and took a sip of the wine before us on the table and took a long, scrutinizing look at me.

"Oh yes," I laughed, somewhat uneasily. "We are still alive. The descendants of Abraham and Moses should have been relegated to the dustbin of history, and yet here we are."

I wasn't sure that he understood, for he continued where he had broken off without as much as a nod toward what I was saying.

"I thought of him often on my wanderings," he said with a wistful look. "The shearing business was good that autumn. In the evenings after stretching out in some barn or wayside inn, I would take out the card he had handed me with an invitation to visit him in Vienna. *Wien!* He described the city in glowing terms. *Ahieser Fortgang*, it read, *Tuch- und Kurzwarenhandlung, Wien-Leopoldstadt.* I have kept it to this day. It will be forever a reminder to me of the horrors I witnessed in that city my companion had glorified as 'the pearl on the Danube.' When winter came, and with nothing to do, I decided to go to Vienna. He received me with obvious pleasure and asked me to help out in his store until spring or summer when I could return to my sheep-shearing trade in the countryside. I gladly accepted his offer and enjoyed his hospitality until March of 1938."

Again a long pensive pause, as if he had to struggle to unlock the chest of memory in his mind.

"Never have I forgotten the Nazi blackguards marching into the city," he finally said. "Their Führer hailed by the populace like the native son who had made good abroad. Never have I forgotten the shrieking barbarians storming into the modest store of my patron on Volkert Square, destroying its shelves and ransacking its wares. Never have I forgotten the sight of the pious Mr. Fortgang being kicked and dragged out into the street. Never have I forgotten the stoic yet pained look as his beard and precious side locks were cut off by the thugs and strewn on the sidewalk. Never have I forgotten the miscreants' pushing him down on his knees, as they did with other Jews, forcing him to scrub the pavement with a toothbrush."

He shook his head vigorously.

"He told me afterwards that he was leaving the city. He would return to his birthplace in the east. I saw him off at the train station with his valise containing few belongings. What became of him, I don't know. Or I should say, I am sure he shared the fate of so many of the others. You know better than I do, professor."

The seneschal paused and closed his eyes. A deep sigh escaped from his lips. He suddenly looked aged by a decade. The long narration of a dreadful memory had obviously drained his energy. Suddenly, he stood up erect with a nod of his head as if he had formed a resolution. He began softly, almost inaudibly.

"There is something else, something I have never admitted, not even to myself. Yet it has been festering in the dark recesses of my mind. The time has come to make a confession of the guilt that has plagued me ever since."

Why to me? I thought. I was not a father confessor. I had very little interest in people's long suppressed guilt feelings or sins. Up to this point, the story was fascinating, especially his encounter with this Ahieser Fortgang, the kind of Jew for whom even most of my compatriots have little love. His portrayal of this character was no doubt idealized—in response to that thought, my alter ego immediately accused me of bigotry, and toward a fellow Jew at that. The hour was advancing, and my body yearned to rest.

The seneschal was too preoccupied with his inner struggle to take note of mine. Still obviously wrestling with his inner self, he raised his arms and blurted out: "I betrayed him!" The words spilled out like retching vomit.

Confronting me full-face now, he muttered something about a Judas. Uncomfortable with this particular allusion, I tried to dissuade him with a few clichés of my own. But he insisted. "Yes, I betrayed him! Like a Judas, I betrayed him. When I saw the gashing wound to his forehead, I made a feeble attempt to fend off his tormentors," he continued in a calmer tone. "My limited German immediately drew their attention, and they poked fun at me and pushed me down on my knees with raised clubs. One of them handed me a scrub brush."

What followed, he related to me in almost breathless haste. He assured them that he wasn't a Jew.

"They replied under vile laughter that there was an easy way to prove this. One of them, spurred on by his comrades, started pulling on my pants. I did not understand at first. Then it came to me. Circumcision had been a practice in Valladine for generations, probably since the beginning. Now the passage in the Bible of Abraham circumcising his son as a covenant with G-d sprung to my mind. I put two and two together. I had to distract them, and the only way I could think of was to lead them to where the old man was hiding a stash of money."

It pained me to see this man in such obvious pain of conscience. His breathing was so heavy I feared he may be having a seizure. I tendered some more wine for him to soothe his spirit.

Ahieser Fortgang forgave him before he departed on the train, but Raymond carried the pangs of guilt over his "cowardly betrayal" with him for the rest of his life. He sought to atone for his sin when he returned home by making it his mission to help refugees from persecution cross the mountains. First, in 1939 at the end of the Spanish Civil War, he guided hundreds to freedom from south to north, and later, after 1940, he helped Jews like us escaping the Vichy regime and the Nazis, taking them from north to south.

"When refugees like you and your family, professor, told us stories of the burning of houses of worship and businesses, brutal attacks and deplorable conditions in camps into which people were herded, I was not surprised. I had seen the signs. No one, not even I, could have foreseen the death mills that were set up in the east as they were revealed at the end of the war. But surprised I was not. To me, it was an almost logical sequence to what I had observed in Vienna.

"And yet, it was all so hard to understand how a human being could act like that toward other human beings. I sought the answers in books, in the writings of wise men. After the war was over, I obtained my father's permission to go and study. First I went to Toulouse and then to Paris. I stayed for almost five years. The Bibliothèque Sainte Geneviève—I am sure you are familiar with that treasure trove of accumulated human wisdom—was practically my home. I sat in on university lectures. Since I didn't have a formal education, I was not able to enroll officially. It was there that I met my wife, Béatrice, who was a philosophy student and a seeker of truth and meaning like me. Eventually, actually after *La Toussaint Rouge*, the massacres that took place at the beginning of November in 1954 in Algeria and the outbreak of the Algerian War, I begged Béatrice to go home with me. I had seen enough of the world. All she wanted was to take her books. *Et violà!* This is our library. Except for some later additions, most of these books belong to my wife. She insisted on bringing them as a condition for cutting herself off from the world and her family.

"So this is the story of my life," he concluded. "After my father's death, I became seneschal and never left the mountain again."

The journey back to his youth had for a moment made him forget the peril his village was facing. It was long past midnight when Alphonse stormed through the door and brought us back to the present with a severe reprimand.

Adverse Winds from Aquilon

Out of the north an evil shall break forth upon all the inhabitants of the land. The seething cauldron! Adverse winds blowing from the northern kingdom of Aquilon! The prophet Jeremiah was far from my mind though on that morning. Only now as I think back and contemplate the events and coincidences, as I wrestle to pour their sequence into a narrative form, am I struck by the irony of the date of the breaching of the gates to the enclave of Valladine, the Jerusalem in the sky, on which began the destruction of a way of life centuries-old, the uprooting of its people, the tribe of the medieval Dina, and its trail of tears down the mountain to the Babylonian captivity near the city of Pamiers.

"By the river Garonne we sat and we wept, remembering our Jerusalem up there in the mountains!" they might have sung, but didn't, unlearned in such matters as they were. And, in the end, the return, a bittersweet return to their Jerusalem. Most of them were unaware of the biblical parallel, which has only now become apparent to me, the chronicler of this saga—bittersweet because once exposed to the outside world, life on the mountain, as it had existed for centuries, could not be regained. Like the purity of a virgin once defiled is irretrievable, the snows of yesteryear had irretrievably melted away.

In the small hours of the 12th of August in the year 1978—was it divine providence or irony that this day too coincided with Tisha b'Av, now 5738 years since the creation of the world?—deafening clatters jolted the inhabitants of Dina's realm from an already fitful sleep. The unheard-of noise struck their hearts with apocalyptic fear. Some whose curiosity eventually got the better of them ventured outside but were immediately swept off their feet. A wind, wayward as the tramontane, whirled through village alleys and pathways, whipping up fields and pastures. A howling flock of birds, more monstrous than they had ever seen, darkened the sky with flapping wings.

I followed Nina and Etoile outside. Alphonse was nowhere to be seen. We had been huddling with the children all night, dozing fully dressed on the floor so we would be ready for whatever was to come. Well, man supposes, and G-d, or whatever force was at work here, disposes. The assault began at an earlier hour and from a different venue than we had expected. Instead of police or army troops invading the territory on foot, a fleet of helicopters came swooping down on the terrified mountain folk, none of whom had ever seen anything like these horrifying birds. We did our best to calm the wailing and lift up the prostrate and guide them back inside their huts. Once they were safe inside, they hurled question upon question at us. Has the day of our doom arrived? Has our end finally come? They pleaded with us, the strangers who had come to their village from the outside world like visitors from another planet, for enlightenment.

It was indeed doomsday for this community, but not in the way anybody could have ever foreseen. Most of the inhabitants had naturally been aware of the existence of a wider world beyond the mountains, a different world, different in customs and guided by a different order. Some had descended to the lowlands on occasion when necessity dictated the acquisition of items that could not be produced within the community. Most found the air down there hard to breathe and ascended as soon as their affairs were complete. They found the people unkind and coarse and frequently dishonest in their dealings. Few nurtured a desire or curiosity in their bosom, not even in their younger years—as had Raymond and Alphonse de Sola—to explore this wider world. Not being wise in the ways of the world, the clamor of fluttering helicopters confirmed their suspicions that the lowlanders had finally found a way to destroy them. The iron birds, as they called them, retreated after a short display of their might to scare the living daylights out of people still living in a pre-modern universe. Nobody doubted that the iron birds would return.

In the meantime, as people are wont to do, blame had to be placed on someone for the terror they had endured. Who had brought strangers into their midst? Who moved freely back and forth between the lowland and the mountain? Who had acquired a foreign wife? Who but the de Solas, Raymond and his brother Alphonse, were guilty on all these counts? But who was the rabble-rouser who shouted out these accusations? The women and I followed the crowd into the great assembly hall. The seneschal and the *sous-viguier* had called them together—now I am more inclined to see it as herding them in—ostensibly in order to calm the spirits. But already on the way in, there was much jostling and grumbling, even some unruly behavior. A rebellious mood pervaded the throng, unlike the sheepishness they had displayed previously.

The one who jumped on the platform before the seneschal and raised his arms was none other than Guilhem de Sola, his brother, loyal servant, and *viguier*. Did he see his chance to seize the moment, to throw off the yoke of subservience to his brother? His eyes glowed rebellion. He fired several shots in the air at once, silencing the clamor of the crowd. Behind him, his myrmidons, wild-eyed and armed with machine-guns and ammunition belts strapped across their chests in the style of Latin American jungle guerrillas, kept the villagers in check with glowering stares. The once loyal soldier pointed an accusing finger at his brothers.

"Traitors! There are the traitors! Arrest them!" His rants quickly won over the fickle mob. Shouts of approval and demands for the arrest of the guilty rang out. Some bold souls even suggested the hanging tree. Surprisingly, the sole objection and call for reason to prevail came from Pierre Lunel, who subsequently was tied up and pilloried together with the seneschal and the *sous-viguier*.

Now, Nina was not one to buckle under when it came to the father of her children. She protested with loud screams and counteraccusations and pummeled the chest of the blackguard who was pushing her back with a barrage of fist blows. Etoile and I, the foreigners who had brought misfortune to the mountain, were held back at the point of several shotguns.

Just then, another swarm of iron birds came swooping down into this melee. The clamor overhead came so close, as if the whole fleet was spiraling down for landing on the roof.

"To the ramparts! To the ramparts!" Guilhelm's shouting, though almost drowned out, was audible enough to rouse his blackguards and a few hardy souls to form a posse. What followed was absolute chaos, total pandemonium. Only from the view of hindsight have I been able to sort out the events. Inside, we rushed over to free the captive leaders. Outside, the rat-a-tat-tat of gunfire lasted about fifteen minutes. Once unfettered, the seneschal and Alphonse made their way to the portal but were held back by the trigger-happy mob. Whether they could have changed the course of events, whether their intervention would have averted the disaster, will never be known but is unlikely.

A gasp, not so much of relief than of apprehension, exhaled from the assembled villagers when the shooting suddenly broke off. Silence at first. The choppers too had ceased sputtering. "They must have landed," Etoile whispered in my ear, squeezing my hand. Then boots grinding the gravel, many boots. I saw them in my mind marching in formation toward the compound. Barking men and dogs. It had been a long time since I had heard this sound. Now they once again evoked the deep fear of goose-stepping uniforms, windows shattering, and doors splintering under the blows of jackboots and axes. Dina's descendants were once again in danger of being evicted, uprooted, subjected to torture, put on trial, and driven from pillar to post. I looked around for Nina. She stood with Alphonse, their two young sons between them, facing the door at the head of the crowd. A dark glower veiled her eyes, her jaw taut, her lips pressed together betraying the strength of mind and undaunted spirit of hers, which I had feared might have been suppressed in this medieval world.

Bright sunlight streamed into the hall as the door flung open wide. I recognized Monsieur Fauré in the midst of the army of troopers gathered in the square, but it was clear that he was not the man in charge. No, the man in charge stepped forward with sovereign self-assurance and somber demeanor. He introduced himself as Inspector Charpentier from Interpol and politely suggested that everybody step outside and line up in the plaza. Images of *Appelplatz* line-ups in Nazi concentration camps rose before my eyes. At this point, the seneschal, who had been very quiet, no doubt still in shock at having been shackled by command of his brother, took control. He raised his arms and walked ahead of his flock out into the sun-flooded morning.

A howl of horror rose up from the rank at the scene that presented itself to their sight. Strewn on the pavement were seven bodies, five clad in the leather attire of the blackguards and two in French police uniforms. Among the dead was Guilhem de Sola, *viguier* of Valladine. The situation was obviously very grave, but also unmistaken. As the inspector explained, Guilhem and his men had opened fire at the troops as they were disembarking from the helicopters that had landed in a field. To the charges of murder of the hikers over a period of several years, the investigation of which had brought the police to the mountain, would now be added the slaughter of two officers of the law.

The seneschal, still looking like a magician or a medieval alchemist in his black velvet robe, stepped forward. He greeted the inspector, spreading his arms as wide as eagle's wings.

"Dear Inspector, let me welcome you and your entourage to our humble realm!"

Rather than appeasing the inspector, the seneschal's sugary words got his ire up. Any discerning observer could see that the inspector who had just lost two men, and even if he hadn't, was not the kind of man inclined to engage in the theatrical banter of medieval courtier games.

"Are you the man in charge here?" he bellowed.

"Indeed, Your Lordship. I am Raymond de Sola, seneschal and overlord of this fiefdom. We are pleased to receive you as our honored guests."

The inspector's clean-shaven face turned red as a tomato, ripe to the point of bursting. "Will someone get this guy to cut the crap? This is a murder investigation—six murders plus two new ones as of this day!"

Why did the seneschal behave this way? What did he presume to gain by playing what would appear to a modern man a buffoon?

Here I thought I had gotten to know this man as a rational human being who had chosen to live in the backwoods of this mountain world on principle. Now he had me totally baffled. The situation had come down to a matter of life and death. This was no longer a game. Shouldn't he have enough sense to realize that the French authorities would not play around with murder, especially when it came to an ambush on its officers? I decided to do what I could to allay the inspector's anger. Nothing I said could make the situation any worse, so I thought.

"Inspector Charpentier," I stepped up to him, "maybe I can be of assistance in clarifying this matter."

"And who are you? Another court jester?"

"I am Henry Marcus, professor in the history and culture of medieval France at the University of Chicago. My work in this field is recognized worldwide, which can easily be determined by a search at any library."

I had spoken with all the dignity I could muster in my best French. Under the circumstances, I didn't mind sprinkling my tone with a bit of academic haughtiness with the intent of impressing the inspector. In the corner of my eye, I caught a glimpse of Etoile rolling her eyes heavenwards and vigorously shaking her head. By the time her silent message that I was as pompous as the seneschal sunk in, it was too late. What had made me think I could intimidate or impress Interpol with my credentials? Instead of helping, I had made things worse. I had flunked my own test.

"I know this man! He's the one who tried to deceive us. He tried to erase the tracks that would lead us to the perpetrators." But Monsieur Fauré's reedy voice was no match for the inspector's roar.

"Never mind that now! Enough of this farce! Professor, whoever you are, go back in line with the rest of the suspects.

You, Seneschal, or whatever you fancy yourself to be, I give you twenty-four hours to bury your dead and get your people together. Everybody here will report in this square at eight o'clock tomorrow morning—this includes women and children. No dogs or other animals. Only one suitcase or bag with bare necessities is permitted. Due to lack of cooperation, this nest of lunatics is herewith subject to dissolution!"

The inspector's plan, as he stated, to deport an entire population from its home was simply mind-boggling. But I had wasted any standing I might have had, though it's unlikely that I ever had any. This inspector wasn't impressed by titles or credentials, especially academic ones. Was there no one else to stand up? I looked around. Where was Alphonse? Just then he crossed the plaza with resolute strides. He assumed a wide stance in front of the inspector, looking him straight in the eye.

"Who will take care of our livestock while we are away?" he demanded to know.

"And who are you?"

"I am Alphonse de Sola, the seneschal's brother. I am a veteran of the wars in Indochina and North Africa. I had an agreement with Monsieur Fauré that no one would be harmed."

"He promised to cooperate," piped Fauré. "There would be no shooting."

"I'm sorry about this incident. A few hotheads took matters into their own hand. It was unforeseen and unauthorized." Alphonse apologized, but he gave no sign of weakness, I was proud to note. He held fast. No buckling under for him.

"All right, then you will be in charge," the inspector concluded. "You heard the order! Eight o'clock sharp tomorrow morning!"

He turned abruptly. Bending down at the waist and holding on to his hat, he made his way toward the helicopters. The rotors had already been set in motion; their giant windmill arms churned up clumps of earth and flung them into the faces of the approaching officers. The police casualties were loaded aboard on covered stretchers. The ranking officers in civilian clothes followed behind. The villagers fixed their gaze at the sky, mouths agape, until the iron birds had dwindled from sight, consumed by the sun's rays like the Dioscuri, and the noise had ebbed to a faint hum.

The uniformed troops who stayed behind meanwhile began setting up camp in a sheep meadow close to the plaza, without so much as requesting permission and with total disregard for the inhabitants and the livestock. They strutted about with miens of superior disdain like conquerors of a foreign land. Valladine had been placed under control of a foreign occupation force without a formal declaration of war or an armistice. Occupiers and villagers glowered at each other with silent suspicion.

Several requests by Alphonse for more polite consideration were rebuffed. He was told to do as ordered or else. The commandant reminded me of those old colonialists, of whom he may well have been a relic, to whom the subjugated natives of the lands of their conquest were naughty children who had to be kept in check with terror tactics. The Germans termed their tactics of controlling the native population in their African colonies a policy of "*Schrecklichkeit.*" The French and British weren't as blunt, but their methods in their respective "spheres of influence" were no less frightful for the natives.

The next command was for surrender of all weaponry—firearms, knives, hoes, scythes, pitchforks, and anything else that could be used in combat.

So Alphonse told the people to ignore the barbarians and go about doing what needed to be done with dignity.

"They have the upper hand right now, and we must do as we are told," he told them, "but the onus is on them. If they take us to court, the French legal system will be more understanding. I'm certain of that."

They nodded their willingness to obey, but their dull faces showed how baffled they were about what he termed the legal system. He tried to explain as best he could and in simple words a concept that was completely beyond their ken and experience. He spoke calmly, soothingly as one does to frightened children. Thus reassured for the time being, they went about their tasks.

Was he really certain French justice would exonerate them? I had my doubts. In fact, I doubted very much that any judge would be inclined to be lenient toward a band of uncivilized mountain dwellers, outlaws in some sense, accused of serial murder and armed resistance resulting in the death of two police officers. By the same token, I had no doubt that these villagers had nothing to do with the crimes and that the actual perpetrators had been Guilhem and his blackguards. I was therefore pleased to hear the seneschal, who was regaining his composure, order the arrest and incarceration of the surviving thugs over their protests of innocence and assurances they had not fired any shots at the police.

"Since Guilhem is dead," he told me, "the rest of them might try to hightail it out of the village after dark on the Spanish side."

Mention of the Spanish side of the mountain came up again later that evening, though in a different context. The day had been taken up primarily with the somber task of disposing of the remains of their brother Guilhem, who had fallen, yeah, given his life, the seneschal emphasized at the ceremony, in defense of his mountain home. He spoke slowly, enunciating every word with heavy breath. His lids veiled his eyes, and his head hung languidly to the side. The past twenty-four hours had placed the weight of senescence on his sagging shoulders. A funeral pyre had been erected in a place reserved for such ceremonies at the far end of the valley. The body was completely incinerated and the ashes left to be carried off by the wind. Nearby was a small cemetery so ancient the inscriptions on the toppled gravestones had been rendered illegible by the elements. Several centuries back when faced with shrinking land for farming and grazing, the community decided on cremating the dead even though it went against Christian practice. The names were immortalized on the wall of a small shed.

Immediately after the funerary rites, Alphonse hurried back to the village. It was now up to him to console the people and counsel them on the ordeal they were facing. Nina and Etoile returned to the house to look after the children and pack what they deemed necessary. I stayed behind with the seneschal, who sat hunched up on the ground in front of the charcoal remains of the pyre, his eyes wistfully fixed on the dying embers. Not wanting to intrude on his meditations, I wandered over to the little cemetery. The number of people buried there was hard to determine. By my rough estimate, there were two hundred gravesites, more if the sites had been staggered. The graves were not clearly demarcated, and the moss-covered, crudely fashioned headstones tumbled any which way, some stretched out on the ground, others holding each other up in crooked position like a procession of blind beggars lost in darkness.

These silent witnesses to the past awoke my researcher's instinct, and I started to examine some of the headstones more closely. To no avail! My attempts to make out the lettering met with little success. Centuries of erosion from wind, rain, and ice had turned the carvings too shallow to yield a single distinct name or date. Disappointed, I sat down on a stone that had conveniently fallen into vertical position and thus provided a weary wanderer with a place of rest. My thoughts drifted back to what I had learned about this place, this oddest and yet most wondrous place called Valladine—the valley of Dina. Somewhere here in this earth rested the bones of the woman who had called herself Dina. I was sure. But where? Did it matter to know the exact spot? Hardly. Suddenly I was overcome with the kind of awe I often felt in archives when the past became present to me. I may not have been able to find a marker indicating the location of her resting place, but I still felt her presence. Without forethought, I rose and fumbled for the *kippah* I always carried in my pocket. Facing east, I began to say the words of the Kaddish. I spoke softly, intoning each cadence with the ardor and precision of an actor reciting a Shakespearian monologue. I repeated it twice, once for Dina and once for her three sons.

My thoughts wandered back to that hotel room in Toulouse when I first became acquainted with Dina and her life, which so closely mirrored the fate of her people in the diaspora. I thought of Tisha b'Av without being aware that this was the actual day. In the course of those past few years, I had lost track of the landmarks in the Jewish calendar. And now I was here walking the earth of her promised land. I was moved to sink down and kiss the ground, but was held back by a gentle hand on my shoulder.

"What are you doing?" said Etoile. "We are waiting for you."

"It just occurred to me that she probably lies somewhere here in this little acre littered with illegible stones."

"Yes, I've thought about it too. Nina took me to this place earlier. We said Kaddish for her together."

"So you got ahead of me," I said in a snit.

"You were closeted most of the time with the seneschal. We didn't want to get in the way of your manly tête-à-tête. You must have noticed that the medieval mindset is still very much alive around here. The seneschal may be a charming man, but even his wife tells stories of how women are kept in their place under his reign."

"So you have been closeted with the women!"

"What else was I to do? I assure you the encounter with these women was as fascinating and fruitful as your *entretrien* with the seneschal."

Now all this was coming to an end. How much more we could have enriched our knowledge of the lives of these people and of history had we had but more time, had we not left a trail behind us for the hounds to follow?

"Do you think it's our fault?" I asked.

"Our fault for what? You mean it's our fault, all this upheaval?"

After a pensive pause, she added: "In a way, I guess we are responsible. But we did nothing willful. The real culprits are the hotheads who murdered the hikers. Without those murders, the police would never have had reason to snoop around and track our peregrinations. No, I really don't think so." She shook her head as if to convince herself of the truth of her statement. "But it's sad, very sad. Who knows what lies ahead? I feel sorry for the people whose lives are about to be destroyed."

We held each other as we walked back to the village. We halted for a moment as we passed the pyre. It had by then become completely extinguished, leaving behind the acrid smell of cold embers.

"All this time, I've hardly been thinking of Dina's codex," I said. "Now I'm wondering what she would think about all that's happening. I have a real yen to get back to her, to read through her book once again."

"Won't you have a chance when you translate it? You still plan to do that, don't you?"

"Yes, of course. But the text poses many questions. Maybe a comparison with the chronicle can help solve some of the more puzzling aspects."

"You mean as to its authenticity?"

"Yes, there are parts—you hinted at some already—that raise questions as to her authorship; whether it really could have come from her pen; whether she could actually have experienced all she said she did. She was after all a fairly unsophisticated waif. Better educated than other women of the time, but still, in modern jargon, her development had been arrested by the circumstances she found herself in. Then there are the historical events she relates. I don't doubt her relationship with the priest. That certainly came from the depth of her soul. But other episodes …"

"Like the encounter in prison with Baruch le Teutonic?" Etoile said.

"Yes, it just seems far too much of a coincidence, don't you think?"

"The dates are right, but Nina and I have the same doubt about this. The same goes for her literal citation of the verses from Lamentations without resort to a Tanakh, as she says herself. A bit too remarkable—wouldn't you agree?—that she should have remembered them word for word and in Hebrew? There must have been another much more learned redactor. Maybe one who had the luxury of copying from the text directly."

I just nodded and swallowed hard on the yellow bile churning my stomach. Jealous and irked about having been left out of the discussion the two apparently had, I sulked like a schoolboy for the rest of the way.

Nina met us at the door as we were about to enter the great house. She placed a finger on her lips, signaling us to enter quietly. Inside, we found the entire de Sola clan assembled. Raymond and Alphonse spoke simultaneously to the women and children, among them Guilhem's widow and her brood.

"Descending on the Spanish side in the dark of night is out of the question. It would be a reckless disregard for the safety of the children." Béatrice, the seneschal's wife, whose self-effacing, guarded bearing had previously reminded me of Renaissance portrait paintings, was clearly in a defiant if not combative mood. "Besides, it would be shameful and cowardly for us to run away and leave the rest of the citizens of Valladine in the lurch. This suggestion is simply preposterous." Nina and the other women, even the children, clapped their hands.

"All right, I give up. We thought of your welfare," said Alphonse, throwing his hands up in the air. "Women can be very stubborn."

The seneschal was not so easily dissuaded. "Women have to do as they are told," he insisted.

"That's a very medieval attitude," said Nina. "The world has moved on in the last few centuries. We now have equal rights!"

"How dare you?" It was clear nobody had ever dared speak to the seneschal in such a defiant manner. Under different circumstances, even Nina would unlikely have been so bold. But it was equally clear on this night that the seneschal was no more. He was simply Raymond de Sola. He was stripped of all attributes of a feudal lord and potentate whose word is the people's command.

"Professor, listen to this." He turned to me in a last-ditch attempt to reassert his authority. "If we are to regain control over our domain here on the mountain, it is imperative for the de Sola bloodline to be preserved. We cannot permit our progeny to languish or come to harm in a French prison. I am prepared to give my life, but these children must live. These are the inheritors of our centuries-old traditions. It is their duty to carry on. This cannot be the end of Valladine!"

I was taken aback to have the onus of ombudsman in the dispute placed on me, the outsider. From what I gathered, the details of which were later confirmed, he and Alphonse had plotted, or decreed in their style, to have the women and children, some like the seneschal's offspring were in young adulthood, escape into Spain at the risk of the descent on the steep and rugged southern side, which required special climbing skills in the daytime and was definitely perilous at night. But that was not the primary objection to this plan. It simply boiled down to their unwillingness to accept special treatment, Nina explained to us later, when the entire village was slated to be taken into custody and possibly be charged with murder. A noble, commendable stance, no doubt!

But here was a man, brought to his knees by the precipitate events, the same man I had come to admire a short while before for his strength and regal bearing—the man who had inspired such loyalty and awe among his subjects. Now he was broken, his world was being swept away; the city of refuge on the mountain far off the evils of the world, to which he had been witness in his youth, this city of dreams that held out the promise for a better world than existed elsewhere, this city was to be no more. Moreover, as far as anyone remembered, reaching back into time immemorial, the House of the de Solas had ruled over this piece of earth and its inhabitants as if it was their fiefdom. He would face the accusers, the French authorities, and if need be, he would shoulder the burden of guilt and the shame his overzealous brother, whose ashes were now mingled with the dust of the mountain, had brought upon the house that Dina and her descendants built.

I understood this much—the house, the de Sola clan, had to be preserved. He could not relinquish it all. He was ready to bear the consequences, to abdicate, he told me later when it was all over. He had an almost mad obsession with preserving the lineage, the bloodline, the line of descent—how many times did he mention these terms!—with the deluded dignity of a medieval monarch. His sons and the sons of his brothers had to be saved from harm at all cost. Unlike his wife and the other women of the household, he seemed to have little concern for what would happen to the common people of the domain. There was a contradiction in his thoughts, which he was unable to fathom even when I gently tried to point it out. As for Alphonse, it was my impression he too was bound by the concept of family honor and a sense of duty that obligated him to support his older brother. By tradition, he could not go against him.

The debate about various matters, possible strategies and subterfuges, went on until deep into the night. All idle chatter when nobody found any sleep on this eve of "expulsion and exile." Those were Nina's words, true to her flair for the melodramatic. Neither her life, nor mine nor Etoile's for that matter, was on the line. We were in the rather more comfortable position of lookers-on, spectators of a drama unfolding on the stage of history, even though the bond we had formed with individual players was of a more personal nature than for common spectators. This was especially true for my cousin Nina whose metamorphosis into a Valladinian was near completion. She tended to the physical and emotional needs of her fellow mountaineers cowered together in the great assembly hall, holding on to their meager bundles as they anxiously awaited the break of dawn. Eventually, the debates ebbed. There was nothing more to thresh out. Any further talk about what lay ahead would be idle chatter.

Béatrice and Nina continued their ministrations, comforting the anxious mother and the weeping child here, the elderly man or woman incapable of grasping what was being done to them there. *Naomi and Ruth*, I thought as I was dozing off. A dream came to me. Nina was gathering sheaves of grain in an expansive field of gold. She was talking to a woman resembling Béatrice in her gracious bearing, though her face was blurred, telling her something to the effect: "Your people are my people, and your G-d is my G-d." I must have been threshing about in my sleep, for I woke with a start when Etoile poked me in the ribs. "Your trumpet is bringing the house down," she laughed.

"Did you have to wake me? I had a beautiful dream," I retorted.

"What about?"

"I won't tell you if you take this kind of attitude," I grumbled. "But if you really want to know, it was about golden cornfields. In their midst was Ruth, the Moabite, ancestress of King David, with Naomi her mother-in-law. The two were gathering sheaves of grain."

"And Ruth said to Naomi …"

"Yes, she did. But the most intriguing thing about the dream was that Ruth clearly had the face of Nina, and Naomi, though in less sharp focus, had the gestalt of Béatrice. What do you make of this?"

"That you are an incorrigible dreamer? But, I admit, it sounds like a beautiful dream, and I'm sorry for interrupting. Listening to you, it sounded more like a dream about the trumpets of Jericho."

Before I could give her my dream interpretation, namely that Nina was a modern-day Ruth, that she had been transformed into a Valladinian, just as Ruth had become an Israelite, a blast of trumpets, ear shattering like those of Jericho, ripped through the air. Since it was the crack of dawn, the sun had not yet risen and, therefore, did not stand still. Etoile pointed out that my analogies were inside out; but what did it matter.

Shouts and stomping boots preceded the entry of Captain Charpentier's storm troopers into the hall where the masses were huddling. The ensuing chaos was calmed with a few salvos in the air that stirred them into grabbing their permitted bundles and stampeding outside where they lined up in the plaza as ordered. Then came the long wait, nobody knew for what or for whom. The prisoners, for that's what they were now, stood silently casting wistful looks at the sky where the sun began its daily rise, a scene so familiar to them, daubing village and peaks with bands of vermillion glory. The sun should have stood still in its orbit, not to assure the enemy's victory, but to shed its light on the injustice being done here. Collective guilt and collective punishment!

The only voice of protest echoing from the cliff face surrounding the crater was that of Nina.

"Why are you all so docile?" she shouted in Occitan. "Resist! You needn't follow those henchmen like sheep! Lie down in their path! Refuse to move!"

"We are unarmed. They took everything from us that could serve as a weapon." Pierre Lunel left his place in line and started toward Nina.

"We don't need arms. We'll just have to form a chain of nonviolent resistance. If they start shooting, our blood will be on their hands."

Nina was still a child of the sixties' civil rights movement in America. But this was a French murder investigation. Alphonse, whose mind was unclouded by ideologies and who had most likely never heard of Martin Luther King, had a much better grasp of the reality of the situation at hand. He understood that one doesn't mess with a stronger adversary, in this case the French police.

Pierre Lunel was ordered back in line with his family. Nina's indomitable spirit was dampened, if only temporarily. Just then, the captain came over, alerted by the disturbance. His strutting stride on the gravel crunched every beating heart. As it turned out, he was from a northern province and did not understand the ancient language of Languedoc, so Alphonse had an easy time persuading him that it was a mere squabble. We held our breath for a moment longer lest there was a native of these parts among his men who was wise to the dialect and caught on to Nina's call to resist. Our fear proved unwarranted, however, and we let out a hushed sigh of relief.

Another hour went by. The sun moved slowly to its high point in the cloudless sky. I saw Nina chomping at the bit. This was no way to treat a girl from New Jersey. Flanked by his two giant snowballs, Alphonse stood guard over the flock. From time to time, he shot a warning glance at his wife to keep her calm. Just as she made another move toward the colonialist taskmaster, the by-now familiar buzz of twirling rotors broke into the monotony, faint at first from far away, but soon closer and finally with deafening crescendo. Deus ex machina was never more fitting! Only in this case it spelled doom for the captives rather than liberation. The return of the iron birds winging in the top honchos! Hovering overhead for a moment, blades rotating, one of the choppers descended in a straight line down, like a cormorant darting into the sea for prey. Four more followed. Together they filled the valley with a howling wind symphony. As on the day before, they landed in the nearest pasture, carelessly churning up huge clods of earth, causing sheep and cattle to clamber up a crag for their lives.

From the first two aircraft issued, as expected, officers or officials in gray suits, their number larger than the day before. One could have thought there was no case of greater importance on the police dockets. The rather bizarre scene made me suspect it was curiosity about this archaic place that made them scramble to be in on it rather than a fervor for justice to be done.

Our colonialist captain bowed and scraped to his superiors. He waved his hands wildly at us while conferring with them. Since we had been standing around without food or water since early morning and were rather befuddled and acquiescent in our fate, I couldn't imagine what there was to discuss with such urgency. Maybe his duty dictated to report about Nina, the one rebel in our midst. Whatever it was all about, it looked to me like a lot of imperious shuffling for position. Who will be hailed for his service to honor and fatherland? Who among them will be decorated with the Grand Croix of the Order of the Légion d'Honneur for his discovery of this uncharted piece of French soil? Who among them will go down in history as conqueror of Valladine? My heart went out to Inspector Fauré. By all rights, he should receive credit for the discovery through his tenacious advancement of the murder investigation. Without his ingenious trickery, these men would not be standing on the soil of our Shangri-La. Instead, the valiant bloodhound cut a rather meek figure in the shadow of all those officious eminences, contenders for *la gloire de la douce France.* The murder investigation had to take backseat to the advancement of French glory, for the time being at least.

Meanwhile, to my surprise, the cormorants kept coming. Four more swooped down, one after the other. They spewed out what in the blinding midday sun appeared to be an army of soldiers crouching under the rotating blades. Once they reached the open field, rather than lining up in military formation, they swarmed all over. Then there was another troop in civilian clothing that pushed toward us. We were blinded by lights flashing into our faces. As they came closer, juggling for position, I realized they were brandishing cameras. Word of the discovery of a medieval village high up in the mountains had apparently been leaked to the press, and as a result, we were inundated with a species of snoopers called journalists. The villagers, who had never seen such devices and took them for pistols or such, raised their arms to shade their eyes against the blitzing fireworks. This was too much for Nina. She may have seen the wisdom of holding back when confronted with the police—but the press? This was an outrage beyond, above and beyond …!

"Paparazzi! Damn paparazzi! Get the hell out of here!" She was no longer shouting. She shrieked uncontrollably. I had never seen her so beside herself with anger and disgust. Yet, after the ignominy that had been poured on the inhabitants of Valladine in the past two days, I delighted in her pouring chamber pots of epithets in the finest New York street slang on the heads of the gatecrashers. As one might expect though, the presence of an American woman, and a feisty one at that, in this godforsaken outpost made the story only more intriguing for the sensation hunters.

Then the order went out for the departure. Once again, the villagers clutched their bundles and lined up. Ahead of the flock, the seneschal shuffled along stoically with his family in tow. He had been very quiet, seemingly reconciled to whatever was to come. All dealings with the officials were left to his brother. There was a brief squabble about whether Alphonse could bring his dogs. He could not. And who would look after the livestock? This was of no concern to the police. *These people really know how to make friends and influence people,* I thought to myself. How different matters could have been had they shown just an ounce of courtesy. This wasn't a conquest of a colonial empire. France had been out of that business for almost two decades, but the mentality was apparently long in waning. The uniforms flanked the captives, and the press brought up the rear, merrily snapping away at the wretched lot. This formation would be hard to maintain once we started the descent along the sloping mountain paths. But why give them advance warning?

Etoile and I walked behind Nina and her children. She was still snorting with indignation. "Did you get the pictures?" she asked Etoile, who nodded. We had brought along a small, unobtrusive camera to establish a record of village life. The rolls of film would have to await development for the time when we returned to the flatland. Now they came in handy for recording the behavior of the police, the lord and masters, and the rudeness of the sensation-seeking press during the forced evacuation of Valladine. The codex and the chronicle that the seneschal had entrusted to me for safekeeping were stashed away in Etoile's backpack, out of the hands of any possible marauders.

We moved on. Alphonse was leading the way through the opening in the rock wall hidden behind the waterfall and out down the sloping abyss. The people followed not knowing where the journey would take them. Would they eventually rebel? The way the Israelites rebelled against Moses in the desert. So far, they simply shuffled along, following their leader. The children too were remarkably docile, especially the older ones. The younger children were under the care of Nina and Béatrice. Etoile too lent a helping hand by carrying a toddler part of the way and soothing anxiety about this journey into the unknown.

A line from Paul Claudel's epic poem about the desert wanderers came to my mind. I had always liked it for the starkness of its rhythm, evoking silent acquiescence: *"Et l'on entend le bruit d'un peuple qui marche."* The sound of a people on the move, indeed. Etoile pointed out the speciousness of my analogy when I cited the phrase to her.

"Moses was the liberator, not the captor of the people," she said.

Of course she was right again. A more fitting analogy would be the Babylonians taking the Jews to the banks of the river Euphrates. But I liked Claudel's poetic cadence.

Foxes Walk on Dina's Mountain

"The camp of Le Vernet covers about fifty acres of ground.
The impression on approaching it was a mess
of barbed wire and more barbed wire.
It ran all around the camp in a threefold fence and across
it in various directions, with trenches running parallel. The
ground was arid, stony, and dusty when dry, and deep in mud
when it rained, knobbly with frozen clods when it was cold.
Le Vernet was the worst camp in France. As regards
food, accommodations, and hygiene, Le Vernet was
even below the level of Nazi concentration camps."
—from Arthur Koestler's *Scum of the Earth*

The barbed wire was gone. The trenches were filled in with debris. The ground was still arid and dusty this many summers later. The deafening clangor had subsided. The stench rising from latrines and the rot of diseased men, withered corpses, that once putrefied the air had long been dispelled by purifying mountain winds. The rattling shrieks from the throats of the wretched, the anguished, the distressed, the famished, the ailing, the infirm, the lepers, the meek, muffled protests from the miserable heap of humanity once detained here, had faded out into eerie stillness. Rows of barracks that once housed refugees from Franco's Spain, veterans of the International Brigades, as well as common French criminals, antifascist intellectuals fleeing persecution, Comintern agents, and Jewish refugees from all over Europe caught in Vallat's net, had been razed to the ground. At the time of our arrival, the place was slated to be spruced up as a public museum, a place people could enter into, through the preserved wooden posts of the entryway, and learn of man's inhumanity to man, so the slogan went.

Le Vernet, a camp that was set up and run by the French authorities, was what they called a "punitive camp." The reasons for this are not entirely clear. One section was indeed reserved for criminals, but most of those incarcerated there fell into the broad category of "undesirables"—those deemed anti-France—who had been caught in a vast net of Vichy police *rafles* and sent to the gulag of camps in the Midi. The small, red brick railroad station and a cattle car were still there as an exhibit to testify to the constant shuttling of humans that once was the daily routine at its ramp. Most of those taken from the hellhole of Le Vernet were dispersed to other camps. Transports of Jews invariably went to the "East"—to the mythical destination of "Pitchi Poï" or somewhere in the Reich. By June 1944, Le Vernet was certified to be *judenrein*. The last transport, known as the "Ghost Train," had left the station: destination Dachau in Bavaria.

It was to this locale the French authorities saw fit to shuttle the uprooted inhabitants of Valladine. As unbelievable as it may seem, like most of the interned who had preceded them some thirty years before, they too had fallen victim to what Koestler had termed "traditional French xenophobia." In the present situation, it made even less sense than it did in that earlier time, in the days of war. It simply boggled the mind why this place was chosen, except perhaps for its proximity to the town of Pamiers. Pamiers of all places!

Conditions at the camp were better and more sanitary. Food and lodgings, while plain, were adequate, but it was an unjust imprisonment nevertheless.

"You and Mademoiselle Assous are free to leave," the camp commandant told me when I broached the question with him why these people were kept in a camp—and in this particular camp.

"With all due respect," I replied, "that is not important at the moment. My concern is the welfare of these people who have been uprooted at gunpoint and callously tossed into a world entirely foreign to them. Again, I demand to know, why have they been put into a concentration camp, and what is the charge against them?"

My voice must have betrayed my irritation about his evasive response. He dropped his military correct manners and pointed out with a cutting tone: "You should be concerned about your own status. As a foreign national, you have no right to make any demands, which may be grounds for deportation."

Rather condescendingly, he added that these backwoods medievals could hardly have any association with the past of this camp and should be happy to live in modern housing courtesy of the government of France. Courtesy had nothing to do with any of this. His superior tone was a sharp break from the cordiality he had displayed when we first met. The hope I had nourished then of finally dealing with a man of civilized disposition, of a post-colonial mentality so to speak, was utterly dashed.

"As a historian, may I remind you that Vichy is past history?" I knew it was unwise to defy the powers that be, but he had gotten my ire up. This was one of the rare occasions in my life when I followed my impulse without regard for the consequences. I still look back on this incident with pride, especially since it gained me the admiration of the two loves of my life, Etoile and Nina, when I later related the exchange to them. Both vowed to take up the fight against the commandant and the entire police and military establishment of France should it become necessary.

Fortunately, the plans they hatched for organized resistance were never put to the test. There never was a call for blowing up bridges or ammunitions depots, nor did it become necessary for them to assassinate high-ranking officers as their loftiest dreams inspired them to do. The next day, the commandant's stance had changed completely. In a friendly, even conciliatory manner, he explained to us, not without a blink of personal skepticism, the why and wherefore of the government's internment policy. I like to think that mention of the wartime collaborationist French government and its xenophobic policies had made him run scared. The prospect of me dropping hints to the media, which had already taken an extraordinary interest in this case, of Vichy conditions at the camp, I am sure played its part.

In fact, it was the sensational discovery of a hitherto unknown medieval tribe on sovereign French territory and the charges of murder against the inhabitants that had made it necessary to move the trial from Toulouse to Pamiers, the commandant explained. But even in that town, not enough safe housing space was available. Some brilliant anonymous chap, of unknown administrative echelon, had conceived of the idea to build temporary shelter at the old abandoned camp which was about to be revamped and made a memorial site for tourists. The advantages were clear, yet the commandant struggled to make us see the wisdom of the decision. The area could be enclosed with a fence, to be sure without the barbed wire of the past, for safety. Also, the section chosen for this purpose was not the original cesspool where criminals, dissidents, the refuse of Europe, and Jews had been kept, but the less odious *Quartier Français*, across the road dissecting the camp, where the Vichy guards had been quartered. Whoever the chap was who came up with this idea had to be slapping his knees with delight. Maybe a promotion was even in the offing. But this was of no concern to us. We had to make the best of the circumstances we were in.

"The question remains," Etoile insisted, "why were these people taken from their home in the first place?"

"I'm a public servant who was ordered to this post. I had no say in any of this." The commandant was a man in his fifties and probably close to retirement. Why should he jeopardize his pension after a lifetime of service by asking too many questions of his superiors? These were my thoughts, but Etoile was not ready to relent.

"You must have some idea. Maybe to exploit them for a sensationalist freak show or circus exhibit?"

"Who alerted the paparazzi and helicoptered them in?" Nina demanded to know. "Just look out there. Here too, ceaseless flashing of cameras. Telephoto lenses zeroing in like sharp-shooting guns."

"I had no part in any of this. But I'm doing all I can to keep the press at arm's length."

"What did they tell you about the purpose? Did they tell you anything about who these people are? They must have said something about why they are reopening an old concentration camp." The furies wouldn't let go of the hapless chap.

"Well then," the commandant spoke slowly, obviously trying to stay calm. "I was told that they are mountain dwellers and that they are being held as material witnesses in a murder investigation. That's all. My orders state that they are to be treated with respect and provided with comfort and adequate meals. I didn't know there were that many," he added. His frustration over having been settled with a thankless task was clearly written in his angered red face.

"Believe me, we understand your predicament," I began, speaking in a deliberately conciliatory tone. What purpose would be served to gain his enmity? But the ladies weren't satisfied yet.

"We know about the murders." Etoile made a dismissive gesture. "If they are witnesses, then who is on trial? Do they have any perpetrators?"

"There are two men under interrogation by the prosecution right now. One, I'm told, calls himself 'seneschal,' and the other is his brother."

"What?" This was enough to make Nina fly off the handle. I had to physically restrain her to keep her from assaulting an officer of the law. I tried to explain to her the simple fact that an interrogation about the murders, which no one denies occurred, is to be expected. It seems perfectly reasonable therefore that they should start with questioning those in charge.

"Which side are you on, Henner?" she asked in English.

"I'm on the side of reason. Rash attacks against the man in the middle will get us nowhere."

We went on bantering back and forth in English for a while. She accused me of bowing to authority like the Germans under Hitler, an accusation that didn't go over well with me. The rest was too ugly and ridiculous to relate in a permanent record. Eventually Etoile stepped in and pulled us apart like a referee separates two exhausted pugilists clinging to each other and trying to land a few more weak blows. We retreated into separate corners and sulked for a while.

"The whole thing is pissing me off," Nina sniffled finally, still sulking but calmer. "In a wink, they destroyed my world. I just can't believe it."

"I'm on your side," I said, "but let's see what develops. And remember, it's not just your world. Our friends are the truly deprived here, and they need our help in this strange new world."

We settled into one of the prefabricated cabins. We had hot water and electricity, and with dividers around the cots and blankets that afforded some privacy. It wasn't the Ritz, but in many ways the lodgings held more comfort than those in the mountain village. There were no refrigerators or kitchen facilities, so food was brought in daily from somewhere. Institutional chow that tasted accordingly. The Valladinians didn't seem to have much of a problem with that particular aspect of their new existence. They had never seen or tasted pork chops and so didn't know what they were ingesting. Etoile and I, and to some degree Nina as well, shied away from the *treife* stuff. After a few days of overcooked vegetables and stale bread, a solution had to be found.

Since we were, as the commandant had told us, free to leave the camp, we considered having our meals somewhere outside. But we had no transportation and didn't really want to cut ourselves off from the people who had become our companions.

"Leave it to me," declared Etoile. "I'll take care of it."

I didn't inquire further, probably because I didn't really want to hear about her solution, at least not that evening.

As I had feared, by noon the next day, Etoile's solution arrived at the camp in a rattling, fume-spewing pickup truck. With the triumphant air of a conquering hero, flashing a big smile at the gathered crowd outside, the Tunisian jack-of-all-trades ploughed a passageway through the sea of photographers with his chariot like Moses, or Charlton Heston, crossing the parted sea. He came to a halt at the gate where Etoile welcomed him with a flurry of hugs and kisses. I kept my distance. She was quite capable of arranging unlimited access for her *copain* to the camp with the commandant. It all worked to everybody's satisfaction. Even I benefitted and so had to put on a happy face.

The Tunisian became our lifeline to the outside world. He brought us whatever we needed, in the food department above all else. Even on days when his services were not required, he hung out at the camp. He befriended the interned as well as the guards. The Valladinians appreciated the endless little favors he did for them to make their lives in this strange world just a bit more bearable. He endeared himself to the commandant and the guards by alleviating the boredom of their duty, whiling away the hours with playing shesh besh with them often well into the night.

We all kept busy with the same tasks. The Valladinians had many anxious questions about a world they did not understand. Nina and Etoile did their best to explain and allay their fears. They set up a makeshift school for the children, a kind of one-room schoolhouse for all ages. The primary subject of instruction, reasonably enough under the circumstances, was French. My two ladies showed quite a bit of ingenuity in devising an elementary curriculum. As the only other person fluent in both Occitan and French, I too was drafted for the effort. As I watched my pupils eagerly lapping up what was taught, an old American saying came to mind: "How'd you keep 'em down on the farm, once they've seen gay Paree?" But then, would there even be a farm for them to return to? Nothing would be as it once was, as it had been for centuries. A deep sense of irretrievable loss filled me with great sadness.

There was one more Nina outburst of indignation, this time quite justifiably so. I almost regretted having collected some newspapers from the commandant. It would have been much better had the authorities kept us in the dark about what was going on beyond the parameter of the camp. But the police who started this proceeding seemed to have forgotten about us once we had been dropped into the camp like so much refuse into a garbage dump. They may not have been thinking of it this way, but it certainly felt like it to us. They were too busy with their investigation and interrogation to give us any consideration. Raymond and Alphonse insisted, as matter of honor and stubbornly so, on being put up on whatever charge against them. As happens so often, the news was leaked to the press first. The seneschal and *sous-viguier*, both now clung to those titles, had been charged with murder and were being held in prison at Pamiers, we read in one of the morning papers.

"Pamiers of all places!" She couldn't have been more outraged. "Is the Inquisition back in town? Is the long arm of Jacques Fournier reaching out to destroy us?"

"Accused put in irons!" screamed the tabloid headlines, and "Incarcerated in the dungeon of Pamiers!" Never mind that there were no functional dungeons in Pamiers anymore. But the press had apparently done some history homework and dug up sensational tidbits about the town's past. Someone's imagination had made the connection with the inquisitor who in the fourteenth century had stamped out the last vestiges of Catharism in the foothills of the Pyrenees beyond the bloody Albigensian Crusade. Their memory was likely aided by current efforts of the local office of tourism to promote the Ariège region as the land of the mysterious Cathars. Some even tried to lure visitors with promises of the famous Cathar cuisine! From there, it was but a short leap for the general public to revel in the romance of Valladine, which they soon painted as the last outpost, a hidden nest, where heresy, once thought totally eradicated, had nonetheless perdured into the twentieth century. The public was no doubt titillated.

Our commandant took it upon himself to make some inquiries about the situation of the prisoners of Pamiers. *La dame américaine* was making his life unbearable, he reported to his superiors. *Insupportable*! The response coming back was to be patient and maintain calm among the internees, as they were now called. The prosecution was gathering evidence. And the wheels of justice, as we know, turn ever so slowly. Where this evidence was being gathered was not clear. The supposedly material witnesses being held at the camp did not speak French and would need our help were they to be interrogated. Maybe the foxes were foraging Dina's mountain for tangible proof. Why start there? Don't ask. I am not a mind reader.

A Pyrenean Chronicle

With all the commotion, we still had more time on our hands than we knew what to do with; time, I suggested, that could be put to better use, which in turn would provide us with some distraction from that which we were powerless to change and especially would keep Nina from bouncing off the walls. The task we gave ourselves was more than a mere pastime; it was to be our long delayed return to Dina and her world. Thus, in a shanty illuminated by a naked bulb at the former concentration camp at Le Vernet, in proximity to the bishopric of Pamiers, the former seat of the Holy Inquisition, we embarked on the translation of Dina's confession into French. The irony of this situation did not escape any of us. We worked through the night with little time for sleep, and yet the next morning we taught the children and generally saw to the needs of the internees, refreshed and with more élan than we had ever had before. The importance of our undertaking never seemed to us more urgent.

The necessary equipment—typewriters, paper, reference works, writing pads, even pen and pencil—as well as the original transcription we had placed in the bank safety deposit box at

Albi, were retrieved and delivered to us courtesy of our Tunisian factotum, as I dubbed him now unkindly and ungratefully, but never out loud. We divided the text among us and set to work. However, it was inevitable that some questions would arise, and a closer examination, *analyse de texte*, became necessary for the prospective readers' understanding and ours. Fortunately, the original codex as well as the other chronicle the seneschal had entrusted me with was in Etoile's rucksack. Nina now objected to any modernist probing of Dina's motivations—she had by this time abjured all feminist paradigms and hidden underlying meanings or alternative redactors—and insisted that the writing should be taken at face value. What she wrote is what it was. However, Etoile and I still had enough of the scholarly detective in us to be stirred by questions and puzzled by coincidences to want to probe further. There was one more squabble between the two ladies.

"Don't you think that there are things described here that just couldn't have happened that way—not exactly that way, at least?" asked Etoile. "You even admitted earlier that you felt this to be the case."

"What do you mean?" Nina wrapped herself sulking in a mantle of obstinate fundamentalism. "Now I changed my mind."

Since time was once again pressing, Etoile relented. "Let's just go on with translating then," she conceded.

Later when she explained to me why she had given in so easily, I came to admire once again her astuteness of mind. It was as simple as that. Long debates would slow us down in producing a French translation that we hoped might help the defense in the case against our friends.

"So we have to choose our battles," Etoile concluded. "It is clear that Nina is not willing to give an inch. She is too involved emotionally. I would even say, she identifies with Dina too closely to have an objective perspective. There will be plenty of time for debate later."

She was right, of course. And yet, I couldn't help but feel a deep sense of loss. The person Nina had become was alien and distant to me, even more so than the one I had met in Albi when she first engaged my help. At that time, she was still filled with enough scholarly fervor to take risks. She had enough spunk to run away from the mountain, driven by a desire to bring this extraordinary medieval Jewish woman to the attention of the world. What had happened since then? What did they do to her? At what point did she lose her curiosity, her inquisitive spirit about the human hand and actions that formed the world in the past? When did she cease to be a historian? Maybe it was a temporary condition brought on by too much stress and strain. So I hoped. Not that I hoped for the return of the Nina in her incarnation of world traveler with feminist paradigms in her briefcase—I had always regarded this as a passing phase, if not a fad. No, it was the questioning Nina, the Nina who always saw three sides to a problem I missed. Most of all, I wanted the Nina who was bursting with creative energy. Maybe it was too much to ask for the child to be reborn.

While my thoughts were thus preoccupied, I reached for the codex containing Dina's confession to her sons. Heedless, but with the habitual care of the scholar, I began to turn over the sheets of parchment. The Hebrew letters danced before my eyes like a passel of Hasidim at a Shabbat service. Slowly they came into focus. As I began to read, I was impressed by the precision with which the symbols were drawn, almost with the neatness of a Torah scroll. Only a trained scribe could have produced such perfection. Other pages clearly came from a more amateurish hand. The contrast was as obvious as night and day. Only our great haste in transcribing the text could have made us overlook what was now so glaringly evident. I felt my heart pumping with double capacity. This was a discovery I could not wait to share with Etoile.

As luck would have it, I found her alone typing away in the adjacent cabin. Nina was getting her children ready for bed. Etoile admitted that she too had noticed the evenness of many passages but for good reasons didn't want to dwell on it. The possibility of another redactor had occurred to us before, as we discussed at the cemetery, but then our suspicion was based on the content of the text itself. Now we seemed to have actual physical proof.

"This is really fabulous!" she exclaimed. "It confirms our hunch about an alternate redactor."

"Look at this!" I said, holding the codex up to the dim light in the cabin. "Even in this light, you can see some overwriting. You know what?" My heart was now racing, and I was breathless.

"Henri, please sit down and have some water," I heard Etoile say as if from far away. I did as she said and caught my breath.

"This is a historian's dream—a palimpsest! Imagine, Etoile, a palimpsest!"

"I am as excited as you are, but we cannot talk to Nina about it. Not now, under the current circumstances. Later when all is behind us, she will understand, and I am sure she will share our excitement in this discovery."

"Somehow I doubt that any of Dina's sons had the skill to make these insertions. They were mere shepherd boys and relatively uneducated," I mused.

"So was Rabbi Akiba."

"Yes, but …" We looked at each other and burst out laughing.

"Maybe a closer look at the chronicle will yield some clues."

"Not tonight. Nina will be back soon, and we still have to meet our daily quota."

Etoile, always the rational, the restrained one, at least when it came to work discipline. Yet, we didn't make much progress with the translation that night. Nina was tired and asked to be excused. Something seemed to weigh on her mind, but I didn't dare to ask.

Etoile and I continued for a while longer but soon called it quits as well. We held each other closely embraced, but sleep did not come until dawn. Motionless and without speaking, we listened to the drumbeat of our hearts. A great adventure lay ahead. Together we would float down the river of time, cutting through uncharted territory waiting to be explored. This was the historian's spice of life. Alas, for now the journey was only in our dreams.

In mid-September—right at the time of the Jewish Days of Awe, it flashed through my mind—the trial began in Pamiers. The tribunal gathered with great fanfare. Missing were only drum rolls and clarion calls. The pompous entry of the red-robed magistrate and the black-robed jurists into the packed courtroom—people literally hanging from the rafters—resembled more a carnival pageantry than the opening of a murder trial. True, it is not uncommon for such trials, especially one appealing to the prurience of the common folk, to be conducted in an atmosphere of hype and hysteria. In this instance, however, it can be categorically stated that this trial was not like any other trial. In fact, I don't think it was a trial at all in the sense of the commonly held definition.

Attendees of the proceeding, both inside and outside the halls of justice, came from far and wide, from various French regions and foreign countries. They came by train, plane, bus, and automobile, bicycle, motorbike, and for all I know by oxcart or hay wain.

Residents from towns and villages all around hoofed or thumbed it. Hotels and boarding houses within a radius of thirty miles were booked out. Habitual newshounds, stringers, and pundits blocked entrances and telephone lines. Then there were the plainly curious rubbing elbows with sensation and thrill seekers, the highbrow and the lowbrow, the scholarly types and the popularizers. Academicians from fields beyond history and anthropology swarmed over the Episcopal See of Pamiers which had not been heard from in world affairs since the Inquisition had left town and Jacques Fournier had moved to the papal palace in Avignon. Surveying the crowd from a hidden place, I espied a legation of colleagues from the American Academy of Medieval History, emeriti of the most eminent American institutions of higher learning.

Earlier that morning, we had been roused by the camp guards. The commandant wanted to see us. Himself half-asleep, unkempt, and unbuttoned, he informed us that the day was finally here. We were to be taken to Pamiers. The curtain on the long-awaited public drama was finally to rise. We were to keep ourselves in abeyance as witnesses for either the prosecution or the defense. The commandant didn't know and didn't care about details. All he wanted was to go back to bed. He was tired after gaming through half the night. The three of us—Nina, Etoile, and I—were transported in a vehicle that resembled a rundown paddy wagon with flapping back doors. A rattling noise behind us drew my attention, and sure enough, the pickup truck was hard on our tail. Etoile nodded when I pointed to it. Yes, she knew. He was following her order to stay close by, just in case. Just in case of what? But I knew better than to ask.

The first witness called by the prosecution, or the jurists who postured as prosecution, was to our surprise Pierre Lunel, one of the few Valladinians who spoke a modicum of French, enough to understand and be understood. Under questioning from said *procureur*, he described the social arrangements in Valladine, the hierarchy at the top of which was the hereditary position of the seneschal.

"Is this seneschal, as you call him, present here in the courtroom?"

"Yes, right there on the accused's bench. But he shouldn't be there."

"What do you mean? Why not? Didn't you say he is all-powerful? A kind of tyrant?"

"Only to some extent. There's also a council of advisors."

"Of elected officials?"

"The seats are passed down from generation to generation."

"Ah, very interesting. Not exactly a model of democracy," the *procureur* mumbled in the direction of the magistrate.

"What do you mean?" Lunel looked confused. "I'm not sure what you want me to say. Our order has existed for centuries. It has worked fine and still does. Nobody complains."

Thinking back to the rather raucous communal dinners Nina described, and which we had opportunity to experience ourselves, this statement didn't quite reflect the reality of the mountain community. Pierre Lunel obviously refused to be coaxed into airing the family dirty linen in public.

"We have no wars or feuds," he added, "unlike what's been happening down here in the flatland. We know about your endless bloody battles down in the flatlands over the centuries. We have no torture chambers or concentration camps."

This remark earned him boisterous applause from the audience. Thus encouraged, he continued: "The seneschal is an honorable man, and so is the *sous-viguier*. They would never kill anyone."

"Not even intruders who might expose the existence of your little realm to the outside world?"

Pierre Lunel shook his head vigorously. No, never. It occurred to me that he was an odd witness for the prosecution. Maybe this wasn't a criminal trial at all. Maybe this was a clever ruse, an exposition of a backwoods community, an oddity arrested in time, in the guise of a murder trial. A bizarre way of going about it. If true, it was no doubt concocted by some twisted judicial mind like those on display in this courtroom. My hunch was to be confirmed at every twist and turn as the theater of the grotesque unfolded.

"So you want us to believe that this Valladine was a perfect utopia where social harmony reigned supreme for centuries?" another black robe spewed his derision.

"Your fancy words may not be familiar to me, but I understand enough what's behind them. Yes, that's the way it is—or was, until you intruded on our domain."

Which jurist played what role was not clear even to the discerning eye. As far as my eye could see, there was no actual defense. Just a team of *avocats* vying with each other in strutting their brilliance. The presiding magistrate too threw in his piece of wisdom from time to time. The questioners consistently steered the witnesses back to testify on what life was like in the community. The murdered hikers and police officers seemed of secondary, if of any interest at all.

La femme américaine or *l'Amércaine* became the star witness and the subject of scrutiny from the populace and the press. The fact that she was rumored to have lived among the savages for many years and was amorously involved with one of the accused added a note of titillation. Nina showed her disdain for the sensationalists with nary a glance in their direction. As for the jurists, who for their part were not above exhibiting a prurient strain, she threw them a few scraps about her personal life—yes, she was the wife of Alphonse de Sola, and yes, she was born in Valladine under somewhat unusual circumstances. Other than emphasizing the fact that both accused men had helped many refugees escape from the police of Vichy France, she divulged little. She was much more interested in establishing the right of the Valladinians to their land in the mountains. All in recognizing it as part of the territory of France, to be sure. Nobody ever denied this. The brave Valladinians have always considered themselves French, she declared. This may have been a slight exaggeration, but as we know, Nina was never above resorting to hyperbole to make a point.

By way of making her point more forcefully, she took out our translation of Dina's letter to her sons.

"I have here in my hand," she exclaimed, holding up the bundle of papers, "the written testimony of the woman, a Jewish woman, who founded Valladine seven hundred years ago."

The jurists fell over each other to grab the document and be the first to enter it as an exhibit for the proceedings. The magistrate looked at it briefly and then ordered it to be handed back to the witness.

A hush went through the crowd in the courtroom as she began to speak. Seven hundred years ago! Words spoken with deliberateness to dramatic effect. Nina had not lost her knack from her teaching days for spellbinding an audience. Even the magistrate and jurists pricked their ears, listening for the hum of the shuttle flying across the loom of time.

From an array of illustrative swatches that she plucked from Dina's account, Nina stitched together a broad tableau of a turbulent time. She evoked images of heretics, persecutions and inquisitors, tortures, and burnings at the stake with vivid strokes.

"And then there was this young Jewish girl who was caught in a maelstrom of evil and injustice." Nina pointed an accusing finger at the evil king of France, a libidinous priest, and superstitious peasants who made this woman's life a "living hell," as she put it.

One person who came off fairly well in Nina's rant was the bishop of Pamiers, who, she stressed, made it possible for her and her offspring to seek the freedom of a new life in the mountains.

"This is how Valladine came to be," she concluded, "and it has continued to exist unchanged for centuries as a model of cooperative living, of peaceful living, of self-sufficiency."

At this point, wild applause erupted in the audience.

"Do you have anything to add?" the judge asked her after quiet returned to the courtroom.

"Only one thing, a word of advice for our time," she said. "Call it a utopia, but the civilized world can learn a thing or two from these brave people, especially from their cooperative social and economic organization, and their peaceful way of resolving conflicts."

It was overwrought and overstated in typical Nina fashion, but a crowd-pleaser nevertheless.

Etoile and I testified briefly. The star of the proceedings was Nina, which was only as it should be. The prosecutor questioned Etoile about life in what, he said, had been described as a medieval village. Based on the knowledge she had gained from her studies of this period, was it her opinion that it was really authentic? She confirmed that here was a textbook example of life in a medieval village, a living laboratory for medievalists to study. At least it had been, she added, until now. Just as a specimen under scientific investigation can become corrupted and contaminated by improper or careless handling, the pristine village environment had already suffered through the interference from the authorities. She concluded with a plea not to disturb life on the mountain any further, lest it be destroyed forever.

"Nice try, but fat chance," I whispered when she returned to the bench on which we were rather uncomfortably seated. For some bizarre reason, the word *Eselsbank* popped into my head. I had wiped the "donkey's bench" from my memory for good, so I thought. This bench was located in the farthest corner of every German classroom, slightly elevated so all could see "the donkey," primarily underachievers set up for shame and ridicule. Only, I wasn't an underachiever. I could read and write and do long division before any of the towheads in the second grade. I was the untouchable, the pariah, the leper, the Ahasver, the Jew. Now, more than forty years later, in a French courtroom, why should this donkey feeling of being pilloried and scorned come over me again? Maybe this trial too was contrived to set a bunch of outcasts up to ridicule.

"I know it's no use," Etoile whispered back, "but I had to say something."

My testimony was brief and limited to the kindness the seneschal had shown the Jews during the war. While the modern French state packed "undesirable foreign elements" into sports stadiums and from there on to cattle cars in which they were shuttled like so much cargo across Europe to that mythical land of no return called "Pitchi Poï" somewhere in the east, the people of Valladine saved lives by helping the many who were fleeing the Vichy authorities across the mountains. And the Nazis, of course, I added quickly in response to the prosecutor's raised eyebrows and glowering gaze as if he were reprimanding a schoolboy who had given the wrong answer to a simple question.

Although they addressed me with the honorific "Monsieur le Professeur," no one deemed it necessary to call on me as an expert witness in the history of medieval France, of which they were no doubt aware. I cannot deny the sting I felt to my ego. My affection for Etoile brought out my more magnanimous side. After all, she was French, had studied at a French university; her credentials were entirely French. So why shouldn't the French trust her word and expertise more than mine? Nonetheless, the entire spectacle was beginning to grind on my nerves. I realized it was nothing but a contrived media event with a plot as transparent as that of a medieval farce! The outcome was easily predictable, and I was itching for it to be over already. But there was more to come. What would this spectacle be without putting on display the man who represented as close as one was ever likely to get to a flesh-and-blood medieval monarch or at least a feudal lord.

"Let my people go!" These weren't exactly the words he used, but he did have something of a Moses about him as he rose to address the court. The seneschal had regained his dignity, I was happy to note. He too gave a brief rundown of the history of his mini-realm from his perspective and then he threw down the gauntlet at the French authorities.

"You have no right," he intoned, "to uproot these people and destroy their lives by taking away their rights based on a centuries-old covenant with the founders of our colony."

"No one, and certainly not the Republic of France is intent on infringing or taking away an ancient right," interjected the judge.

"Then why did you bring us here?" the seneschal retorted. "Why did you treat us as criminal outcasts? Why did you put my people into a concentration camp?"

"You must remember, we had a murder investigation going that seemed to require a more drastic measure to prevent the guilty from eluding justice," the magistrate stuttered and stammered.

"But the guilty had already been identified," the seneschal retorted. "As you know, most of them were killed when your police stormed our village."

A brief fracas initiated by Monsieur Fauré ensued at this point.

"How do we know, Your Honor," he shouted, "that these were all the guilty? How do we know there wasn't a conspiracy to commit murder of anybody who got too close to this mountaintop paradise?"

Calls for the inspector to pack up and go home came from the audience. Sympathies were all on the side of the Valladinians.

The magistrate threatened to clear the courtroom. Not even the sound of a needle dropping could have been heard when he issued his verdict: "Raymond de Sola, you are herewith ordered to take your people home!"

Jubilation and pandemonium broke out in the courtroom and flowed over to outside the courthouse.

"I had been waiting patiently," the inspector told me years later over a cup of coffee back in Oloron Sainte Marie. "I thought once the circus was over, the jurists would get down to the real business at hand, which was the murders. Imagine my disappointment when the presiding judge ordered the detainees released and the proceedings closed without as much as giving any consideration to the murders. I felt I had to do or say something. But, you were there, professor; you know what happened."

"Well, you know," I started to reply, but he went on.

"Just dismissed the charge with a flippant gesture." Monsieur Fauré made a corresponding motion with his hand. "Such are the people who sit on the bench in France nowadays making life and death decisions. These are the types entrusted with upholding the law. The law! They don't give a damn about the law. Publicity—that's the name of the game. Well, he and those jurists got plenty of it. Makes you wonder what our *patrie* is coming to."

I listened attentively to the inspector's laments. He didn't seem to take into consideration whose side I was on, but he had gained my respect in the time he had been doggedly pursuing his case. Now he needed someone to talk to, to unload his soul, to lay out his theory about the series of crimes, and I was happy to play Dr. Watson to his Sherlock Holmes. He had, of course, a very different take than what it turned out to be. His thinking ran along more conventional lines of smugglers and brigands, professional criminals waylaying innocent vacationers. The ultimate truth of the matter was too fantastic for any human mind to conceive of, he had to admit.

Considerable time had passed since the *soi-disant* trial at Pamiers. Most members of the tribe of Dina had returned to the mountain. I am saying most because a goodly number of the younger folk wanted to see gay Paree first, which is as one might expect. Would they be repelled by civilization and its morals, or lack thereof—as the seneschal once was in his youth—and return to the mountain? Somehow I felt the lure of Babylon was likely to be too great for many to resist.

My encounter with the inspector took place long after my own life had collapsed around me. I always knew that the end of Valladine and our work on Dina's codex would also spell the end of my love affair with Etoile. Deep down, I knew that one day she would marry the Tunisian mechanic, even though I didn't know then that they had been betrothed since childhood. What a strange arrangement for a modern, educated woman! But she didn't seem to mind.

At first we went back to our cottage of blissful memories to finish translating Dina's codex into French. The work progressed slowly due to her frequent absences on teaching assignments and revisions of her dissertation for publication and, I presume, trysts with my rival. My offer to help with her work was rejected. I noticed that her heart was no longer in our task to which we had given so much. She was carving out her own niche in medieval studies.

"Dina Miryam belongs to you and Nina," she said one day.

This was an odd statement and clearly not true. She had put her heart and effort into this just as much as we had. Her remark could only be a prelude to the end. She was letting me down gently. Was she trying to soften the blow? I surrendered my head to the chopping block.

"Will you come to the wedding?" she asked.

"We'll see," I said. When the day came, I was far away from Toulouse and the Languedoc.

So, long after all this happened, on a return trip to the country, I took a detour to Oloron Sainte Marie. I found the inspector at the coffeehouse where we had breakfast together years before.

"We were playing a cat and mouse game then," I said laughing.

"Who was the cat and who the mouse?"

"You were the cat. Definitely. And a very sly one at that."

"Ah, *oui*!" He intertwined his fingers and stretched his arms far with a distant look at the mountains. A self-satisfied smile flushed his face.

"I used every trick I could think of, but you still slipped through my fingers."

"Not for good. You finally tracked us down all the way to the mountain top."

He nodded pensively. It was clear to see, he still carried a chip on his shoulder.

"Guilhem de Sola, whom they called the *viguier*," I said, "he was obsessed with keeping intruders away. Unlike his brothers, he had never left the mountain except to buy pistols and shotguns from Spanish arms dealers. In time, he accumulated a considerable arsenal. I'm sure the seneschal did not know how far his brother was willing to go to protect the home turf. So Guilhem went out in a blaze of fire, if not glory. To us moderns, it's almost like a Hollywood movie, but for the seneschal and his people, it was the end of their world."

While I was speaking, the inspector's lips had tightened, and his eyes narrowed to a squint. He began to rock back and forth in his chair. His eggs and coffee were getting cold.

"I guess the case is closed then," he said with a tone of finality. He turned toward the waiter. "Let's have two more breakfasts over here for two very hungry souls."

"No, no, it's on me," he protested when I reached for my wallet. "And no more tricks from anybody. You know, this could be the beginning of a beautiful friendship," he added with an impish smile. We both burst out laughing. The image of the two of us walking arm in arm into the fog, Casablanca style, was not altogether unappealing.

We chatted a while longer. He asked about my *copine* and Nina. Both were doing well, I assured him without going into details. I told him I had come to France for the publication of my translation of Dina's tale into French. He was almost ecstatic when I handed him a copy and insisted that I inscribe it for him. Then he turned it over a few times lingering over the front cover. A collage of images of mountains, a forlorn-looking wench with a bonnet, shadowed by a Dracula look-alike holding a Cathar cross over her, was printed over with the title: *La concubine du curé cathare.*

"Interesting title!" The inspector held the book at arm's length with raised eyebrows. "But I shall look forward to reading it."

"Believe me," I said not without embarrassment, "I had nothing to do with it. It's appalling to me, but at least now everybody can get to know Dina's remarkable story."

My protests against the sensationalist title had been overridden by the French publisher. "If you like alliterations it's not bad," the inspector tried to console me.

I could only foresee with dread what title American publishers might adopt for the English translation. Nina was not one to take any crass vulgarization of Dina Miryam's life lying down without a fight.

CODA

Valladine Redux

Israel, May/June 1982

I set out in my Land Rover in the early morning hours of a pleasant day in late May. A few miles up the road, I stopped to take in the spectacle of Dawn slowly lifting her rosy fingers from behind the eastern mountain range, daubing the damp, breathing desert in a vermilion glow. Since taking up residence in the southern Negev, the eternally recurring cycle of sunrise in the east and sunset in the west, both clearly visible from my abode at the kibbutz, has never failed to overwhelm my senses and stir my soul. Against my previous habits, I have become an early riser, a very early riser. On occasion, I even don tallit and tefillin, face east and say the morning prayers.

On that morning, however, I had no time to linger. I was on my way to the airport up north. Since he had announced his visit to the Holy Land, I had been seized by a strange apprehensiveness. Several years had passed since the day when he had gathered his flock and returned them to the mountaintop. We, including Nina, stayed behind in the flatland. The work still ahead of us then was better done in a place that afforded access to libraries and archives, as well as specialists in ancient bookmaking for us to consult. He had graciously left the chronicle of Valladine and Dina's codex in our care for further study. Now I was worried. Would I recognize him? What a silly question. Why shouldn't I? People don't change that much, not in three years.

Yet, much had happened in that time! Etoile had married and settled in Toulouse to a life of domesticity as well as scholarship. I couldn't quite imagine the former. Maybe I didn't want to dwell on it. Nina had accompanied me back to the United States while Alphonse returned with their children to Valladine. How odd an experience it was for both of us, especially for her to be back to what was for us the old country! We had literally been to the mountain, away from civilization and the hustle of big cities. The noises of the modern world heightened our sense of disorientation and alienation. We knew that we would never feel at home there again, neither in Chicago nor in New York. We discussed other places, more isolated and remote, for us to settle. After all, it's a big country, we told ourselves. There are vast spaces and high mountains. It had to be a place where Alphonse and the children could feel at home as well.

"Some remote place in the Rocky Mountains, far from the madding crowd, for example, would be ideal," she said over coffee and scrumptious cake at Aunt Hedy's dining table in New Jersey. It was like old times, and Aunt Hedy was in heaven. Yet, I felt a long "but" coming from across the table. After some hems and haws, she finally came out with it: "I want to raise my sons as Jews," which promptly earned her a big hug from her mother. "In all these years, I always felt that something was missing in my life, despite my love for Alphonse. I don't know that I could have stayed in Valladine forever. Alphonse understands. He's willing to go along."

"So then all is well," I stated.

"Not exactly, at least not with settling here, even though I love this country. As you know, Jewish communities in America are concentrated in the cities. I don't believe there is a sizable *kehilla* in, say, rural Idaho or Montana. So where can one find a place remote enough, give the children a Jewish education, raise sheep for a living, and still be in relative proximity to the amenities of civilization?"

"That's easy enough," I said.

There was, of course, only one answer. And so we all, Aunt Hedy included, who was beside herself with joy, came to settle in the land of Israel. Alphonse became an observant Jew and settled in a far corner of the Golan Heights, adjacent to the Lebanese and Syrian border, an ideal place for raising sheep. Nina bought an apartment in the center of Jerusalem for her mother and sent her boys to yeshiva. Aunt Hedy moved out within a short time, however. She found a home for elderly German Jews, congenial companions who still knew how to recite the poetry of Goethe, Schiller, and the venerated Heine of their youth by heart and were not shy about correcting each other if one of them made a mistake or had a lapse of memory.

Nina and the boys commuted on weekends from Jerusalem to the Golan. Weekdays she worked on the story of Dina and Valladine at the Hebrew University. Having had my fill of lofty heights of any elevation, I chose to settle in the desert. A kibbutz in the Arava region was just far enough, though not too far out of reach, from that madding crowd we all have come to dread so much but couldn't do completely without.

"Such is the beauty of Israel!" Nina exalted. We were sitting on the porch of my modest hut one day, looking out on the sunset over the desert during one of our get-togethers to work on the Valladine project. "It's like Valladine redux!"

"What do you mean?" I asked.

"Israel! It's like Valladine, a refuge, a sanctuary from the evils of the world!"

I wasn't going to get into this debate and point out the difference.

Our project was finished now. Well, one could say it had at least progressed far enough for a presentation to the public. Nina had arranged a symposium at the Hebrew University for that purpose. However, the powers that be apparently deemed the vagaries in the life of one medieval Jewess of insufficient academic interest to warrant an entire symposium. There was a lot of back and forth from which Nina mercifully shielded me. The compromise, a not altogether displeasing one to her or me, was a two-day conference on the broader topic of Jewish women in medieval France. It gave her an opportunity to invite her friend Etoile to speak about her research on Rashi's daughters. A colleague from the United States was to speak about two medieval Jewish women, one from the German Empire, the other from the kingdom of Aragon. The language of the conference was to be French with some English and Hebrew translations available.

To give her presentation a real-life fillip, or as one might say in German, to make it more *lebensnahe*, she came up with the idea of inviting the seneschal. My skepticism that he was not likely to venture down the mountain to undertake the journey, by airplane of all things, to be her show-and-tell object was quickly dispersed. He accepted, and now I was on my way to fetch him from the airport and bring him to Jerusalem. I cannot deny that I was looking forward to greeting the man whose almost otherworldly demeanor and imposing presence had once inspired me to call him *stupor mundi*.

I recognized him right away. *Stupor mundi* hadn't changed much at all. He strode through the swinging doors with the aplomb I remembered from his entry into the grand assembly hall at Valladine. He held his massive frame arrow-straight, convincing me once again that they were growing giants in those mountains. His white hair spilled onto his shoulders from under a broad-brimmed hat, the kind Alphonse favored too. In my mind, I had seen him arriving clad in one of his flowing wide garments. If not the black velvet, which was more fitting for a cooler clime, at least the white linen one with turban, which would give him the aura of a desert sheik. Fortunately, he had more sense than that. He wore a simple shepherd's outfit, coarse homespun trousers and a white linen shirt over which he had donned a bolero type jerkin of sheepskin. He traveled light. His luggage consisted of a leather scrip slung over his shoulder and a small canvas rucksack on his back.

He greeted me with a bear hug and kissed me on both cheeks with a third one added *à la française.* The knot in my stomach began to dissolve almost magically.

"For whom are they building these airplanes? Dwarves?" he thundered as we walked toward my car. He was tall and lanky, and being lanky myself, I could well imagine how cramped in his legs must have been during the flight.

"You have come alone," I remarked as we took the turn to the highway for Jerusalem.

"Yes," he nodded with a sad smile. "My faithful Béatrice wanted our children to get to know Paris. The wonderful, magical city of Paris! They should also meet their relatives, aunts, uncles, cousins, whoever was still alive. Two years have passed since they left the mountain. I doubt they'll ever come back."

"And you? What about you?" I asked.

"My place is in the mountains. That's where I belong, that's where I'll die."

We both fell silent. He cast a wistful look on the parched landscape on both sides of the road. I wondered what was going through his mind. He had closed himself off. Maybe I had been too intrusive. The loss of his family was no doubt very painful. I hesitated to press for more. Fortunately, the traffic required my attention, which gave us some reprieve from having to talk.

As the road made its ascent toward the holy city, it passed through greener pastures. Flowering bushes lining the roadway pleased the eye with their colorful clusters. I wanted to show off my country, impress him with its beauty so different from his mountains, yet equally dear to us. On a sudden impulse, I veered off the highway onto a country road leading to Latrun. I halted on a hill overlooking the terrain that had served as a bitterly contested battlefield going back to the time of Joshua and the conquest of the land. In more recent times, during Israel's war of independence, the most heated fighting had taken place here for control of access to Jerusalem, I explained to the seneschal. He did not ask any questions, which I attributed to the fact that he was not familiar with the history, but he nodded his head and seemed to listen attentively. Thus encouraged, I went on to give him a brief outline of the history of the Jews in this land, spanning over three and a half thousand years, the dispersion and the more recent ingathering of the exiles.

"Nina calls this land our Valladine," I concluded with a chuckle. "What she means is that this is our refuge from a hostile world," I clarified when I saw his puzzled look.

"A refuge from a hostile world," he murmured. "Valladine is no longer a refuge," he added more forcefully, a note of sorrow swinging in his tone. "Everything you predicted, professor, has come true. Valladine has become a hikers' and climbers' attraction. It's the goal of every daredevil in Europe. And many make it. The village is now overrun with strangers."

"How do the natives take it?"

"Many have left the mountain, especially the young. They want to see and experience the world beyond. Quite a paradox, don't you think? The young people from the world below risk their lives, climbing over the most rugged and steepest terrain to reach Valladine. And ours want to escape the mountain. And among those who have stayed, most have found a way to profit from the influx. They've opened eateries and hostelries, even gift shops with handmade *trucs, bric-à-brac*. A regular helicopter run brings all kinds of goods and wares. There's even talk about a cable car service. This would require electricity. No road, thank goodness. The slopes are quite steep, as you know."

"I can see you are not pleased."

"It matters none what I think or feel. Valladine is no longer the fiefdom of its founders. The spell has been broken once and for all. There's no going back to the old ways. But I still have my library, which I hope to enrich during my visit down here. And old Pierre Lunel is still ploughing his fields. We are two relics set in our ways—vestiges of a lost world."

"But you have found the courage to go on this journey to a foreign land in a modern mode of transportation."

"So I did!" he laughed. "How could I pass up an invitation from Nina and the opportunity to see my brother Alphonse? Pierrot could never be persuaded to get into an airplane."

To my questioning look, he clarified: "The old Lunel. His sons and grandsons too have flown the nest."

As we came closer to the city, the road took several steep ups and downs, inclines alternating with declines. Raymond de

Sola pointed to the clutter of rusted tanks and military vehicles alongside the road. I nodded. More reminders of the hard fought battle for our land, I explained. "The battle is not over," I added. "Our enemies are still seeking to destroy us."

I had reserved two rooms at a small hotel not far from the Old City.

"When do we see Alphonse and Nina?"

"We'll visit Nina and the boys tonight. She is making dinner. I'm not sure Alphonse will be there. He's usually with his sheep in an area located on the highest elevation in this country. Nowhere near the majesty of the Pyrenees though."

In the afternoon, we took a stroll through the Old City. I answered his questions about this and that object or scene which caught his eye. He towered over me and took such large strides I had to scurry to keep up. At the Kotel, we put little pieces of paper into the cracks of the last standing wall of King Solomon's temple. He thought it was childish to write little notes to a deity, but then declared it was fun to follow ancient customs. I didn't ask what he wrote.

We garnered two chairs and positioned ourselves in the middle of the square from where we had a good view of worshippers and passersby. He was perplexed by the fence that separated the men and women, which in turn perplexed me since I had seen similar divisions of the sexes in Valladine under his reign. I preferred to let this topic slide and turned his attention to the clusters of young people, male and female, in uniform with rifles slung over their shoulders.

"You see, everybody serves in defense of the country here."

"I can see that." And after a brief pause: "There are no more weapons in Valladine. I guess we no longer need them," he added with a tone of regret or maybe nostalgia for the good old days. "We are now under the protection of the French Republic."

I closed my eyes. It felt good to have him here, to sit with him in this ancient historic spot and soak up the warming rays of the sun. I wondered how he felt about all this, about being here, about a place that must appear rather exotic to him. When I opened my eyes, I found him staring with that wistful look of his at the swarming throngs of men in black suits and hats. I started to explain that these were the very religious Jews, Chassidim and Haredim they were called. But he waved off my attempt to enlighten him.

"I've seen them before," he mumbled. "My friend Ahieser Fortgang was one of that kind. This is how he prayed facing the rising sun, swaying back and forth in his big white shawl with black stripes and dangling threads. He seemed so firm in his faith and at ease in his daily dialogue with his G-d. I see him before me as if it was yesterday. Never forgot. And I betrayed him, left him to the wolves."

I wanted to say something comforting like there was nothing he could have done without risking his own life and even then it would have been for naught. But he would have rejected this as patronizing with meaningless platitudes. It would have been no consolation to him. I felt bad about having for a moment forgotten about the story he had told me of his youthful wanderings, his encounter with the itinerant peddler and his stay with him in Vienna until March 1938. It was not difficult for me to picture him, this man Ahieser Fortgang, whose last name means going away as well as going forward. Seen superficially, Ahieser too seems a fitting name for a wandering Jew. "Ahasver" is the name of a legendary figure in anti-Jewish Christian mythology, the Jew who supposedly refused to give Jesus water as he walked by his house carrying the cross to Golgotha. The similarity of the names surely must be mere coincidence, I thought. Ahieser is biblical, and Ahasver is a Christian invention of debated origin.

I saw no point in sharing these thoughts with my companion. It was also time to return to our lodging and make ready for dinner at Nina's place. So we wandered on through the narrow twisting alleys of the Old City. My mind would not let go yet of the legend though. A question that had bothered me for a long time came back to me. Why was this figure called "wandering Jew" in English and other languages like *"le juif errant"* in French, but in German was called *"der ewige Jude"*—the eternal Jew implying immortality? More likely, what the Christian mind implied here had something to do with the concept of eternal damnation. The Jew was condemned to live forever as was his cousin Lucifer. Something else has always bothered me. In the course of time, the story of this figure was incorporated into Jewish folklore as well. Variations of this legend—better to say myth since it has no proven basis in historical reality—can be found in works of Jewish artists, in novels, paintings, and in the twentieth century in motion pictures. Of course, he was de-demonized and became more the archetype of the outsider, the pariah, a *Randfigur* in society, the exile. I thought of Dina Miryam who was the archetype of the outsider in the village where she was left stranded. Then she founded Valladine, far up in the mountains where she could breathe free. It came to me what Nina meant by saying that the state of Israel is our Valladine even though its physical reality had so little in common with that mountain enclave. Like Valladine, Israel was a fortress, a refuge. But is it impregnable surrounded as it is by those who seek her destruction? Then again, Valladine too proved in the end vulnerable to assault.

My thoughts had wandered far afield into unpleasant territory, and I was startled when we found ourselves in front of our lodgings. I apologized to my guest and begged him not to take my silence in any way as a sign of displeasure with his company. He told me not to worry. He too had been lost in thought stirred by the manifold new impressions that were assailing his senses and forcefully bringing back memories of past events and encounters.

In the early evening, we took a taxi to Nina's place on Har Hatzofim, also known as Mount Scopus, near the university. Nina gave the seneschal a warm, respectful welcome. The two boys ran up to their uncle, their tzitzit and side locks bouncing with exuberance.

"Arnaud! Bernard!" the seneschal called out while pressing them both to his chest. "How big you have grown!"

Aunt Hedy was there. It was her first meeting with this man since he had assisted in the birth of her daughter some forty years before. It was quite an emotional reunion. Aunt Hedy couldn't stop embracing him even though she had to stand on tippy toes to reach his face, which she stroked with an abundance of warmth.

This was not the only emotional reunion that evening. I should have known. As Nina's closest friend, it was natural for Etoile to stay with her while she was in Jerusalem. She greeted me like a friend with whom she had lost touch and was now overjoyed to see again. Like the seneschal and I at the airport, we too kissed the French way, one on the left cheek and one the right cheek, and then one more on the left for good measure, I guess. She was leaning over toward me to bridge the divide between us caused by her considerable girth.

Rather than ignore the indisputable fact that she was with child, I said with all the pluck I could muster: "*Mazal tov!* You look wonderful! When is the blessed event?"

To which she replied while patting her belly: "Not much longer—this summer, sometime in July."

The evening meal started out pleasantly enough. Nina had learned to prepare some Moroccan recipes, a taste her mother, who was raised on such delicacies as Wiener schnitzel and bratwurst (kosher, of course) with steamed potatoes and red cabbage or other overcooked and underseasoned vegetables, was never able to acquire. If it had to be fish on couscous, then it should at least be filet, not some fried leviathan with head, tail, and bones intact. Why all that spicy stuff? The rest of us obviously had more sophisticated palates if one were to judge by the gusto with which we consumed the repast.

Then came the phone call. It was Alphonse. He had called earlier to let Nina know he would be late. She shouldn't keep the guests waiting—go ahead and start the meal without him. Now he couldn't tell when he would be able to leave his post. His post? The newspapers and television news had been filled for weeks already with government warnings about a deteriorating situation in the north of the country. PLO attacks from southern Lebanon against civilian targets in the Galilee had been mounting despite an ostensible ceasefire. The crisis atmosphere heated up amidst amplifying calls for reprisals. Some street corner haranguers called for direct military action to make the Galilee safe once and for all.

I tried to explain the situation to the seneschal as best I could while Nina was on the phone with her husband. We heard her first pleading softly, then demanding with sharper tone that he leave the Golan at once.

"Wars have been fought for decades without you. No need for you to stick your neck out!" she finally screamed into the mouthpiece. "You're not even in the army!"

"Your brother farms sheep near our northern border," I explained. "It gives him a good vantage point on our enemies' movements. The defense forces have used him as a scout—in an unofficial capacity, of course. Knowing Alphonse, I would be surprised if he didn't foray into enemy territory on occasion to gather intelligence."

"He was *our* best scout too," Raymond said wistfully. "Knew the terrain better than anybody. Alphonse knows war better than any of us. He fought in two wars in his youth—Indochina and North Africa."

"Let's stop the reminiscences," Nina cut off the conversation in a brusque tone, unusual for her when addressing the seneschal.

Etoile placed her hand on her friend's arm and forced her to sit down between her sons. "Let me and your mother take care of what needs to be done."

The two women cleared the table and set up water for coffee and brought out the dessert dishes and cups. We ate Aunt Hedy's delicious homemade cake in gloomy silence. My attempts to reach out to Nina were bluntly rebuffed. When we had finished, she apologized with a nod toward the seneschal and asked to be excused for a last review of her presentation in the morning.

Arnaud and Bernard, as the seneschal still called them, although they now went by the Hebrew names Aharon and Baruch, sat with their uncle and chatted away in Occitan.

"You are happy here then?" the seneschal asked them.

"Yes, we are," said Arnaud, the older one. "Life is so different here. The cars and buses in which people get around and all that noise and bustle. It's just nothing like Valladine."

"It's exciting," said Bernard. "But I still think of the mountain and I miss it. It's all so flat here and hot."

"Our father tends his sheep on the highest ground he could find," Arnaud continued. "But what they call high here is nothing more than an anthill. It's just no comparison." He made a dismissive gesture.

They burst out laughing over so much pretention, and both boys expressed the hope to visit their uncle on the mountain sometime soon.

"But otherwise we do like it here," they assured him. "We like our school and all the things we are learning—things we never heard about before and didn't know existed."

"Don't take it wrong, Uncle Raymond," said Arnaud, "but our life in Valladine was so limited. If it hadn't been for our mother, who told us about the outside world and taught us English and stuff like that, we would have grown up as dumb as the other children in the village."

I looked up alarmed at the seneschal, but he didn't seem to take the remark amiss.

"You are right," he agreed. "Living on the mountain deprived you of many things, but there was a reason why we wanted to preserve that world. Now, it's all changed anyway." He threw his hands up into the air. "When you come, you'll be amazed at all the tourists filling the streets."

When the boys had gone to bed, we sat together for a while longer. The seneschal and I sipped some cognac. Etoile had a glass of milk, and Aunt Hedy a cup of tea. We tried to come up with excuses for Nina's behavior, attributing it to the fact that once again the country was on the verge of war, and this time it hit home more closely than ever before.

On the walk back to our lodgings, I felt compelled to explain the politics of our country and its relationship with our neighbors in greater detail, but probably didn't do a good job of it. He nodded pensively every time I reached the end of a sentence, which tended to be lengthy and convoluted and, I suspect, often incoherent. Unable to gauge whether my words had any impact on my companion, I gave up and just broke off in mid-sentence. We walked on in silence. It was a warm spring night. The streets of Jerusalem were teeming with people, many clustered in animated debate. A mood of ominous foreboding filled the air.

"So this is your Valladine," the seneschal said after he seemed to have given the matter some deep thought, however without elaborating further on the validity of Nina's analogy between the land of Israel and the remote outpost in the Pyrenean Mountains by that name.

Pyrenean Chronicles: *Compte Rendu*

One cannot be a good historian of the outward, visible world without giving some thought to the hidden, private life of ordinary people; and on the other hand one cannot be a good historian of this inner life without taking into account outward events where these are relevant. They are two orders of fact which reflect each other, which are always linked and which sometimes provoke each other.

With this quote from Victor Hugo, a historical novelist not a historian, Nina opened the symposium. She appeared composed and unruffled. She had greeted individual attendees with a handshake and a gracious smile. Yet, looking at her sitting up there on the podium from the audience's perspective, I became aware for the first time that she had aged. Her navy blue business suit and her hair tied back in a severe bun made her look more than her forty-some years. Life had wiped the dew of youth off her cheeks. I thought of Dina who had had to endure much more pain at fate's hand than Nina ever had in her lifetime. Did she even reach forty? Dina, that is. We have no date of her passing.

And what are we to make of the omission of her name in the official chronicle of Valladine? Nina was sure to touch on that in her presentation, but I knew there was no definitive answer. All we can do is speculate, or in academician speak "take an educated guess," which is, in reality, a way of hiding our ignorance behind a big fig leaf.

I cast a furtive glance from the side at my companion, the seneschal. I could see him only in profile, which made it hard to read his thoughts and surmise his feelings. His eyes were firmly pinned on Nina. She spoke with that self-assured poise and clarity, even as she spoke in French, which once had earned her the reputation of an academic whiz kid, way back when, in another life. Here in this lecture hall, she was the seneschal, the ruler supreme. This was her moment, and her last hurrah.

The first presenter was Etoile Assous from the University of Toulouse. She spoke of the education of Jewish women in medieval France and in particular about the learned pious daughters of the great Talmudist and commentator Shlomo Itzhaki, better known as Rashi. At least that's how her presentation was billed in the program. I heard very little of what should have been to me a fascinating topic. Instead of the scholar I once was, the expert on the history and philosophy of medieval French Jewry, I had become a jilted lover unable to let go. Rather pathetic, I'd say. All I could do was seek comfort in the immortal poetry of the immortal Goethe: The lines I had heard my mother and aunt recite so often kept crowding my head: *Ich besaß es doch einmal was so köstlich ist, daß man doch zu seiner Qual nimmer es vergißt!* These words went round and round in my head, knowing very well that I never really possessed her, that nobody would ever really possess Etoile, not even the Tunisian mechanic whose child she was carrying. No one ever really possesses a star.

The audience's applause tore me from my stupor, and I joined in with enthusiastic applause, even jumping to my feet, hypocrite that I was. Our eyes met briefly. I thought I detected a glimmer of scorn in hers. But this was probably my imagination projecting onto her feelings I had about myself. She was more likely seeking my opinion with that broad smile of hers. I nodded and gave her a thumbs-up.

The next topic of discussion was billed as "A Saint and a Sinner: The Lives of Dolce of Worms and Doña Lumbre of Zaragossa," which had already aroused my skepticism mixed with the slight sneer I still harbored for feminist studies. Then something almost inexplicable happened. Just a few minutes into it, I felt myself sitting up. In vivid narrative strokes, she presented the audience with an evocative picture of two distinct medieval periods and Jewish communities within which these women lived. When she had finished, I felt humbled. I owed this American woman an apology and an expression of my appreciation. She had opened my eyes and mind to the lives of two medieval Jewish women who were probably right there in front of me, but whom I had so far overlooked probably because they were women. The ladies' husbands, though beyond my immediate ambit of scholarship, were known to me, but the importance of these women in the lives and careers of these men had escaped me.

The saint was Dolce of Worms, the wife of Rabbi Eleazar ben Judah, a leading figure in the pietist movement *Hasidei Ashkenaz,* who lived at the time of the Crusades. Dolce's life came to a tragic end in November 1196. She and her two daughters, Bellette and Hannah, were murdered by two intruders into their home. The motive was said to have been robbery rather than religious fanaticism. Dolce, also known as Dulcea, was a successful business woman and an avid volunteer in community affairs, a true woman of valor. Her husband composed an elegy celebrating her life and accomplishments—he described her as *hasidah* and *zadeket*—structured as an acrostic patterned on the passage about the perfect wife in the biblical book of Proverbs.

The sinner, Doña Lumbre of Zaragossa, lived two centuries after Dolce in the fourteenth-century kingdom of Aragon. She was the wife of Solomon Anagni, a court Jew in the interior decorating business. The scandal centered on allegations of adultery against her. No proof of her guilt actually exists. In all likelihood, the rumors were circulated by Don Solomon's numerous business rivals and enemies within the *aljama* of Zaragossa. The heel of a husband, as I would call him, divorced her anyway without returning a penny of her dowry. The presenter speculated that he may even have been complicit in the plot.

These stories broadened my horizon about medieval Jewish community life. They brought me down from my lofty castle keep of ideas. This was down-to-earth history taken from the teeming bustle of human life. I was willing to do penance at my Canossa for overweening pride. The lives of these women opened up a unique alternate portal onto a world to which I had claimed ownership for decades. Dina had pointed the way. Now these women and Nina affected my conversion, albeit sans postmodern paradigms.

The next morning, Nina took to the podium. As she stood before the audience, she was in full control with her gracious smile. I was glad to note that she had exchanged the blue business suit of the day before for a very becoming, free flowing, white cotton, ankle-length summer gown sprinkled with light blue dots. Furthermore, she let her blondish hair, woven through with silvery filigree, hang loosely about her shoulders.

"Imaginez!" she began, her voice suggestive and mellifluous, beckoning the audience to come along on a journey, a journey seven centuries back in time. "Imagine a young girl, fifteen or sixteen, alone in a hostile land, cut off from her family, from her people, from her religion and tradition! Imagine such a girl, alone, abandoned, and in constant peril of being found out by the powers that be; in constant peril of retribution for just being who she is—a Jewess. Put yourselves into the shoes of such a girl! Just think back forty years. How many Jewish children, many even much younger than sixteen, were left alone in a hostile world? Wherever the armies of Nazi Germany held sway, countless Jewish children were stranded in similar calamitous straights."

Nina scanned the room, making eye contact with everybody in the audience. Her words had taken root like a delicate plant sunk into a receptive soil. Now it needed water and loving care to grow.

"But this is a topic for another conference. Today we are following the journey of a young girl into womanhood in another barbaric period of our history." She sketched in broad outline the historical backdrop within which the drama of our heroine's life unfolds. She made reference to my French translation which was available to the mostly French-speaking audience.

"The story of Valladine, the mountain retreat or enclave, existed shut off from what we would call 'the civilized world at large' almost unchanged in its way of life for seven centuries until it became the focal point of a much publicized trial a few years ago. We are honored here today by the presence of the man who was one of the defendants at that trial in Pamiers, the seneschal of Valladine, Raymond de Sola!"

The standing ovation lasted several minutes. Seeing how embarrassed and perplexed he was, I put a protective hand on his shoulder.

"I am sure the seneschal won't mind if I now turn back to the matriarch Dina and the origin and history of Valladine as much as we have been able to patch it together from the evidence we have, some ample and plenteous and some scanty and threadbare—*embarras de richesses et embarras de pénurie.*"

Nina first turned to the ample and plenteous. "The letter or account of the woman who calls herself Dina," she said, "is a unique mirror into the innermost world of a medieval woman. It is truly '*un mirroir d'une âme pêcheresse*' (mirror of an errant soul) to borrow the title of the work by another medieval woman, one who lived two centuries later, at the beginning of the northern Renaissance, Marguerite d'Angoulême, the queen of Navarre.

"The worlds of these two women may seem light years apart, one Jewish, the other Christian, but they share a passionate desire, reflected in their soul-bearing confessions, to be forgiven for the sins they committed. Marguerite seeks forgiveness from her G-d for sins committed against him. Dina confesses her sins to her sons to gain their forgiveness. Her atonement for the wrong she did them, her sons, through her carnal weakness; the wrong which resulted in their illegitimate birth and status as bastards. She feels deeply that her weakness had made them pariahs among the small-minded peasants.

"More than anything, she regrets that through her failing, let's say improbity, she had deprived her offspring of the connection with her people. To make amends, she states expressly they should know where they came from. This is reminiscent of another Jewish woman who lived four centuries later and under drastically different circumstances. Glickl of Hameln wrote to her children a now famous account of her life, and like Dina Miryam, she enjoins her children never to forget where they came from. She too wants to instill them with pride in their Jewish lineage.

"Their mother, Dina tells them, is not the despised wretch they see before them; no, she is a princess in the house of Israel, and her offspring are princes of the tribe of Judah. For Glickl and her brood of thirteen, this was not difficult to accomplish; not only were they bred and nestled within the bosom of their own Jewish community, their mother and by extension her offspring had far-flung connections, commercial and familial, to practically every Jewish community between France and Poland. Dina had no such resources. She was alone in a hostile world and had to fall back on what she remembered from her childhood. She was fairly well versed in Tanakh; she could read and write Hebrew; and she was familiar with customs and holidays. Not all of this was she able to pass on. But much of it she did, with determination. One of the most dramatic chapters in the account concerns the length to which she was willing to go, and went, to have her sons circumcised. The sign of the covenant was to set her sons apart from the rest of the villagers. It was a sacred duty she took extraordinary steps to fulfill.

"In the mountain community she later founded, the Jewish origins of the customs and ceremonies they practiced may over time have been forgotten and their form altered in many ways, yet circumcision on the eighth day after birth remains to this day the most sacred and faithfully observed practice."

Nina called on the seneschal to confirm the truth of her statement.

"This is absolutely true," he said, "As seneschal, it has been my duty to perform this ritual, which has been practiced for as long as anybody could remember."

"There was one more matter, maybe the most pressing matter, our heroine felt compelled to clear up," Nina continued. "This matter concerned the man she calls 'the priest' and the role she played in his ultimate undoing. This was the man who had caused her perdition and who was the father of her sons. Right at the beginning of her account, she takes note of her sons' questioning looks. She feels compelled to justify her actions—what they are we learn later—which she suspects may seem callous to them. So the letter is in many ways her *J'accuse,* a litany of accusations against the man who made her his whore and enslaved her sexually and otherwise. Pitiless and without mercy for herself or her readers, she lays bare her relationship with the libidinous priest. She holds back nothing about her seducer and herself. She makes us feel the charm and allure of this village Don Juan as well as his perfidy and duplicity. Neither does she spare herself. With astounding frankness, she confesses her collusion in her own corruption due to the 'weakness of her flesh' as she says repeatedly."

A discussion ensued at this point among the attendees who had the French translation available to them. Most of the participants were women scholars, so the question was whether it was rape or seduction or both, and if one or the other, how and why. The debate culminated in a heated dispute over the definition of the terms, which finally broke off unresolved when Nina put an end to it by pointing out that it was inconsequential in the context. Unlike Jacob in the biblical story of Dina, this Dina's father would not likely have taken her back no matter what the circumstances, whether she was forced into it or willingly colluded in her downfall. In the spirit of the time, she was a fallen woman.

"I find the priest to be a rather interesting character," a woman in the audience interjected. "Nowadays we would slap him with the diagnosis of sociopath. He truly thought of himself as invulnerable. He took unwarranted risks and like all narcissists, he eventually became sloppy."

"As tempting as it may be to indulge in psychoanalyzing," Nina retorted, "I would like to leave this, for the time being at least, in abeyance. Maybe some among you will take a crack at it later on in your work. We could read all kinds of metaphoric meanings into their removal to the top of the mountain, away from the madding crowd, so to speak. But let's not stretch the speculating and analyzing too far. The fact is that she took her children to the mountain to found her own community far removed from a world of everlasting strife and discord, of human misery and …"

Nina paused. She leaned forward and let her gaze wander around the room. With knitted brow, she whispered: "Or did she …?"

Before the audience was able to recover from the abrupt ending of this part of the session, she jumped up from her chair on thc podium and cheerfully announced: "Lunch!"

My French translation published a few years earlier consisted merely of Dina's text as found in the codex without annotations or commentary. This was the version most people in the audience were familiar with. It was the story of Dina the Jewish concubine, or kept woman of a Cathar priest, titillating in its details, the stuff novels are made of. Now Nina was poised to present some of the results of our research concerning the origin of the physical object at hand, the codex itself. After the lunch break, she delved right into the subject.

"If anybody asks me or my colleague Professor Marcus whether we believe this fourteenth-century Jewess Miryam de Sola e Lunel, Dina's real name as she tells us, actually wrote the account exactly in the form it exists in this codex, we will have to answer with a definite *no*."

She held up the codex, which had been in front of her on the table. "There's no doubt that this codex was inscribed many years later. The professional analysis we obtained of the parchment and the binding places it at the end of the fourteenth or even more likely at the beginning of the fifteenth century. The binding was probably done in Venice. Interesting! Also, the hand that inscribed the text was that of a skilled Hebrew scribe. The letters are remarkably clean, almost immaculate. Not as perfect as a Torah scroll, but close. There are some mistakes and glitches. After all, it's not a divinely inspired work, but human, all too human.

"Are we saying the whole thing is a hoax, that Dina didn't exist and is a figure sprung from the fertile imagination of a fiction writer? Here too our answer is *no*. Such a possibility would be too cruel to contemplate. We do believe there was such a person who wrote an account of her life for her sons. The mountain village of Valladine, valley of Dina, exists to this day. We also believe she was literate enough to write down her story in Hebrew script, just not in the codex. A few of the pages we were even able to identify as palimpsests, possibly overwriting Dina's original. This may be wishful thinking, but it really doesn't matter. Nonetheless, part of the narrative was definitely inserted by a later redactor. Not an unusual occurrence in those days. Most notable among the passages we consider to have been inserted into Dina's narrative are the verbatim citations from *Echa*, the Book of Lamentations. By her own testimony, she had no books, no Bible available to her. Could she have cited the passages from memory? And in Hebrew? Not likely. Think about it, how many of us who hear this book read year by year could claim to do that? More plausible is that she recounted what happened to her and her family the day after Tisha b'Av, and the redactor took this scenario and couched it in the verses from Lamentations. I'm sure he had the text right in front of him and all he had to do was copy it. I'm using the third person singular masculine in the generic sense here, though I doubt it was a woman.

"The other episode is Dina's account of her encounter with Baruch le Teutonic. Anybody who has studied the history of Jews in medieval France, as Professor Marcus will confirm, will come across this character and his testimony before Jacques Fournier, the bishop of Pamiers who headed the Holy Inquisition. It is almost breathtaking to think, serendipitous indeed, that our Dina should have shared a prison cell with this man. Dina's account of what Baruch tells her about the events in her hometown of Toulouse dovetails precisely with the historical record of his testimony before the inquisitor which is preserved in the archives. There's just too much coincidence here for belief. Then again, the timetable is certainly correct. Baruch bears witness to the massacres of the Jews by the Pastoureaux in Toulouse and the surrounding area before the inquisitor in the early 1320s. We know he was incarcerated for his repeated relapses into Judaism after several conversions to Christianity. This timeline also coincides with the inquisitor's last crusade against the Cathars. Dina may well have met Baruch le Teutonic.

"All in all, the evidence points to a second redactor, someone who had a broader knowledge of the world and Judaism than Dina could have had. The question is, who was he? It is probably safe to assume that he was a Jew and so was the scribe of the codex. Were the presumed redactor and the scribe one and the same person? And how did he, they, come by Dina's epistolary confession?

"Here we resort to the official Chronicle of Valladine for assistance. However, I must warn against too much hope of finding any evidence. Even this document does not exactly overflow with information. It gives us some hints of events from a later period and allows us to speculate further.

"Above all, it has been determined that this chronicle, written in Occitan, is not an eyewitness account. It was not started until somewhere in the late fifteenth or early sixteenth century. The original hand may have had an ax to grind—an agenda to push, as we say nowadays—in starting the account of the creation of Valladine. There are veiled references to *"Josieux"*—not exactly a flattering term for Jews. So the purpose may very well have been to vitiate the Jewish roots of the colony.

"The chronicle backtracks to the year 1348, the height of the Black Death. A clan headed by three brothers, we are told, flees into the mountains to escape the ravages of the pestilence that had already decimated entire towns and villages in Languedoc, as in most other parts of Europe. The brothers, according to this account, gathered about them several hundred people and together they founded the mountaintop village of Valladine. The chronicle gives no explanation of the origin of the name. There is no reference to a person named Dina or Miryam de Sola. As far as the chronicler is concerned, she doesn't exist, never existed. It is not beyond the realm of possibility that the omission was deliberate, that she was written out of the narrative. Certainly he was no friend of the Jews. He faithfully serves up a rehashing of all the timeworn clichés and familiar accusations found in numerous medieval texts: the Jews poisoned the wells, associated and conspired with lepers, desecrated the host, and so on. It's not worth listing them all. The chronicler's disdain for the Jews comes through particularly—the style of writing indicates the same person at work—in his account of the final banishment of the Jews from the kingdom of France in the 1390s. It wasn't the banishment though, or as it was officially designated, Charles VI's refusal to renew the permission for Jews to stay in the kingdom, which was tantamount to expulsion. No, it wasn't the king of France's refusal, but the fact that apparently a goodly number of those thus cast out had found their way to the remote village of

Valladine and settled there that got this redactor's ire up about two centuries later when there were no Jews left in the kingdom. His motives are unknown, and for our purposes they really don't matter.

"Nevertheless, we can glean some valuable information for our inquiry into the origin of the codex. The chronicle confirms a Jewish presence in the mountain enclave at least from the time of the final expulsion of the Jews from the kingdom of France in 1394. There may have been some Jews among those who fled into the mountains during the Black Death. The chronicle dates the founding to 1348, at which time the grim reaper was stalking all of Europe. The entire group of founders may have been Jews who were fleeing not only from the plague but also from the violence of the populace against them. Fleeing to higher ground to escape the plague was not uncommon. Remember Boccaccio and his company of courtiers?

"A later entry in the chronicle speaks of a dispute between Sfarad and Tsarfat over a shrine or sanctuary, probably meaning a house of prayer or assembly. In view of the mass massacres and forced conversions that ravaged Jewish communities all over Spain in 1391 and following, it is not totally out of the realm of possibility that some Spanish Jews sought refuge in the Pyrenees coming from the south. Indeed we know they did. There's quite a bit of movement back and forth of people and livestock over this mountain range that plays a central role in the drama we are trying to unravel—the transhumance, which Dina describes as well.

"At this point, I'd like to beg your indulgence as I take the liberty to give wing to *my* imagination. As historians, we are not supposed to engage in flights of fancy, but I think we have pretty much established the possibility that Dina's letter or epistolary confession to her sons had gotten into the hands of a learned Jew.

Maybe it had been placed into the hands of this Jew by Dina's sons. She told us that she taught them the *aleph-bet*. How well versed they were we don't know. My guess is that their knowledge was rudimentary under the circumstances. Just think of how much Hebrew many of our young people come away with from several years of Hebrew school. That being beside the point, there seem to have been plenty of Jews populating the mountain refuge who had the ability to copy Dina's writing, and no doubt were not above embellishing the narrative here and there, to produce the codex that is now here on the table before us."

She again lifted up the codex in its yellowed white leather binding, now carefully stored in a transparent plastic bag.

"In the course of time, the inhabitants of Valladine forgot their Jewish roots. The Hebrew lettering was to their mind some kind of mystery code, incomprehensible yet sacred. For centuries, the codex was kept in a place of honor in a sealed vitrine in the grand assembly hall, as the seneschal can testify."

Raymond de Sola nodded in agreement.

"My personal connection to Valladine is well known and need not be rehashed here. Suffice it to say that it was my historian's curiosity that drove me to ask the seneschal's permission to take a look inside. It turned out to be a Pandora's Box, if not a can of worms at first. Now with the full translated text at our disposal, we all have come to love Dina. Yet I cannot but feel some guilt for having contributed to, if not caused, the destruction of life as it existed almost unchanged on the mountaintop for so many centuries. I hope the seneschal will find it in his heart to forgive me."

Raymond de Sola responded with a slight shake of his head and dismissive hand gesture. Stunned silence filled the room. A full minute must have passed before somebody rose and pulled the rest of the attendees along into an enthusiastic standing ovation.

Nina stormed out of the room before it abated. She had given a marvelous presentation and held up well to the end. I knew she was rushing to the telephone for news from up north, but the members of the audience, who were not privy to what was going on, were visibly perplexed. I mounted the podium and gave a brief explanation with which everybody could sympathize at this time of threatening national emergency. Concluding the seminar, Etoile and I, and to some extent the seneschal, took some questions, but the mood in the room had tangibly shifted away from the past to present.

In the days that followed the symposium, concern and outrage about continued shelling across the northern border of Israel cast a pall of impending war over the country. Nina was frantically trying to get into contact with Alphonse. Tension rose to a fever pitch when news came from London on June 3 of an attempt on the life of the Israeli ambassador. Nina gave up on telephoning Alphonse. Instead she practically commandeered my Land Rover and headed north. On June 6, the Israel Defense Force launched Operation "Peace for the Galilee" with a full-force invasion of Lebanon. The objective was to dislodge the PLO from their strongholds along the border and push them out of shooting range. How Nina was able, or even whether she was able, to make her way to the Golan along roads packed with mobilized troops heading to the front is still unclear to me to this day. She never spoke about it and refused to answer questions. About a week later—a week during which those of us left behind followed the reports from the north with great anxiety and ill foreboding—she returned in the company of a troop of military guards carrying a plain wooden box. It was flanked by two snow-white whimpering Pyrenean sheep dogs who periodically rubbed their heads against the sides of the coffin.

Alphonse de Sola was laid to rest with full military honors in the cemetery of Mount Herzl in Jerusalem. We sat Shiva, the ritual that is meant to bring comfort to the bereaved. Nina found no comfort. She withdrew from the callers and refused to greet them. The one who might have been a pillar to her, Etoile, had to return, though reluctantly, to France, for her time was fast approaching.

The time had also come for the seneschal to depart. I am not sure he understood why his wish to take his brother's ashes with him to the mountain could not be fulfilled. Either he had forgotten the discussion we once had, back in Valladine, about cremation and the Jewish tradition or, not having seen his brother during his stay in Israel, he did not understand the extent to which Alphonse had become an observant Jew. When I told him that Alphonse would want to rest in the soil of the country for which he gave his life, he nodded ever so wistfully. He returned home, a broken man, in the company of the loyal mountain dogs. I often thought of him, but I never saw him again.

At the end of the year, news reached us through Etoile that the last of the de Solas had joined his ancestors not long after he returned to the mountain where he once reigned like a king.

Ingathering of Dina's Children

Behold, I make thee a new threshing-sledge
Having sharp teeth;
Thou shalt thresh the mountains, and beat them small,
And shalt make the hills as chaff.
Thou shalt fan them and the wind shall carry them away,
And the whirlwind shall scatter them;
And thou shalt rejoice in the LORD,
Thou shalt glory in the Holy One of Israel.
Isaiah 41:15–16

Jerusalem, May 1992

Raymond de Sola was the last seneschal of Valladine, but he and his brothers were not the last of Dina's progeny. Today a proud young offspring, now named Aharon de Sola, having turned eighteen, was drafted into the Israel Defense Force. His younger brother, whose name is now Baruch, is waiting impatiently for his time to come. I saw him off at the Jerusalem station where he mounted the bus with other recruits bound for the induction camp at Bakum. Both boys have been talking almost incessantly for several years now about wanting to serve in the elite force of the Golani Brigade. Their mother would cover her ears at such talk. I know she is proud of her sons who resemble so much their father, strapping and dauntless, the kind they seem to grow in the Pyrenean Mountains. She appreciates their patriotic zeal for their adopted land of Israel. But she is also constantly aware, as we all are, of the Damocles sword perpetually threatening Israel with more wars and possible complete destruction.

Nina has never recovered from her loss. Haunted by intimations of violence and war, she has been sinking deeper and deeper into a welter of despair. For years now, she has been balancing on the edge separating reality from a utopian world of her fantasy.

"I often dream of Valladine. What a perfect world it is—no wars, no conflict!" she tells me sometimes in quiet moments together. I don't dare contradict her. I don't dare tell her that this paradise never really existed, not in the way it figures in her dreams. Nor do I dare remind her that the Valladine of old, in the form it existed, is no more. Somehow she seems to have pushed from her memory the events of the great upheaval that changed life on the mountaintop forever and forced on it an abrupt leap from the medieval to the modern world. She knew it once and dealt with it forcefully then. But widowhood draped her mind with the fragility of a frayed gossamer veil.

The first two years after the death of Alphonse were still marked by a sense of total incomprehension and refusal to acknowledge the loss. For a long time, she could not or would not come to grips with what had happened. It was probably the passing of her mother, my Tante Hedy, and the reality of the double loss that jolted her out of her trance. Before then, she often sprinkled her conversation with hints about the sheep on the Golan that Alphonse had to tend to, though without mentioning his name.

At first, she even travelled as far as Tel Aviv for readings and book signings when the English version of Dina's epistolary came out. Soon after, however, she fell into a marked withdrawal from any kind of public engagement. She began to speak about Alphonse, sometimes obsessively. Why did he abandon her? Why did he have to turn into a warrior? She asked the questions over and over. The man she loved was a peaceful shepherd. As so often I didn't have the courage to shatter the idealized picture she had formed in her mind of the world and of the man she loved. Should I have reminded her of what had made her fall in love with Alphonse? As she had herself confessed in her letters, it was his natural manliness, unpolished, unspoiled by civilization, yet kind and righteous, an image out of the noble savage tradition. I could have reminded her of our biblical ancestors, breeders and keepers of sheep and kine with heifers, red and otherwise, who were skilled in wielding a sword and a spear, even a slingshot, in defense of land and honor. The sons of Jacob, the patriarch, were a bunch of characters not unlike Alphonse, or rather he was much of the same mentality. That is, within limits. I am absolutely certain that Alphonse would never, even had he had the opportunity, have sold a brother into slavery, not even Guilhem. Nor did he ever to my knowledge sacrifice his livestock in a ritual of burnt offering. However, I am reminded of one of the conversations, mostly about the weekly portion, we used to have in his cottage up on the Golan. After we had settled in the land, I frequently accompanied Nina and her children on their weekend jaunts to the Golan. Aunt Hedy would come along on occasion, but usually preferred to stay with her newly acquired German Jewish friends. I guess it was the language or some other affinity.

Where Alphonse had learned to cook dishes redolent of Shabbat dinners past, I never found out. On getting close to the modest cottage, the sweet and pungent aromas beguiled us already from a distance and overwhelmed our senses as we entered the gate to his domain. When we were done with feasting, praying, and singing *zemirot*, I would take the boys out for a stroll under the stars to leave their parents to their shabbes mitzvah. Not since childhood had we enjoyed such a warm sense of family. Thinking back to those days fills me too with nostalgia, as I am sure it does Nina. She had planned to end the weekly separations once the work on the Dina project was done. That it never came to pass left her inconsolable.

But I digress. What came to my mind was the time when Alphonse woke me early on Shabbat morning, before dawn as usual. He would have a hearty breakfast ready to keep up our strength for the seven-mile walk to the nearest synagogue. He would move about the cabin noiselessly like a prowling cat so as not to wake Nina and the children.

On this particular Shabbat, a blasting wind and intermittently gushing rainfall impeded our progress. We reached the synagogue just at the end of the *Amidah* prayer. By the time we had shed our rain gear, dried off, and put on the prayer shawls, the Torah scroll was being taken out and carried around the room in procession. Alphonse's grim mien showed his displeasure at being late. He blamed himself for having missed a good part of the service. I was less ruffled. I was used to it. Where I come from, that is just about the time when most people start drifting in.

It so happened that the reading on this particular Shabbath was the portion "Vayyishlach" from Genesis that contains the story of Dina, the daughter of Leah and Jacob. I couldn't help but let my thoughts wander to our Dina, who had adopted the name of her biblical forebear. But how different are the narratives of these two women! The Torah tells us next to nothing about the inner life of the biblical Dina. By contrast, the medieval Dina's extraordinarily candid confession makes us privy to her innermost feelings as well as the most intimate details of what happened to her. If we compare what we know about both, the trajectory of their fate could not diverge more. The biblical Dina is taken back into her father's household never to be heard from again, except once briefly and much later when the clan moves down to Egypt. The medieval Dina is declared dead by her father and brothers. She is a pariah in the village where she met her defilement and was subjected to years of abuse by her seducer. Yet, neither bondage nor obloquy breaks her spirit. Ultimately she becomes the founding mother of a mountain clan, a tribe, so to speak, whose existence continued for centuries. Her biblical namesake, by contrast, lives out her life sheltered within the bosom of her family as an old maid, for all we know.

Dina Miryam becomes her own avenger for the pain that was inflicted on her. Jacob's daughter's violation is avenged by her brothers in a horrific act of violence. It's the honor of the clan that had to be restored. Dina's thoughts and feelings remain unexplored by the biblical redactor, as do those of her mother Leah. The text and the commentators have plenty to say about Jacob's feelings and anguish, not over his daughter—after all, she "went out," and the implication is she deserved what she got—but about the consequences of her brothers' vengeful action for him and his clan. We moderns tend to cast the story within the frame of our more enlightened perspective, to which I myself am prone, which is to condemn the brothers' action. I was, therefore, surprised to hear the interpretation, or better the gut reaction, to the story of someone who was untainted by our presumably more refined sensibilities.

I had stolen a glance a few times at my companion during the reading. He was hunched up in a huge, black-striped tallit that must have been custom made for his large frame. He was tracing the letters on the page with his finger with a stern look and furrowed brow. I could not but admire his obvious devotion to the Jewish faith which he had adopted only a few years before. His knowledge of biblical Hebrew was still somewhere around bar mitzvah level, but he was of determined mind and made steady progress. We had never become very close. Unlike his brother, the seneschal, he was not given to intellectual discourse. He was quiet and reserved and rarely ventured an opinion. Nina's profound love for him was good enough for me to hold him in high esteem.

On the long way home, I was therefore surprised, quite pleasantly I must say, when he suddenly spoke up and made reference to this particular reading. We were still battling the storm. Our plastic ponchos flapped about our bodies, providing sparse protection from the drenching rain. I, bobbing about like a vessel that had lost its bearing, was at first unable to catch what he was saying or that he was saying anything at all, attributing, as I did, the murmuring I heard to the wind. After a while, I came to realize that it was his words the wind's shrieks were shredding and carrying aloft before they reached my ear. I reached out to get a hold of his arm to make him slow down and promptly slipped in the mud. This mishap at least drew his attention to the fact that not everybody is built like a rock and impervious to the elements. He pulled me up, and I managed to trot alongside him, panting like one of his loyal snowball retainers.

"They were both wrong," he grumbled.

"Who was wrong?" My inquiry elicited an irritated reply.

"The fathers—Ya'akov the Patriarch and Don Elazar. Both are at fault. The one for condemning his sons for avenging their sister's honor and the other for not letting his sons avenge their sister's honor. If we had a daughter and she came into such circumstance, I would expect my sons to act like Shimon and Levi. But her brothers were more concerned about saving their own hide. Ya'akov should have been proud of what his sons did. Would there be a people Israel had they not done what they did, and the two clans had merged as the pact between their father and the father of his daughter's ravager had foreseen?"

I had never thought of it this way. There was a certain compelling logic to his argument, a logic too down-to-earth for *soi-disant* sensitive souls to admit to or even contemplate.

"We don't know anything about the de Sola brothers' intentions," I shifted the conversation to another set of players. "Their sister hoped, as she said, that they would act like Shimon and Levi. Then again, she seems to have been ambivalent about it."

He gave me a puzzled look. I remembered what Nina had said about his concrete way of thinking. Ambivalence was not something he would understand. She was raped by the priest and thus was dishonored. End of discussion. Her own account of what happened was much more nuanced than that. So I tried to explain to him how different was the downtrodden, browbeaten medieval Jew living in constant fear for his life and property from his free-roaming, sword-wielding biblical forebears.

"Ya'akov was not all that different," he said after some consideration. "He was more like a medieval Jew, as you describe him, timid and easily cowed. He too was constantly on the run, fearful for his life and limb, of his brother and everybody else around. The honor of his daughter was nothing to him. His sons, at least those Leah bore him, were of a tougher mettle, dauntless and uncowed."

As we entered upon the dirt path leading to his compound, the rain and wind had let up a little but the clouds in spectacular dramatic formation overhead threatened—or promised, for water starved Israel this weather was a blessing—more downpours.

Inside the roofed courtyard, we shook off our wet garments and pulled off our muddied boots. We were about to enter the house when Alphonse held me back by the arm: "Nina doesn't agree with me on any of this." Placing a conspiratorial finger on his lips, he added in hushed tone: *"Shalom bayit!"*

This was the kind of man who would not shrink from risking his life for what he believed was right. Once he had adopted the Jewish religion and the land of Israel as his homeland, no holds were barred for him. He too was of a tougher mettle. He was still the *sous-viguier* from another era, dauntless and uncowed.

This episode sprang to my mind at the bus station on the day Alphonse de Sola's firstborn entered the army. His sons would carry on his legacy. They were made of the same tough mettle as their father, prepared to put their lives on the line. I had gotten to know them quite well in the years since their father's death. In fact, I had acted as a kind of surrogate father to them. The loss had left their mother for a long time in a state of mental paralysis. She went through a daily routine of feeding and clothing them and getting them off to school, but the joy had gone out of her life. Her mother moved back into the apartment and took on most household chores.

One evening when Nina was out somewhere, Aunt Hedy opened her heart to me.

"This doesn't bode well," she said shaking her head in sorrow. "I've seen her like this before. It's the same melancholy. But where will she run to now that he's gone?"

"You mean her illness when she came back from France?"

"Die Kinder sollten doch ein Trost sein!" As so often when she was distressed, Aunt Hedy resorted to her native language.

"True, from a rational view, she should find some consolation in her children, but at the moment she is not thinking or feeling rationally," I agreed. "The way I see it, though I'm no psychologist, it's not only the loss, but guilt that drives her to distraction."

"What guilt?"

"The guilt, irrational of course, for having lured him from his peaceful mountain enclave and made him settle in this country with its constant threat of war!"

"Hör mir auf mit dem Unsinn, Henner!" Her tone of indignation, as if she was scolding a little boy for using forbidden language, made me cease "the nonsense" as I was told. She would never accept some murky psychoanalysis of her daughter's behavior. Nor would she accept my ridiculous suggestion about guilt and Israel.

At that moment, we heard the front door open and Nina's steps in the foyer.

"Just promise me one thing, Henner," my aunt whispered quickly in my ear. "Don't leave her alone. Take care of her and the boys—when I am gone."

Of course, I promised. I would have done that much anyway. Nobody had ever been nearer and dearer to me than my wondrous cousin Nina.

Nina's mother, my beloved Tante Hedy, passed away a few years later. Following her wish, she was laid to rest next to her dear husband Aaron in New Jersey. I made the arrangements, and we all—that is Nina, the boys, and I—made the journey, our last, to America. After that, I pulled up the stakes in the desert and moved into the apartment in Jerusalem. The boys needed a father, and in spite of my inexperience in this area, I tried my best. Nina settled into a daily routine of keeping house, cooking, cleaning, and the like. She spent much time reading, mostly the kind of literature, if it can be called such, she would have disdained in the olden days. *Schundliteratur* to my mother and aunt. It hurt me to see what I regarded as a withering of her intellect. But then I myself was following a similar path from academic star to ordinary homebody. I played chess with my boys, taught them English, and when the time came for their bar mitzvah, also Haftarah and Torah trope which to my great surprise came back to me very easily. We went hiking and biking, never on the Golan though. So the days, months, and years flowed by like the waters of a quiet river. Nina and I no longer had those debates that once had animated our spirits and not infrequently set us at loggerheads.

I must have been too preoccupied with ordinary matters to take note at first; besides, it was not my habit to spy on her or pry into what she was doing. So it was with great surprise to find her one evening bent over at her desk engaged in writing with a fountain pen in a leather bound notebook.

She looked up startled when I made my presence known and quickly closed the notebook. Then more calmly and apparently reassured, she said: "Oh it's you, Henner."

"You are writing," I stated the obvious.

"Yes," she said. "It gives me peace of mind."

"That's nice." I tried not to appear patronizing. "May I ask …?"

"Yes, sure. I'm working on a novel—historical of course. Stories of love and war and things like that. What else could I write?" Her caustic brief laugh that brought a spark into her blue eyes elicited in me a sense of relief and even hope.

"Actually, this is my second child," she said. "I have another one, a finished manuscript on the shelf in the closet."

"Have you thought of publishing?"

"Not really. It's my private therapy, to keep my mind from withering."

Strange she should use the same word that had previously come to my mind about her.

My fear thus turned out to have been premature. She didn't wither, neither in body nor in soul.

She is still writing. Sometimes I get to read a passage, but no critique is permitted. The pieces I'm fed make me hungry for more. But she's very miserly, and I have to beg like a puppy. Maybe the day will come when she will finally unveil to the public the wonderful tapestries she weaves with such skill and flourish. For the time being, I'm happy for the change this activity has brought to her life and to her disposition, and in a way, to mine as well. Since then, our life together has taken on a lighter, more playful air. Not that all is roses. I can still often see a secret pain in her eyes. The sense of loss will never totally go away. But she has found a medium into which she can pour the entire scale of her emotions. Most importantly, this activity tethers her to life. We chat about all sorts of things, such as the latest good reads, even politics, but no metaphysics. Oftentimes a third person enters our circle, a woman who lived in another time and place some seven centuries ago and yet is so real to us we are certain we can feel her breath: Miryam who took the name of her biblical forebear Dina.

Inspired by Nina's renewed creativity, I too have begun to write again, albeit not in the scholarly style of my former existence. No more conjectures in turgid prose embedded in endless footnotes and references. This book is my tribute to two extraordinary women, my celebration of their lives and the spirit that animated them. Unlike Nina, who keeps her creations jealously under wraps, I gladly share this work with all who are willing to follow me on a journey along the frequently rough and treacherous trajectory into the worlds of Dina Miryam de Sola and Nina Aschauer.

3JED000010016E